Catch nev
episodes

THE NEXT GENERATION

on CTV

... or watch it on demand at CTV.ca

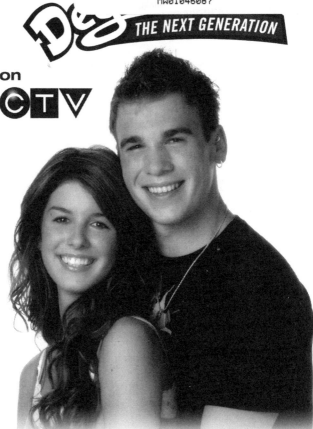

EXTRA CREDIT

A Fenn Publishing Company Ltd. / Madison Press Book

This book is a work of fiction. Names, characters, places and incidents are used fictitiously. Any resemblance to actual events or locales or to persons, living or dead, is entirely coincidental.

Library and Archives Canada Cataloguing in Publication

Torres, J., 1969-
        Missing You / J. Torres, author ; Eric Kim, illustrator.

(Degrassi the next generation : extra credit ; 3)
ISBN-10: 1-55168-301-6
ISBN-13: 978-1-55168-301-0

        I. Kim, Eric, 1977- II. Title. III. Series.

PN6733.T67M48 2007   741.5'971   C2007-901507-7

&⊗ FENN
Fenn Publishing Company Ltd.
Bolton, Ontario, Canada

Distributed in Canada by H.B. Fenn and Company Ltd.
Bolton, Ontario, Canada
www.hbfenn.com

Produced by
Madison Press Books
1000 Yonge Street, Suite 200
Toronto, Ontario, Canada M4W 2K2
www.madisonpressbooks.com

Printed in Canada by Friesens

Degrassi
THE NEXT GENERATION
EXTRA CREDIT

MISSING
YOU

Story by J. Torres

Art by Eric Kim

⊗ FENN

A Fenn Publishing Company Ltd. / Madison Press Book

PREVIOUSLY ON DEGRASSI...

Former class clown and underachiever Gavin "Spinner" Mason has been trying to clean up his act since the school shooting that put his friend Jimmy Brooks in a wheelchair. When a new "girl" friend, Darcy Edwards, introduces him to Friendship Club, a Christian students' organization, Spinner finds God — but Darcy soon finds out about Spinner's promiscuous ways. Their on-again, off-again relationship is now off again, but Spinner means to change that....

Model student and overachiever Liberty Van Zandt is probably the last girl anyone expected would get pregnant before graduation. When J.T. Yorke, the baby's father, turned to selling prescription drugs as a fast way of making money to help out, she broke up with him and announced she would give the baby up for adoption. At the end of the school year, Liberty seems to be holding up rather well, all things considered. But if anyone has proven that looks can be deceiving....

ACT 1

"Put on the whole armour of God,
that ye may be able to stand against
the wiles of the devil."

— *Ephesians* 6:11

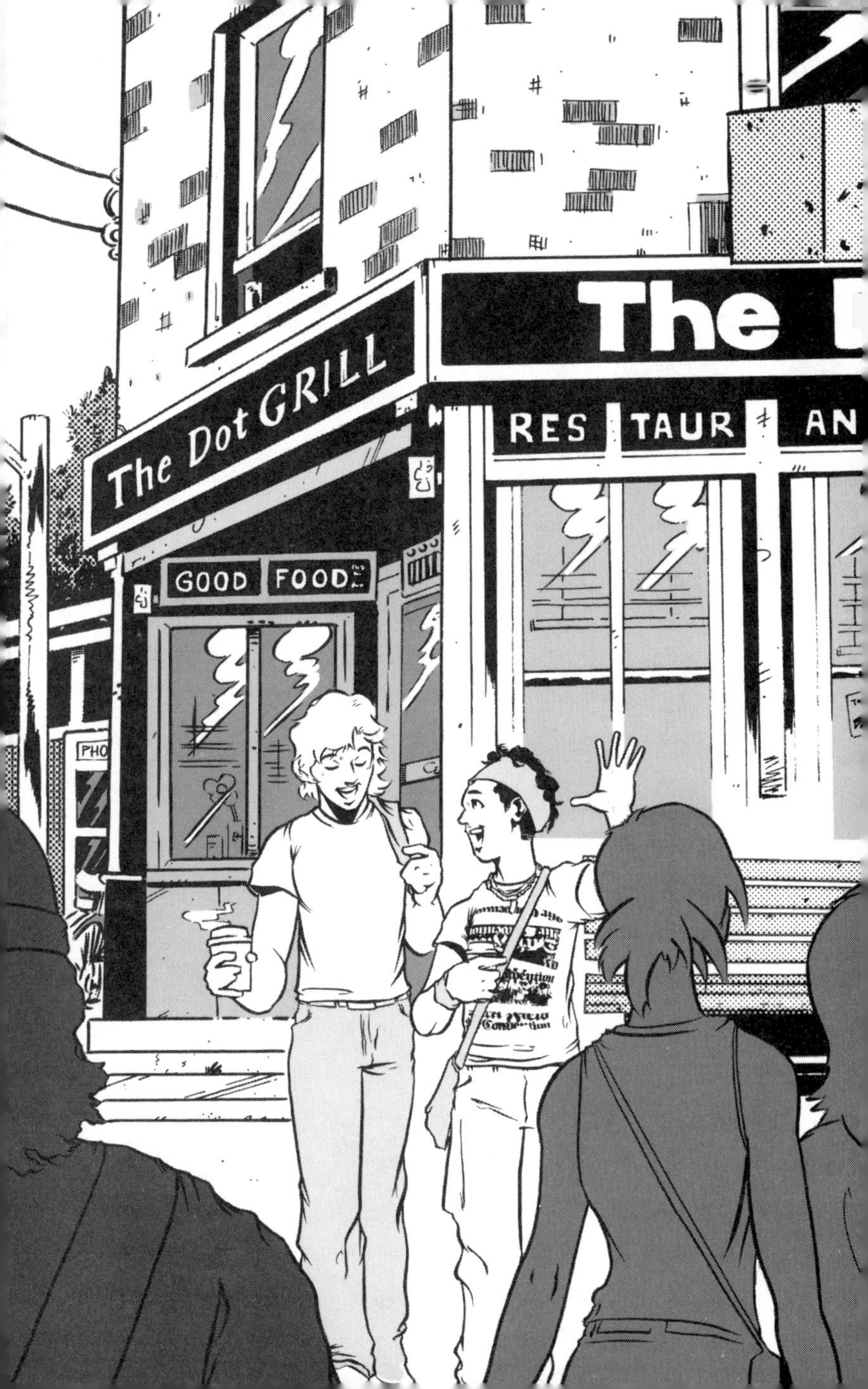
The Dot GRILL
GOOD FOOD
The
RES TAUR AN

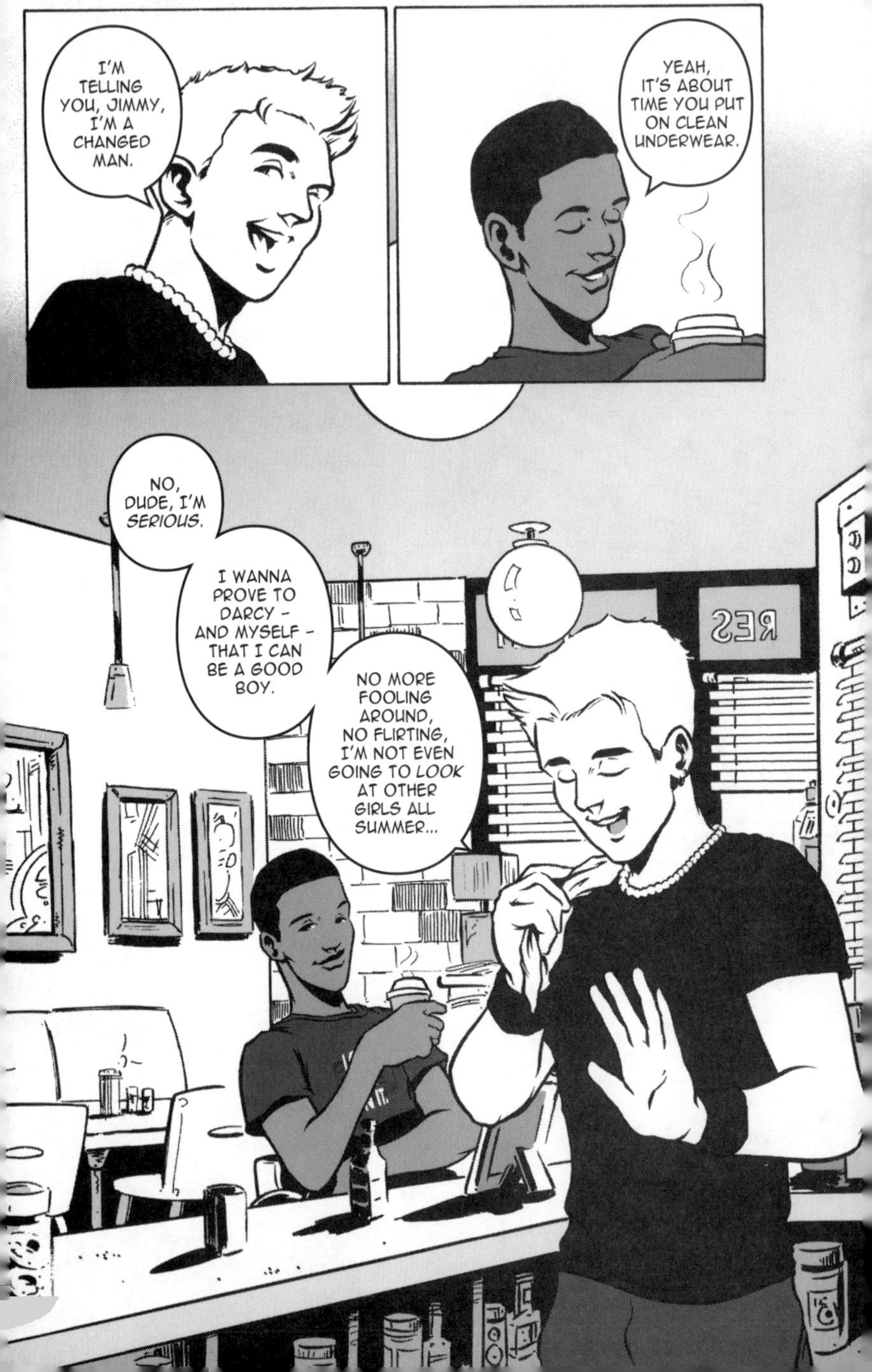
I'M TELLING YOU, JIMMY, I'M A CHANGED MAN.
YEAH, IT'S ABOUT TIME YOU PUT ON CLEAN UNDERWEAR.
NO, DUDE, I'M *SERIOUS.*
I WANNA PROVE TO DARCY - AND MYSELF - THAT I CAN BE A GOOD BOY.
NO MORE FOOLING AROUND, NO FLIRTING, I'M NOT EVEN GOING TO *LOOK* AT OTHER GIRLS ALL SUMMER...
RES

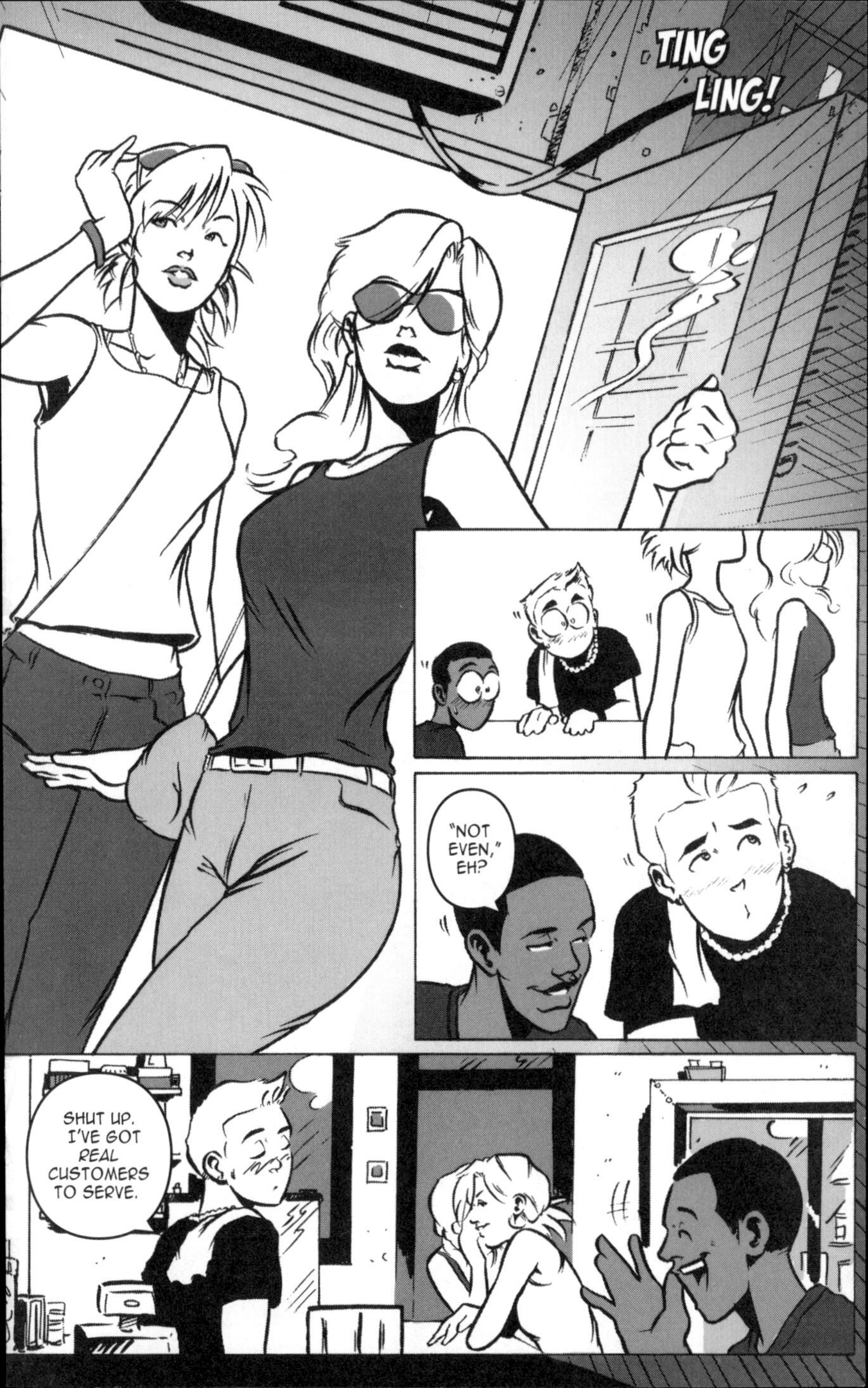
TING
LING!
"NOT EVEN," EH?
SHUT UP. I'VE GOT REAL CUSTOMERS TO SERVE.

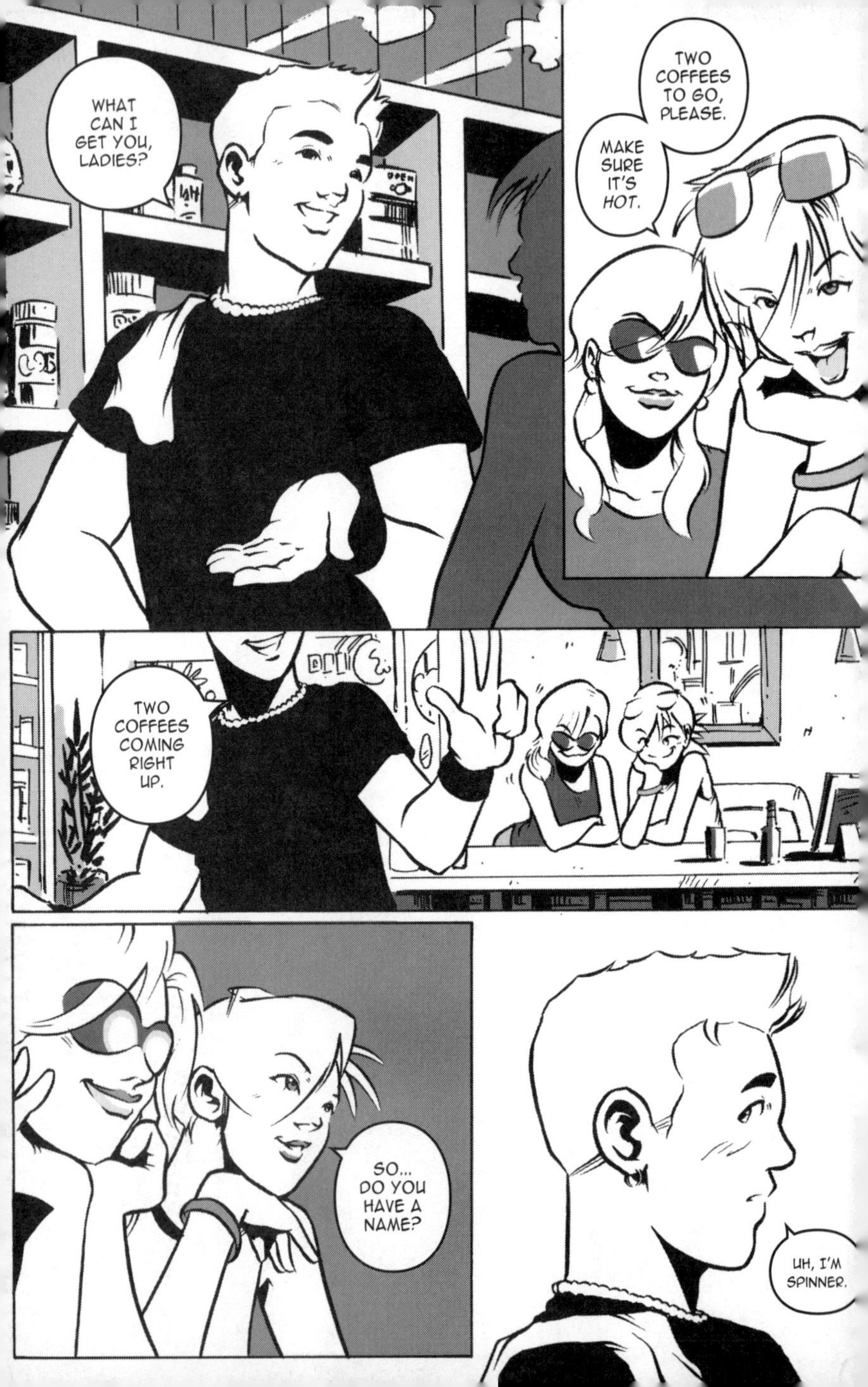
WHAT CAN I GET YOU, LADIES?
TWO COFFEES TO GO, PLEASE.
MAKE SURE IT'S *HOT*.
TWO COFFEES COMING RIGHT UP.
SO... DO YOU HAVE A NAME?
UH, I'M SPINNER.

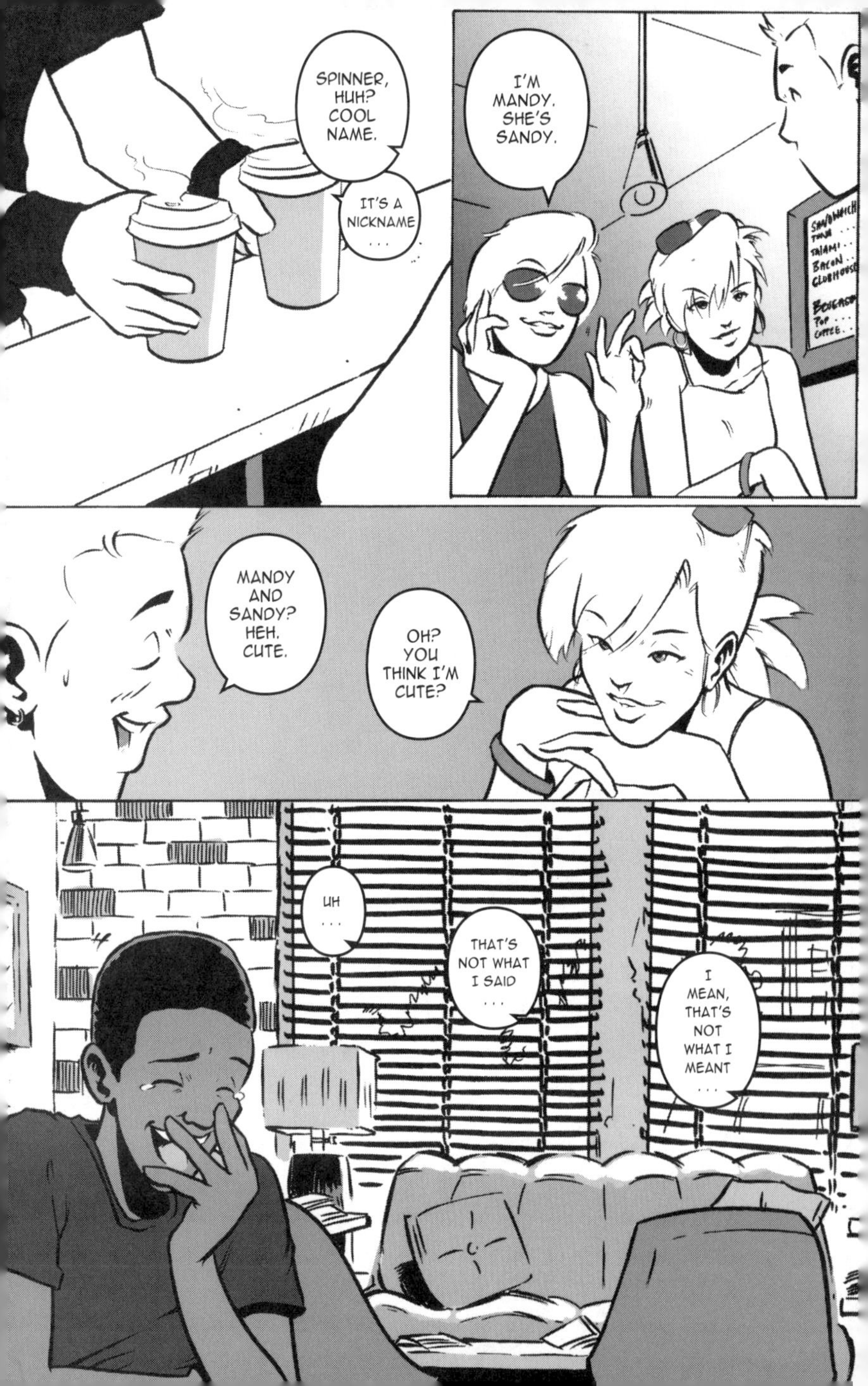
SPINNER, HUH? COOL NAME.
IT'S A NICKNAME . . .
I'M MANDY. SHE'S SANDY.
MANDY AND SANDY? HEH. CUTE.
OH? YOU THINK I'M CUTE?
UH . . .
THAT'S NOT WHAT I SAID . . .
I MEAN, THAT'S NOT WHAT I MEANT . . .

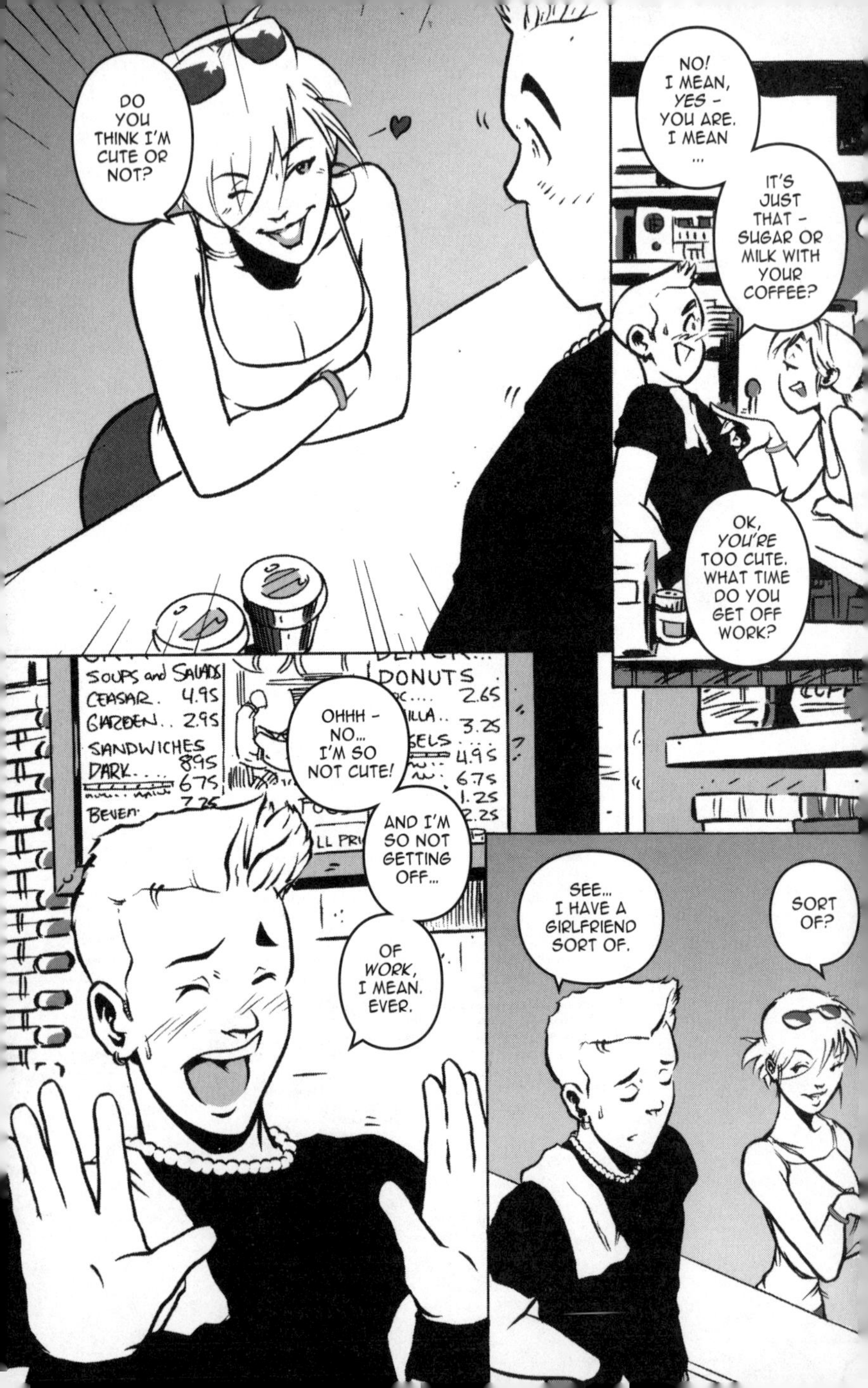
DO YOU THINK I'M CUTE OR NOT?
NO! I MEAN, *YES* - YOU ARE. I MEAN ...
IT'S JUST THAT - SUGAR OR MILK WITH YOUR COFFEE?
OK, *YOU'RE* TOO CUTE. WHAT TIME DO YOU GET OFF WORK?
SOUPS and SALADS
CEASAR. 4.95
GARDEN.. 2.95
SANDWICHES
DARK.... 8.95
DONUTS
2.65
3.25
OHHH - NO... I'M SO NOT CUTE!
AND I'M SO NOT GETTING OFF...
OF *WORK*, I MEAN. EVER.
SEE... I HAVE A GIRLFRIEND SORT OF.
SORT OF?

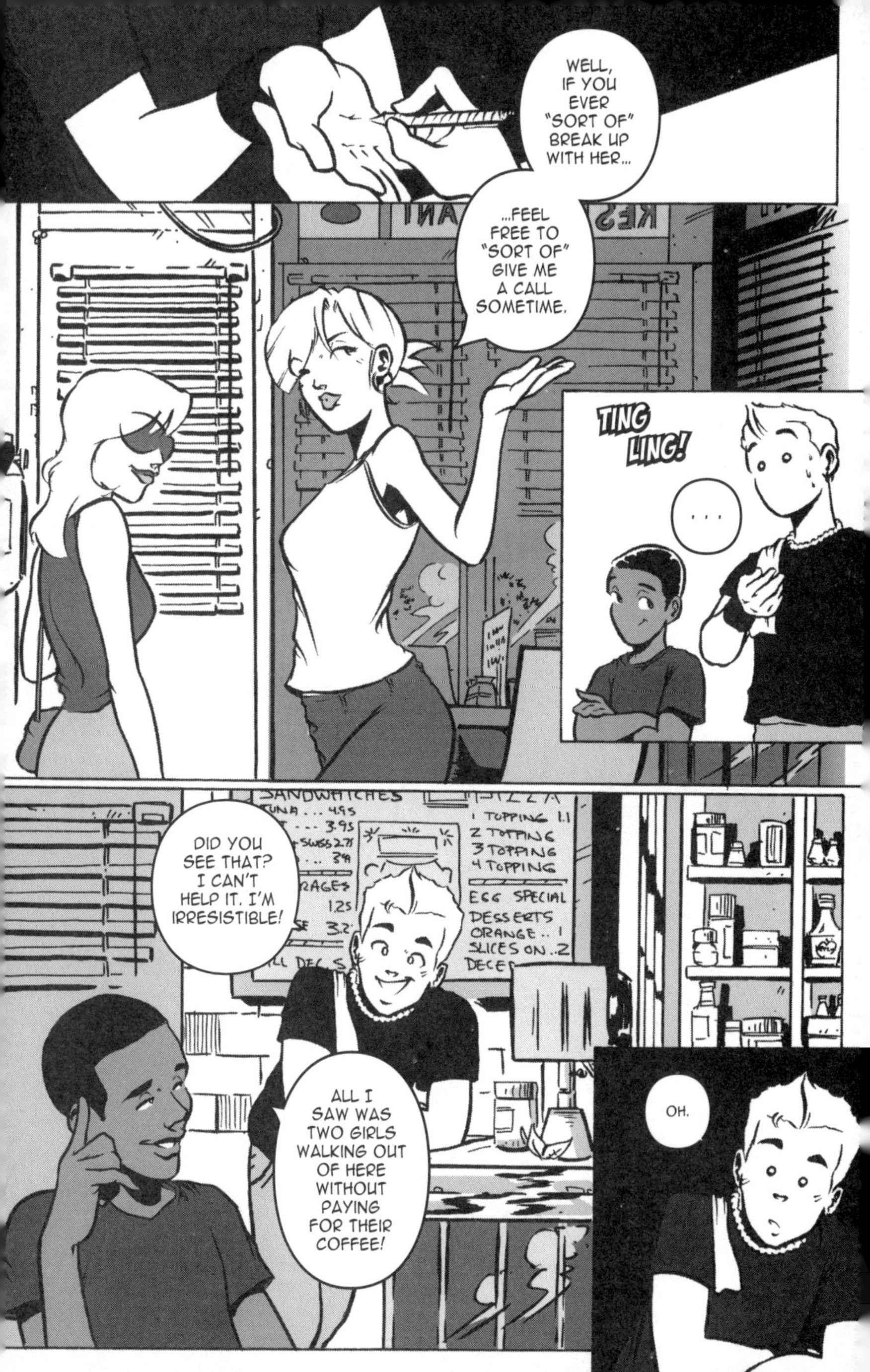
WELL, IF YOU EVER "SORT OF" BREAK UP WITH HER...
...FEEL FREE TO "SORT OF" GIVE ME A CALL SOMETIME.
TING LING!
. . .
DID YOU SEE THAT? I CAN'T HELP IT. I'M IRRESISTIBLE!
ALL I SAW WAS TWO GIRLS WALKING OUT OF HERE WITHOUT PAYING FOR THEIR COFFEE!
OH.

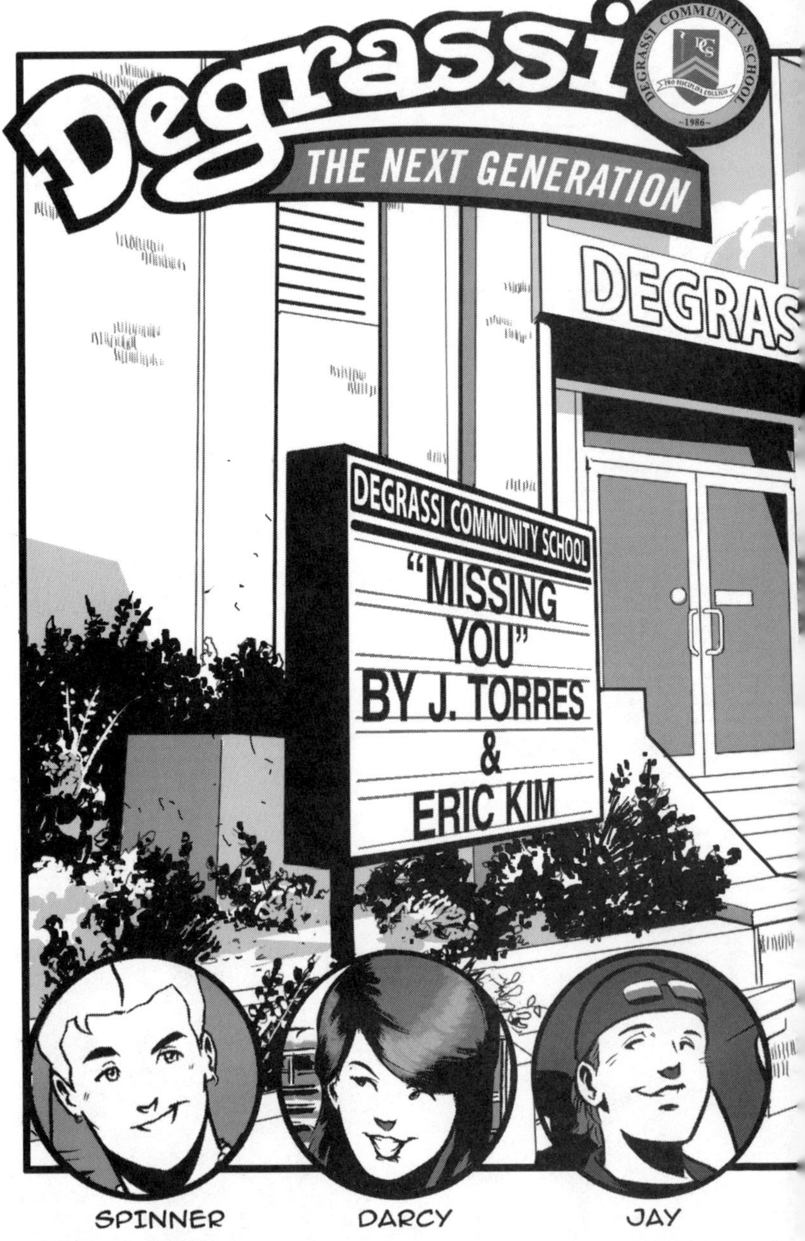
Degrassi
DEGRASSI COMMUNITY SCHOOL
PRO DISCIPULA COLLIGO
~1986~
THE NEXT GENERATION
DEGRAS
DEGRASSI COMMUNITY SCHOOL
"MISSING YOU"
BY J. TORRES
&
ERIC KIM
SPINNER
DARCY
JAY

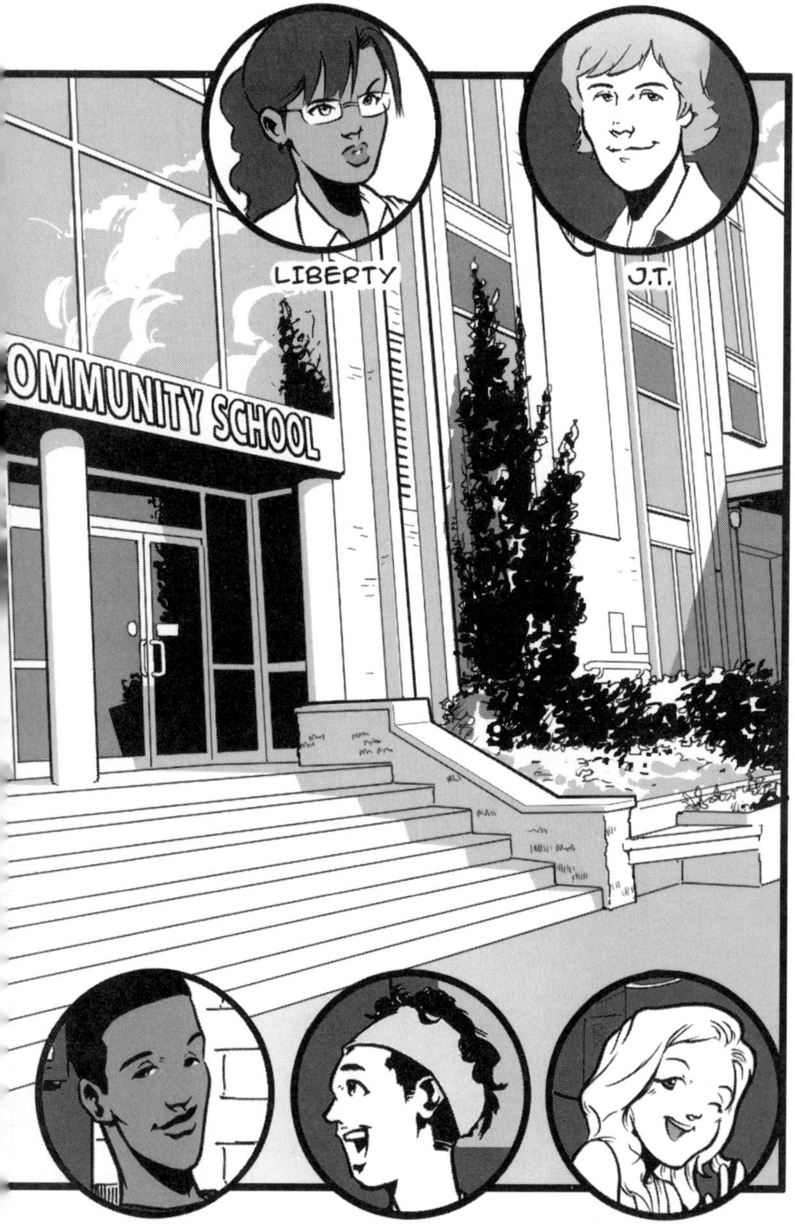
LIBERTY
J.T.
OMMUNITY SCHOOL
JIMMY
MARCO
PAINGEL

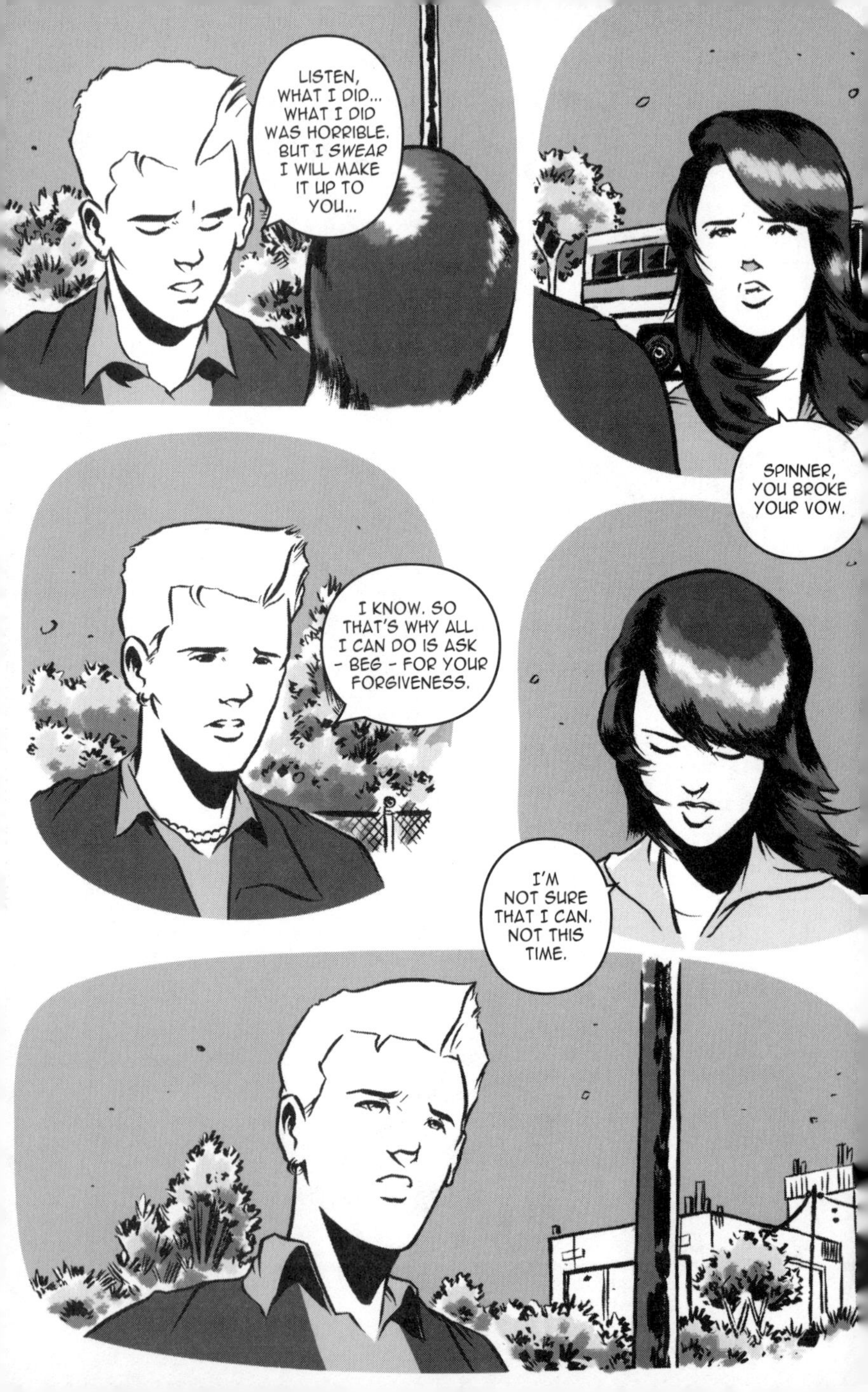

LISTEN, WHAT I DID... WHAT I DID WAS HORRIBLE. BUT I *SWEAR* I WILL MAKE IT UP TO YOU...
SPINNER, YOU BROKE YOUR VOW.
I KNOW. SO THAT'S WHY ALL I CAN DO IS ASK - BEG - FOR YOUR FORGIVENESS.
I'M NOT SURE THAT I CAN. NOT THIS TIME.

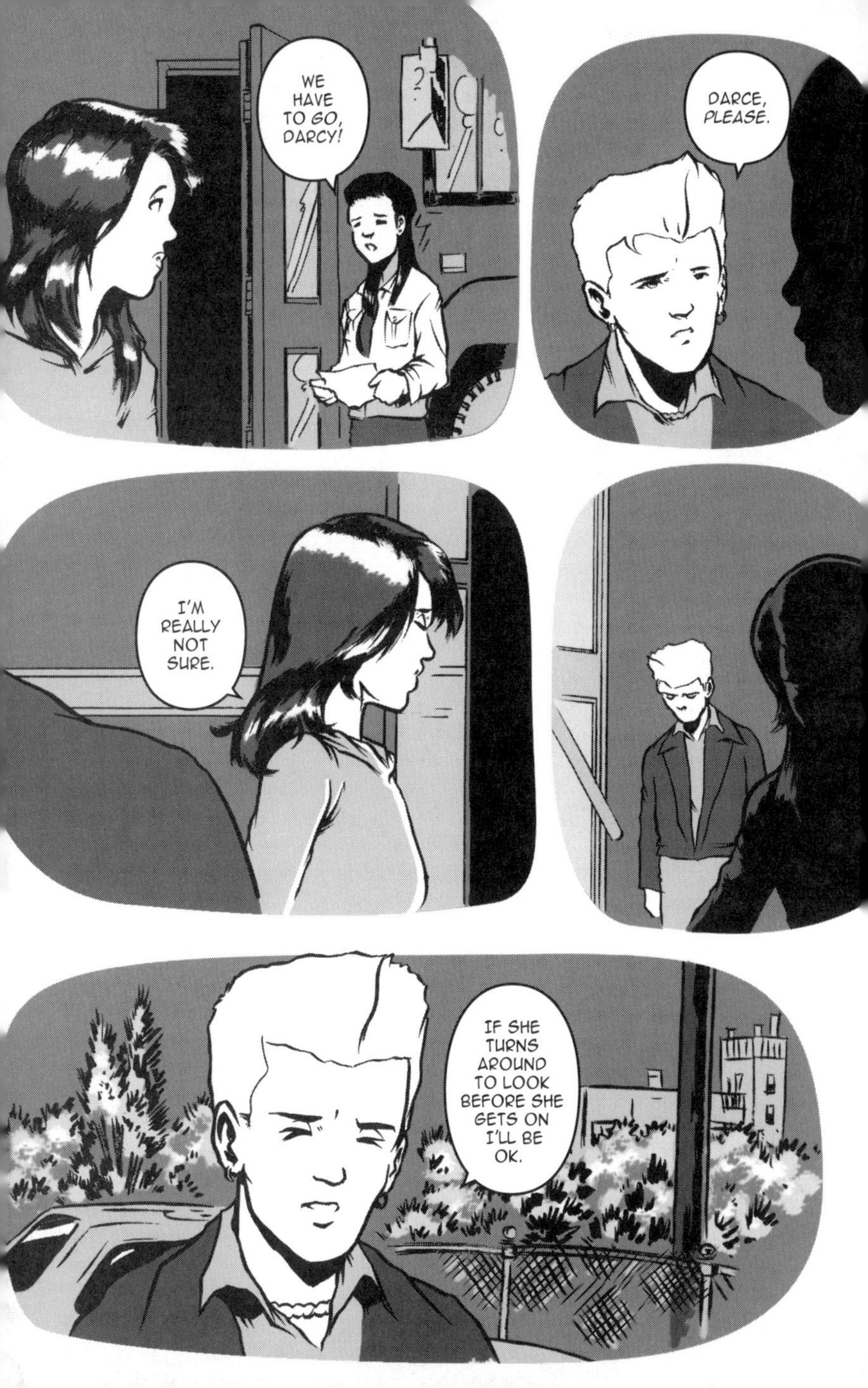
WE HAVE TO GO, DARCY!
DARCE, PLEASE.
I'M REALLY NOT SURE.
IF SHE TURNS AROUND TO LOOK BEFORE SHE GETS ON I'LL BE OK.

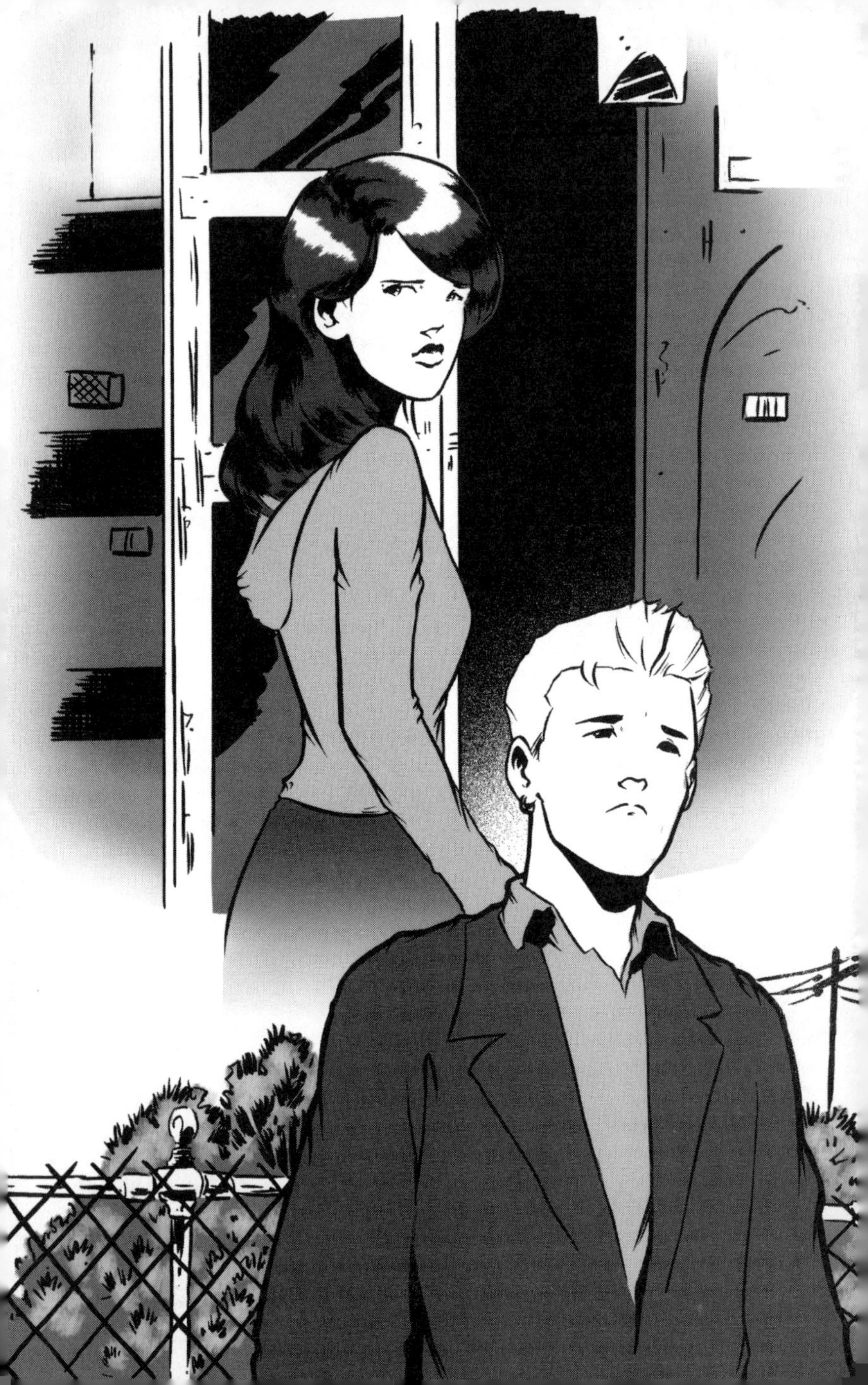

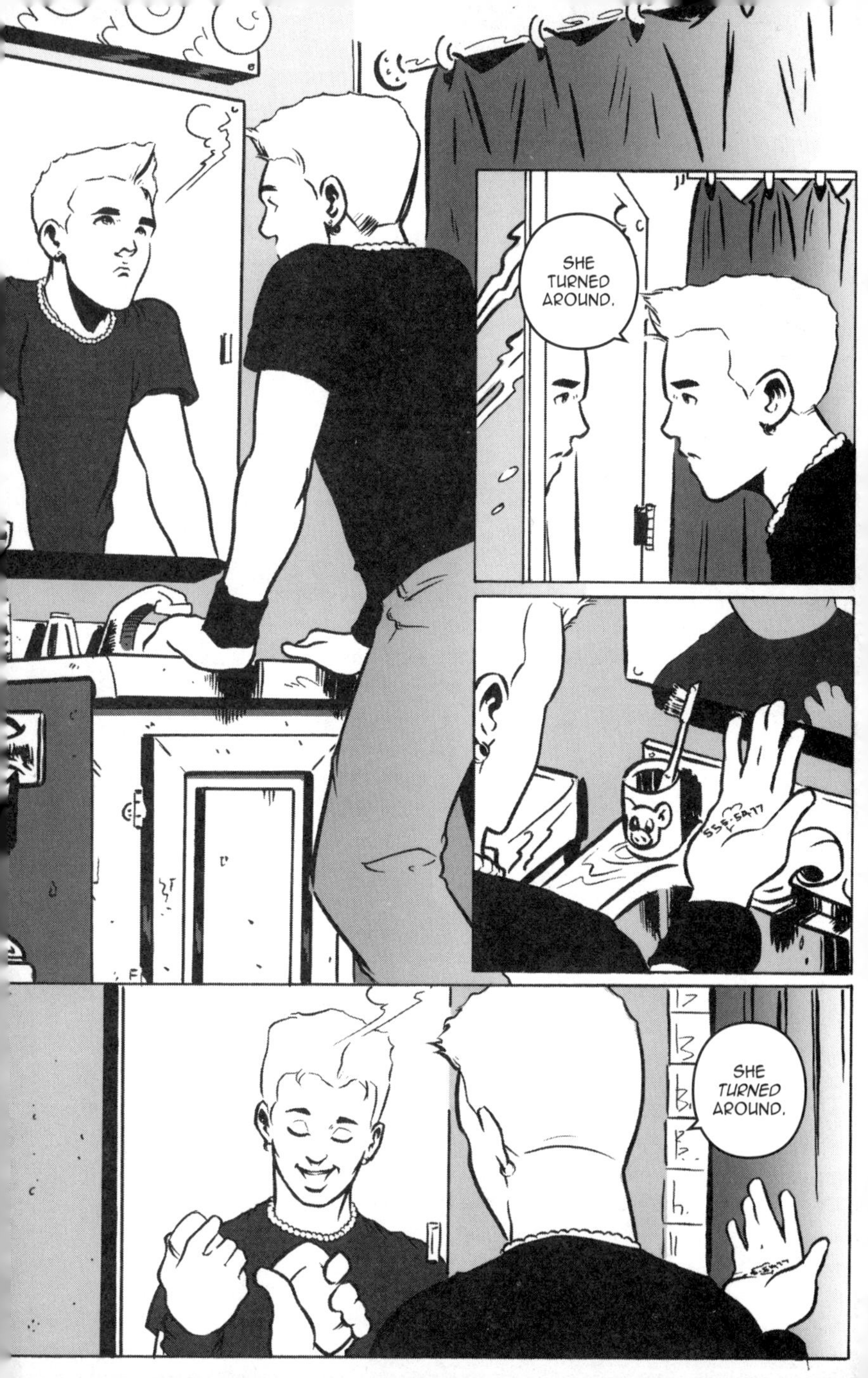
SHE TURNED AROUND.
SHE TURNED AROUND.

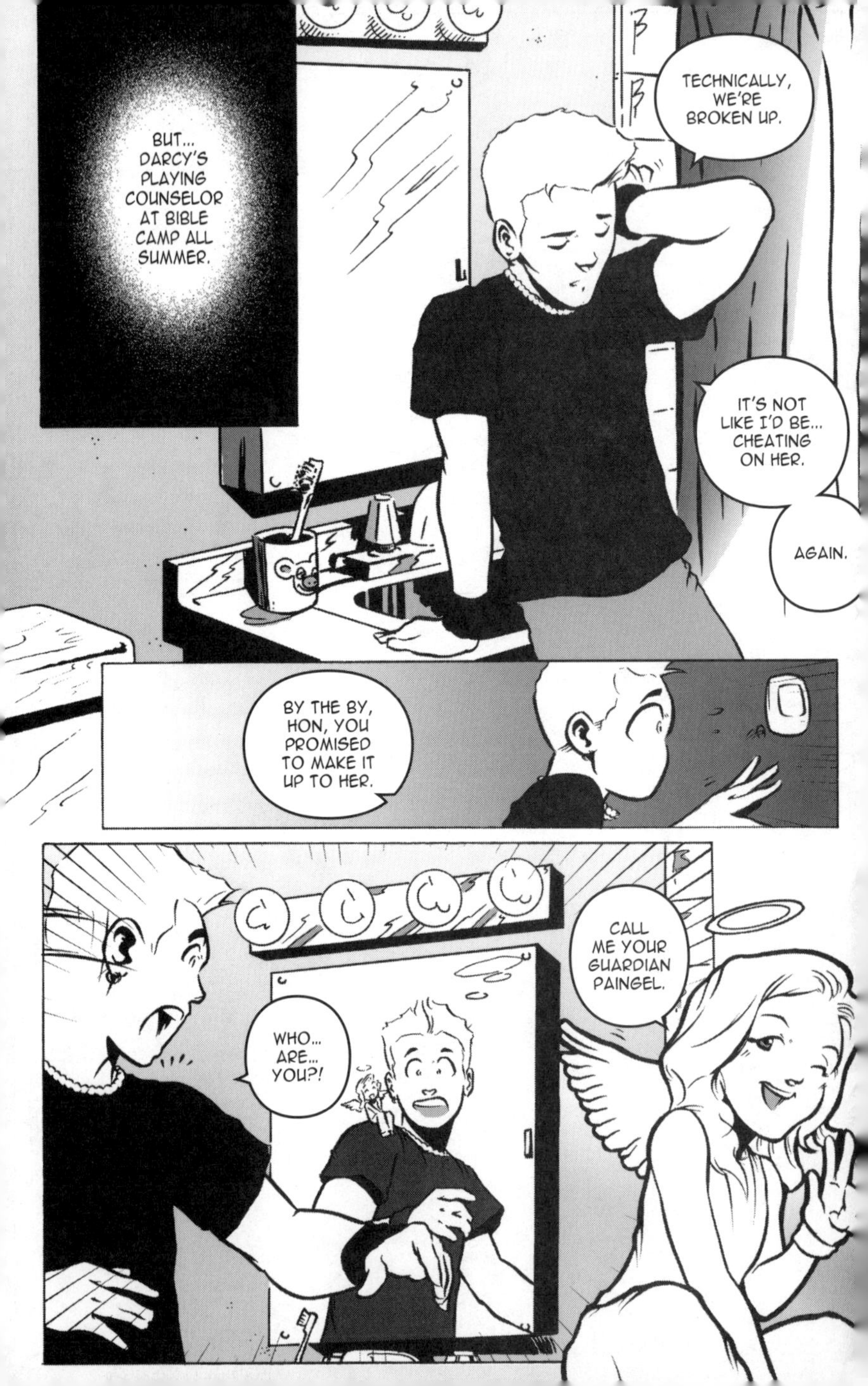
BUT... DARCY'S PLAYING COUNSELOR AT BIBLE CAMP ALL SUMMER.
TECHNICALLY, WE'RE BROKEN UP.
IT'S NOT LIKE I'D BE... CHEATING ON HER.
AGAIN.
BY THE BY, HON, YOU PROMISED TO MAKE IT UP TO HER.
WHO... ARE... YOU?!
CALL ME YOUR GUARDIAN PAINGEL.

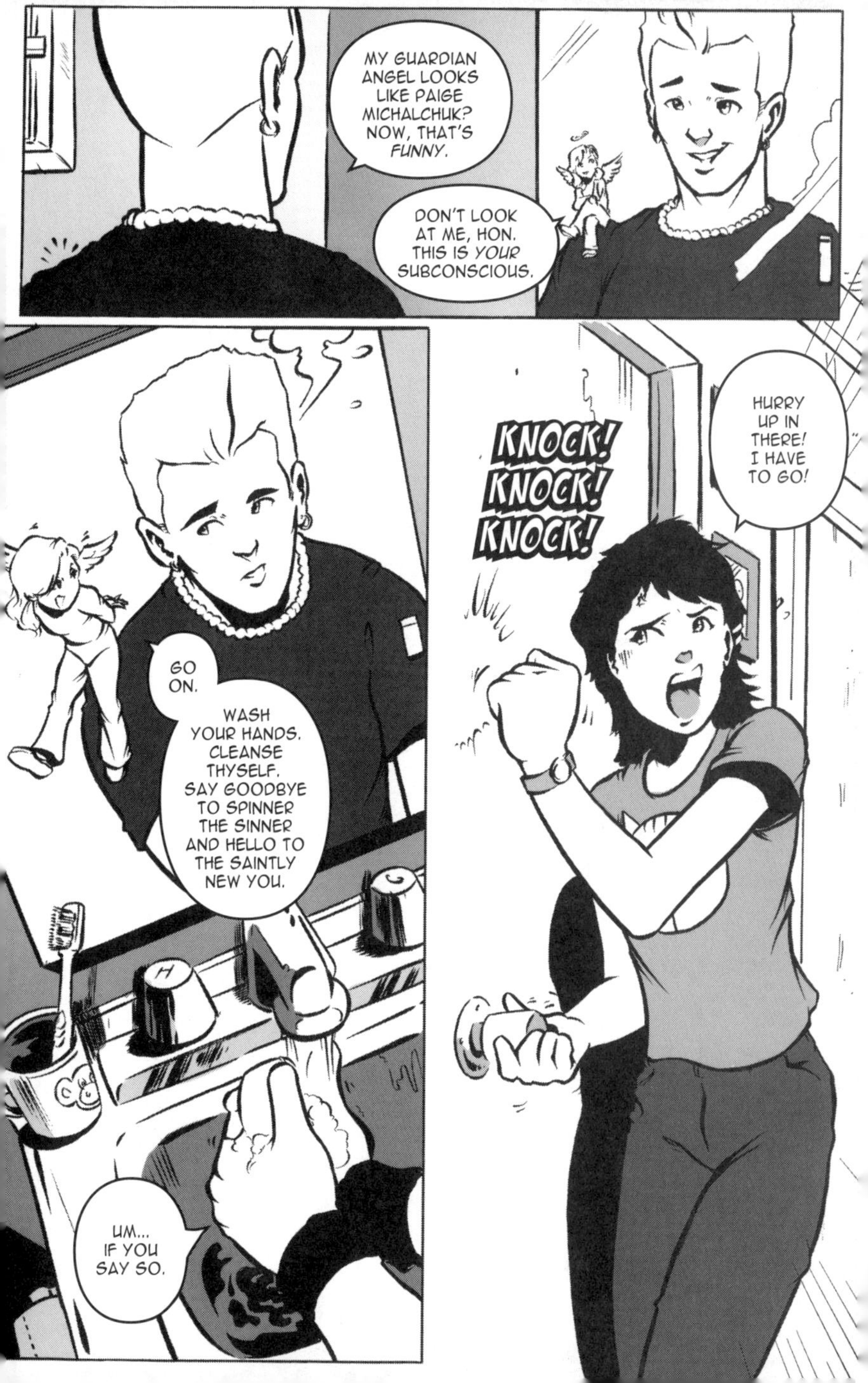
MY GUARDIAN ANGEL LOOKS LIKE PAIGE MICHALCHUK? NOW, THAT'S *FUNNY*.
DON'T LOOK AT ME, HON. THIS IS *YOUR* SUBCONSCIOUS.
GO ON.
WASH YOUR HANDS. CLEANSE THYSELF. SAY GOODBYE TO SPINNER THE SINNER AND HELLO TO THE SAINTLY NEW YOU.
UM... IF YOU SAY SO.
KNOCK! KNOCK! KNOCK!
HURRY UP IN THERE! I HAVE TO GO!

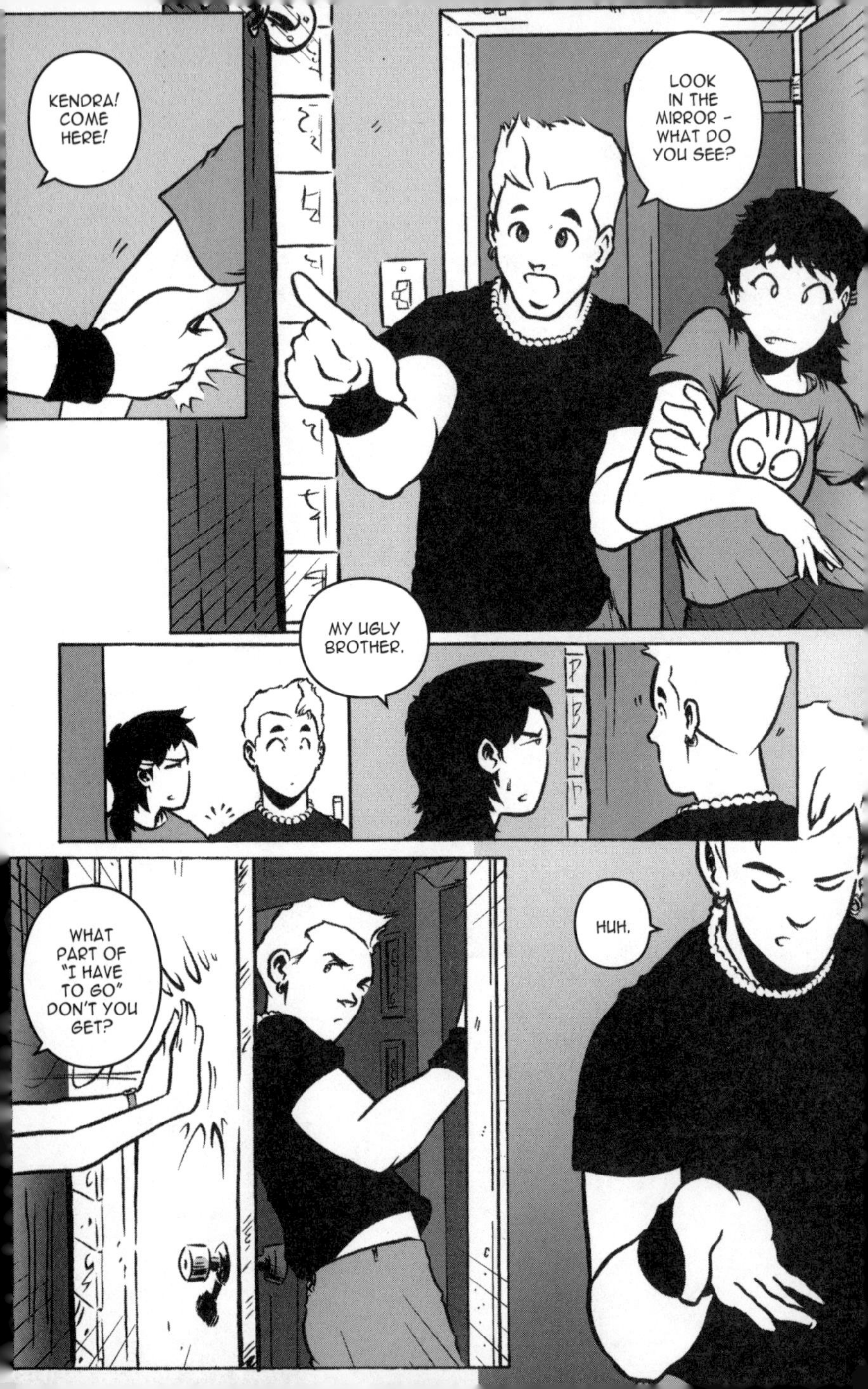
KENDRA! COME HERE!
LOOK IN THE MIRROR - WHAT DO YOU SEE?
MY UGLY BROTHER.
WHAT PART OF "I HAVE TO GO" DON'T YOU GET?
HUH.

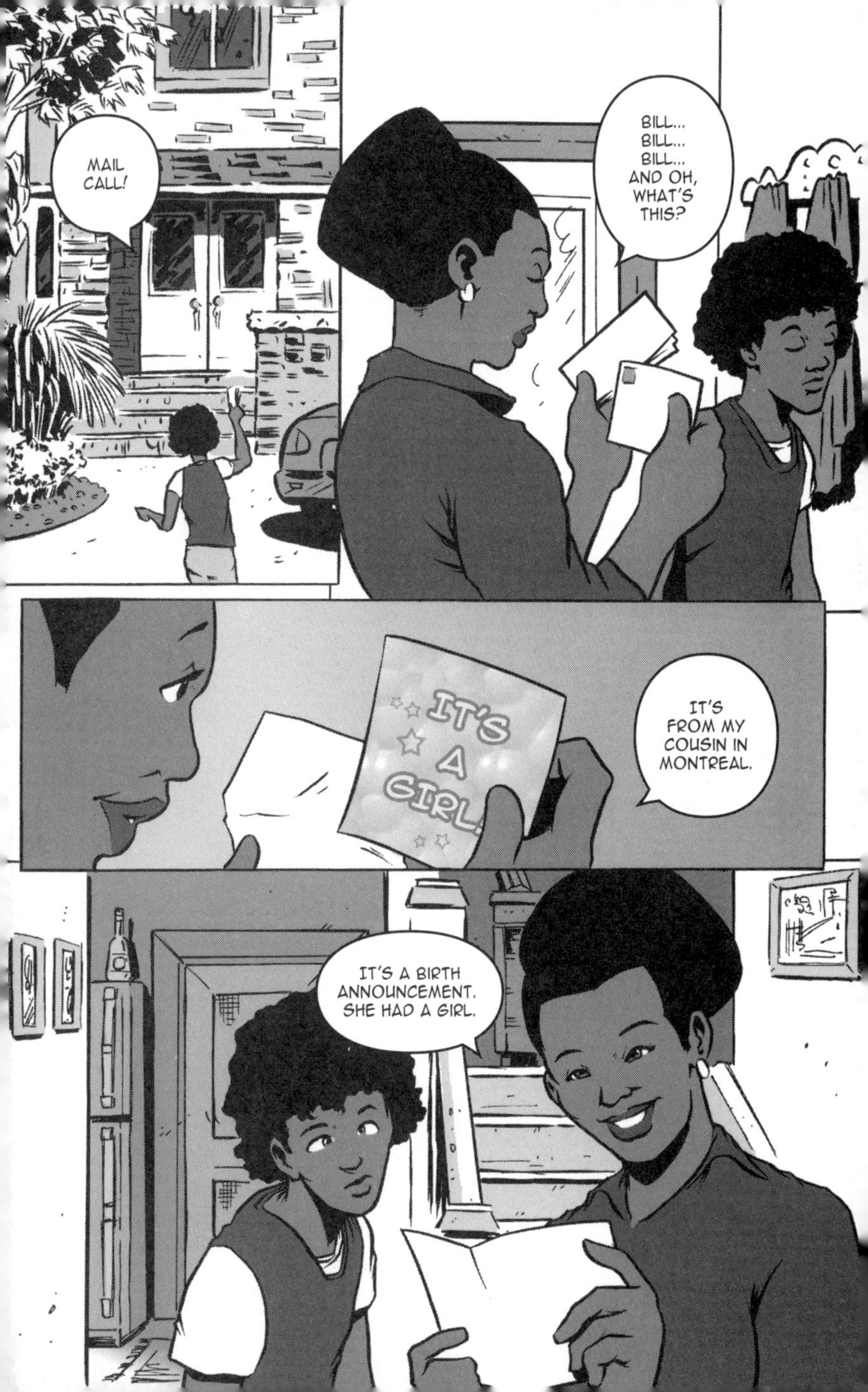
MAIL CALL!
BILL... BILL... BILL... AND OH, WHAT'S THIS?
IT'S A GIRL!
IT'S FROM MY COUSIN IN MONTREAL.
IT'S A BIRTH ANNOUNCEMENT. SHE HAD A GIRL.

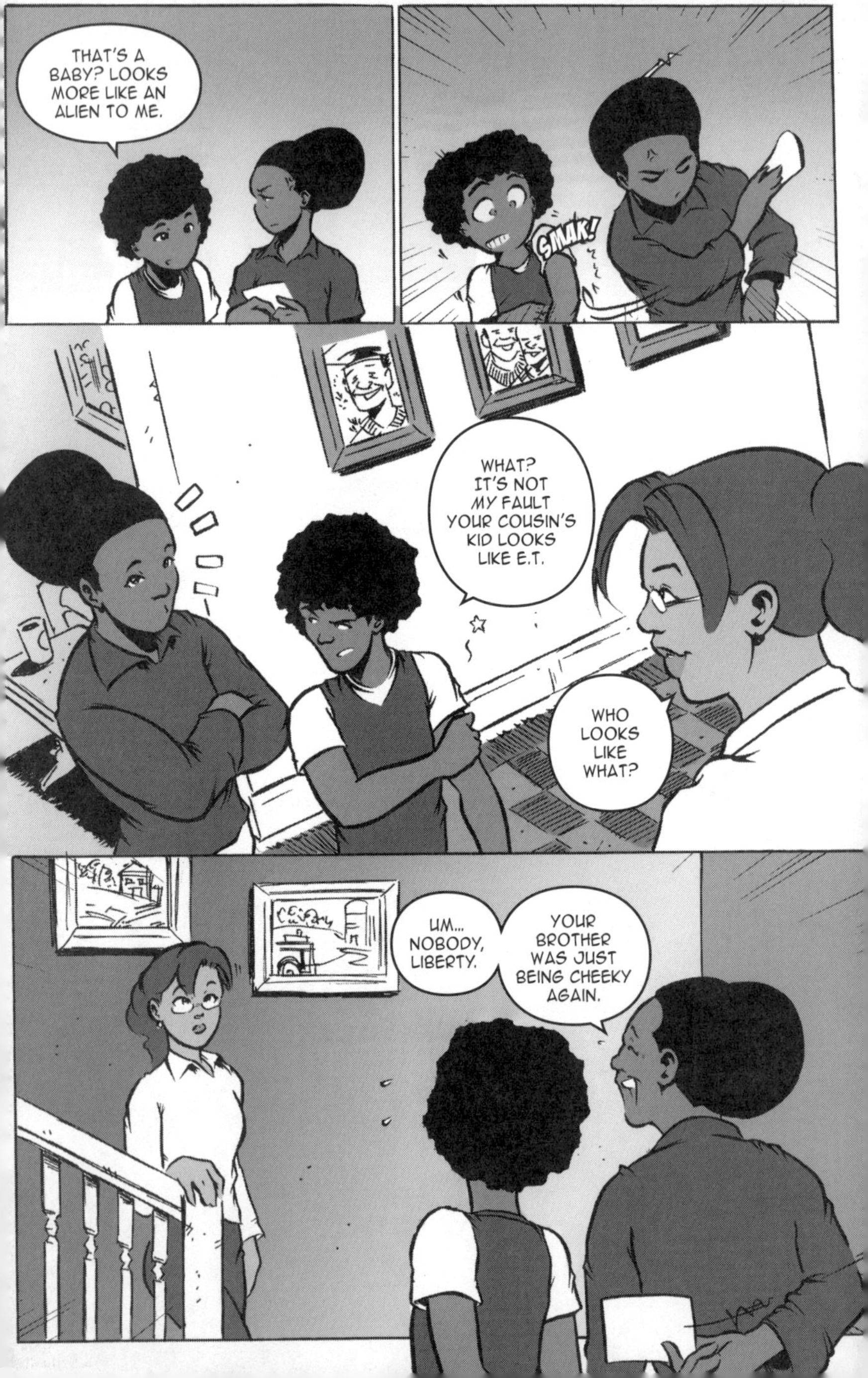
THAT'S A BABY? LOOKS MORE LIKE AN ALIEN TO ME.
SMAK!
WHAT? IT'S NOT MY FAULT YOUR COUSIN'S KID LOOKS LIKE E.T.
WHO LOOKS LIKE WHAT?
UM... NOBODY, LIBERTY.
YOUR BROTHER WAS JUST BEING CHEEKY AGAIN.

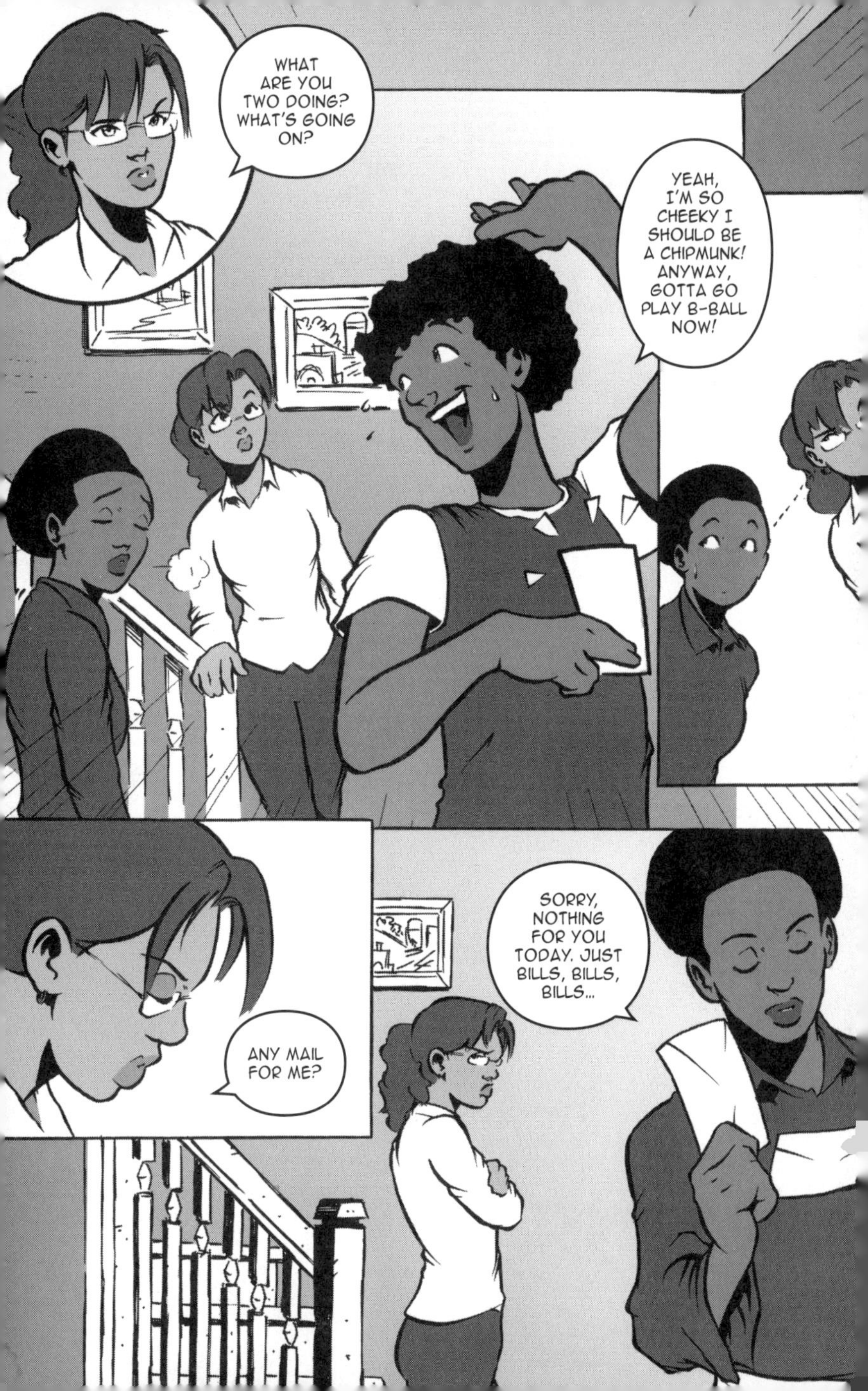
WHAT ARE YOU TWO DOING? WHAT'S GOING ON?
YEAH, I'M SO CHEEKY I SHOULD BE A CHIPMUNK! ANYWAY, GOTTA GO PLAY B-BALL NOW!
ANY MAIL FOR ME?
SORRY, NOTHING FOR YOU TODAY. JUST BILLS, BILLS, BILLS...

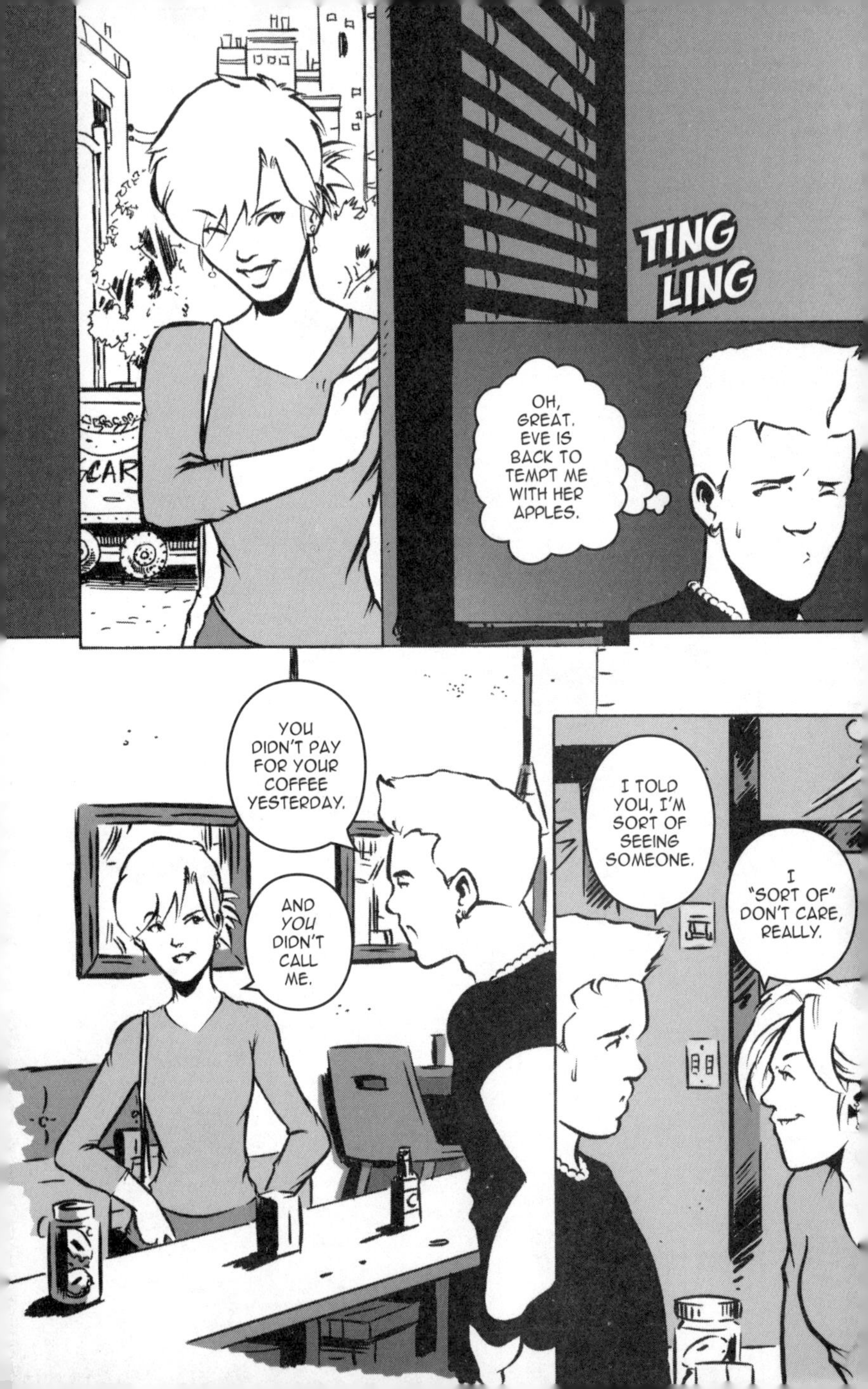
TING LING
OH, GREAT. EVE IS BACK TO TEMPT ME WITH HER APPLES.
YOU DIDN'T PAY FOR YOUR COFFEE YESTERDAY.
AND YOU DIDN'T CALL ME.
I TOLD YOU, I'M SORT OF SEEING SOMEONE.
I "SORT OF" DON'T CARE, REALLY.

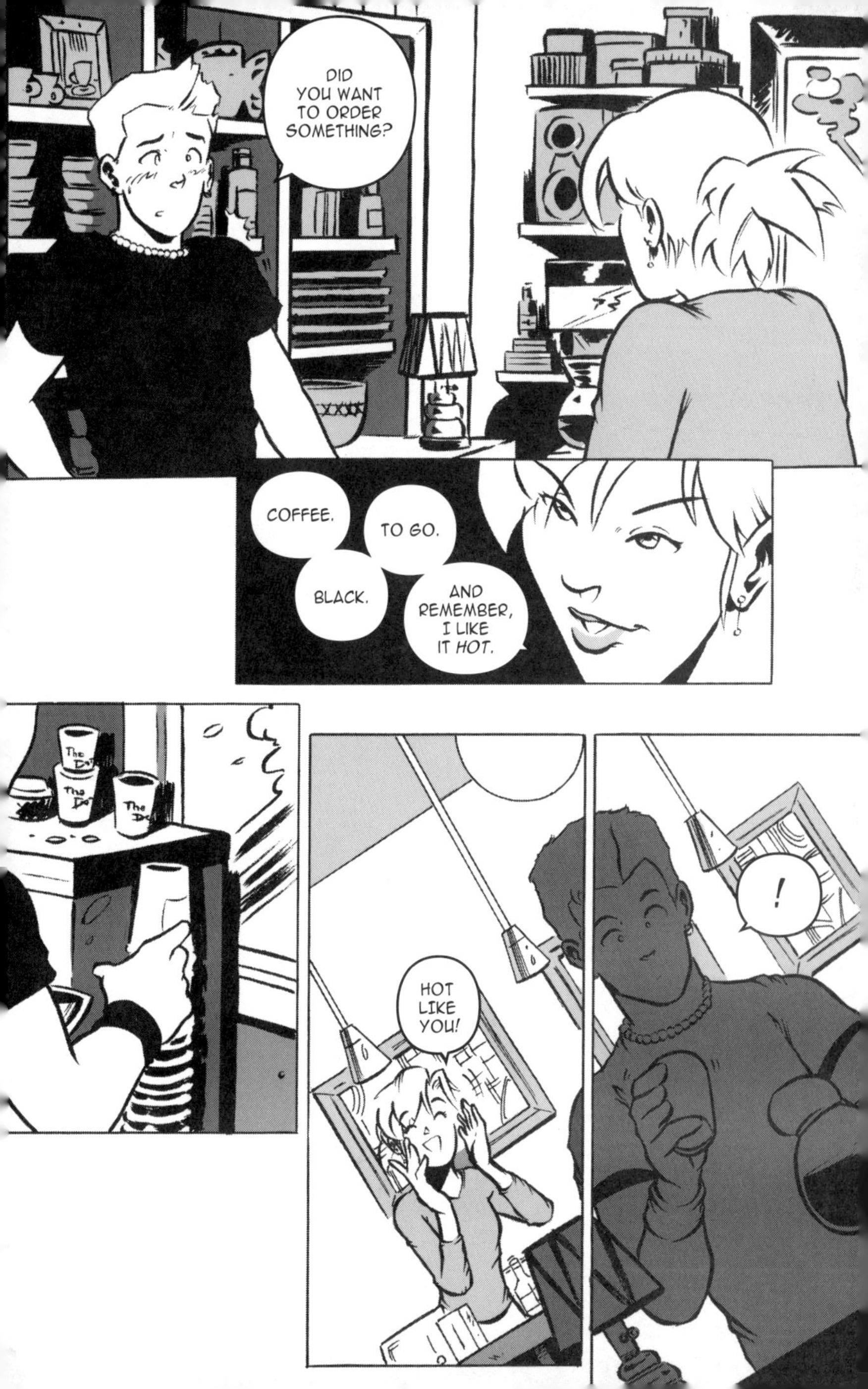
DID YOU WANT TO ORDER SOMETHING?
COFFEE.
TO GO.
BLACK.
AND REMEMBER, I LIKE IT *HOT*.
HOT LIKE YOU!
!

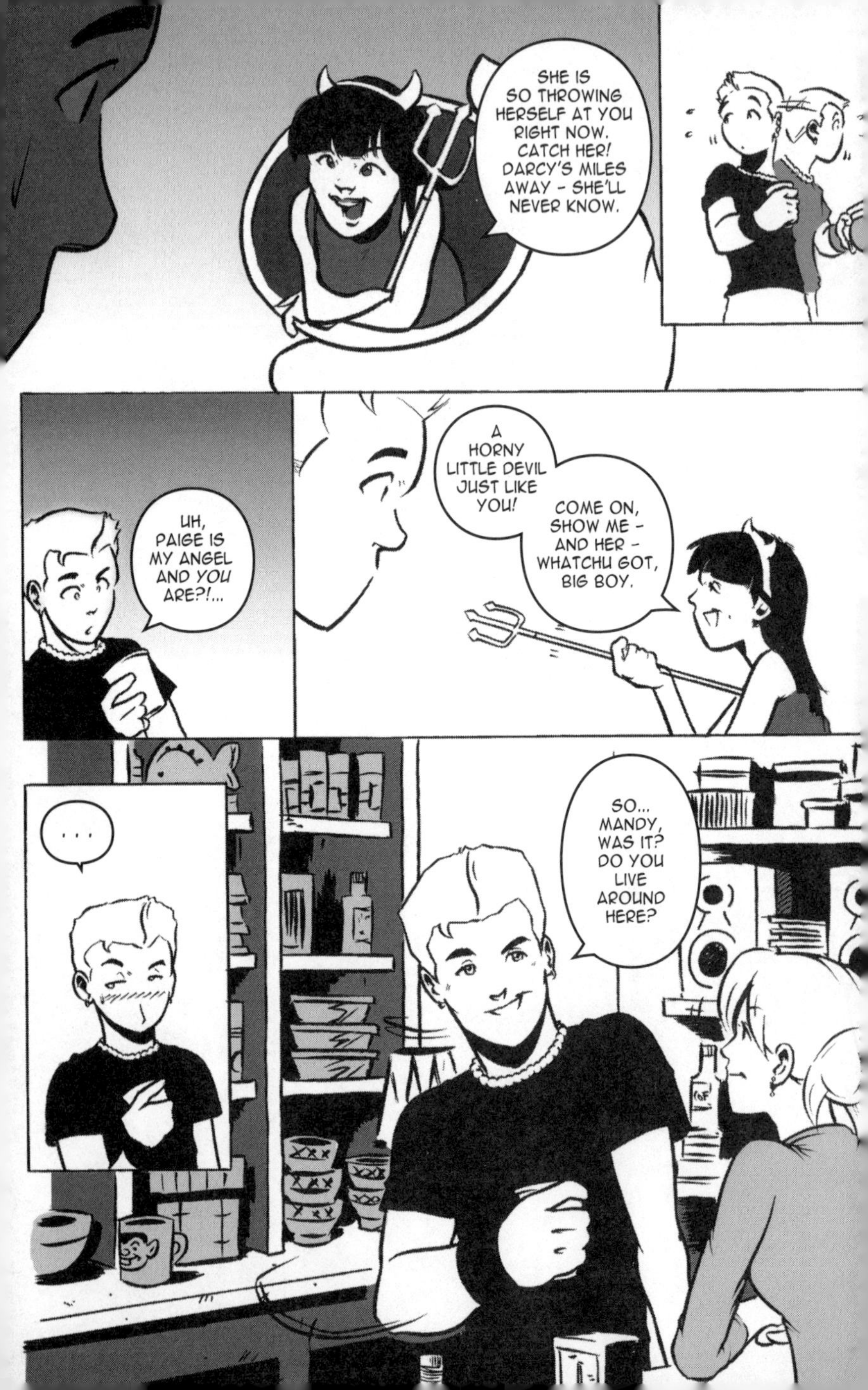
SHE IS SO THROWING HERSELF AT YOU RIGHT NOW. CATCH HER! DARCY'S MILES AWAY - SHE'LL NEVER KNOW.
UH, PAIGE IS MY ANGEL AND YOU ARE?!...
A HORNY LITTLE DEVIL JUST LIKE YOU!
COME ON, SHOW ME - AND HER - WHATCHU GOT, BIG BOY.
...
SO... MANDY, WAS IT? DO YOU LIVE AROUND HERE?

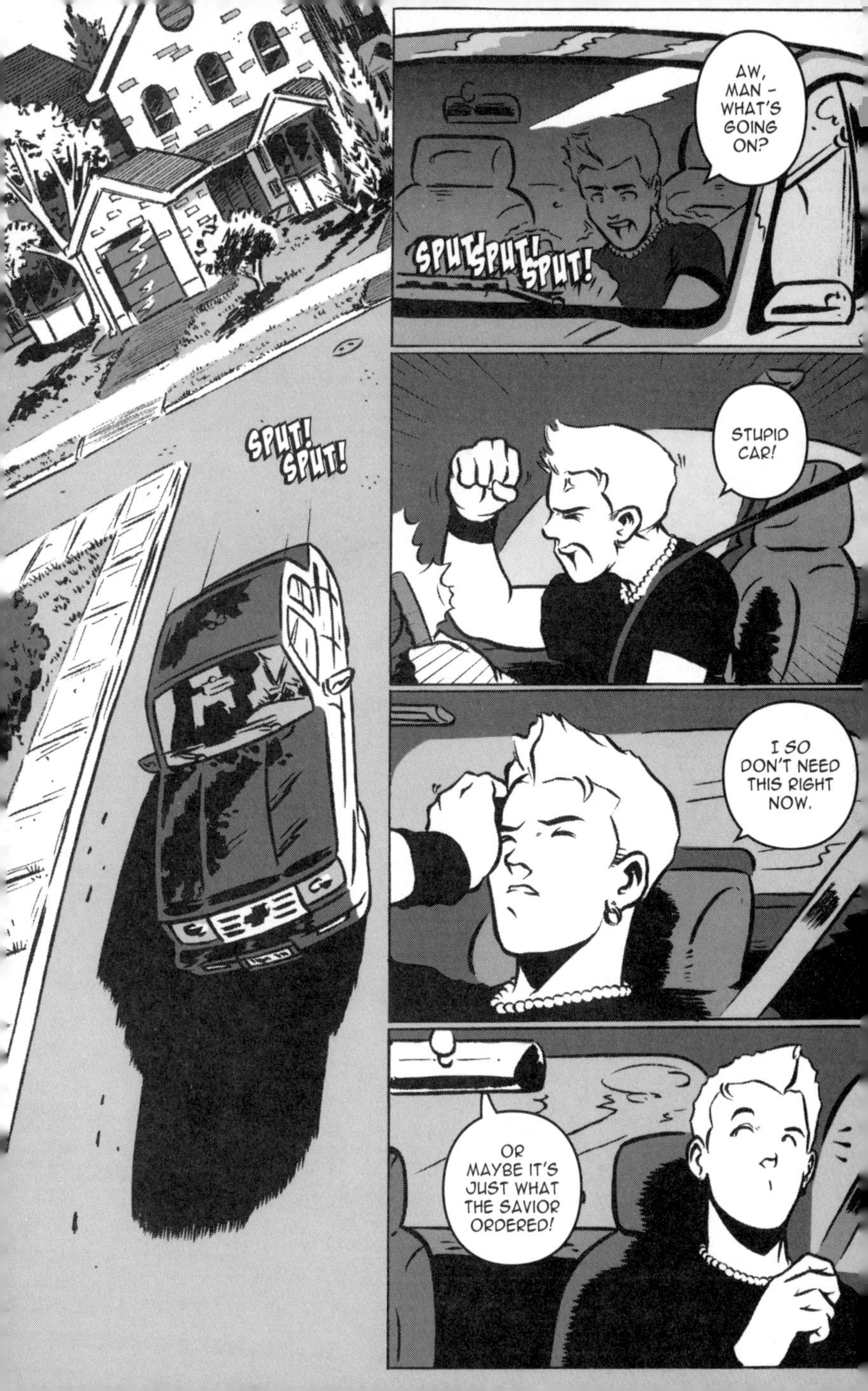
SPUT! SPUT!
AW, MAN - WHAT'S GOING ON?
SPUT! SPUT! SPUT!
STUPID CAR!
I SO DON'T NEED THIS RIGHT NOW.
OR MAYBE IT'S JUST WHAT THE SAVIOR ORDERED!

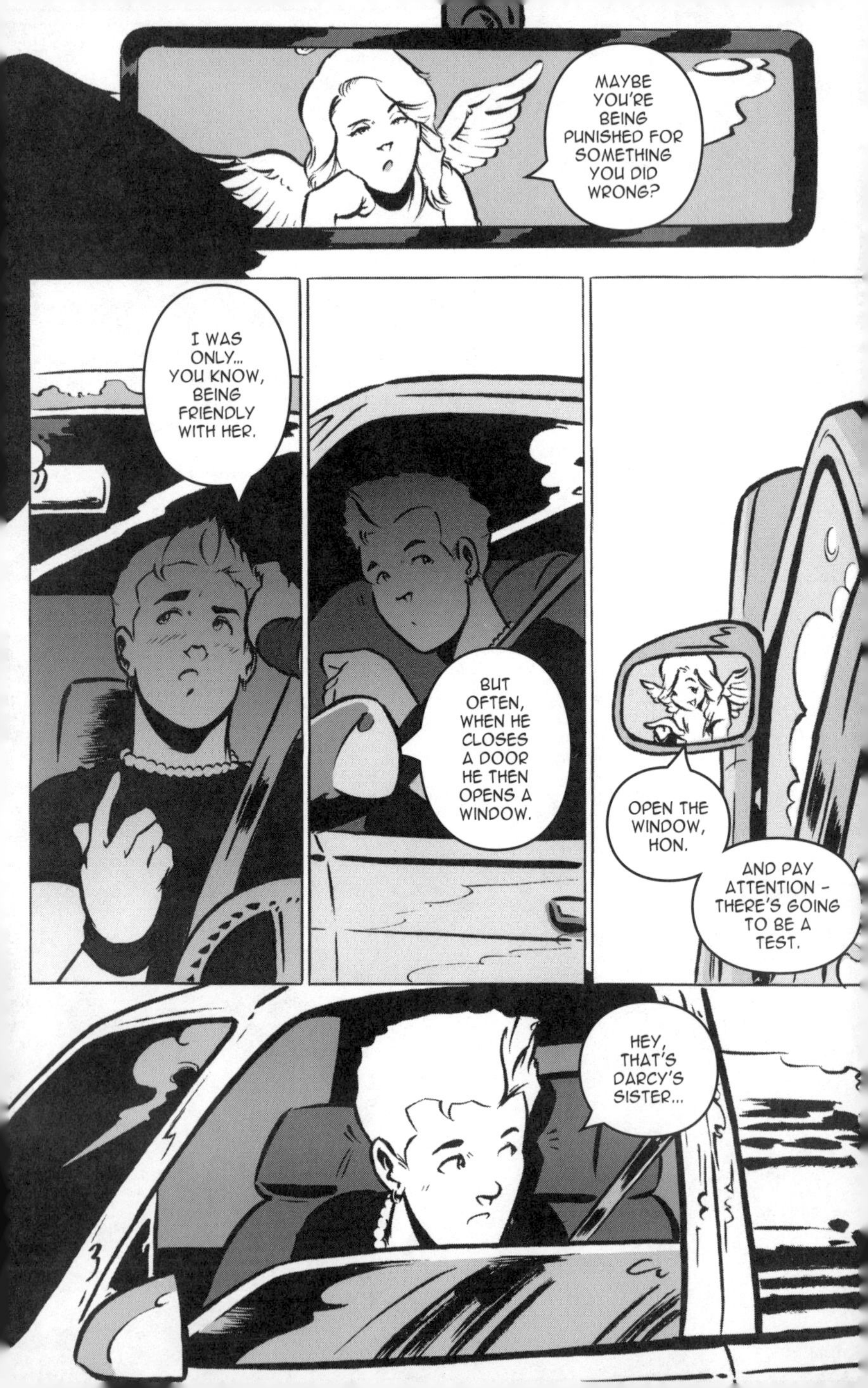
MAYBE YOU'RE BEING PUNISHED FOR SOMETHING YOU DID WRONG?
I WAS ONLY... YOU KNOW, BEING FRIENDLY WITH HER.
BUT OFTEN, WHEN HE CLOSES A DOOR HE THEN OPENS A WINDOW.
OPEN THE WINDOW, HON.
AND PAY ATTENTION – THERE'S GOING TO BE A TEST.
HEY, THAT'S DARCY'S SISTER...

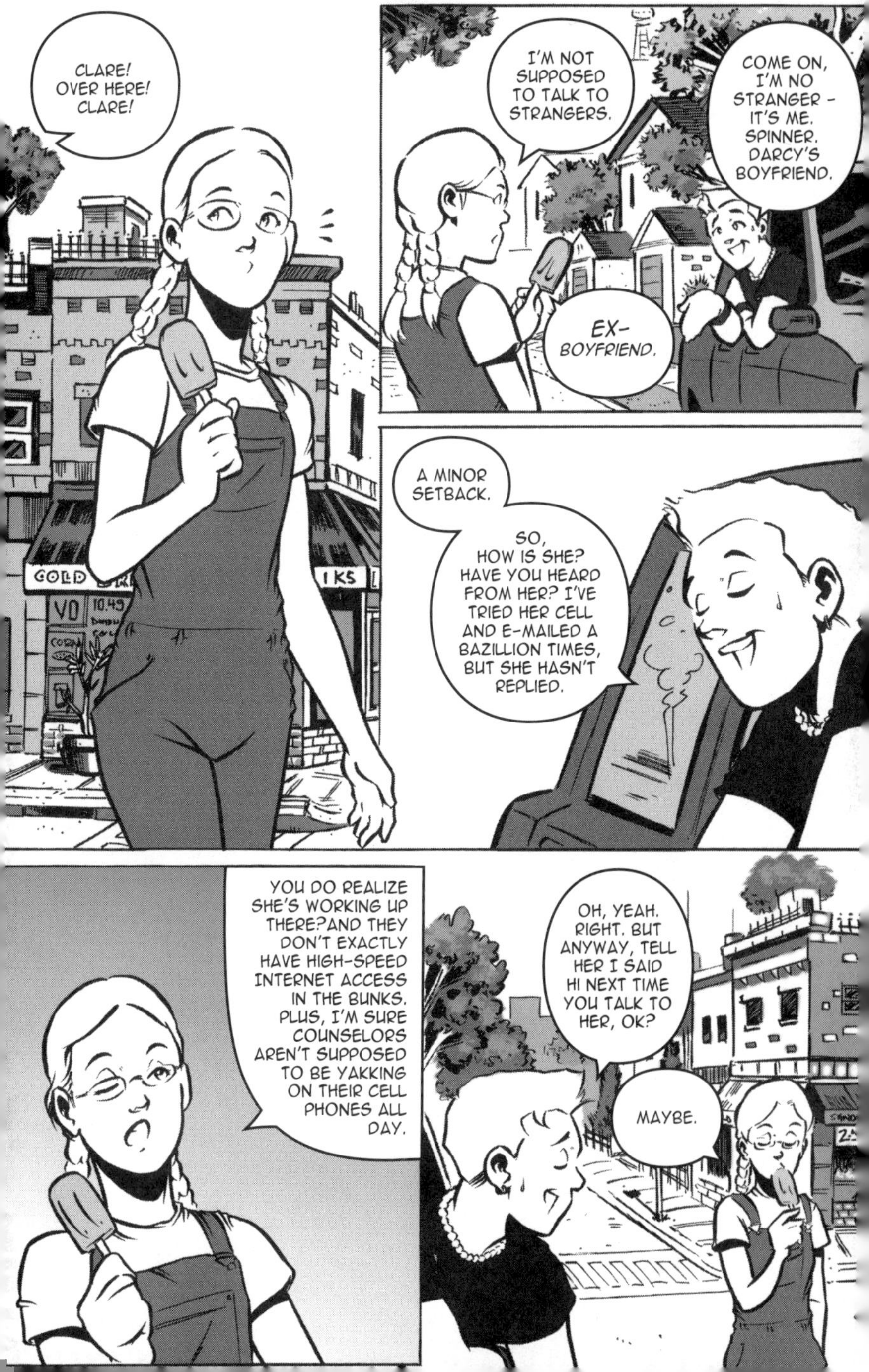
CLARE! OVER HERE! CLARE!
I'M NOT SUPPOSED TO TALK TO STRANGERS.
COME ON, I'M NO STRANGER - IT'S ME. SPINNER. DARCY'S BOYFRIEND.
EX-BOYFRIEND.
A MINOR SETBACK.
SO, HOW IS SHE? HAVE YOU HEARD FROM HER? I'VE TRIED HER CELL AND E-MAILED A BAZILLION TIMES, BUT SHE HASN'T REPLIED.
YOU DO REALIZE SHE'S WORKING UP THERE?AND THEY DON'T EXACTLY HAVE HIGH-SPEED INTERNET ACCESS IN THE BUNKS. PLUS, I'M SURE COUNSELORS AREN'T SUPPOSED TO BE YAKKING ON THEIR CELL PHONES ALL DAY.
OH, YEAH. RIGHT. BUT ANYWAY, TELL HER I SAID HI NEXT TIME YOU TALK TO HER, OK?
MAYBE.

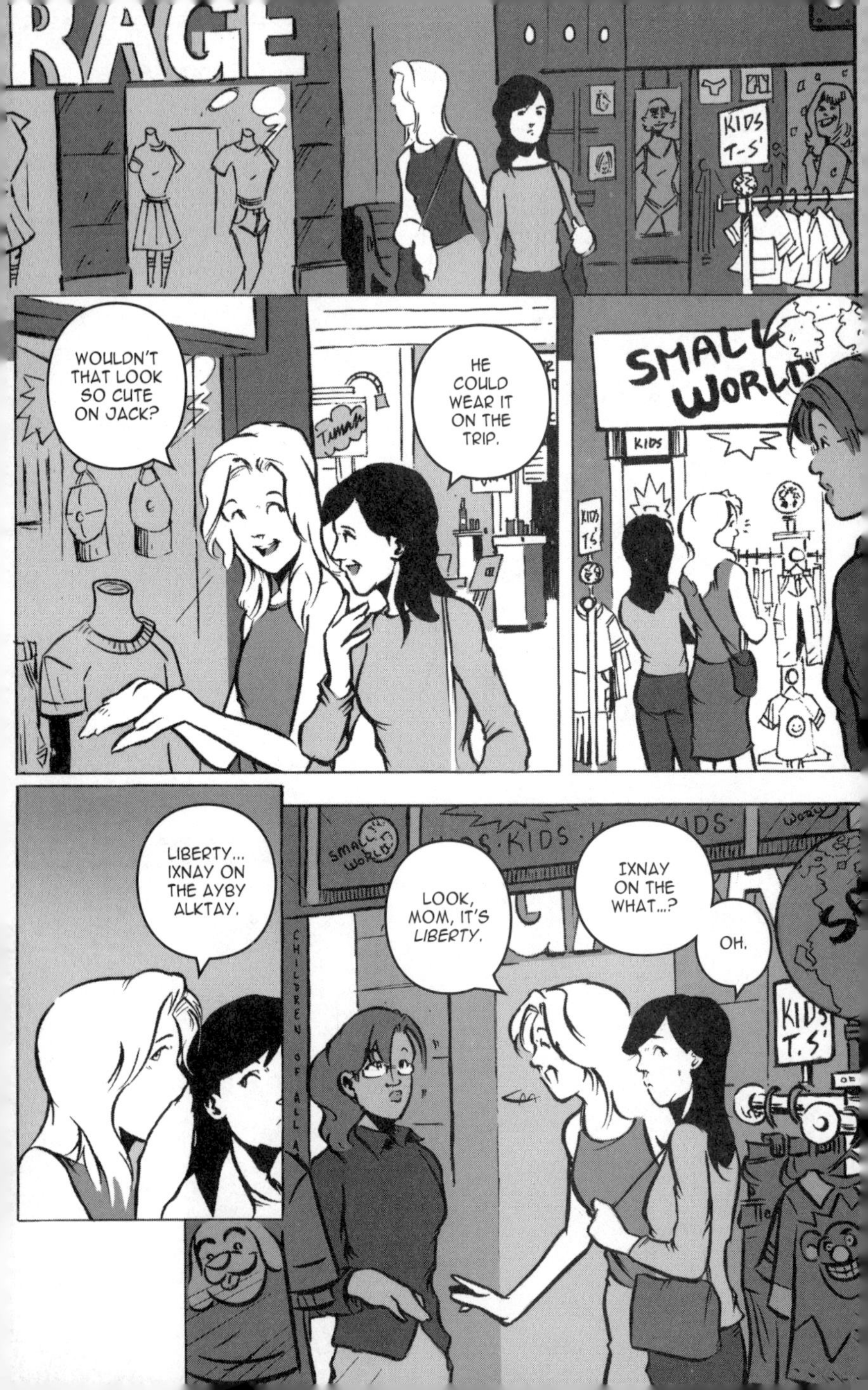
RAGE
KIDS T-S'
WOULDN'T THAT LOOK SO CUTE ON JACK?
HE COULD WEAR IT ON THE TRIP.
SMALL WORLD
KIDS
KIDS T.S'
LIBERTY... IXNAY ON THE AYBY ALKTAY.
SMALL WORLD
KIDS
LOOK, MOM, IT'S *LIBERTY*.
IXNAY ON THE WHAT...?
OH.
KIDS T.S'

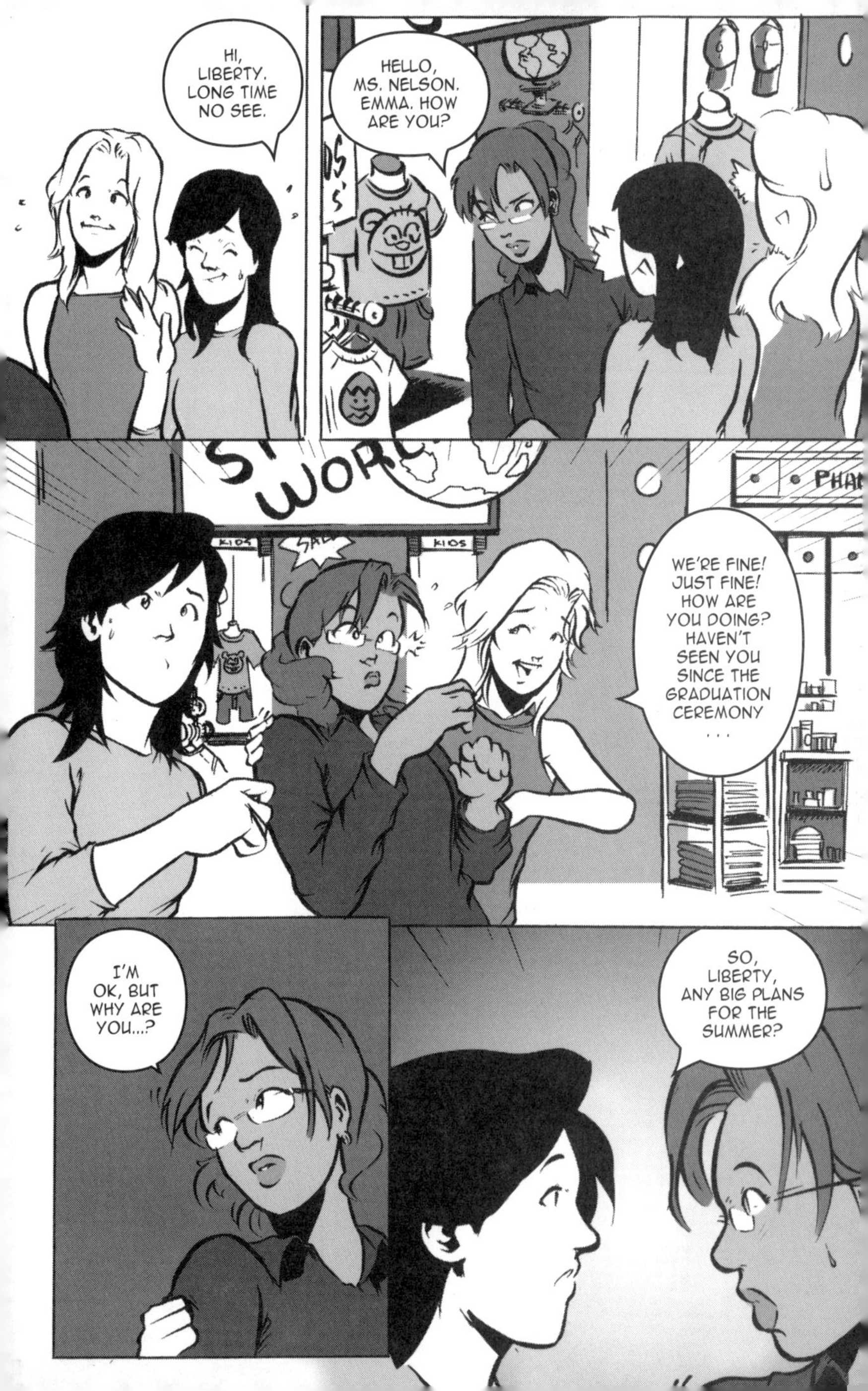
HI, LIBERTY. LONG TIME NO SEE.
HELLO, MS. NELSON. EMMA. HOW ARE YOU?
WE'RE FINE! JUST FINE! HOW ARE YOU DOING? HAVEN'T SEEN YOU SINCE THE GRADUATION CEREMONY . . .
I'M OK, BUT WHY ARE YOU...?
SO, LIBERTY, ANY BIG PLANS FOR THE SUMMER?

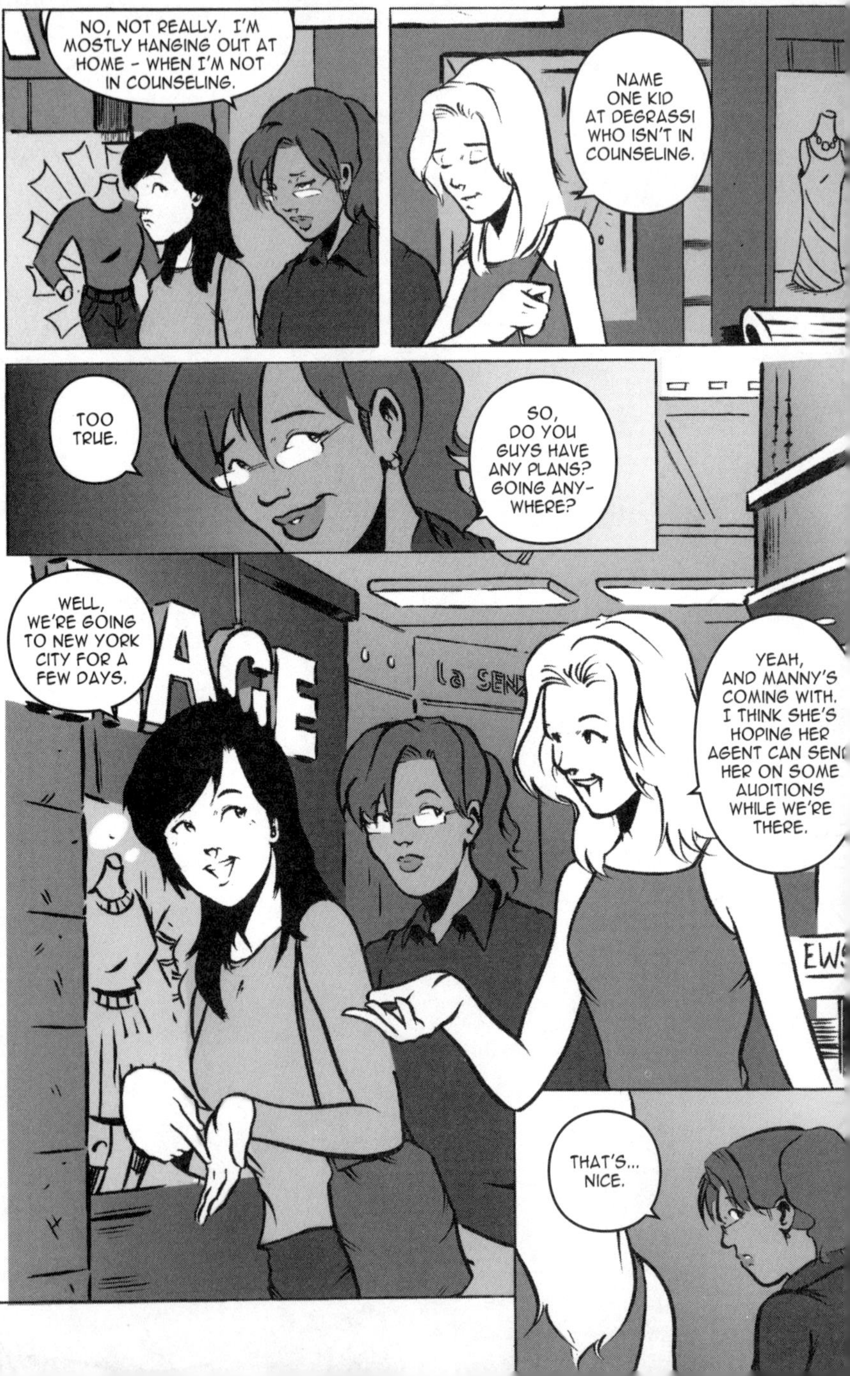
NO, NOT REALLY. I'M MOSTLY HANGING OUT AT HOME - WHEN I'M NOT IN COUNSELING.
NAME ONE KID AT DEGRASSI WHO ISN'T IN COUNSELING.
TOO TRUE.
SO, DO YOU GUYS HAVE ANY PLANS? GOING ANY-WHERE?
WELL, WE'RE GOING TO NEW YORK CITY FOR A FEW DAYS.
YEAH, AND MANNY'S COMING WITH. I THINK SHE'S HOPING HER AGENT CAN SEN HER ON SOME AUDITIONS WHILE WE'RE THERE.
THAT'S... NICE.

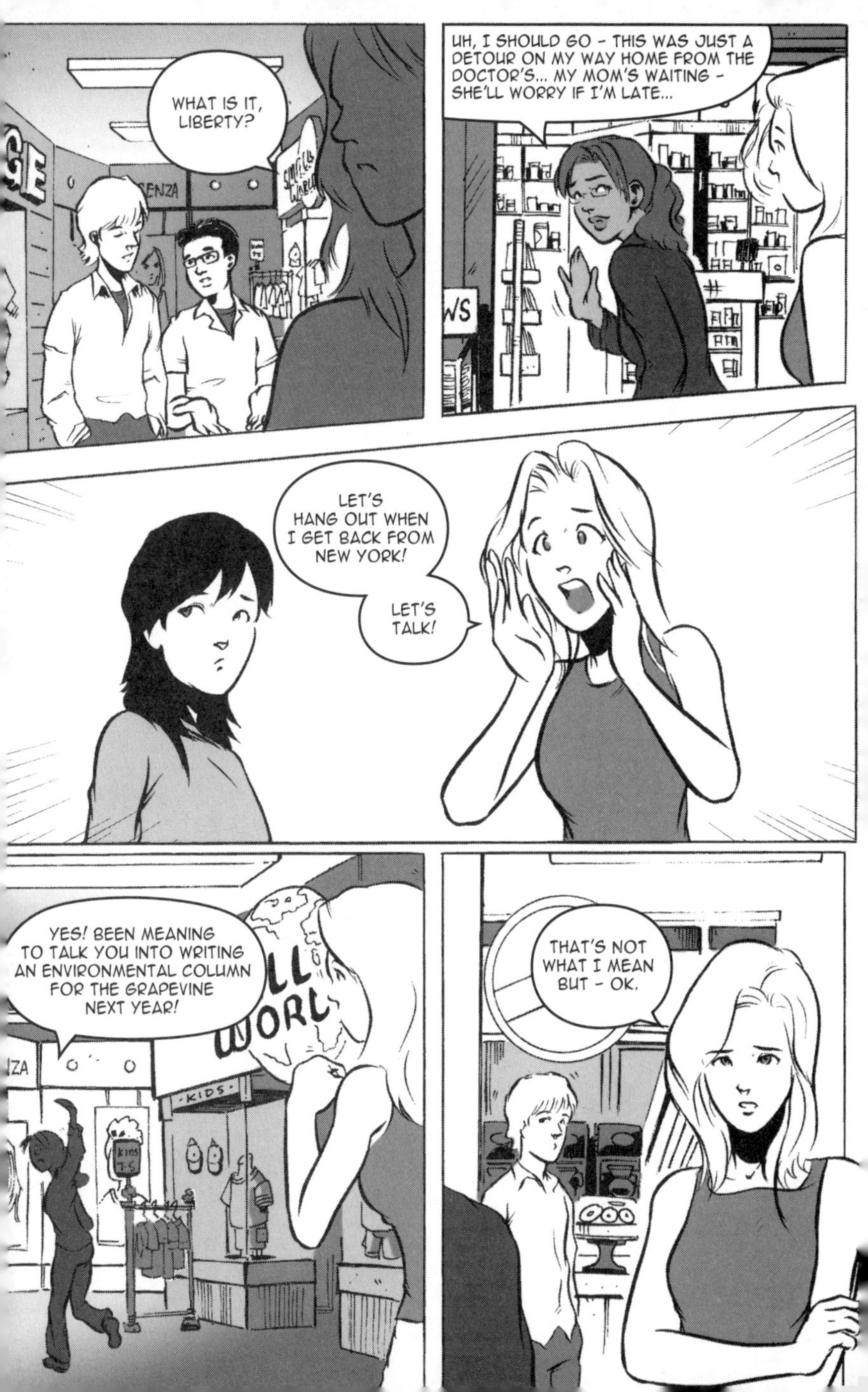
WHAT IS IT, LIBERTY?
UH, I SHOULD GO - THIS WAS JUST A DETOUR ON MY WAY HOME FROM THE DOCTOR'S... MY MOM'S WAITING - SHE'LL WORRY IF I'M LATE...
LET'S HANG OUT WHEN I GET BACK FROM NEW YORK!
LET'S TALK!
YES! BEEN MEANING TO TALK YOU INTO WRITING AN ENVIRONMENTAL COLUMN FOR THE GRAPEVINE NEXT YEAR!
THAT'S NOT WHAT I MEAN BUT - OK.

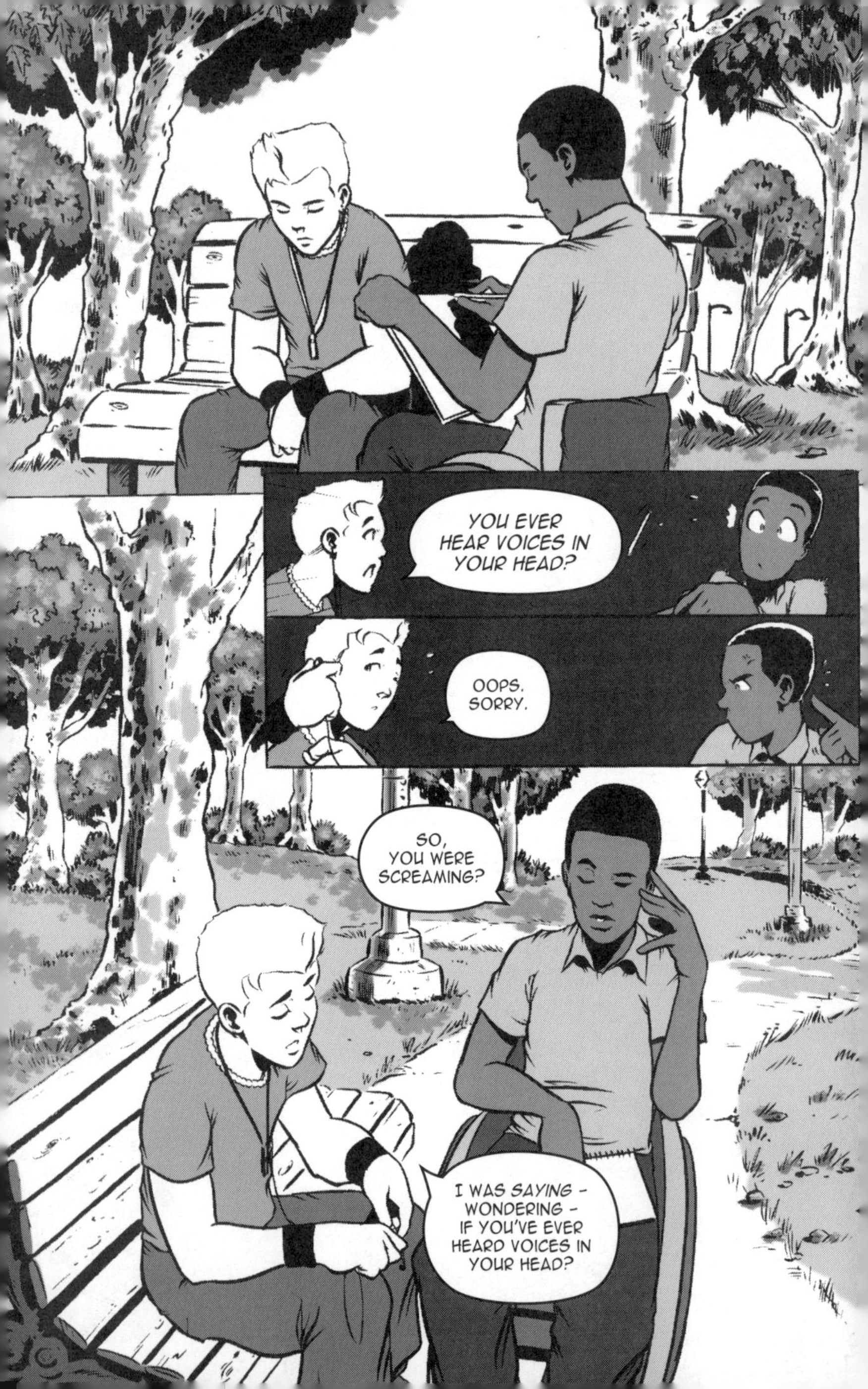
YOU EVER HEAR VOICES IN YOUR HEAD?
OOPS. SORRY.
SO, YOU WERE SCREAMING?
I WAS SAYING - WONDERING - IF YOU'VE EVER HEARD VOICES IN YOUR HEAD?

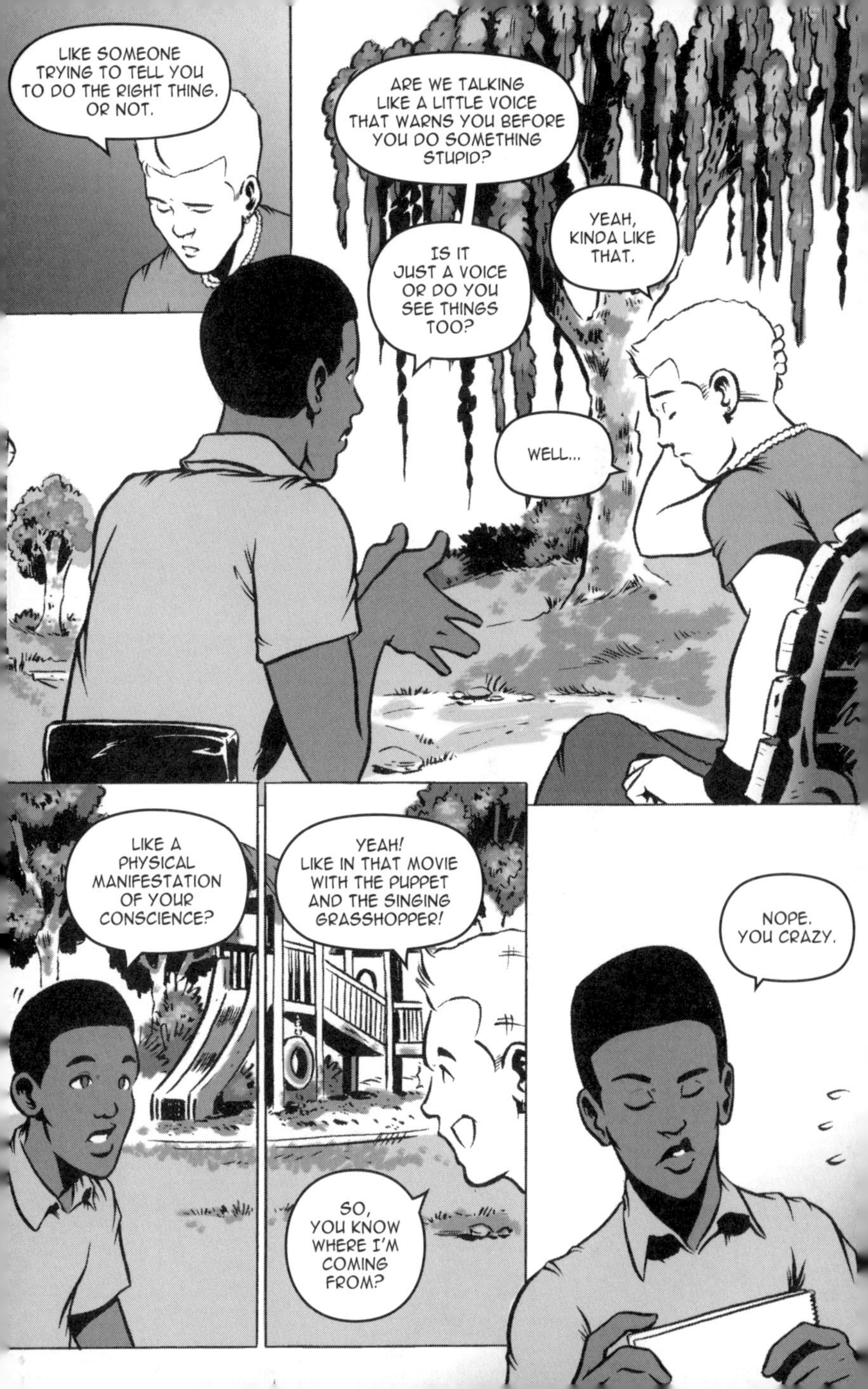
LIKE SOMEONE TRYING TO TELL YOU TO DO THE RIGHT THING. OR NOT.
ARE WE TALKING LIKE A LITTLE VOICE THAT WARNS YOU BEFORE YOU DO SOMETHING STUPID?
YEAH, KINDA LIKE THAT.
IS IT JUST A VOICE OR DO YOU SEE THINGS TOO?
WELL...
LIKE A PHYSICAL MANIFESTATION OF YOUR CONSCIENCE?
YEAH! LIKE IN THAT MOVIE WITH THE PUPPET AND THE SINGING GRASSHOPPER!
SO, YOU KNOW WHERE I'M COMING FROM?
NOPE. YOU CRAZY.

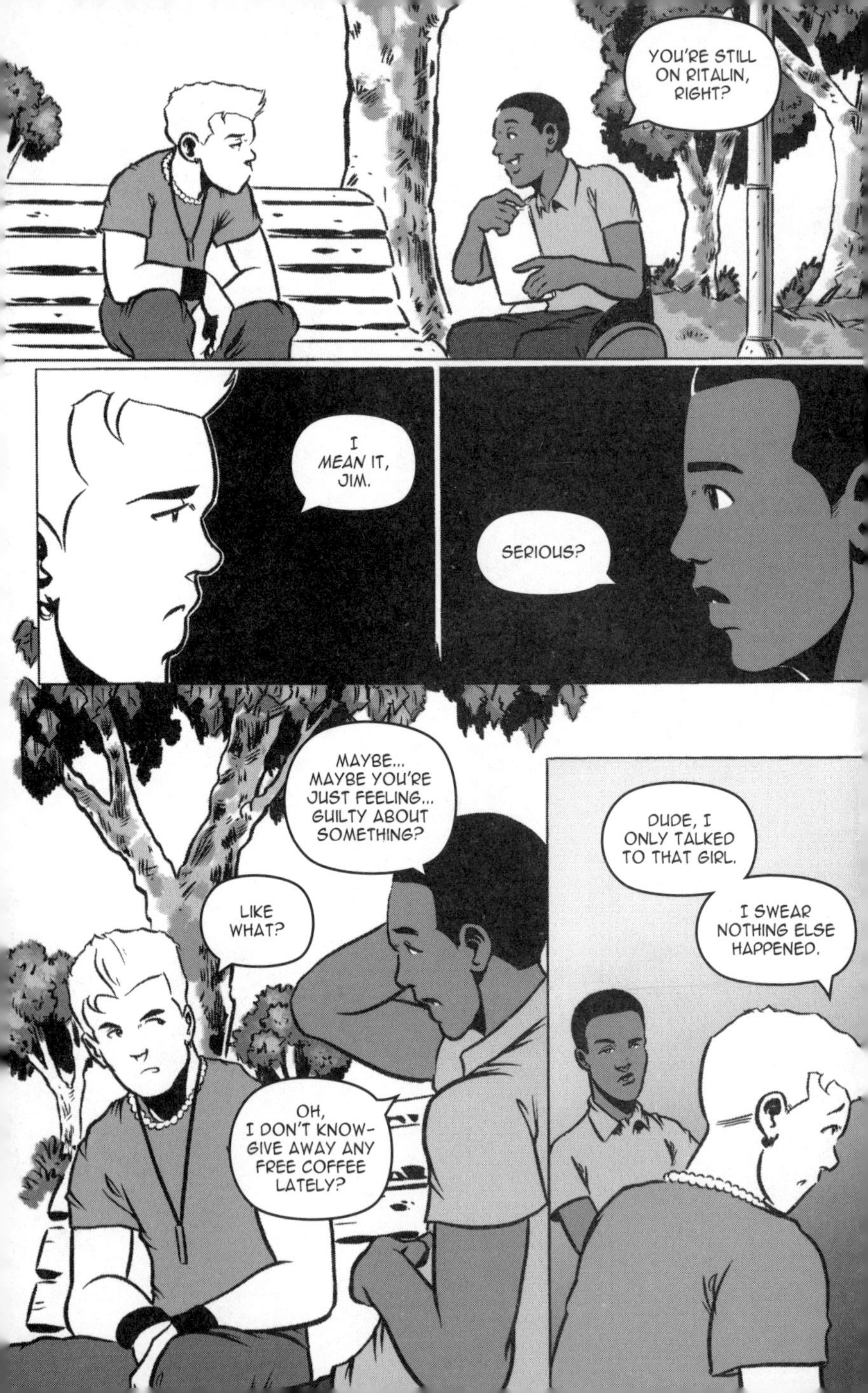
YOU'RE STILL ON RITALIN, RIGHT?
I MEAN IT, JIM.
SERIOUS?
MAYBE... MAYBE YOU'RE JUST FEELING... GUILTY ABOUT SOMETHING?
LIKE WHAT?
OH, I DON'T KNOW- GIVE AWAY ANY FREE COFFEE LATELY?
DUDE, I ONLY TALKED TO THAT GIRL.
I SWEAR NOTHING ELSE HAPPENED.

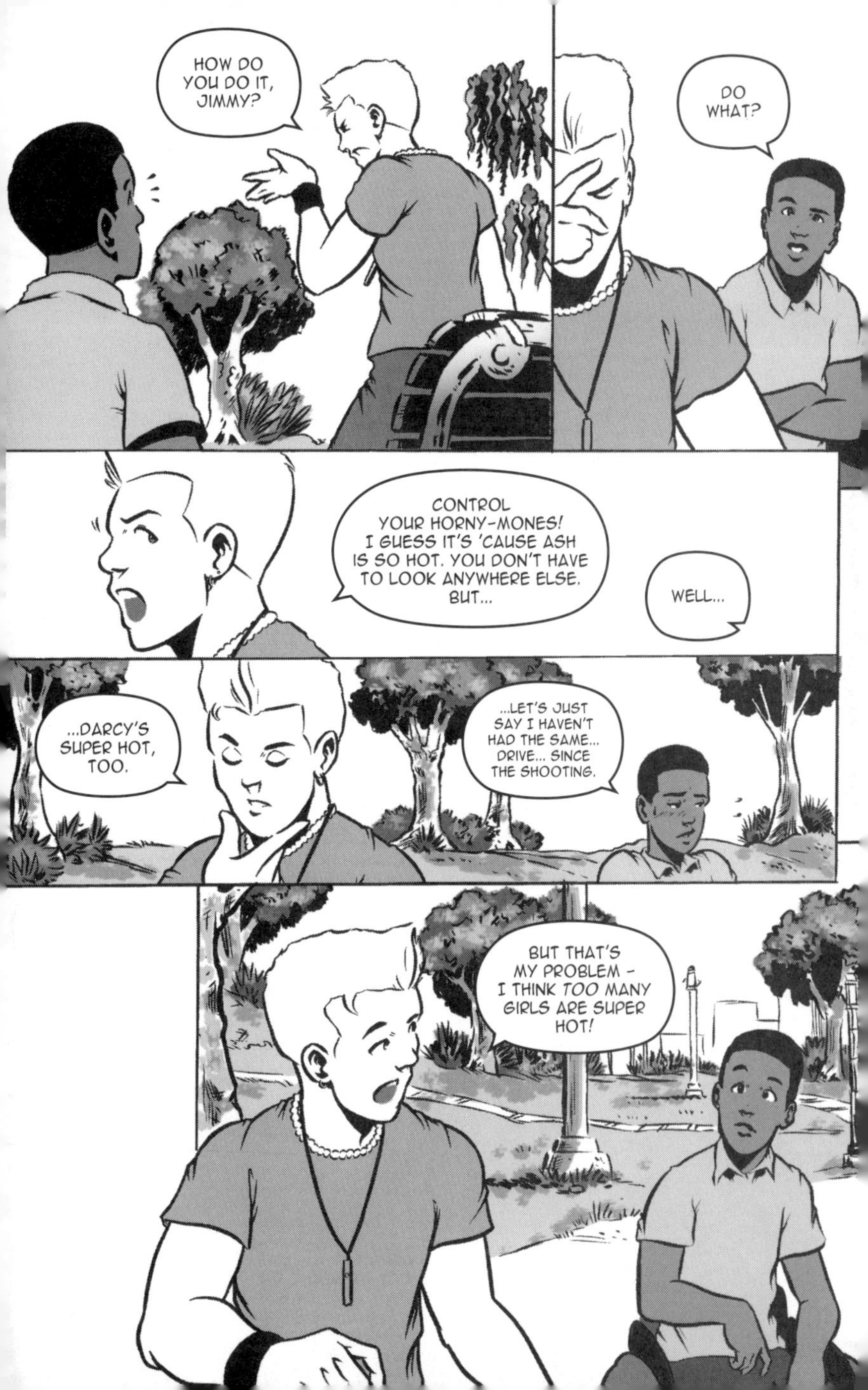
HOW DO YOU DO IT, JIMMY?
DO WHAT?
CONTROL YOUR HORNY-MONES! I GUESS IT'S 'CAUSE ASH IS SO HOT. YOU DON'T HAVE TO LOOK ANYWHERE ELSE. BUT...
WELL...
...DARCY'S SUPER HOT, TOO.
...LET'S JUST SAY I HAVEN'T HAD THE SAME... DRIVE... SINCE THE SHOOTING.
BUT THAT'S MY PROBLEM – I THINK *TOO* MANY GIRLS ARE SUPER HOT!

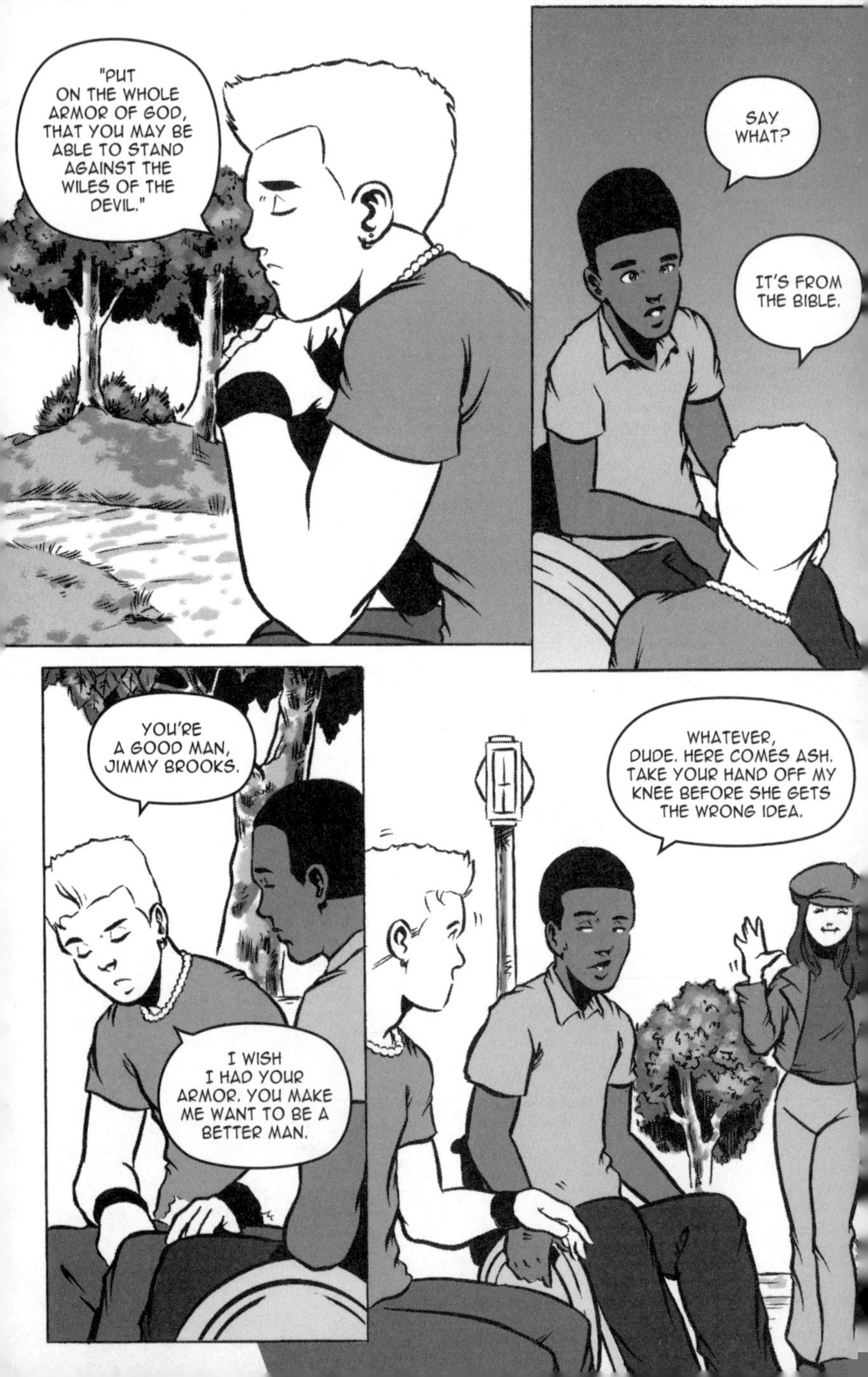
"PUT ON THE WHOLE ARMOR OF GOD, THAT YOU MAY BE ABLE TO STAND AGAINST THE WILES OF THE DEVIL."
SAY WHAT?
IT'S FROM THE BIBLE.
YOU'RE A GOOD MAN, JIMMY BROOKS.
I WISH I HAD YOUR ARMOR. YOU MAKE ME WANT TO BE A BETTER MAN.
WHATEVER, DUDE. HERE COMES ASH. TAKE YOUR HAND OFF MY KNEE BEFORE SHE GETS THE WRONG IDEA.

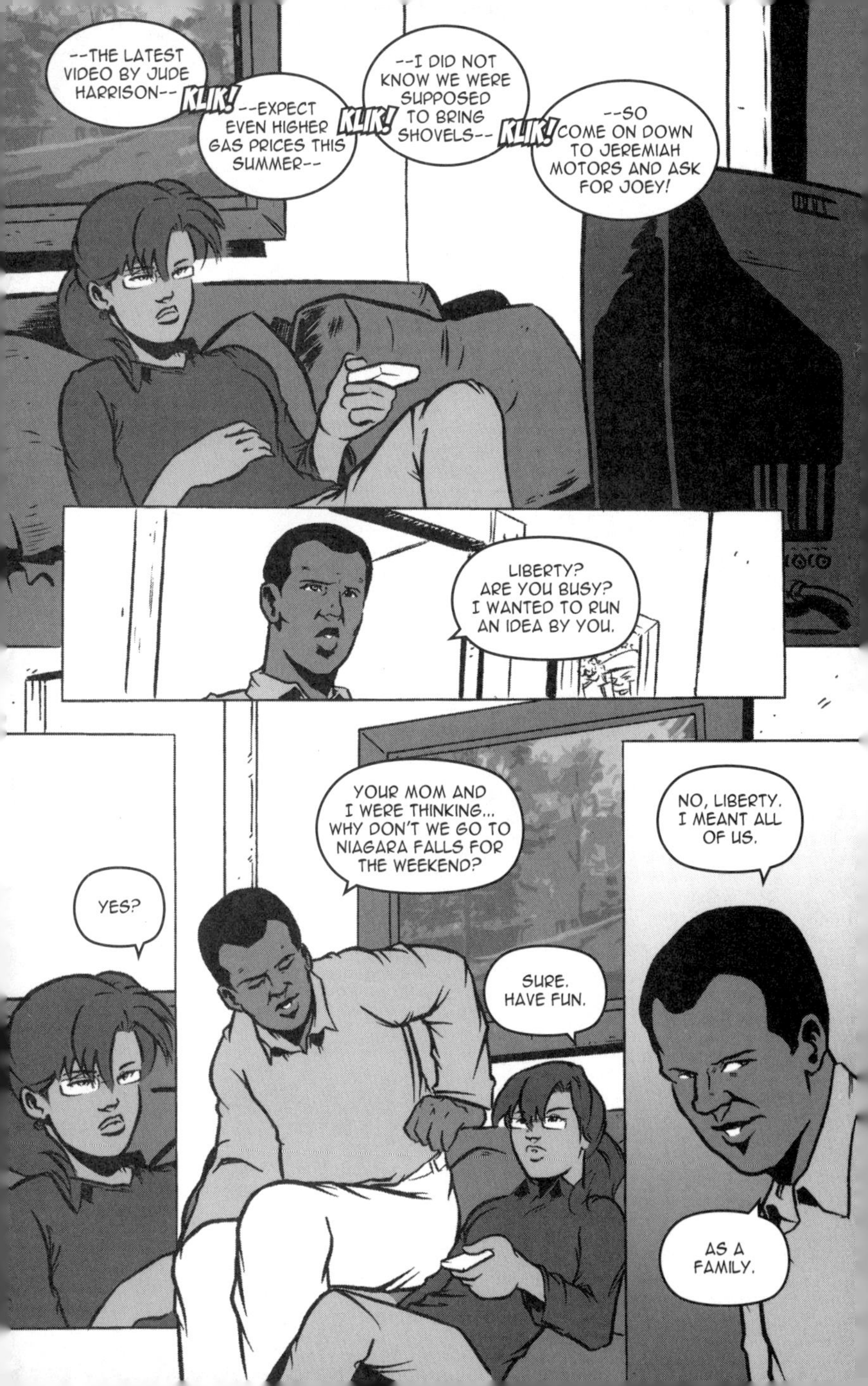
--THE LATEST VIDEO BY JUDE HARRISON--
KLIK!
--EXPECT EVEN HIGHER GAS PRICES THIS SUMMER--
KLIK!
--I DID NOT KNOW WE WERE SUPPOSED TO BRING SHOVELS--
KLIK!
--SO COME ON DOWN TO JEREMIAH MOTORS AND ASK FOR JOEY!
LIBERTY? ARE YOU BUSY? I WANTED TO RUN AN IDEA BY YOU.
YES?
YOUR MOM AND I WERE THINKING... WHY DON'T WE GO TO NIAGARA FALLS FOR THE WEEKEND?
SURE. HAVE FUN.
NO, LIBERTY. I MEANT ALL OF US.
AS A FAMILY.

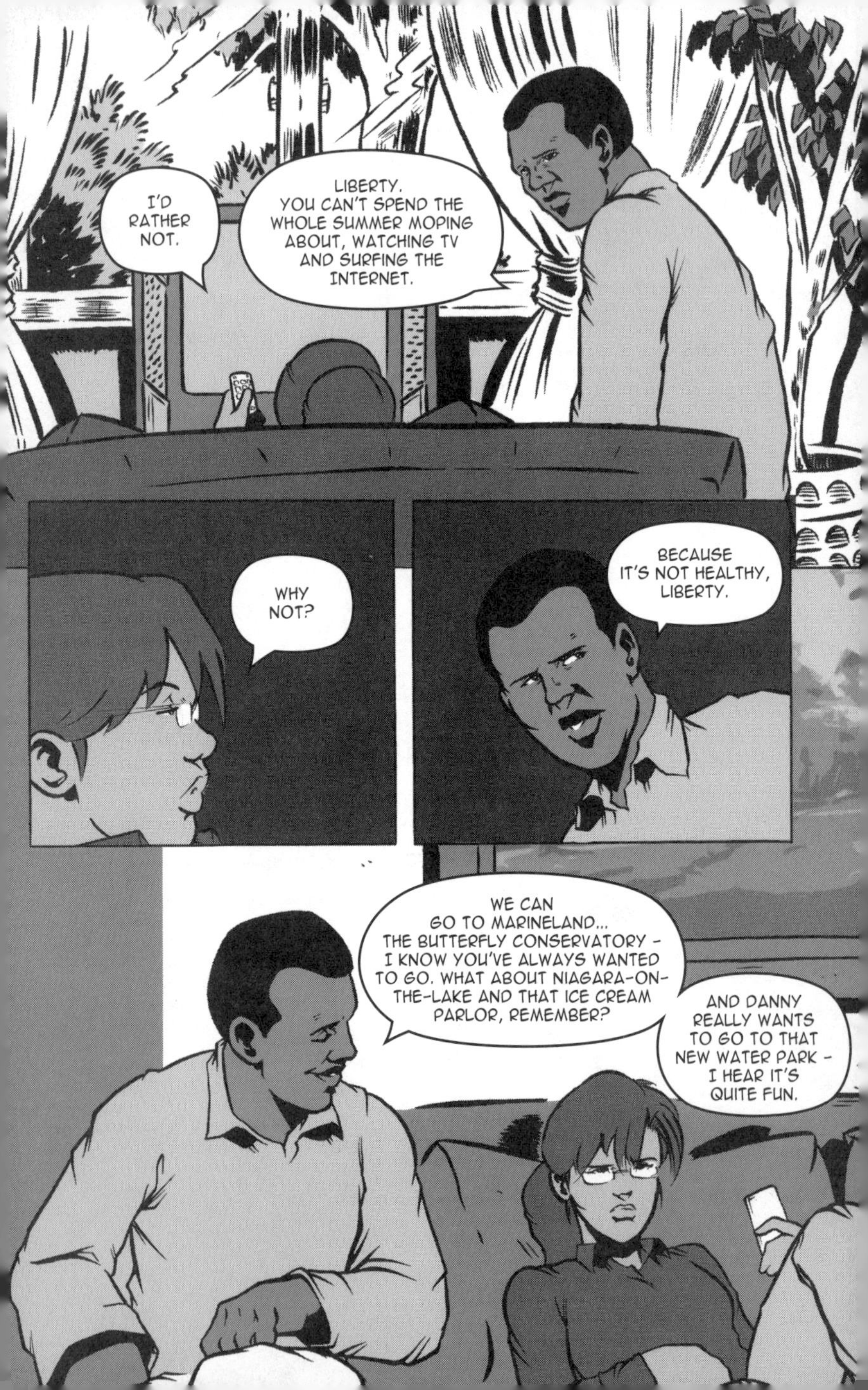
I'D RATHER NOT.
LIBERTY. YOU CAN'T SPEND THE WHOLE SUMMER MOPING ABOUT, WATCHING TV AND SURFING THE INTERNET.
WHY NOT?
BECAUSE IT'S NOT HEALTHY, LIBERTY.
WE CAN GO TO MARINELAND... THE BUTTERFLY CONSERVATORY - I KNOW YOU'VE ALWAYS WANTED TO GO. WHAT ABOUT NIAGARA-ON-THE-LAKE AND THAT ICE CREAM PARLOR, REMEMBER?
AND DANNY REALLY WANTS TO GO TO THAT NEW WATER PARK - I HEAR IT'S QUITE FUN.

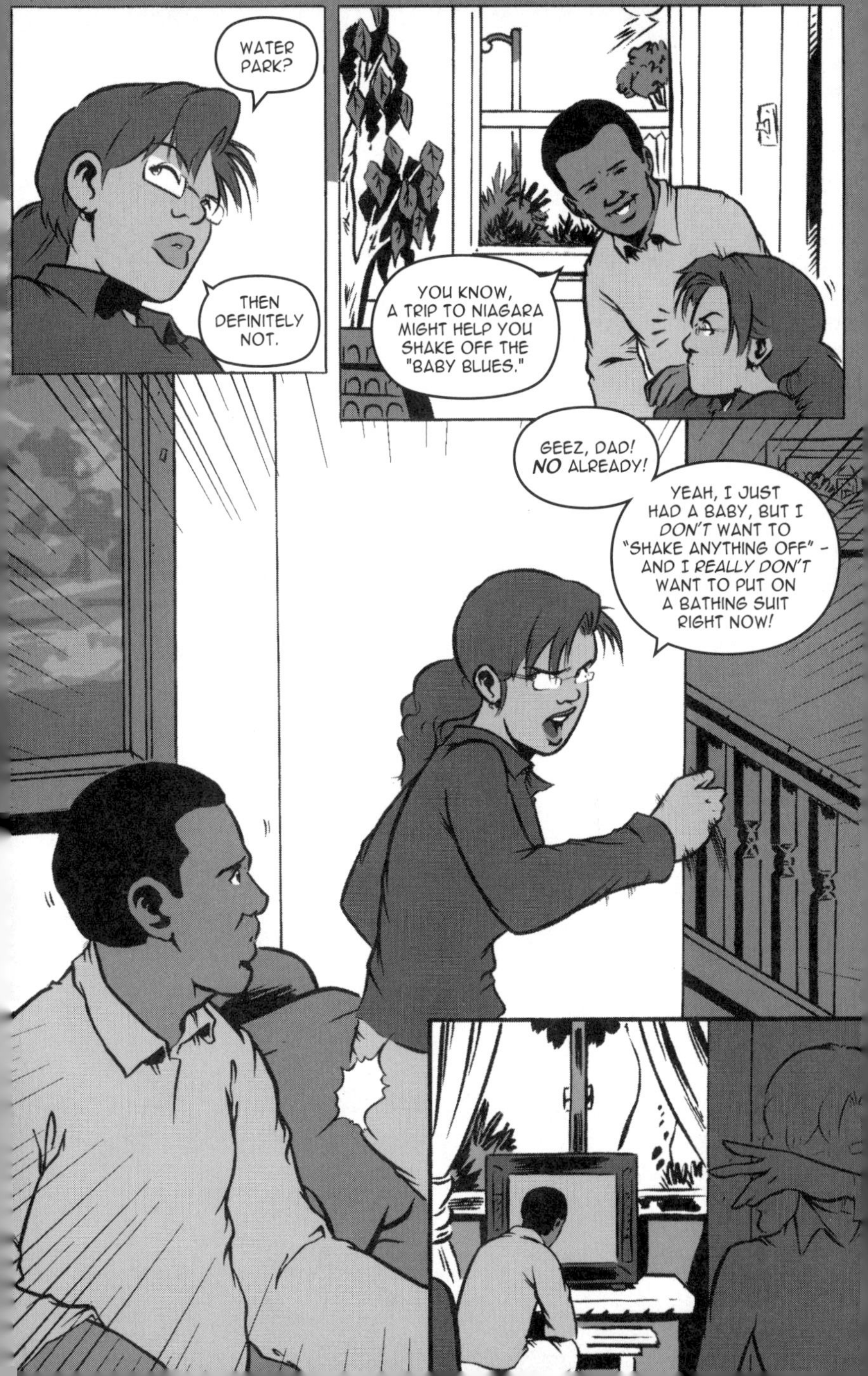

WATER PARK?
THEN DEFINITELY NOT.
YOU KNOW, A TRIP TO NIAGARA MIGHT HELP YOU SHAKE OFF THE "BABY BLUES."
GEEZ, DAD! NO ALREADY!
YEAH, I JUST HAD A BABY, BUT I DON'T WANT TO "SHAKE ANYTHING OFF" - AND I REALLY DON'T WANT TO PUT ON A BATHING SUIT RIGHT NOW!

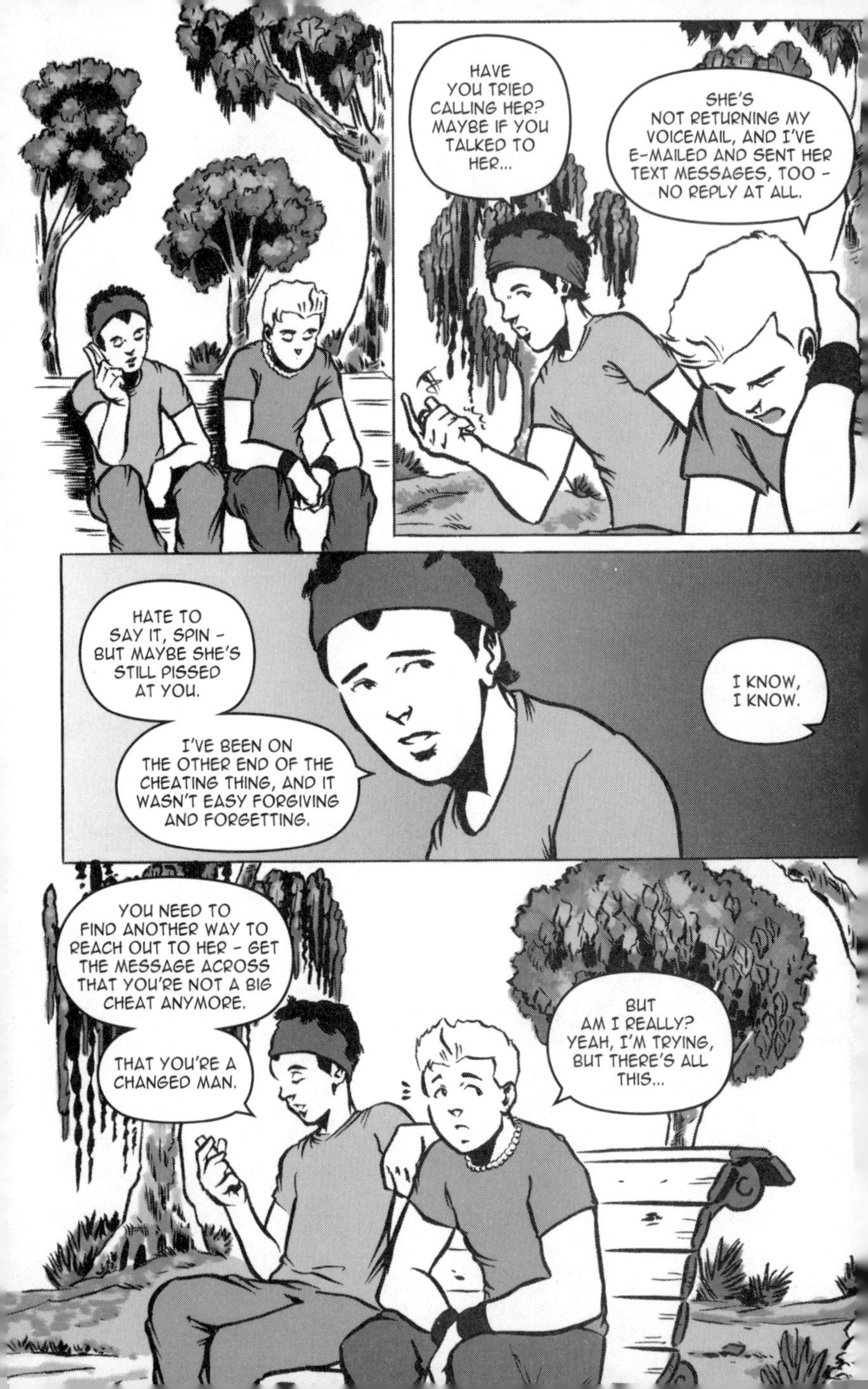
HAVE YOU TRIED CALLING HER? MAYBE IF YOU TALKED TO HER...
SHE'S NOT RETURNING MY VOICEMAIL, AND I'VE E-MAILED AND SENT HER TEXT MESSAGES, TOO - NO REPLY AT ALL.
HATE TO SAY IT, SPIN - BUT MAYBE SHE'S STILL PISSED AT YOU.
I'VE BEEN ON THE OTHER END OF THE CHEATING THING, AND IT WASN'T EASY FORGIVING AND FORGETTING.
I KNOW, I KNOW.
YOU NEED TO FIND ANOTHER WAY TO REACH OUT TO HER - GET THE MESSAGE ACROSS THAT YOU'RE NOT A BIG CHEAT ANYMORE.
THAT YOU'RE A CHANGED MAN.
BUT AM I REALLY? YEAH, I'M TRYING, BUT THERE'S ALL THIS...

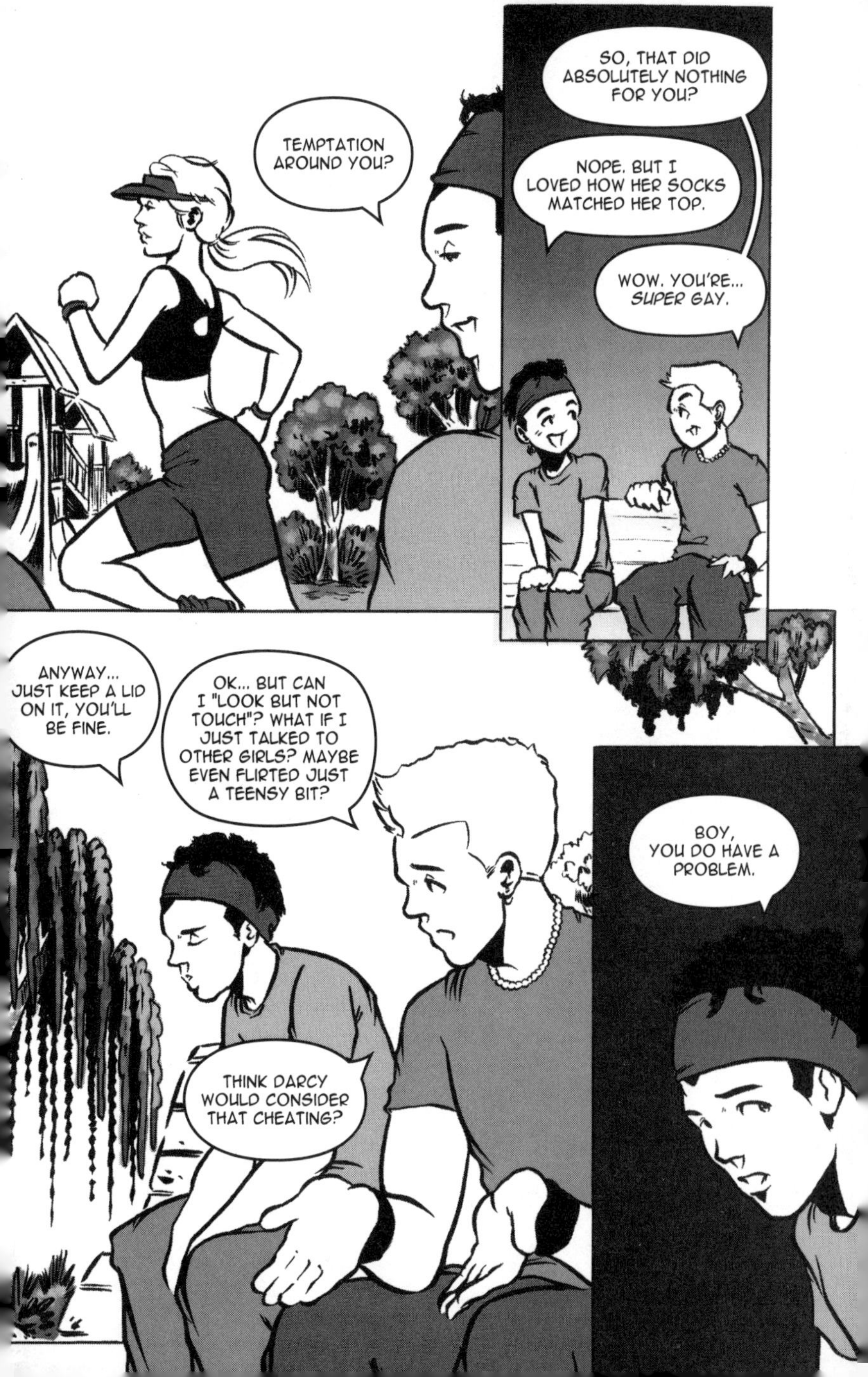
TEMPTATION AROUND YOU?
SO, THAT DID ABSOLUTELY NOTHING FOR YOU?
NOPE. BUT I LOVED HOW HER SOCKS MATCHED HER TOP.
WOW. YOU'RE... SUPER GAY.
ANYWAY... JUST KEEP A LID ON IT, YOU'LL BE FINE.
OK... BUT CAN I "LOOK BUT NOT TOUCH"? WHAT IF I JUST TALKED TO OTHER GIRLS? MAYBE EVEN FLIRTED JUST A TEENSY BIT?
THINK DARCY WOULD CONSIDER THAT CHEATING?
BOY, YOU DO HAVE A PROBLEM.

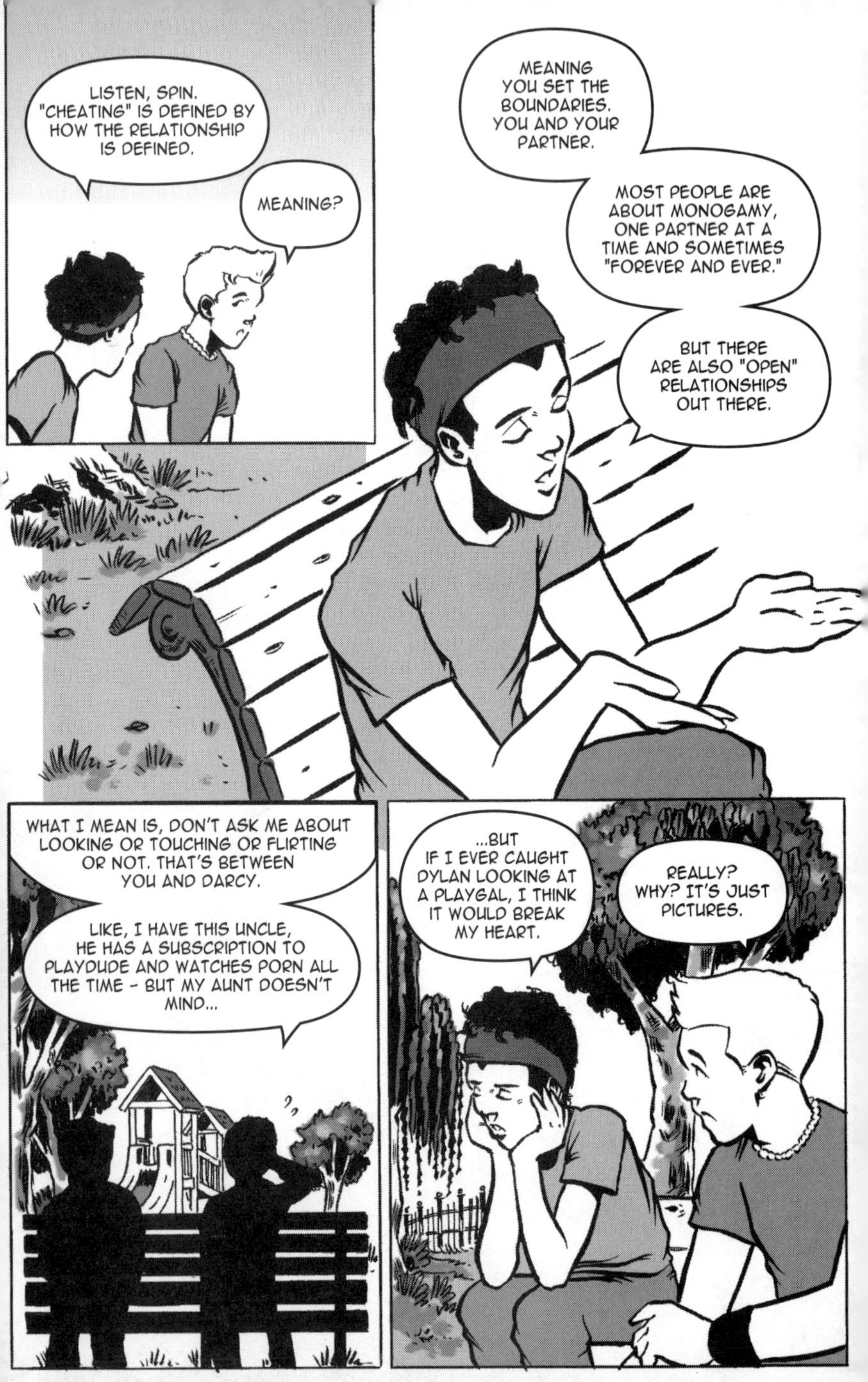
LISTEN, SPIN. "CHEATING" IS DEFINED BY HOW THE RELATIONSHIP IS DEFINED.
MEANING?
MEANING YOU SET THE BOUNDARIES. YOU AND YOUR PARTNER.
MOST PEOPLE ARE ABOUT MONOGAMY, ONE PARTNER AT A TIME AND SOMETIMES "FOREVER AND EVER."
BUT THERE ARE ALSO "OPEN" RELATIONSHIPS OUT THERE.
WHAT I MEAN IS, DON'T ASK ME ABOUT LOOKING OR TOUCHING OR FLIRTING OR NOT. THAT'S BETWEEN YOU AND DARCY.
LIKE, I HAVE THIS UNCLE, HE HAS A SUBSCRIPTION TO PLAYDUDE AND WATCHES PORN ALL THE TIME - BUT MY AUNT DOESN'T MIND...
...BUT IF I EVER CAUGHT DYLAN LOOKING AT A PLAYGAL, I THINK IT WOULD BREAK MY HEART.
REALLY? WHY? IT'S JUST PICTURES.

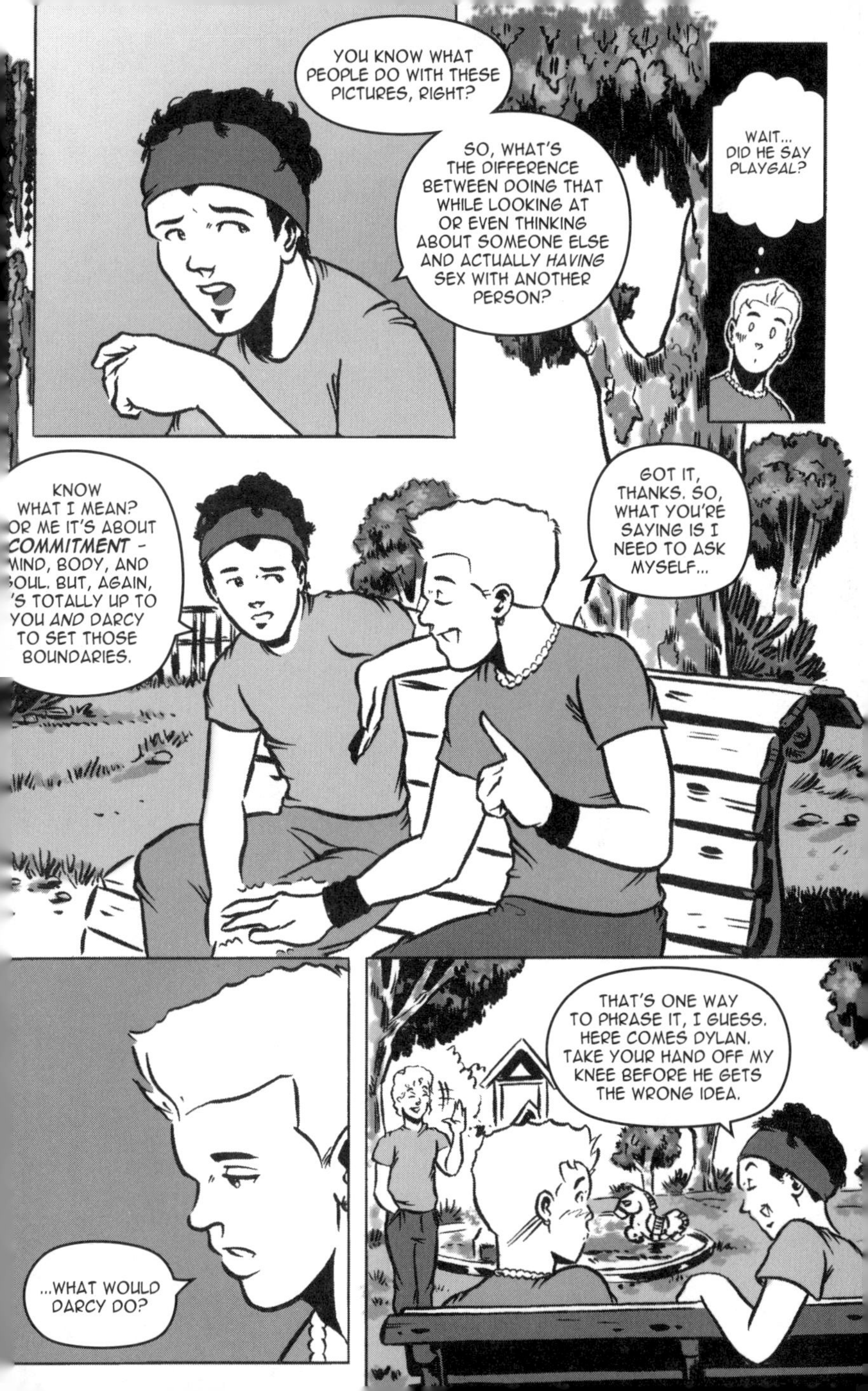
YOU KNOW WHAT PEOPLE DO WITH THESE PICTURES, RIGHT?
SO, WHAT'S THE DIFFERENCE BETWEEN DOING THAT WHILE LOOKING AT OR EVEN THINKING ABOUT SOMEONE ELSE AND ACTUALLY *HAVING* SEX WITH ANOTHER PERSON?
WAIT... DID HE SAY *PLAYGAL*?
KNOW WHAT I MEAN? OR ME IT'S ABOUT **COMMITMENT** - MIND, BODY, AND SOUL. BUT, AGAIN, 'S TOTALLY UP TO YOU *AND* DARCY TO SET THOSE BOUNDARIES.
GOT IT, THANKS. SO, WHAT YOU'RE SAYING IS I NEED TO ASK MYSELF...
...WHAT WOULD DARCY DO?
THAT'S ONE WAY TO PHRASE IT, I GUESS. HERE COMES DYLAN. TAKE YOUR HAND OFF MY KNEE BEFORE HE GETS THE WRONG IDEA.

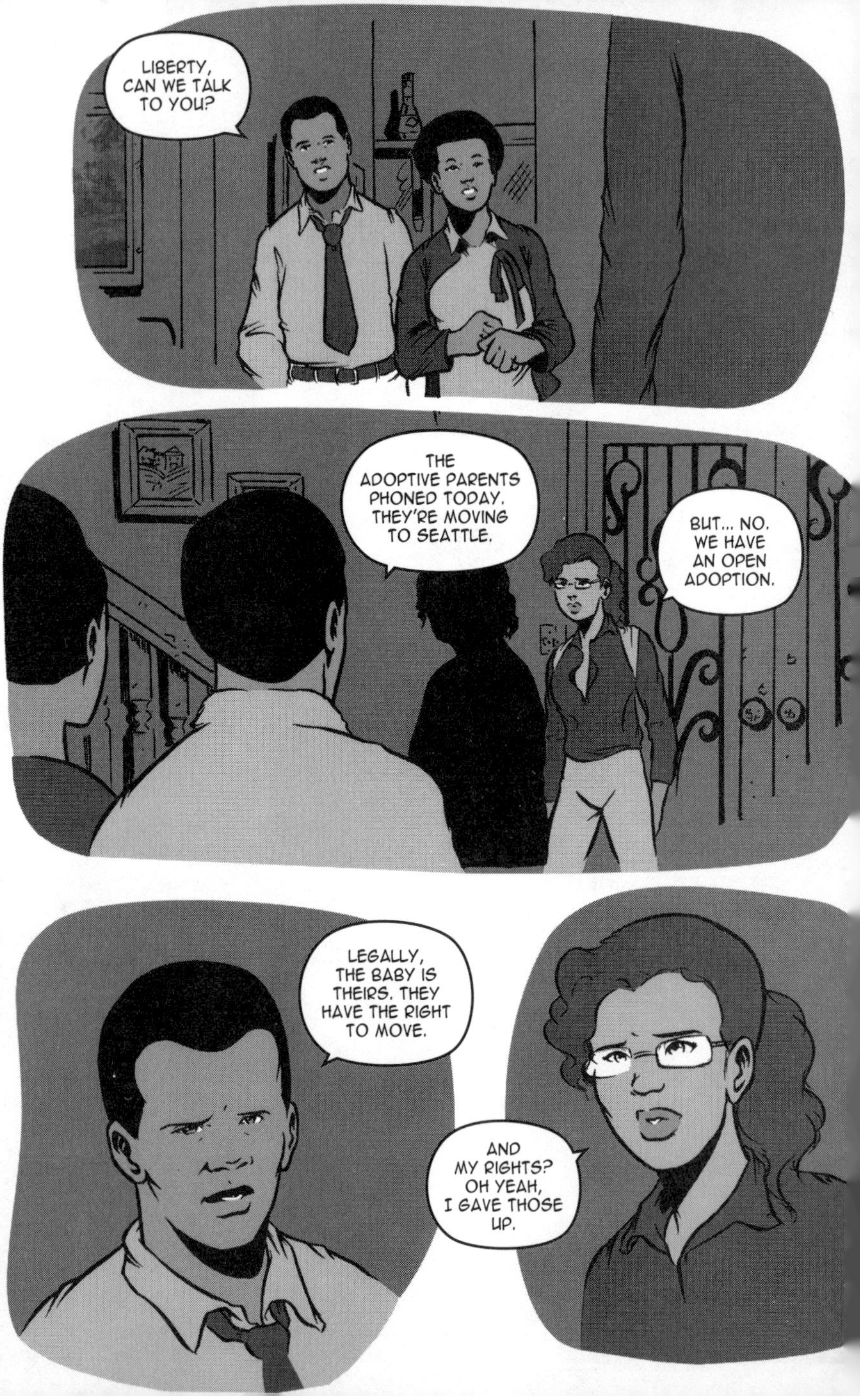

LIBERTY, CAN WE TALK TO YOU?
THE ADOPTIVE PARENTS PHONED TODAY. THEY'RE MOVING TO SEATTLE.
BUT... NO. WE HAVE AN OPEN ADOPTION.
LEGALLY, THE BABY IS THEIRS. THEY HAVE THE RIGHT TO MOVE.
AND MY RIGHTS? OH YEAH, I GAVE THOSE UP.

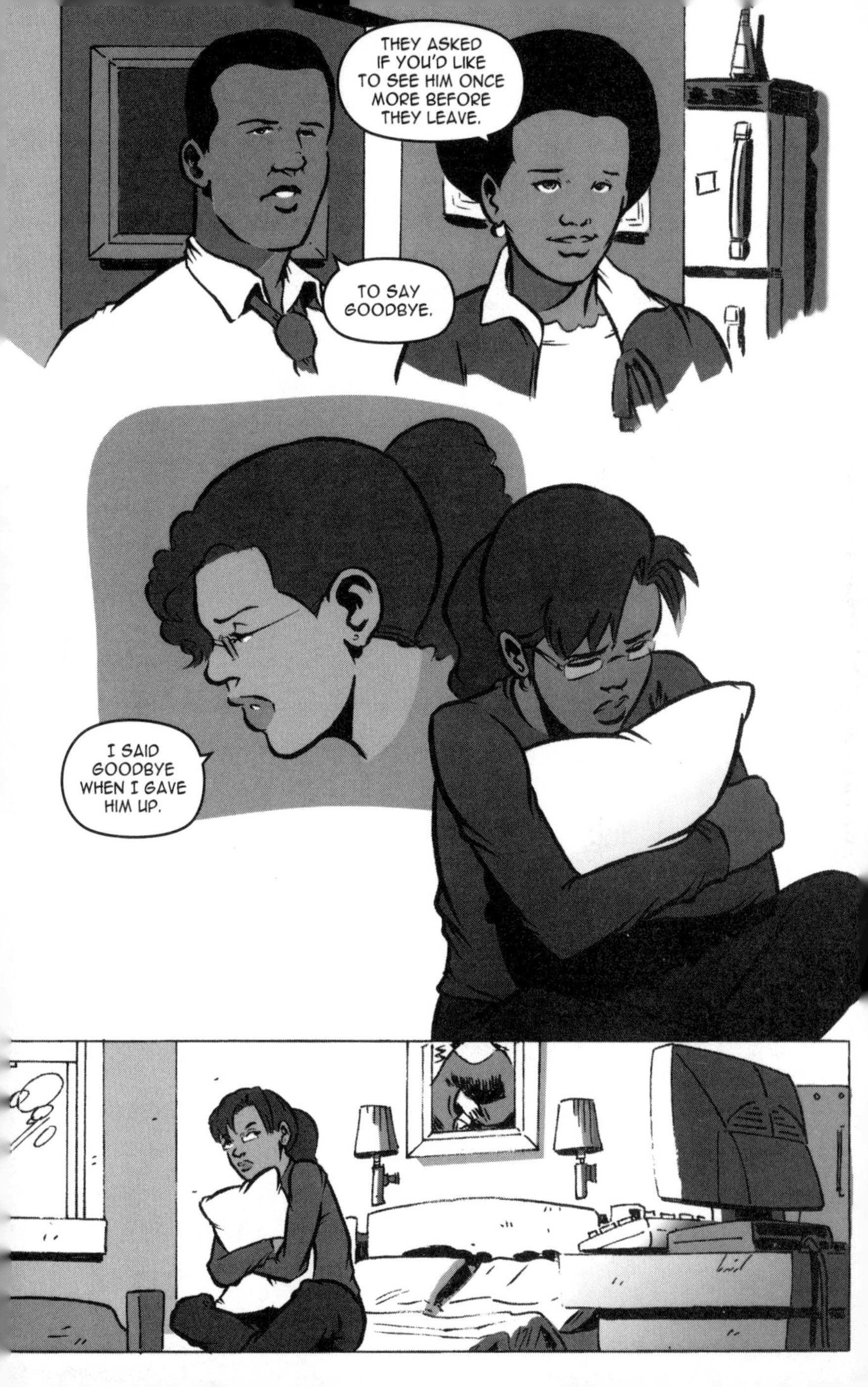
THEY ASKED IF YOU'D LIKE TO SEE HIM ONCE MORE BEFORE THEY LEAVE.
TO SAY GOODBYE.
I SAID GOODBYE WHEN I GAVE HIM UP.

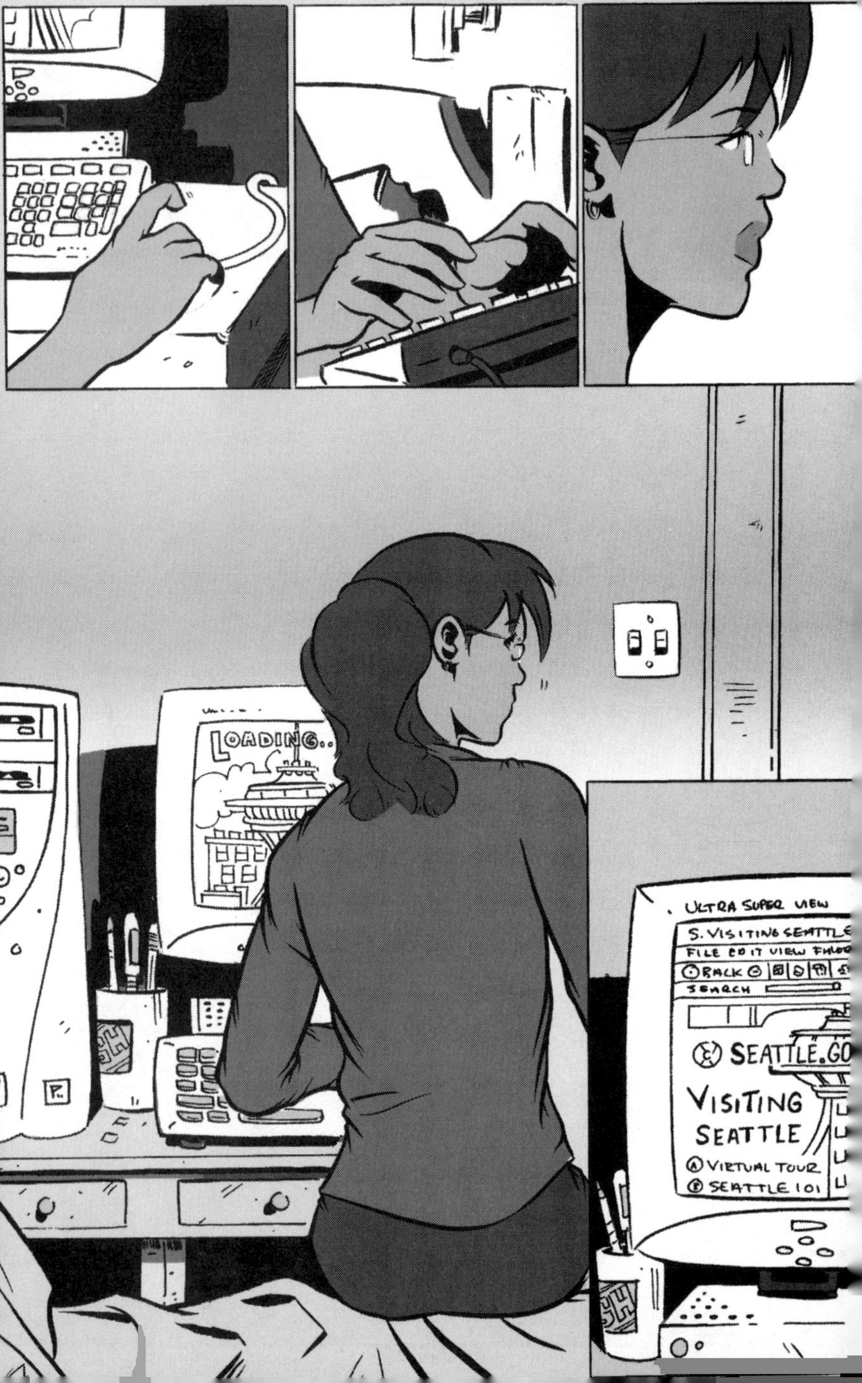
LOADING...
ULTRA SUPER VIEW
BACK
SEARCH
VISITING SEATTLE
VIRTUAL TOUR
SEATTLE 101

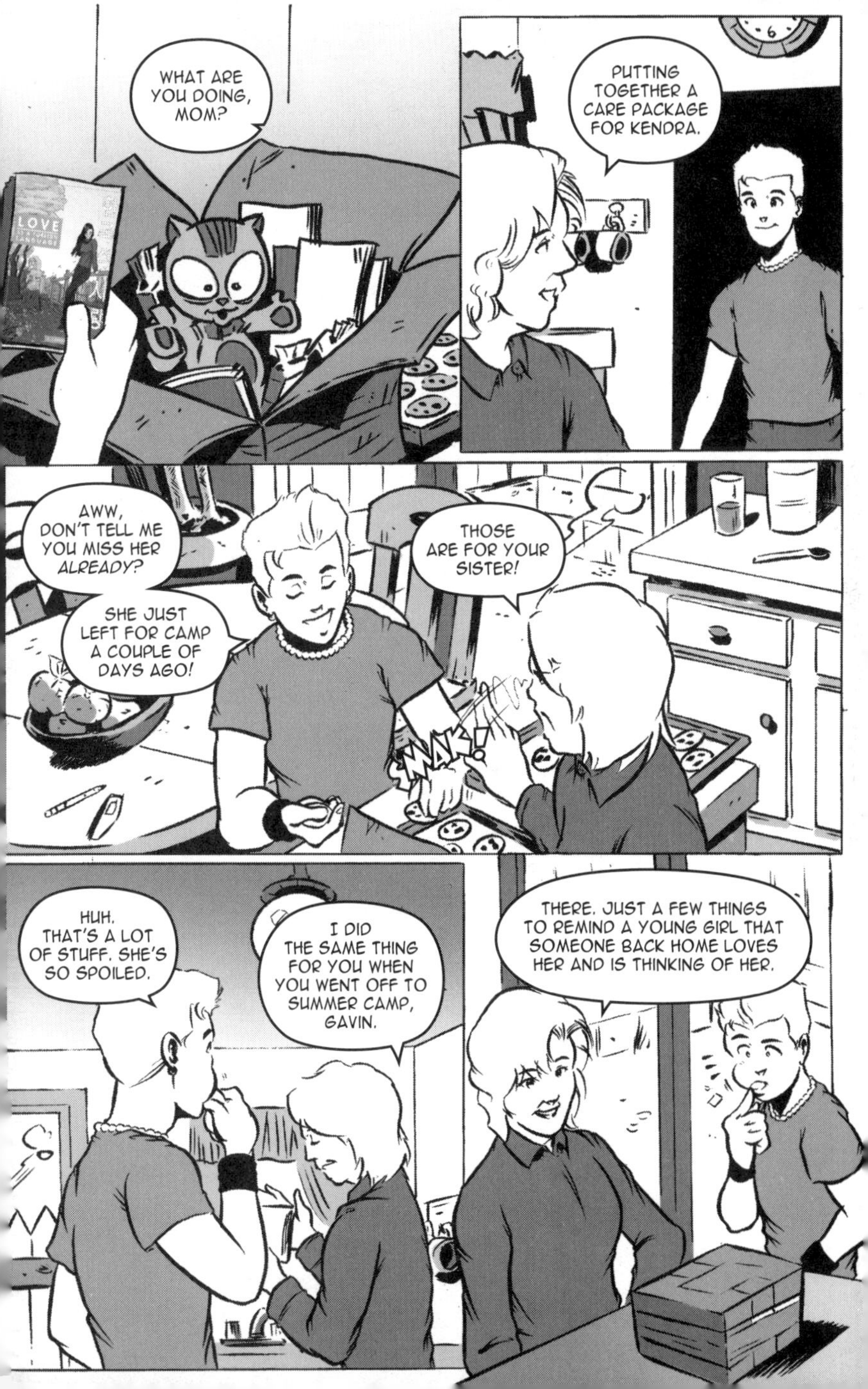
WHAT ARE YOU DOING, MOM?
LOVE
PUTTING TOGETHER A CARE PACKAGE FOR KENDRA.
AWW, DON'T TELL ME YOU MISS HER ALREADY?
SHE JUST LEFT FOR CAMP A COUPLE OF DAYS AGO!
THOSE ARE FOR YOUR SISTER!
SMAK!
HUH. THAT'S A LOT OF STUFF. SHE'S SO SPOILED.
I DID THE SAME THING FOR YOU WHEN YOU WENT OFF TO SUMMER CAMP, GAVIN.
THERE. JUST A FEW THINGS TO REMIND A YOUNG GIRL THAT SOMEONE BACK HOME LOVES HER AND IS THINKING OF HER.

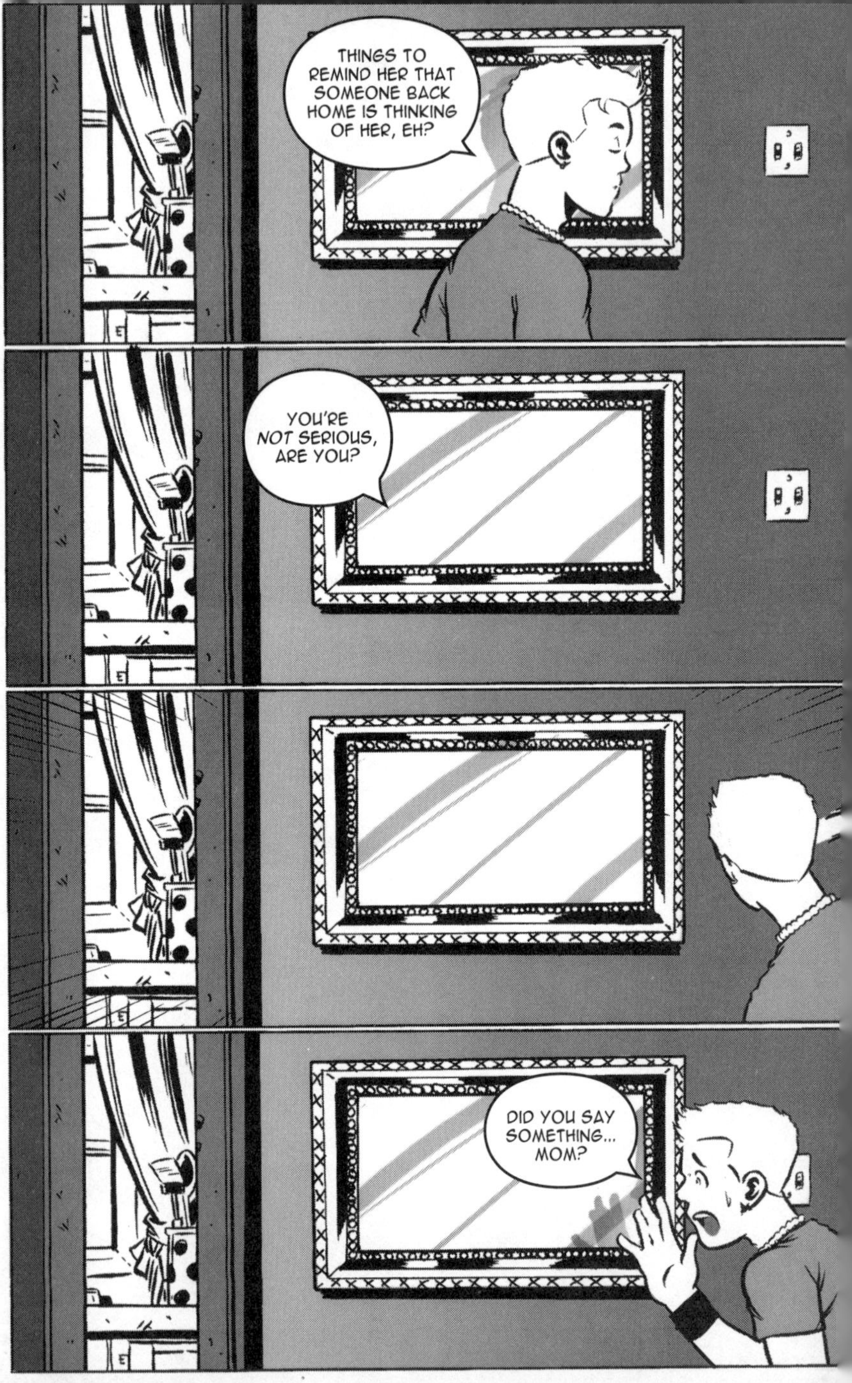
THINGS TO REMIND HER THAT SOMEONE BACK HOME IS THINKING OF HER, EH?
YOU'RE NOT SERIOUS, ARE YOU?
DID YOU SAY SOMETHING... MOM?

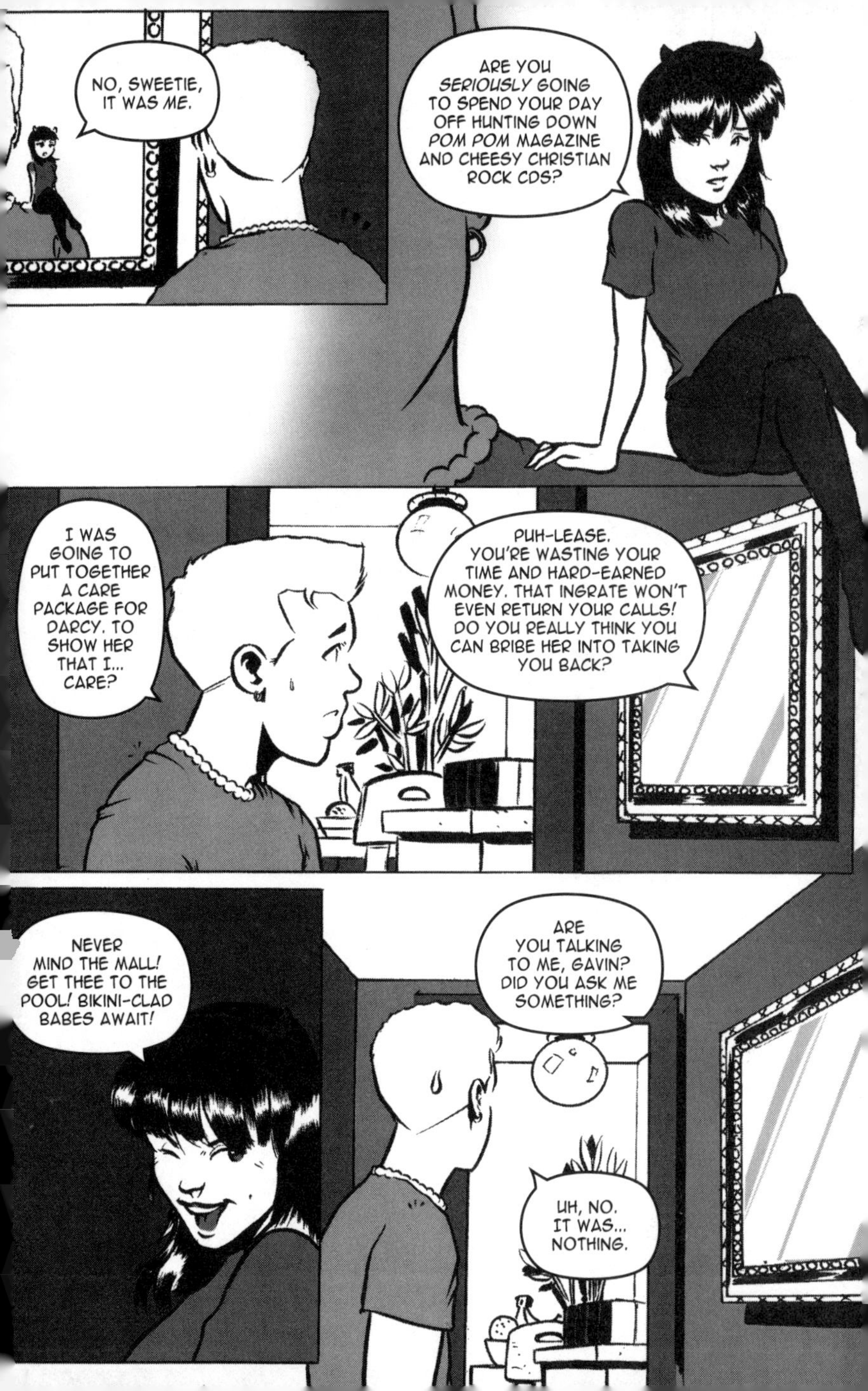
NO, SWEETIE, IT WAS ME.
ARE YOU SERIOUSLY GOING TO SPEND YOUR DAY OFF HUNTING DOWN POM POM MAGAZINE AND CHEESY CHRISTIAN ROCK CDS?
I WAS GOING TO PUT TOGETHER A CARE PACKAGE FOR DARCY. TO SHOW HER THAT I... CARE?
PUH-LEASE. YOU'RE WASTING YOUR TIME AND HARD-EARNED MONEY. THAT INGRATE WON'T EVEN RETURN YOUR CALLS! DO YOU REALLY THINK YOU CAN BRIBE HER INTO TAKING YOU BACK?
NEVER MIND THE MALL! GET THEE TO THE POOL! BIKINI-CLAD BABES AWAIT!
ARE YOU TALKING TO ME, GAVIN? DID YOU ASK ME SOMETHING?
UH, NO. IT WAS... NOTHING.

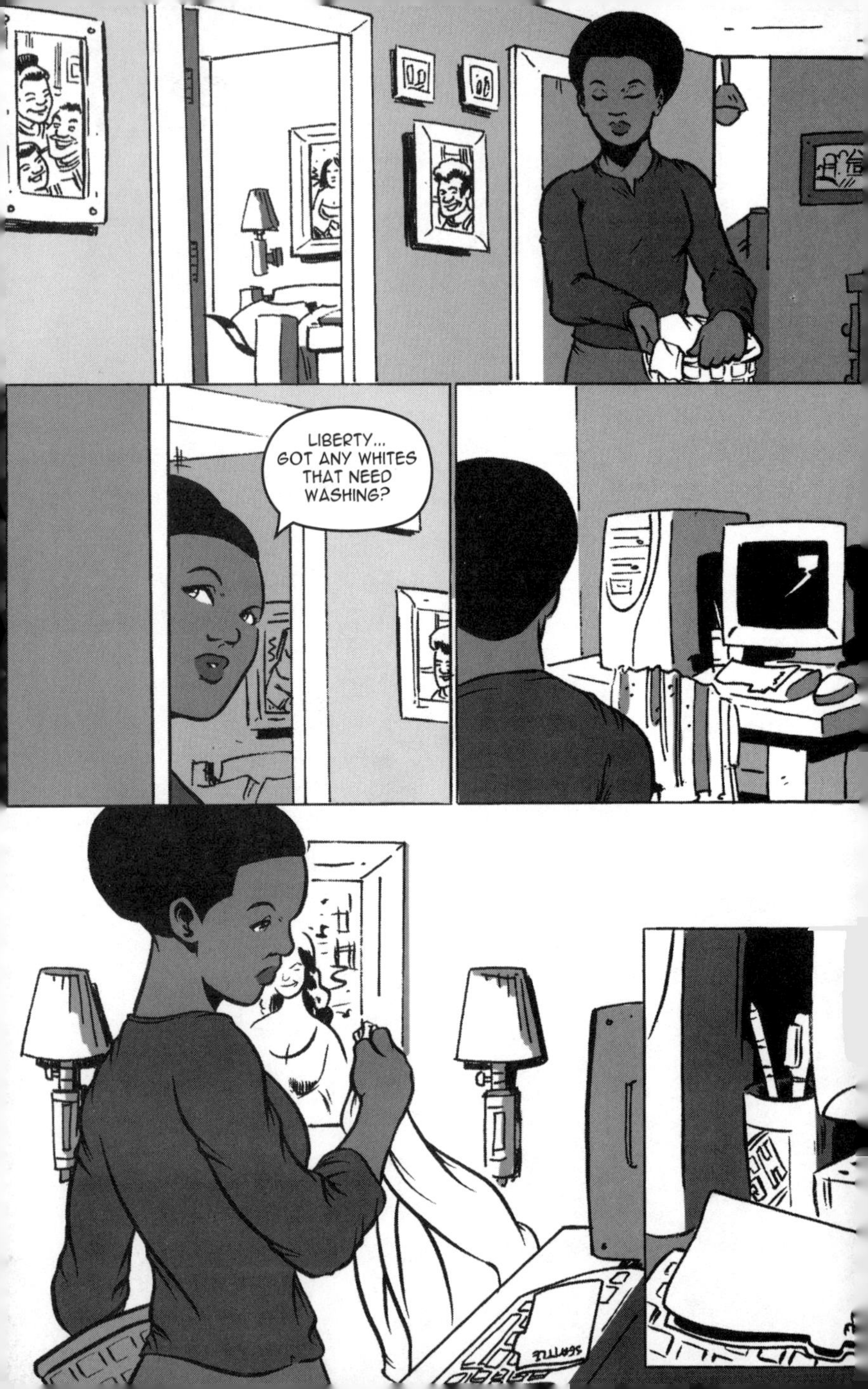
LIBERTY...
GOT ANY WHITES
THAT NEED
WASHING?

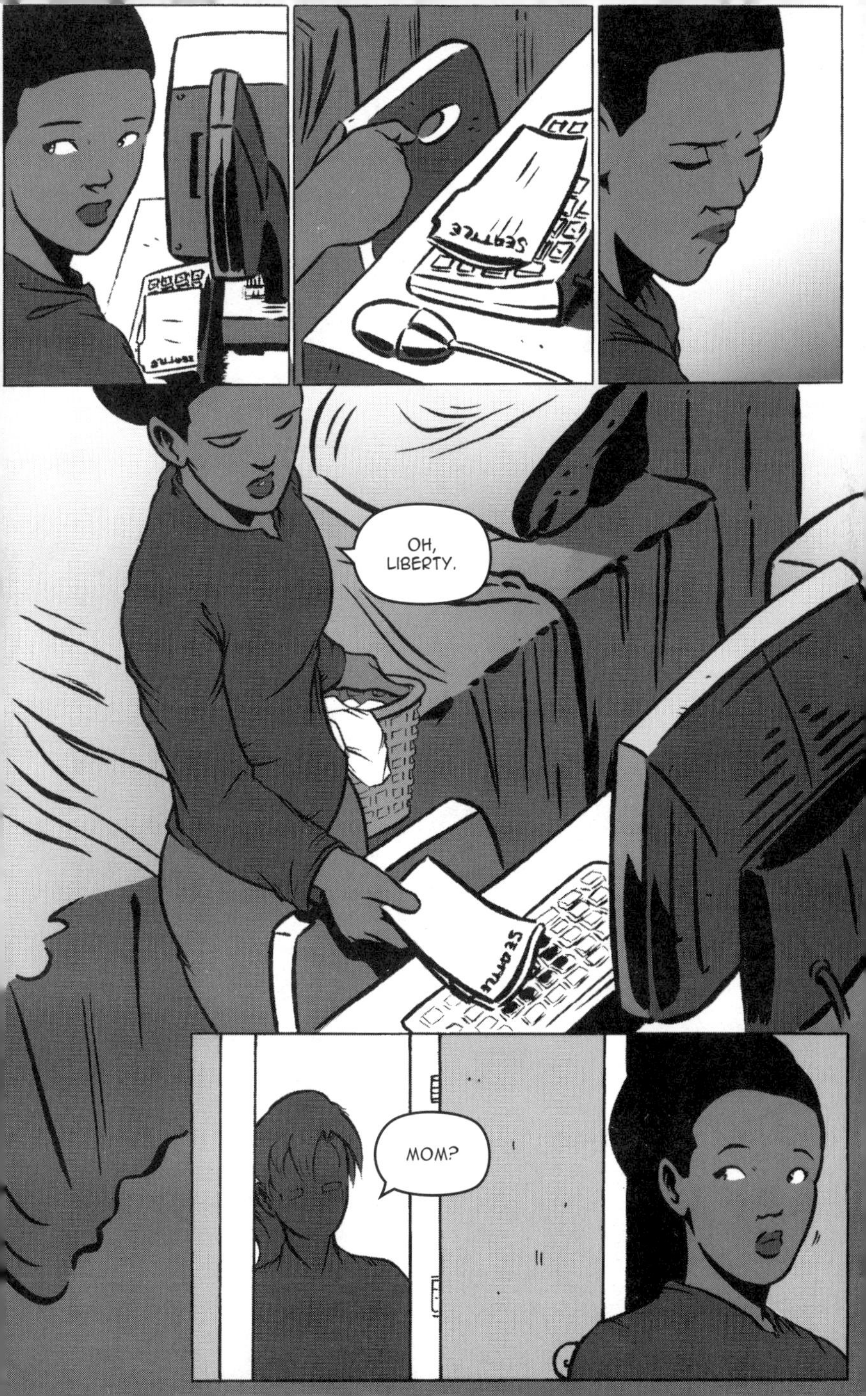
SEATTLE
OH, LIBERTY.
MOM?

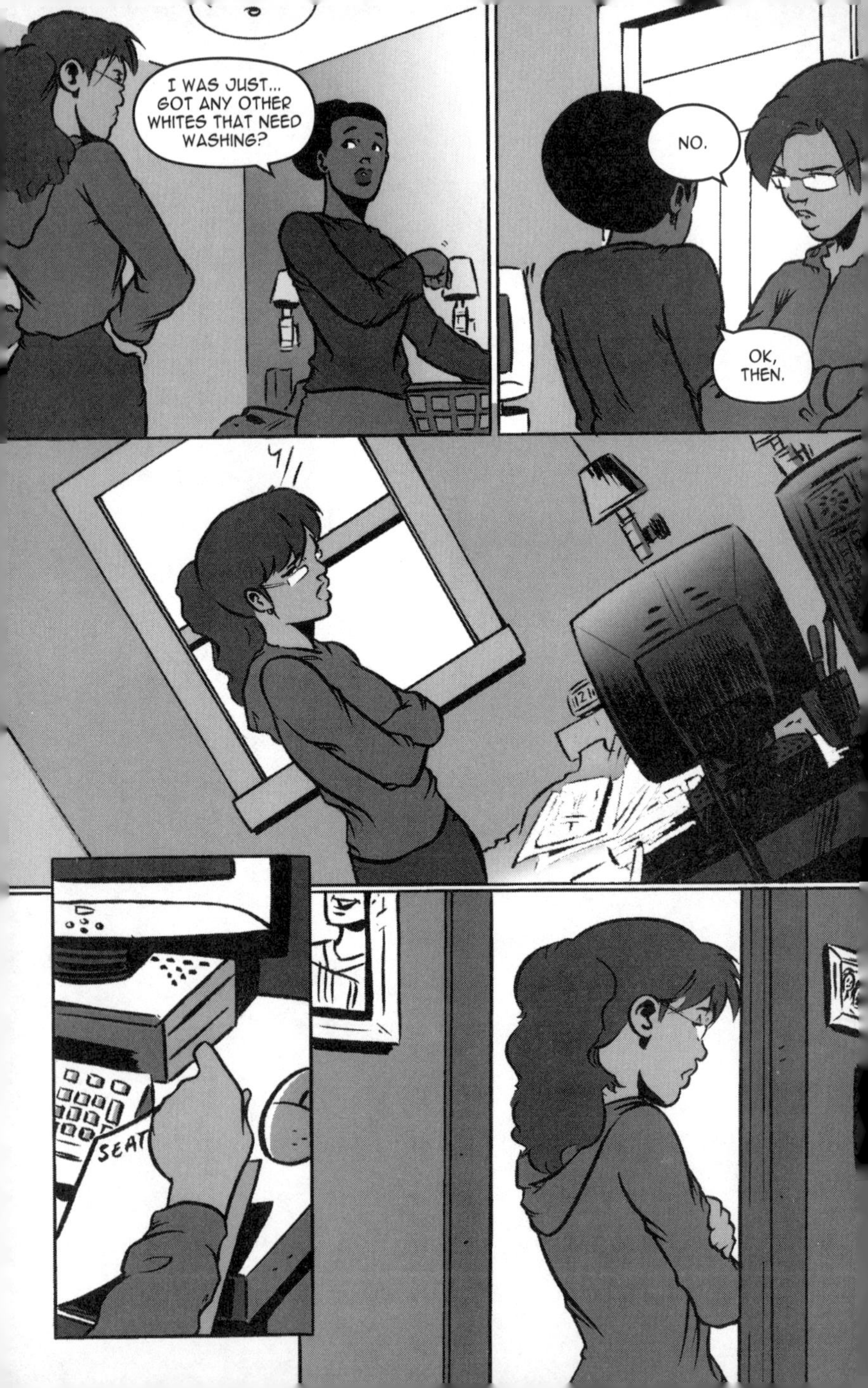
I WAS JUST... GOT ANY OTHER WHITES THAT NEED WASHING?
NO.
OK, THEN.
SEAT

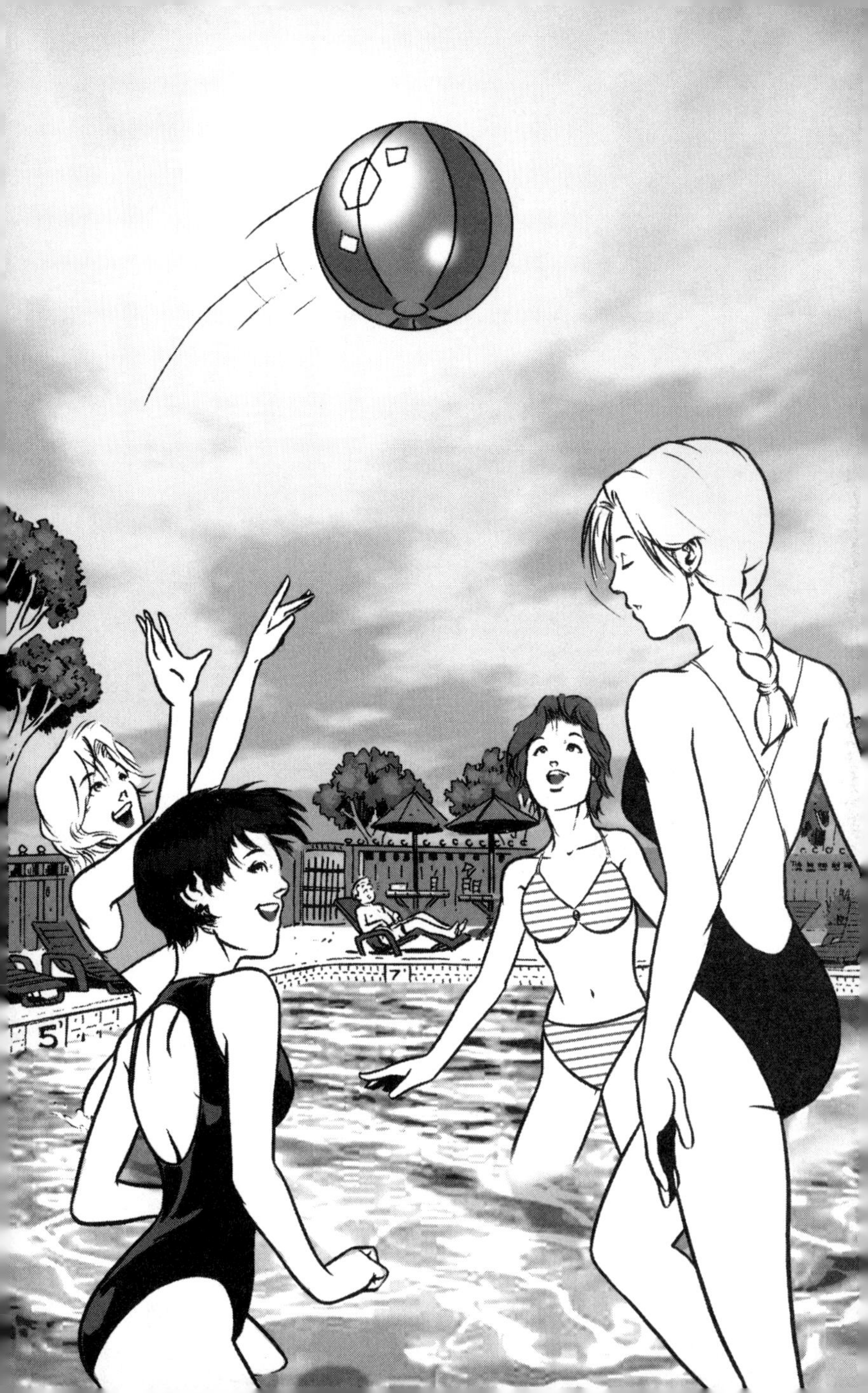
5
7

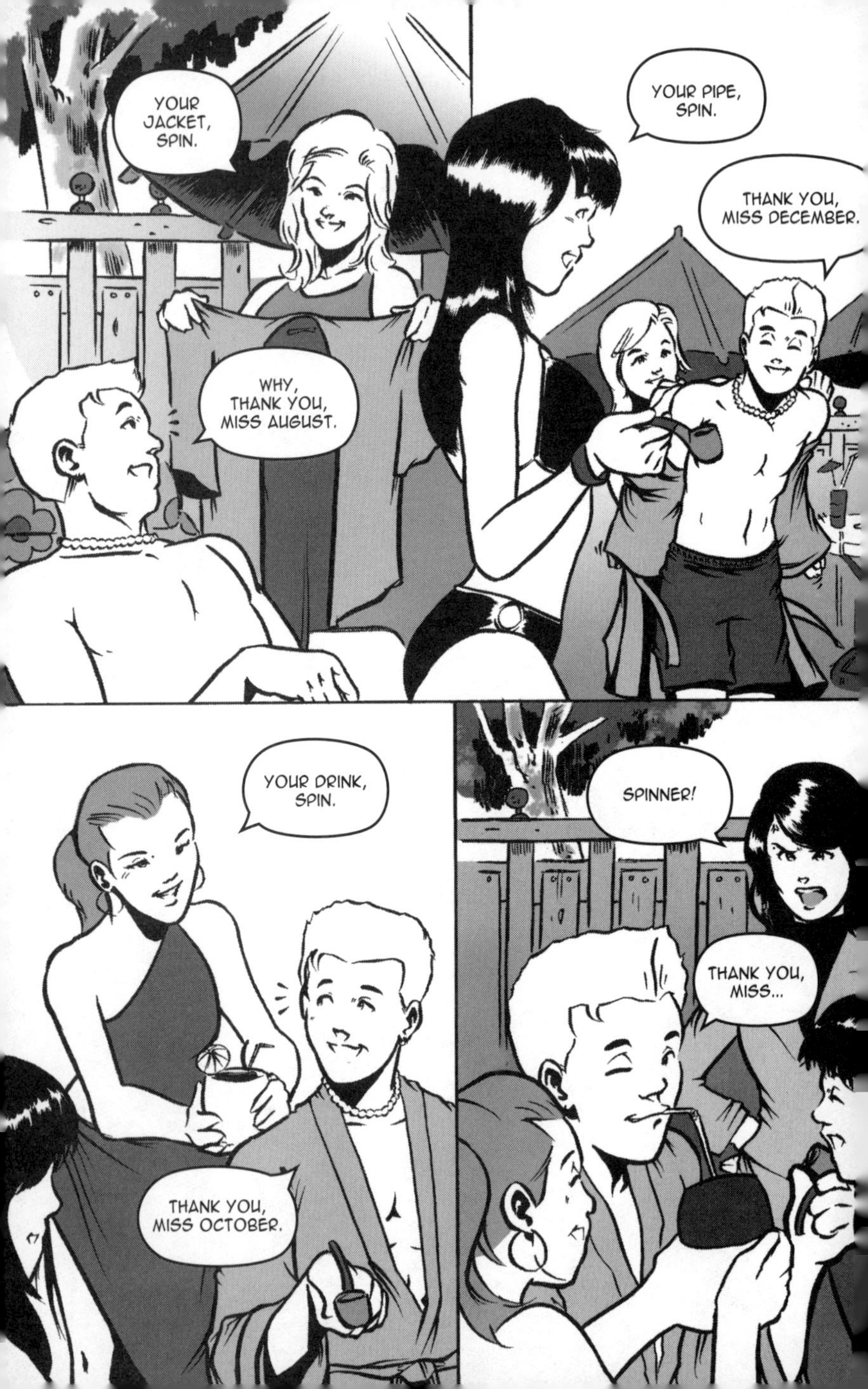
YOUR JACKET, SPIN.
WHY, THANK YOU, MISS AUGUST.
YOUR PIPE, SPIN.
THANK YOU, MISS DECEMBER.
YOUR DRINK, SPIN.
THANK YOU, MISS OCTOBER.
SPINNER!
THANK YOU, MISS...

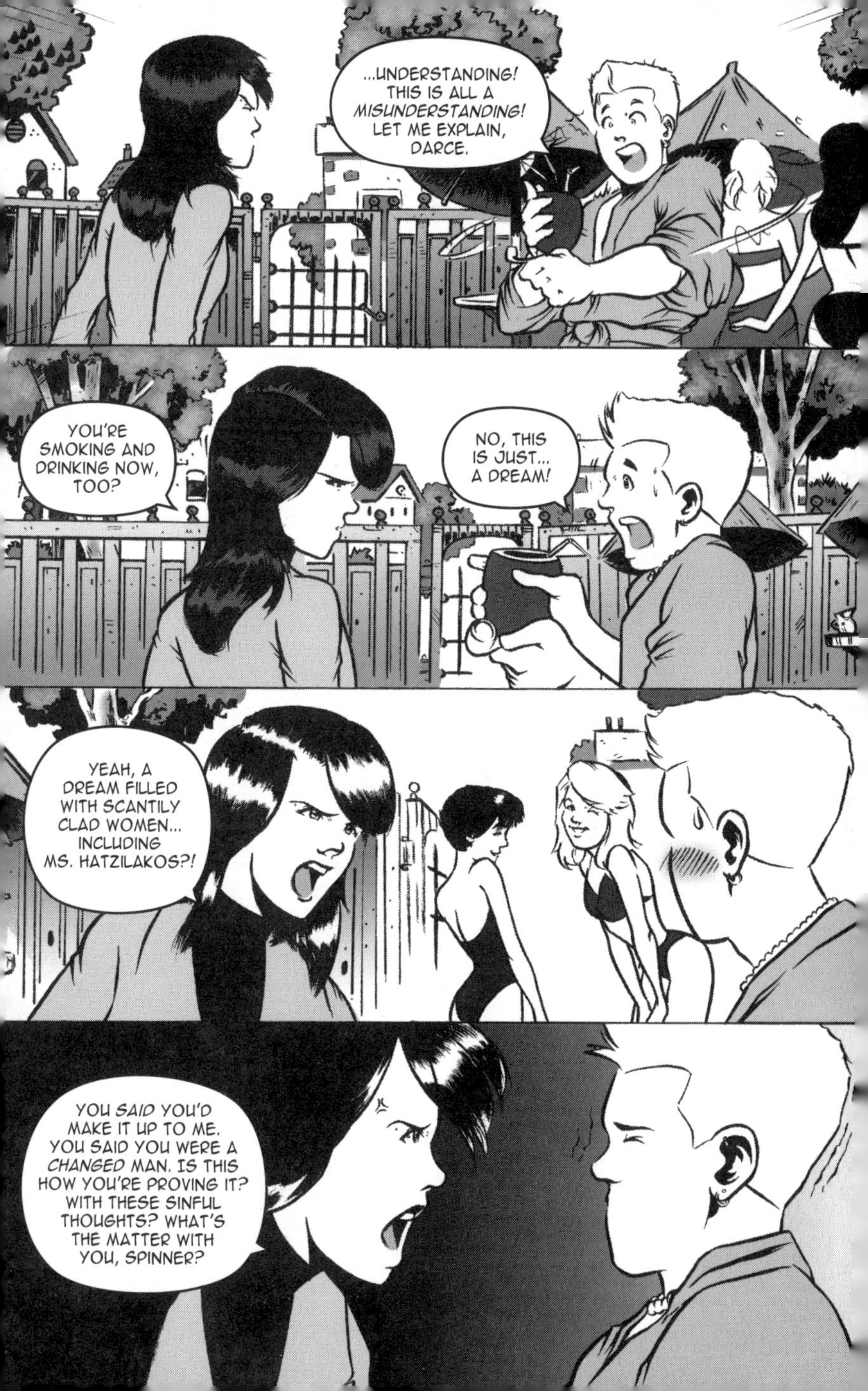
...UNDERSTANDING! THIS IS ALL A *MISUNDERSTANDING!* LET ME EXPLAIN, DARCE.
YOU'RE SMOKING AND DRINKING NOW, TOO?
NO, THIS IS JUST... A DREAM!
YEAH, A DREAM FILLED WITH SCANTILY CLAD WOMEN... INCLUDING MS. HATZILAKOS?!
YOU *SAID* YOU'D MAKE IT UP TO ME. YOU SAID YOU WERE A *CHANGED* MAN. IS THIS HOW YOU'RE PROVING IT? WITH THESE SINFUL THOUGHTS? WHAT'S THE MATTER WITH YOU, SPINNER?

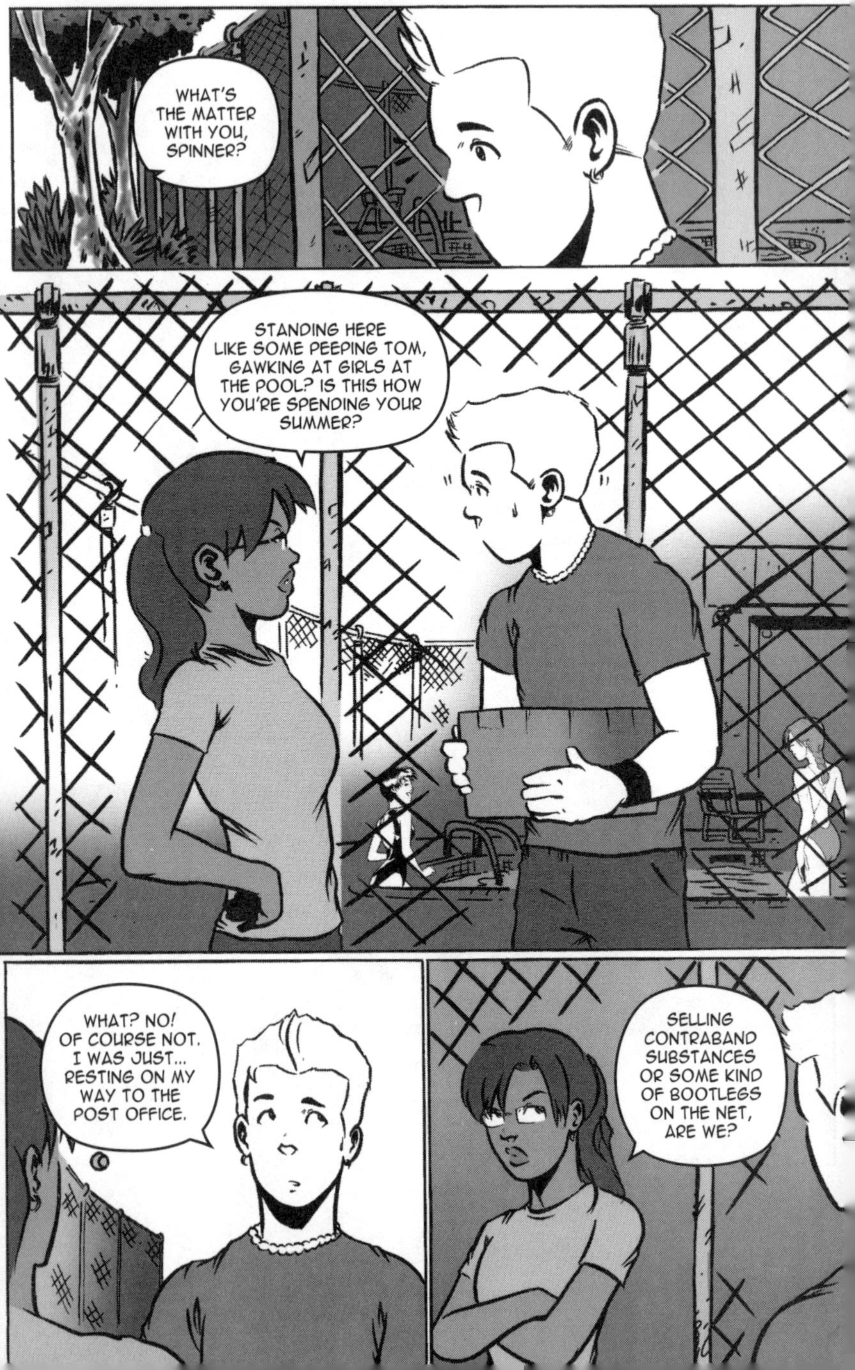
WHAT'S THE MATTER WITH YOU, SPINNER?
STANDING HERE LIKE SOME PEEPING TOM, GAWKING AT GIRLS AT THE POOL? IS THIS HOW YOU'RE SPENDING YOUR SUMMER?
WHAT? NO! OF COURSE NOT. I WAS JUST... RESTING ON MY WAY TO THE POST OFFICE.
SELLING CONTRABAND SUBSTANCES OR SOME KIND OF BOOTLEGS ON THE NET, ARE WE?

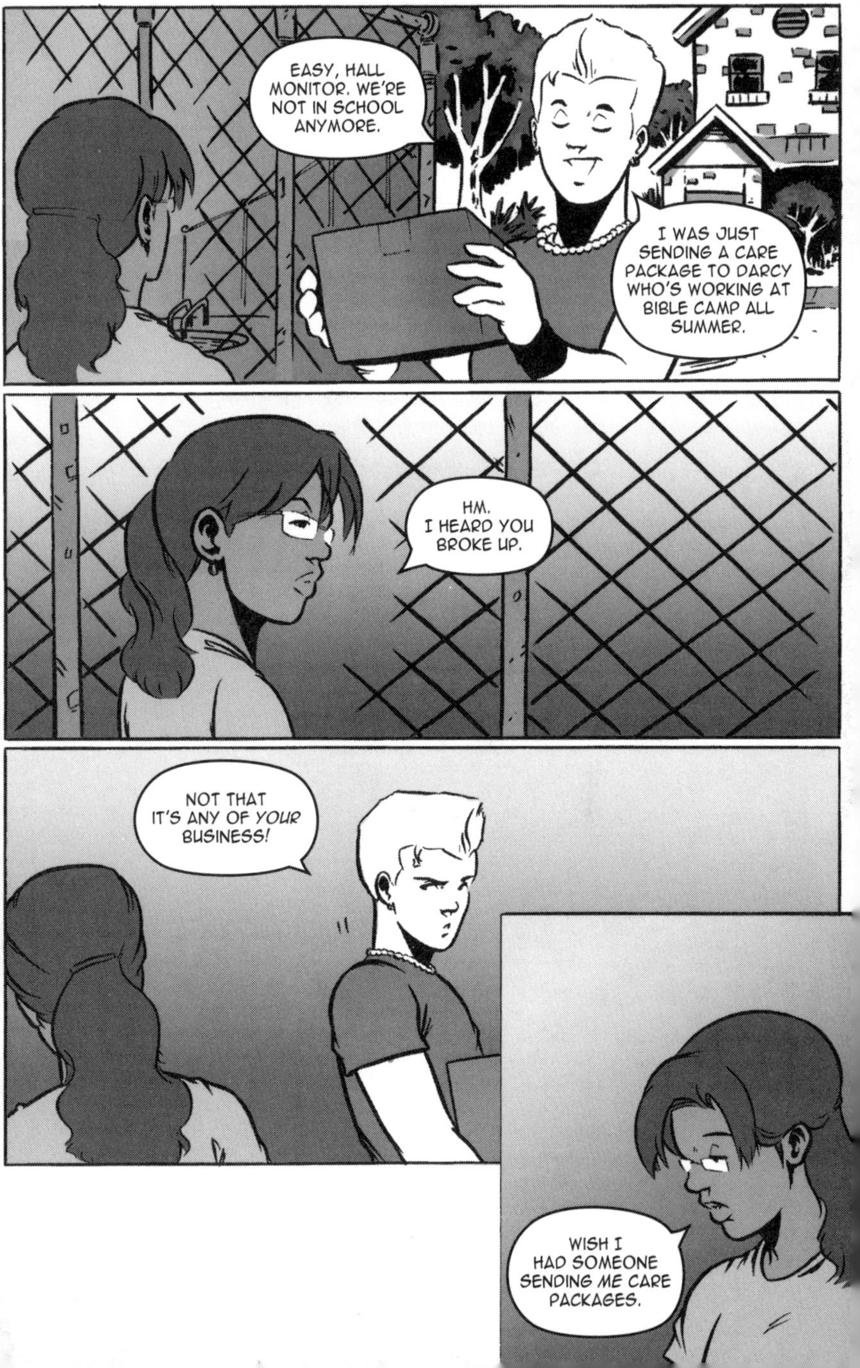
EASY, HALL MONITOR. WE'RE NOT IN SCHOOL ANYMORE.
I WAS JUST SENDING A CARE PACKAGE TO DARCY WHO'S WORKING AT BIBLE CAMP ALL SUMMER.
HM. I HEARD YOU BROKE UP.
NOT THAT IT'S ANY OF *YOUR* BUSINESS!
WISH I HAD SOMEONE SENDING *ME* CARE PACKAGES.

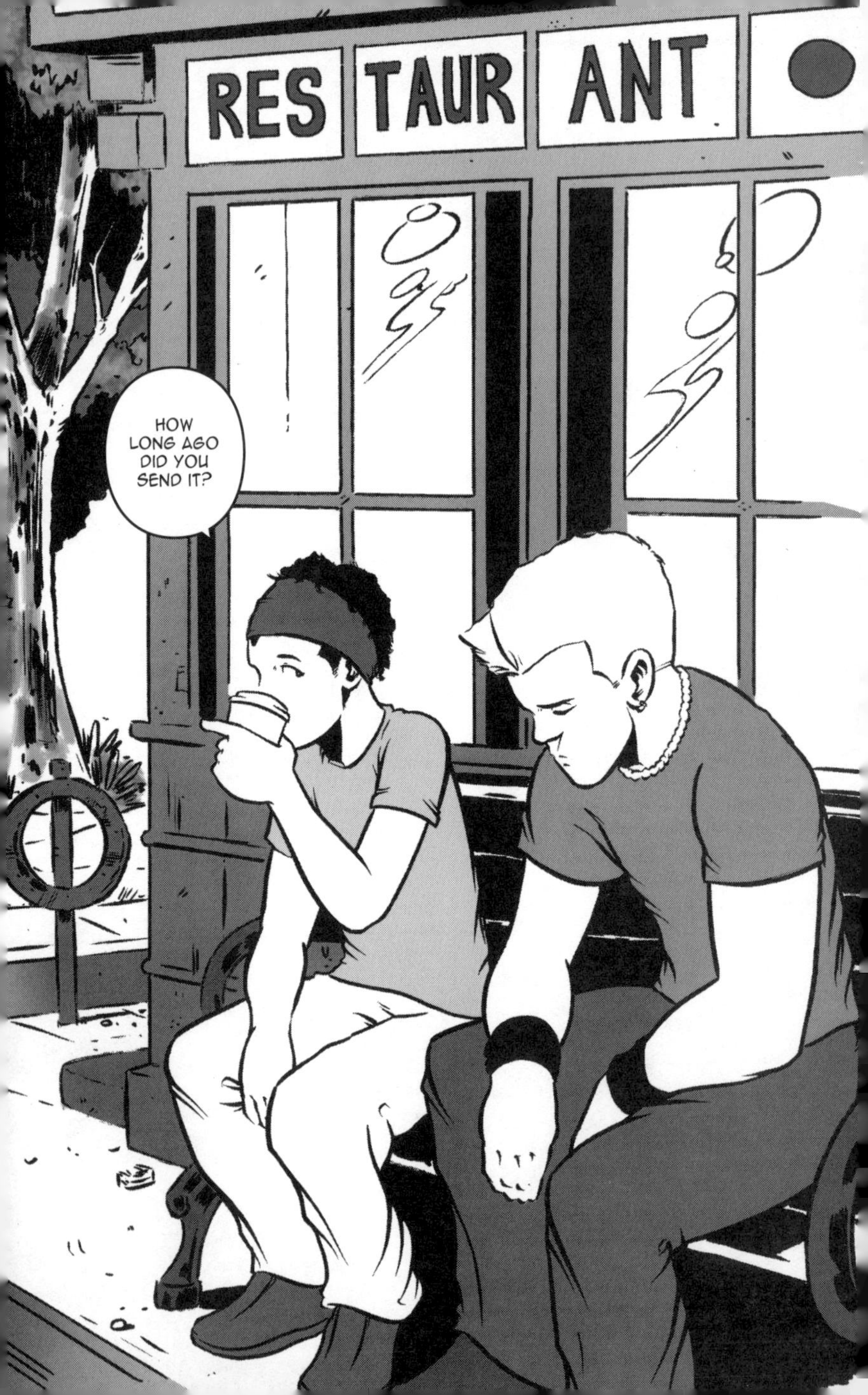
RESTAURANT
HOW LONG AGO DID YOU SEND IT?

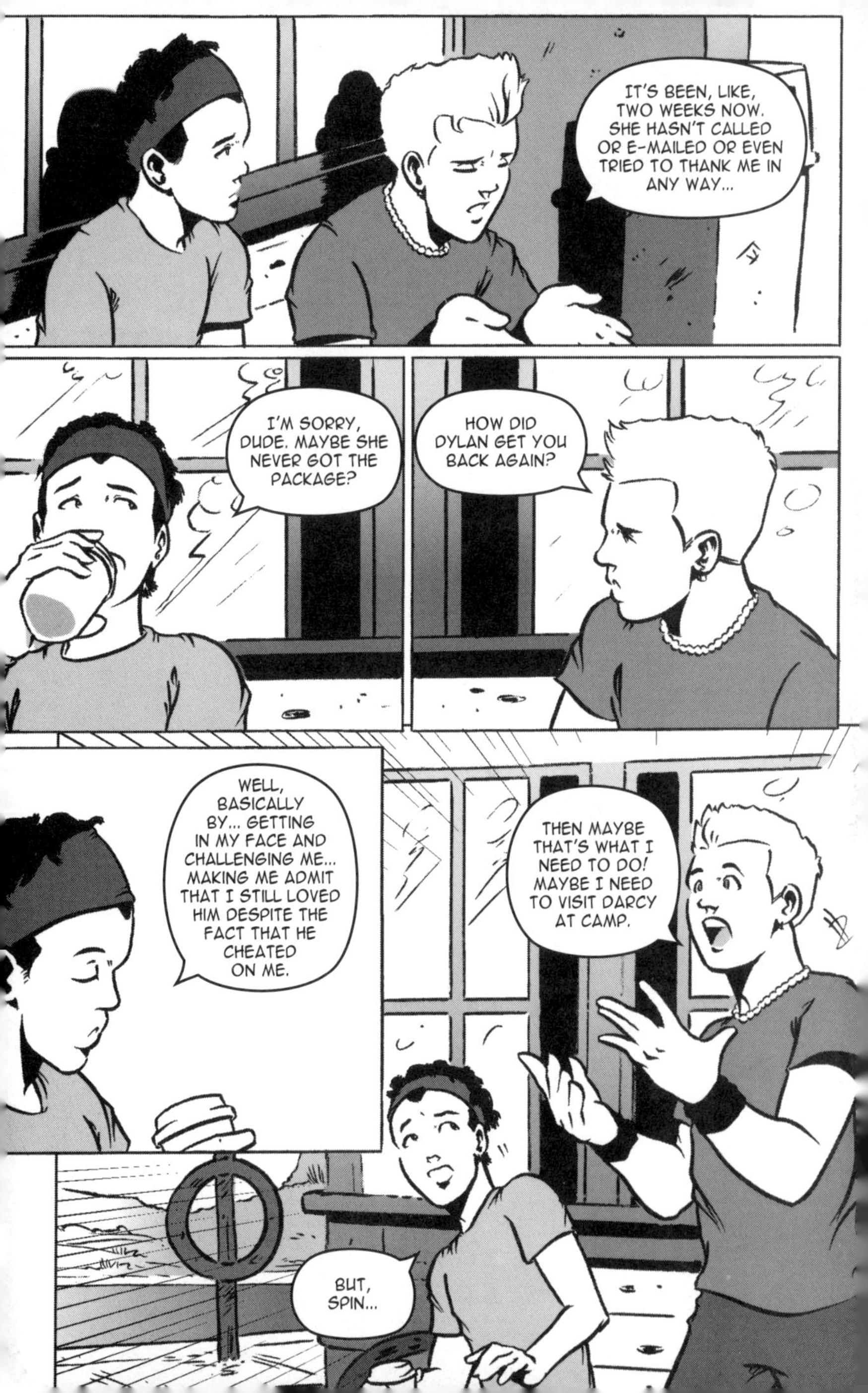
IT'S BEEN, LIKE, TWO WEEKS NOW. SHE HASN'T CALLED OR E-MAILED OR EVEN TRIED TO THANK ME IN ANY WAY...
I'M SORRY, DUDE. MAYBE SHE NEVER GOT THE PACKAGE?
HOW DID DYLAN GET YOU BACK AGAIN?
WELL, BASICALLY BY... GETTING IN MY FACE AND CHALLENGING ME... MAKING ME ADMIT THAT I STILL LOVED HIM DESPITE THE FACT THAT HE CHEATED ON ME.
THEN MAYBE THAT'S WHAT I NEED TO DO! MAYBE I NEED TO VISIT DARCY AT CAMP.
BUT, SPIN...

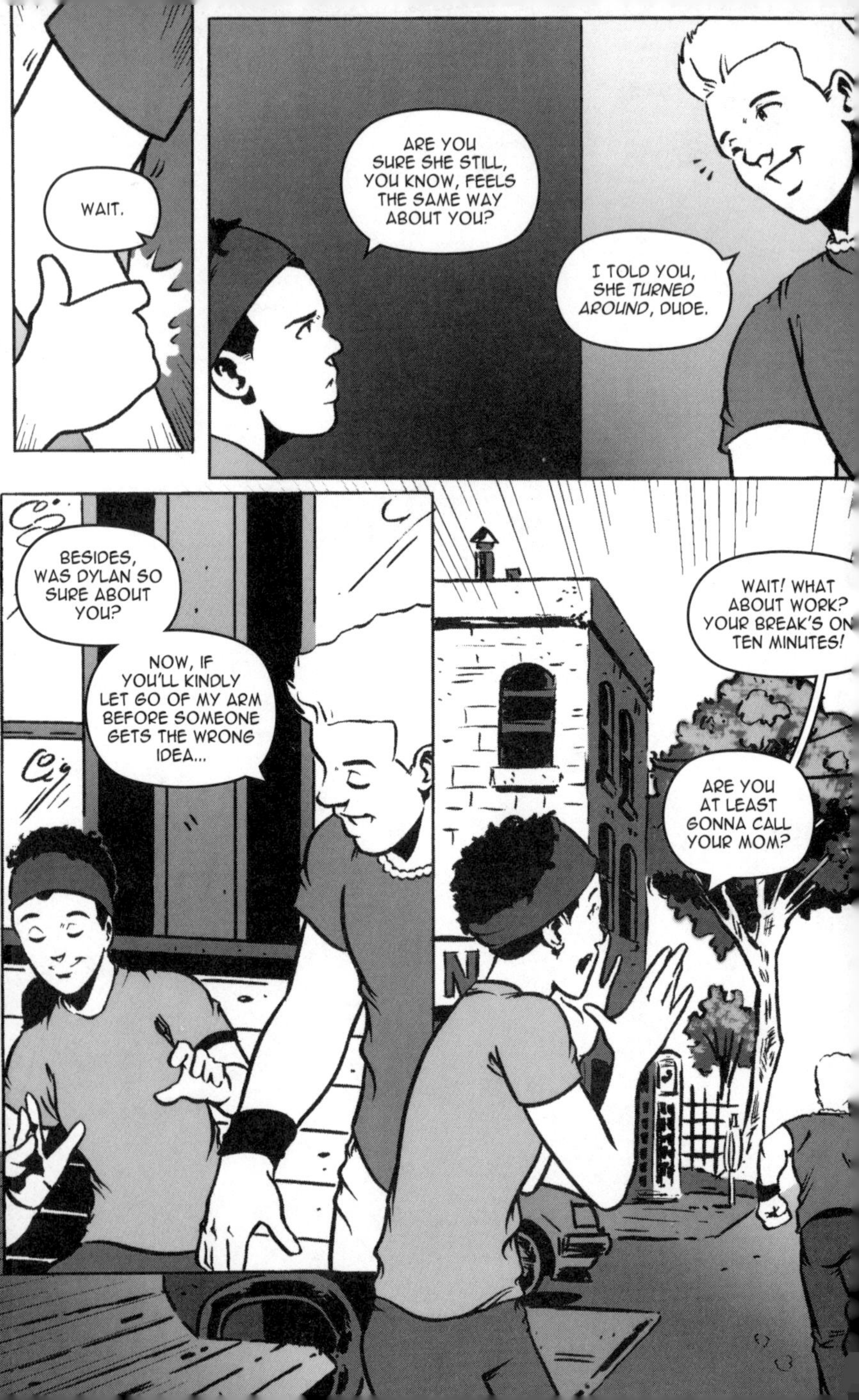
WAIT.
ARE YOU SURE SHE STILL, YOU KNOW, FEELS THE SAME WAY ABOUT YOU?
I TOLD YOU, SHE *TURNED AROUND*, DUDE.
BESIDES, WAS DYLAN SO SURE ABOUT YOU?
NOW, IF YOU'LL KINDLY LET GO OF MY ARM BEFORE SOMEONE GETS THE WRONG IDEA...
WAIT! WHAT ABOUT WORK? YOUR BREAK'S ON TEN MINUTES!
ARE YOU AT LEAST GONNA CALL YOUR MOM?

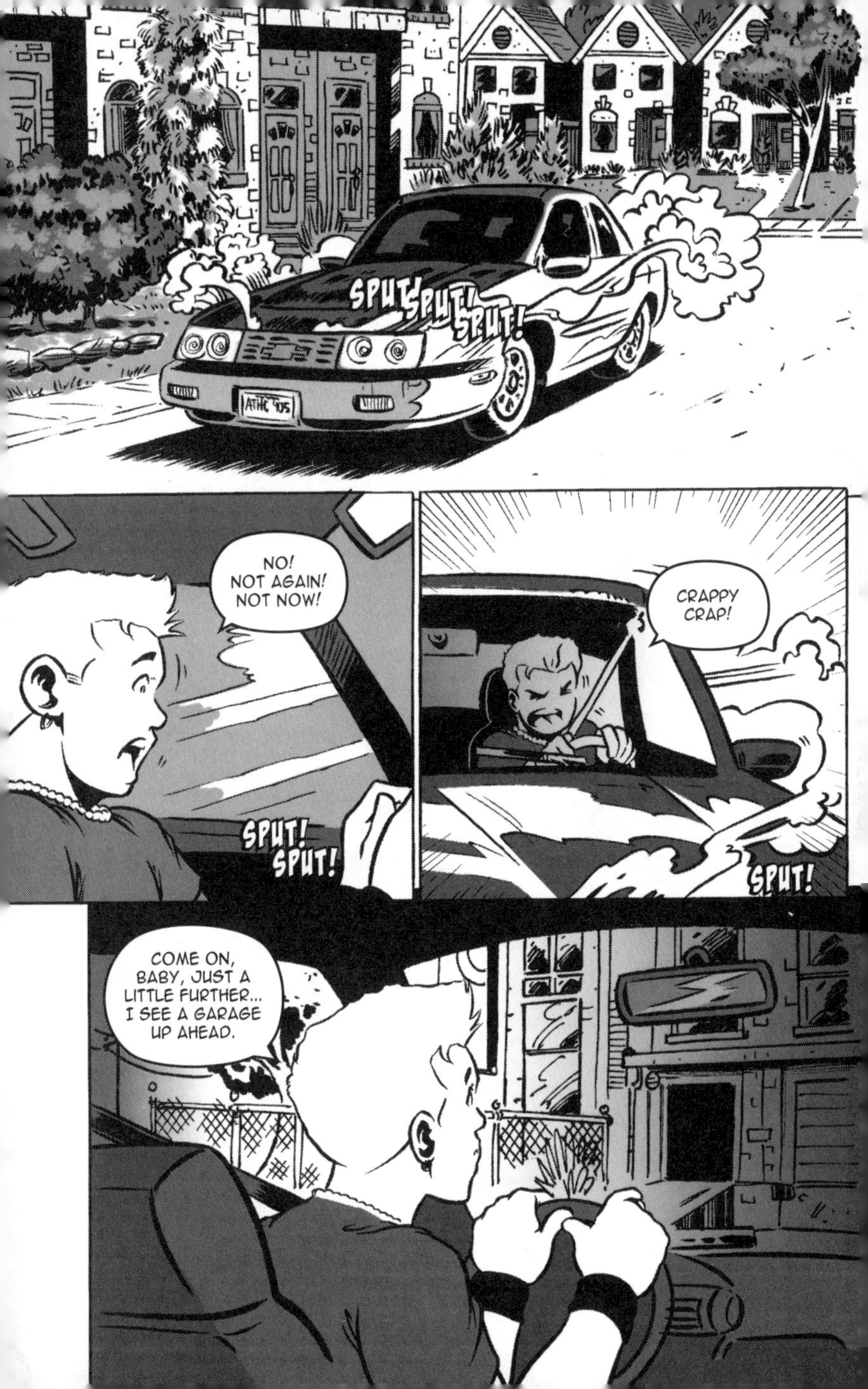
SPUT! SPUT! SPUT!
ATHC 905
NO! NOT AGAIN! NOT NOW!
SPUT! SPUT!
CRAPPY CRAP!
SPUT!
COME ON, BABY, JUST A LITTLE FURTHER... I SEE A GARAGE UP AHEAD.

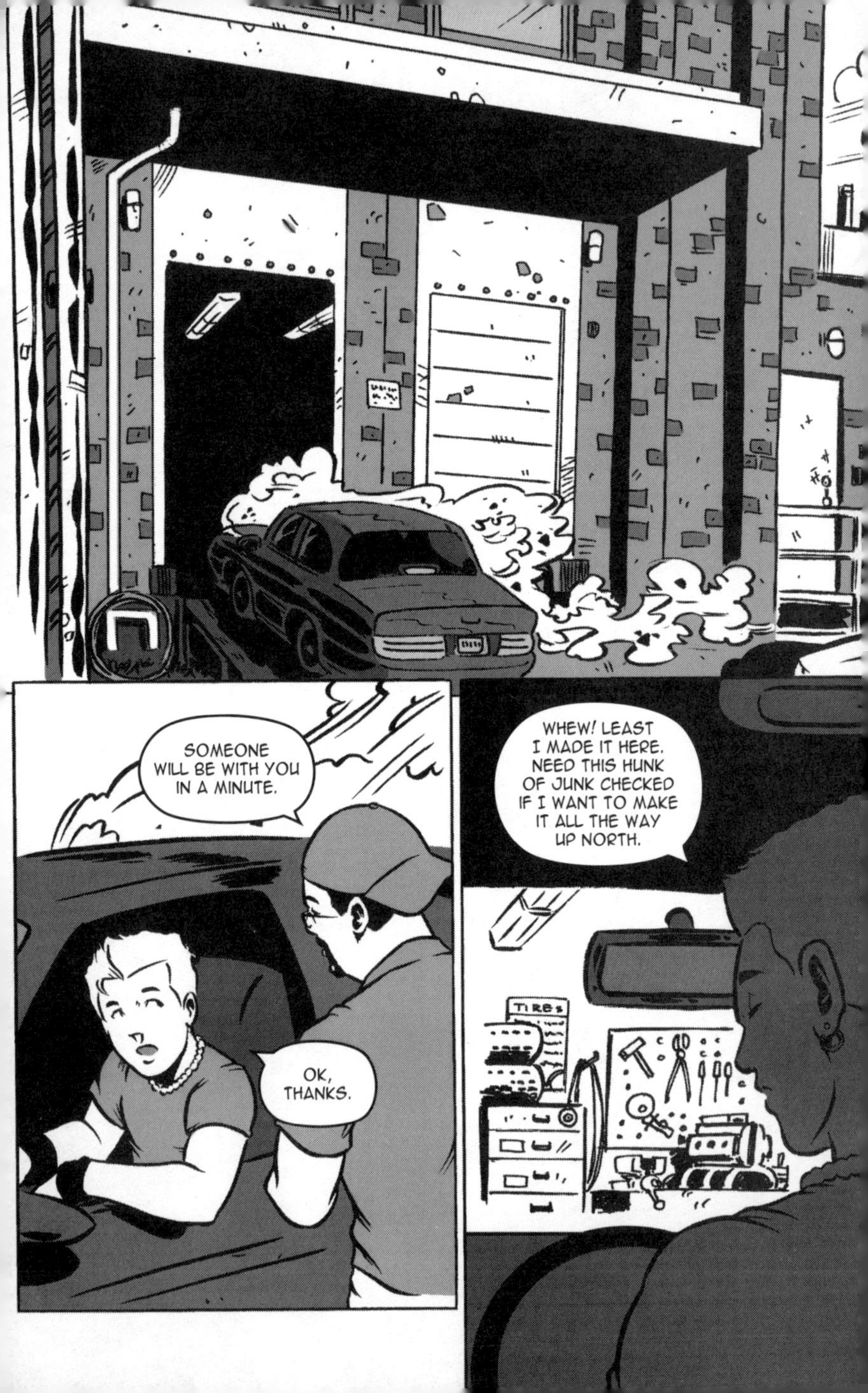
SOMEONE WILL BE WITH YOU IN A MINUTE.
OK, THANKS.
WHEW! LEAST I MADE IT HERE. NEED THIS HUNK OF JUNK CHECKED IF I WANT TO MAKE IT ALL THE WAY UP NORTH.
TIRES

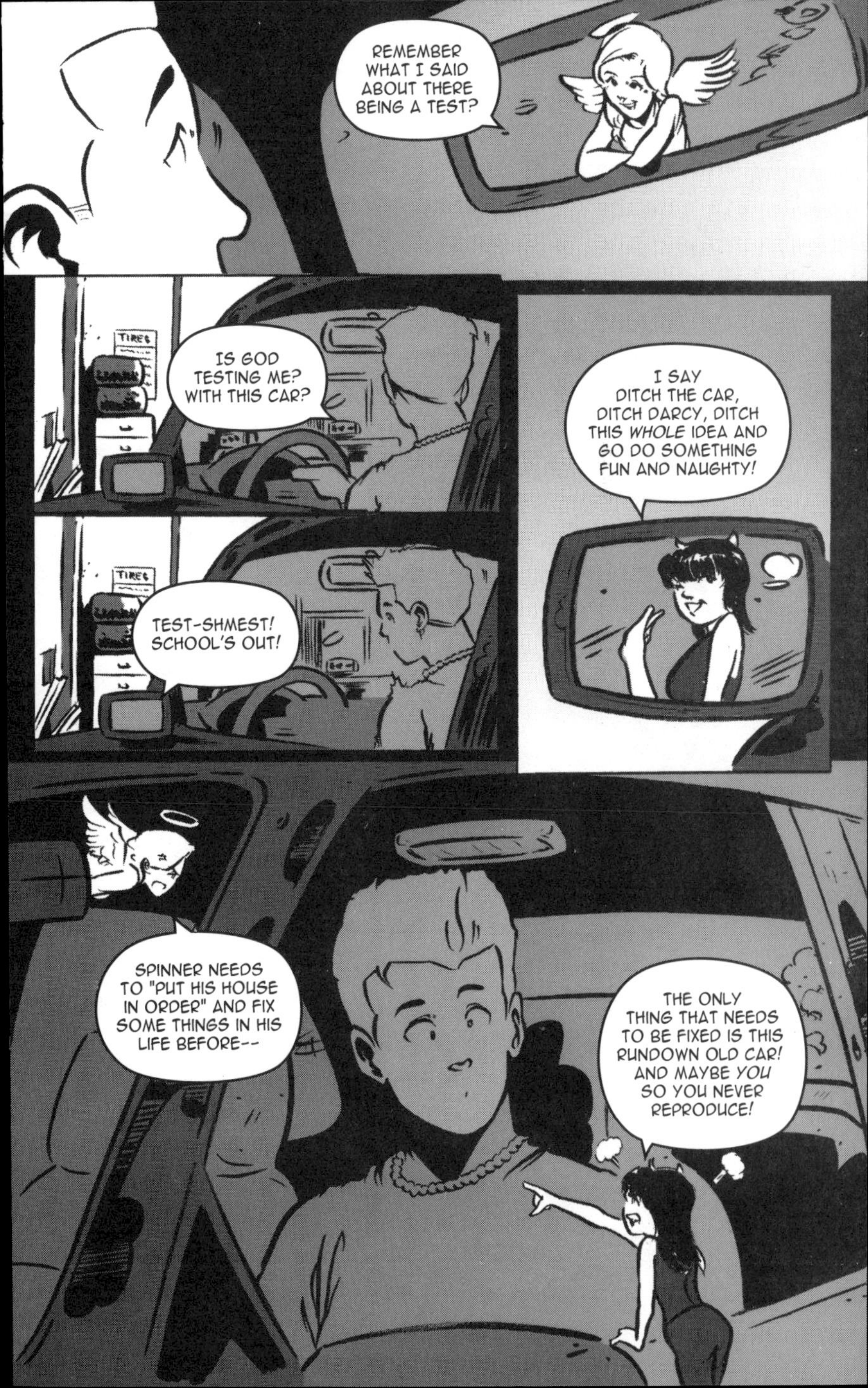
REMEMBER WHAT I SAID ABOUT THERE BEING A TEST?
TIRES
IS GOD TESTING ME? WITH THIS CAR?
I SAY DITCH THE CAR, DITCH DARCY, DITCH THIS *WHOLE* IDEA AND GO DO SOMETHING FUN AND NAUGHTY!
TIRES
TEST-SHMEST! SCHOOL'S OUT!
SPINNER NEEDS TO "PUT HIS HOUSE IN ORDER" AND FIX SOME THINGS IN HIS LIFE BEFORE--
THE ONLY THING THAT NEEDS TO BE FIXED IS THIS RUNDOWN OLD CAR! AND MAYBE *YOU* SO YOU NEVER REPRODUCE!

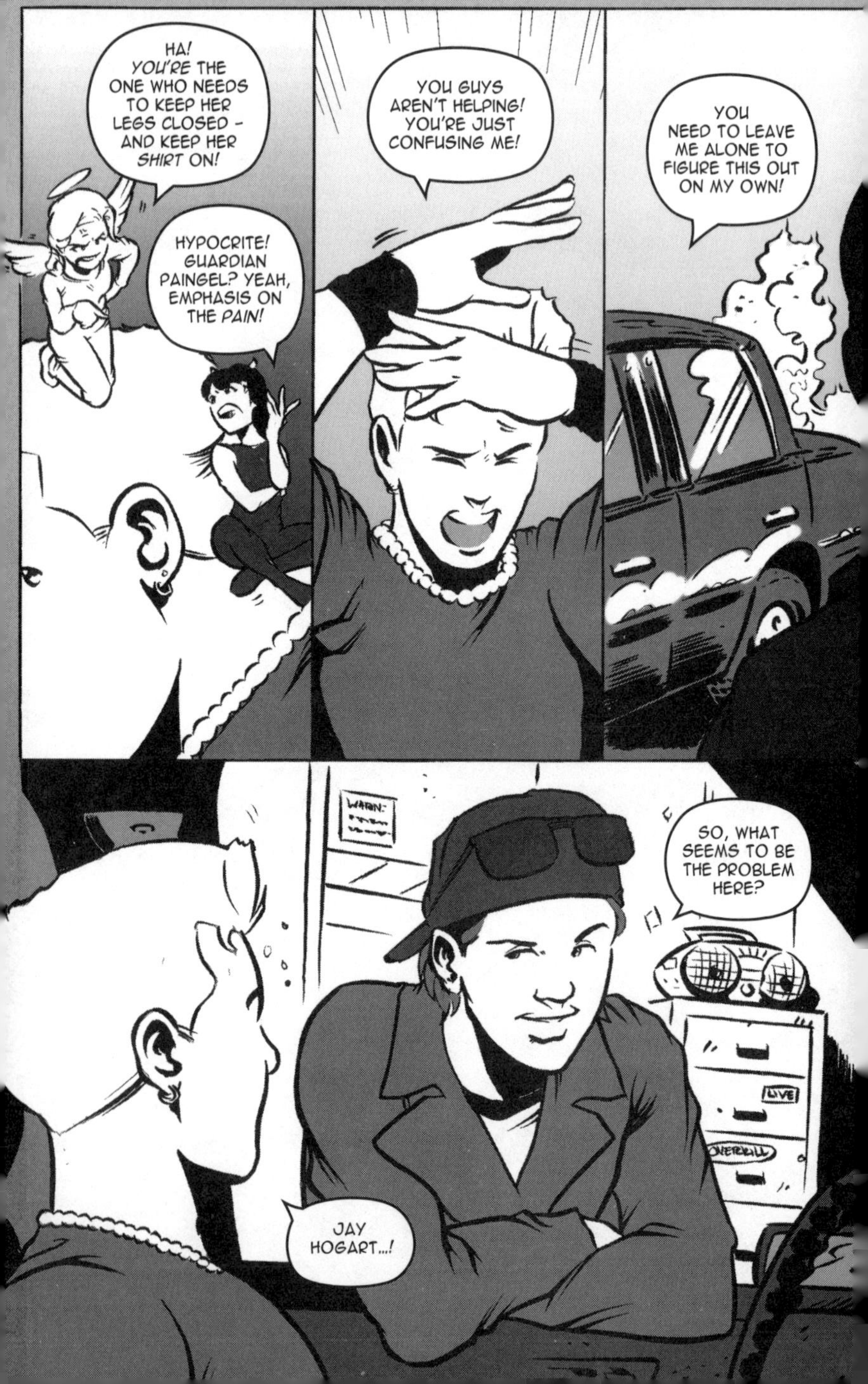
HA! YOU'RE THE ONE WHO NEEDS TO KEEP HER LEGS CLOSED - AND KEEP HER SHIRT ON!
HYPOCRITE! GUARDIAN PAINGEL? YEAH, EMPHASIS ON THE PAIN!
YOU GUYS AREN'T HELPING! YOU'RE JUST CONFUSING ME!
YOU NEED TO LEAVE ME ALONE TO FIGURE THIS OUT ON MY OWN!
SO, WHAT SEEMS TO BE THE PROBLEM HERE?
JAY HOGART...!
LIVE
OVERKILL

ACT 2

"Sometimes I just like to steal."
— Jay Hogart, *The Diary of Jay Hogart*

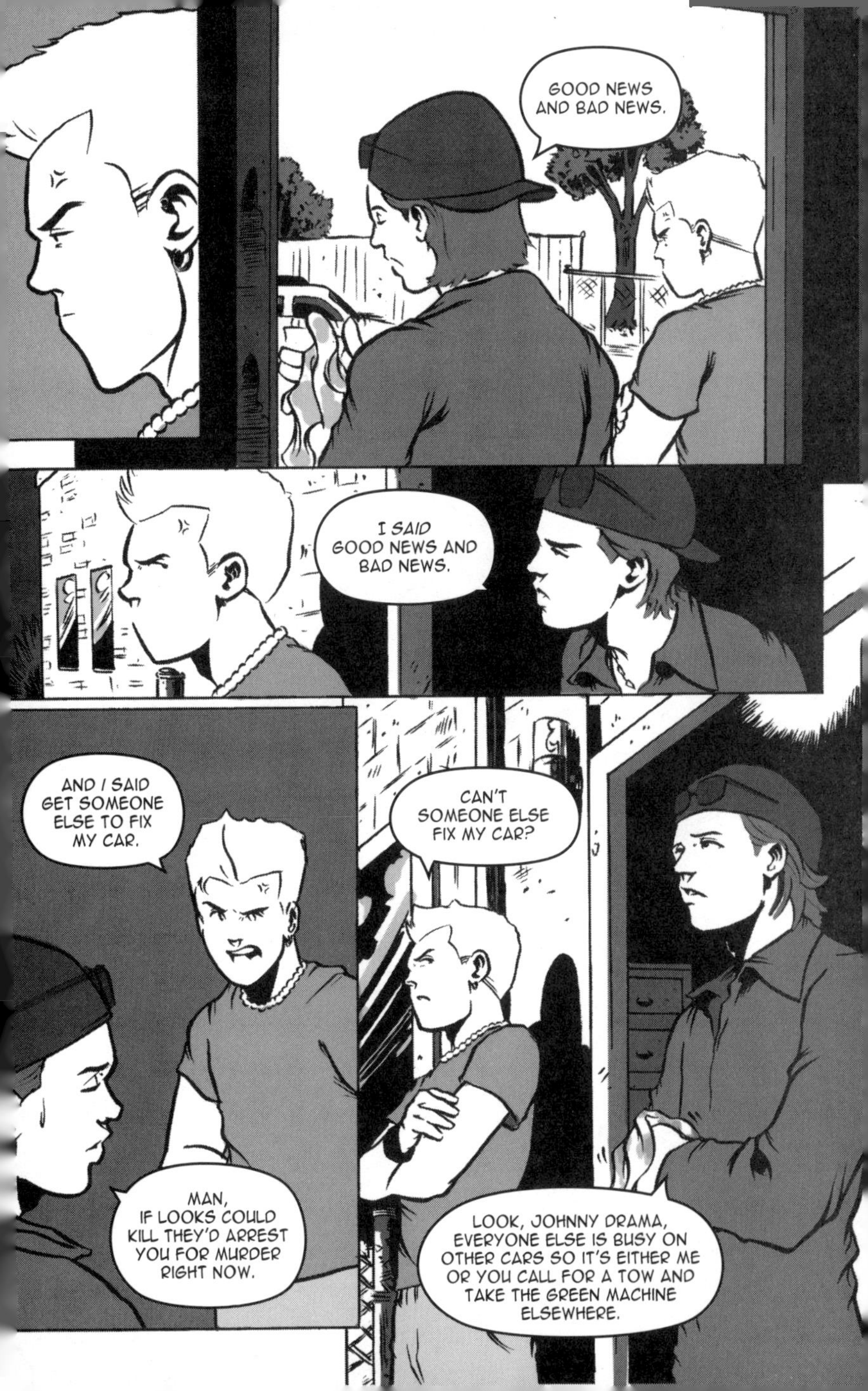
GOOD NEWS AND BAD NEWS.
I SAID GOOD NEWS AND BAD NEWS.
AND I SAID GET SOMEONE ELSE TO FIX MY CAR.
MAN, IF LOOKS COULD KILL THEY'D ARREST YOU FOR MURDER RIGHT NOW.
CAN'T SOMEONE ELSE FIX MY CAR?
LOOK, JOHNNY DRAMA, EVERYONE ELSE IS BUSY ON OTHER CARS SO IT'S EITHER ME OR YOU CALL FOR A TOW AND TAKE THE GREEN MACHINE ELSEWHERE.

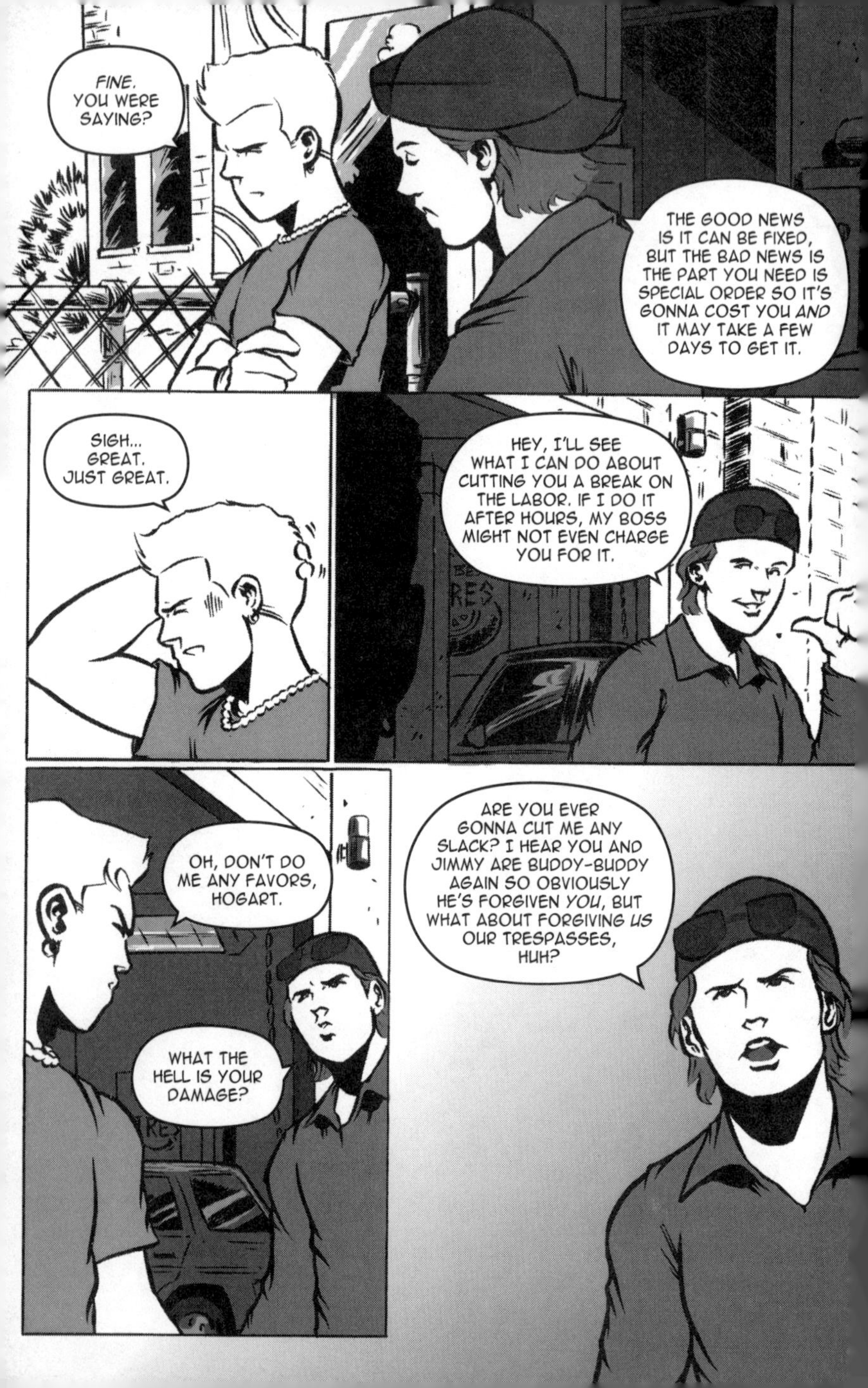
FINE. YOU WERE SAYING?
THE GOOD NEWS IS IT CAN BE FIXED, BUT THE BAD NEWS IS THE PART YOU NEED IS SPECIAL ORDER SO IT'S GONNA COST YOU *AND* IT MAY TAKE A FEW DAYS TO GET IT.
SIGH... GREAT. JUST GREAT.
HEY, I'LL SEE WHAT I CAN DO ABOUT CUTTING YOU A BREAK ON THE LABOR. IF I DO IT AFTER HOURS, MY BOSS MIGHT NOT EVEN CHARGE YOU FOR IT.
OH, DON'T DO ME ANY FAVORS, HOGART.
WHAT THE HELL IS YOUR DAMAGE?
ARE YOU EVER GONNA CUT ME ANY SLACK? I HEAR YOU AND JIMMY ARE BUDDY-BUDDY AGAIN SO OBVIOUSLY HE'S FORGIVEN *YOU*, BUT WHAT ABOUT FORGIVING *US* OUR TRESPASSES, HUH?

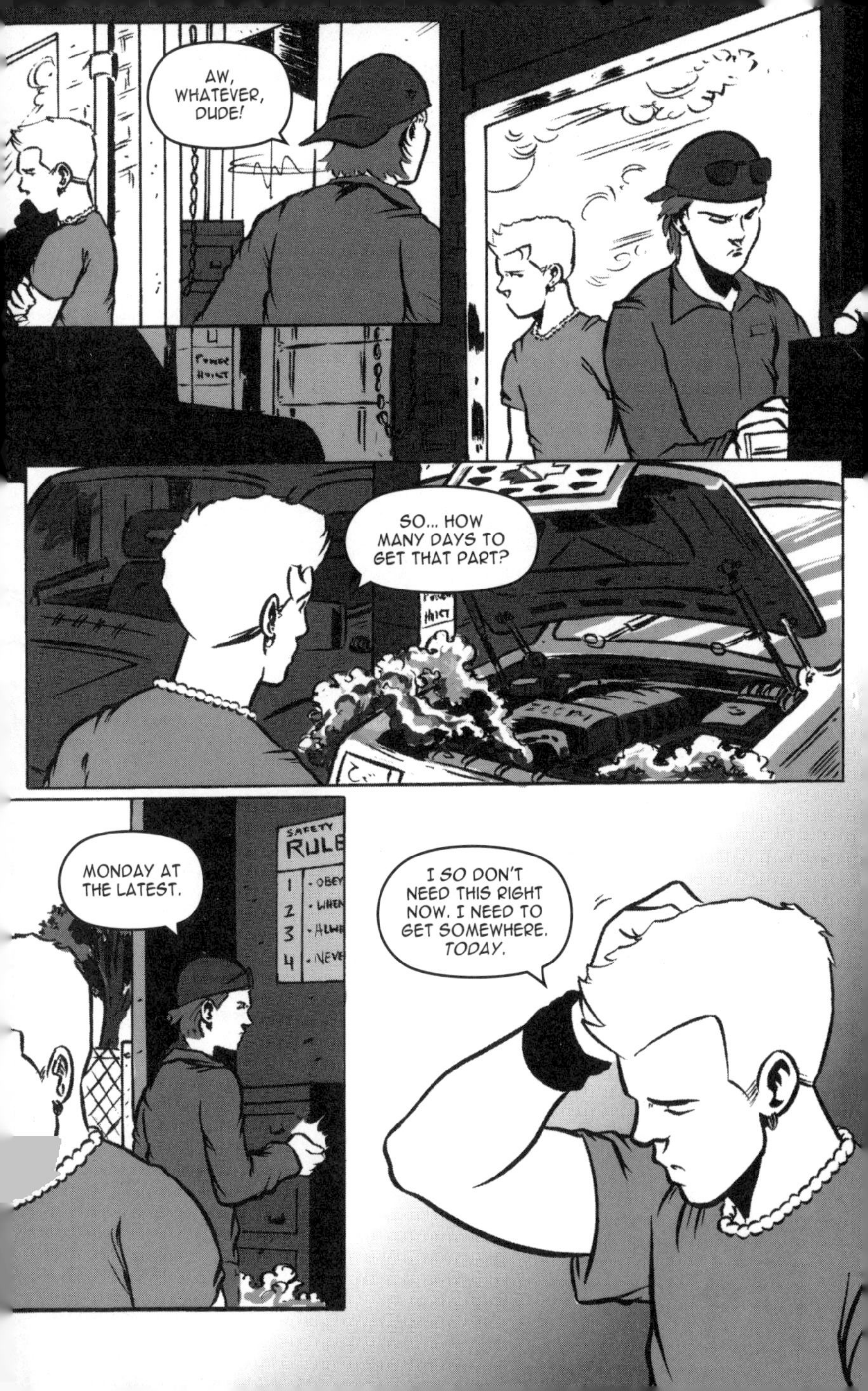
AW, WHATEVER, DUDE!
SO... HOW MANY DAYS TO GET THAT PART?
SAFETY
RULE
MONDAY AT THE LATEST.
I SO DON'T NEED THIS RIGHT NOW. I NEED TO GET SOMEWHERE. *TODAY.*

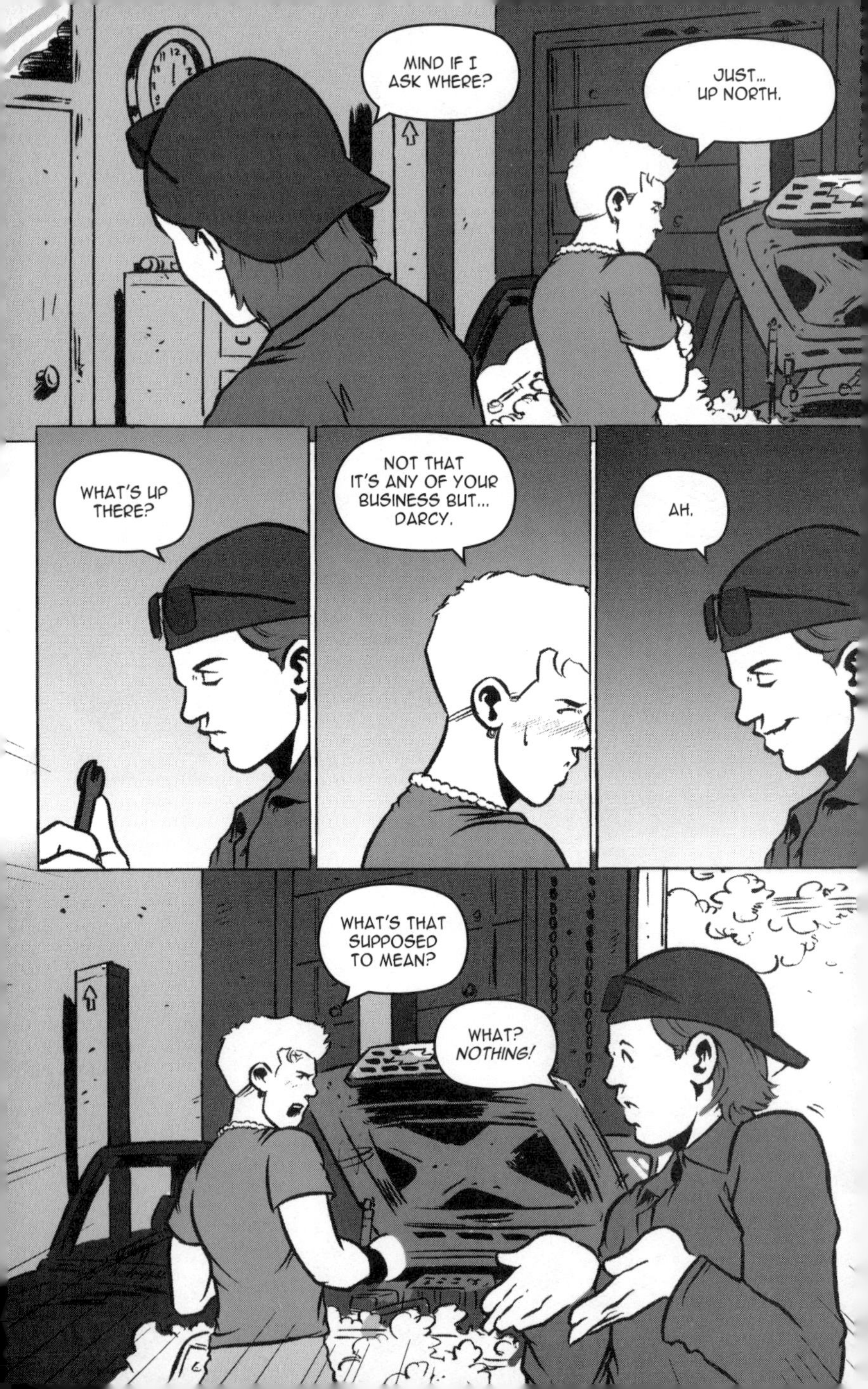
MIND IF I ASK WHERE?
JUST... UP NORTH.
WHAT'S UP THERE?
NOT THAT IT'S ANY OF YOUR BUSINESS BUT... DARCY.
AH.
WHAT'S THAT SUPPOSED TO MEAN?
WHAT? *NOTHING!*

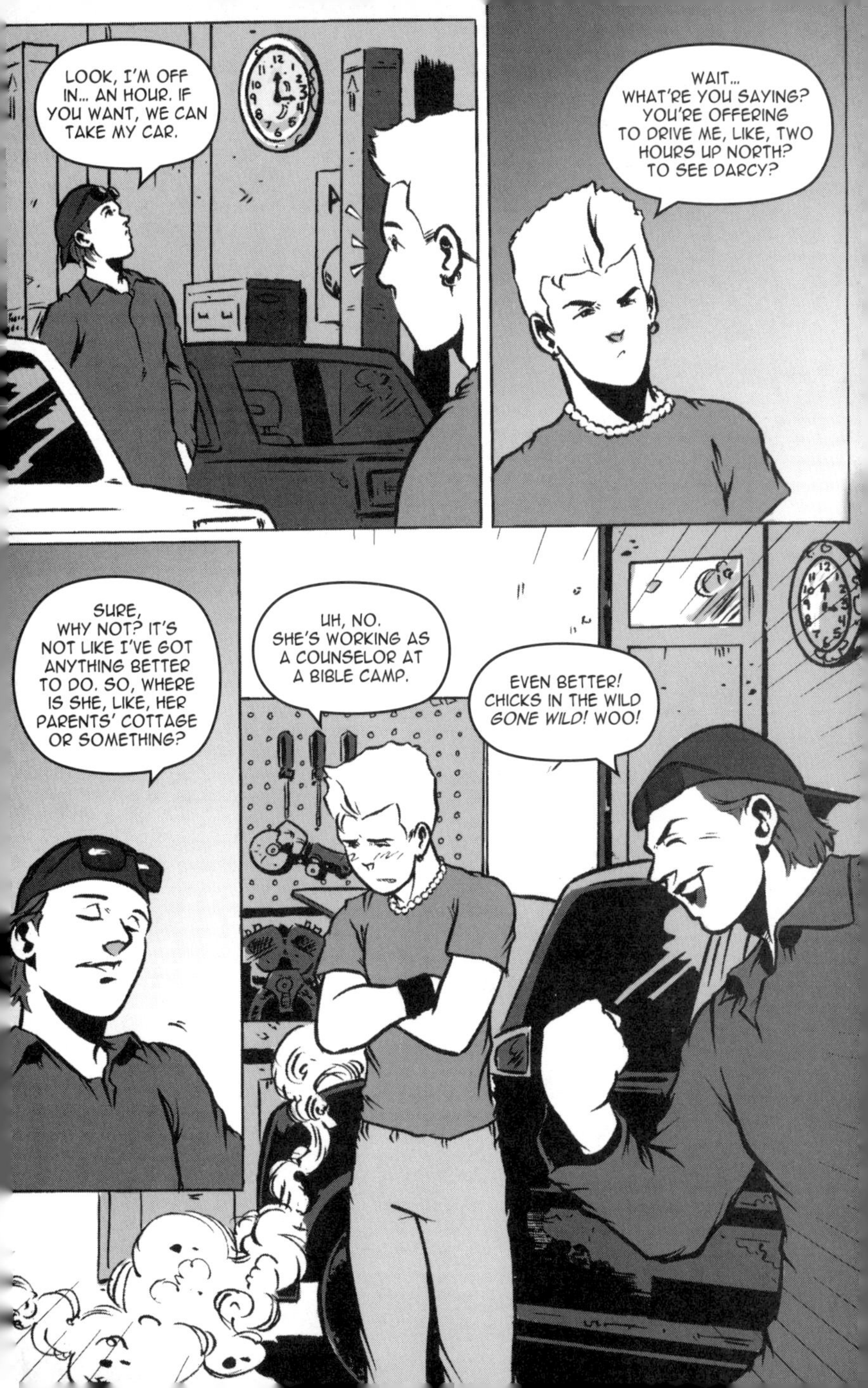
LOOK, I'M OFF IN... AN HOUR. IF YOU WANT, WE CAN TAKE MY CAR.
WAIT... WHAT'RE YOU SAYING? YOU'RE OFFERING TO DRIVE ME, LIKE, TWO HOURS UP NORTH? TO SEE DARCY?
SURE, WHY NOT? IT'S NOT LIKE I'VE GOT ANYTHING BETTER TO DO. SO, WHERE IS SHE, LIKE, HER PARENTS' COTTAGE OR SOMETHING?
UH, NO. SHE'S WORKING AS A COUNSELOR AT A BIBLE CAMP.
EVEN BETTER! CHICKS IN THE WILD *GONE WILD!* WOO!

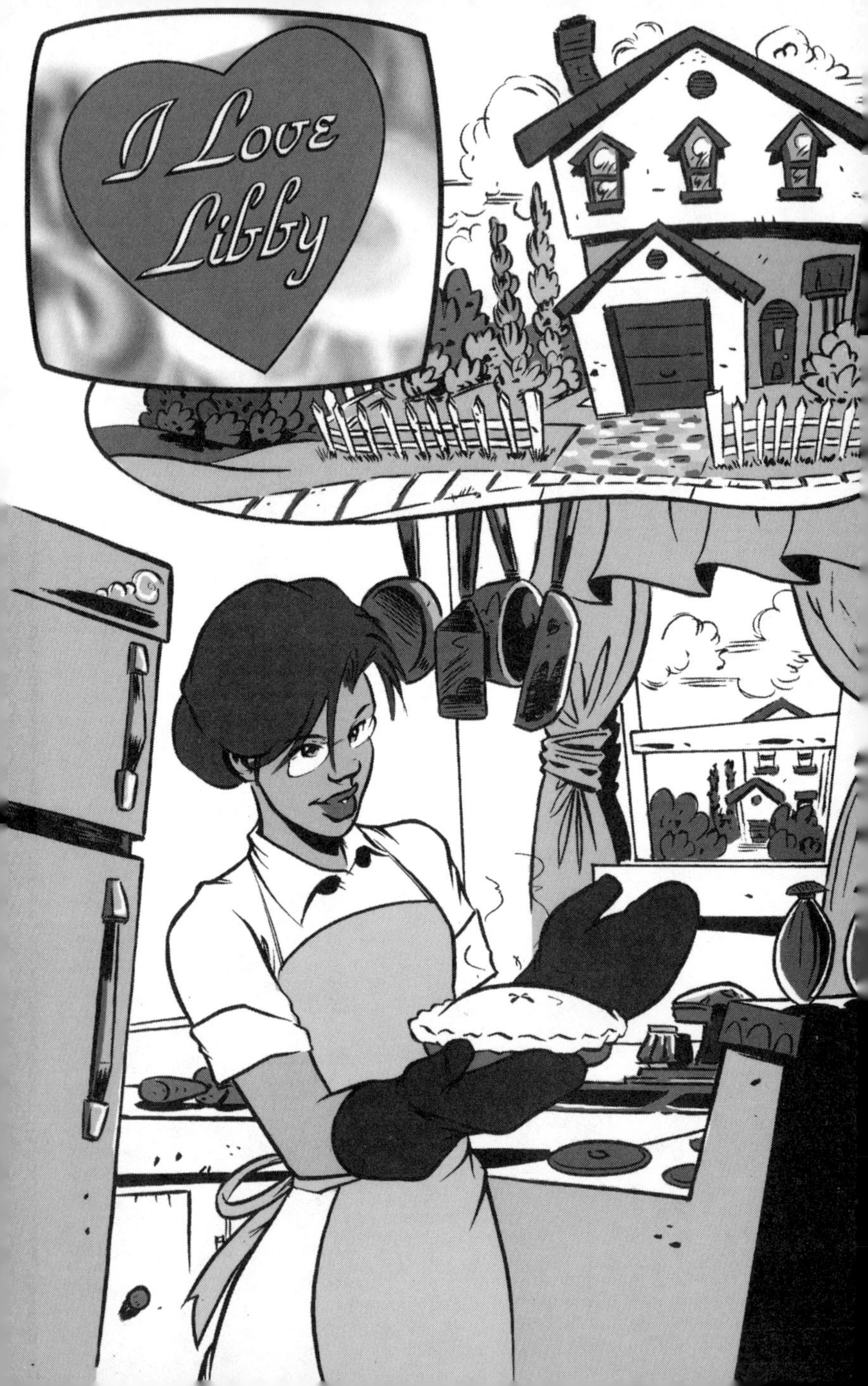
I Love Libby

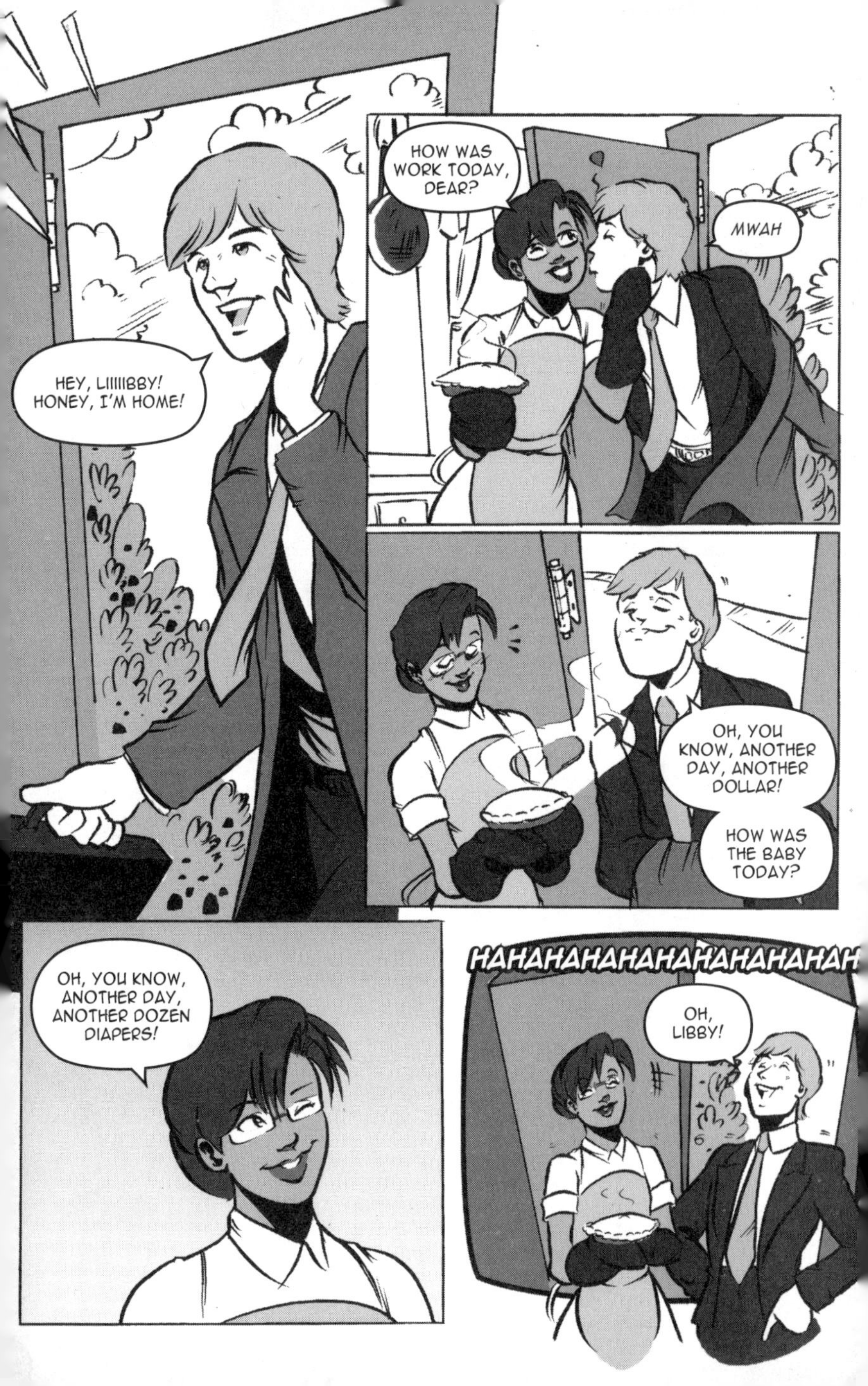
HEY, LIIIIIBBY!
HONEY, I'M HOME!
HOW WAS WORK TODAY, DEAR?
MWAH
OH, YOU KNOW, ANOTHER DAY, ANOTHER DOLLAR!
HOW WAS THE BABY TODAY?
OH, YOU KNOW, ANOTHER DAY, ANOTHER DOZEN DIAPERS!
HAHAHAHAHAHAHAHAHAHAH
OH, LIBBY!

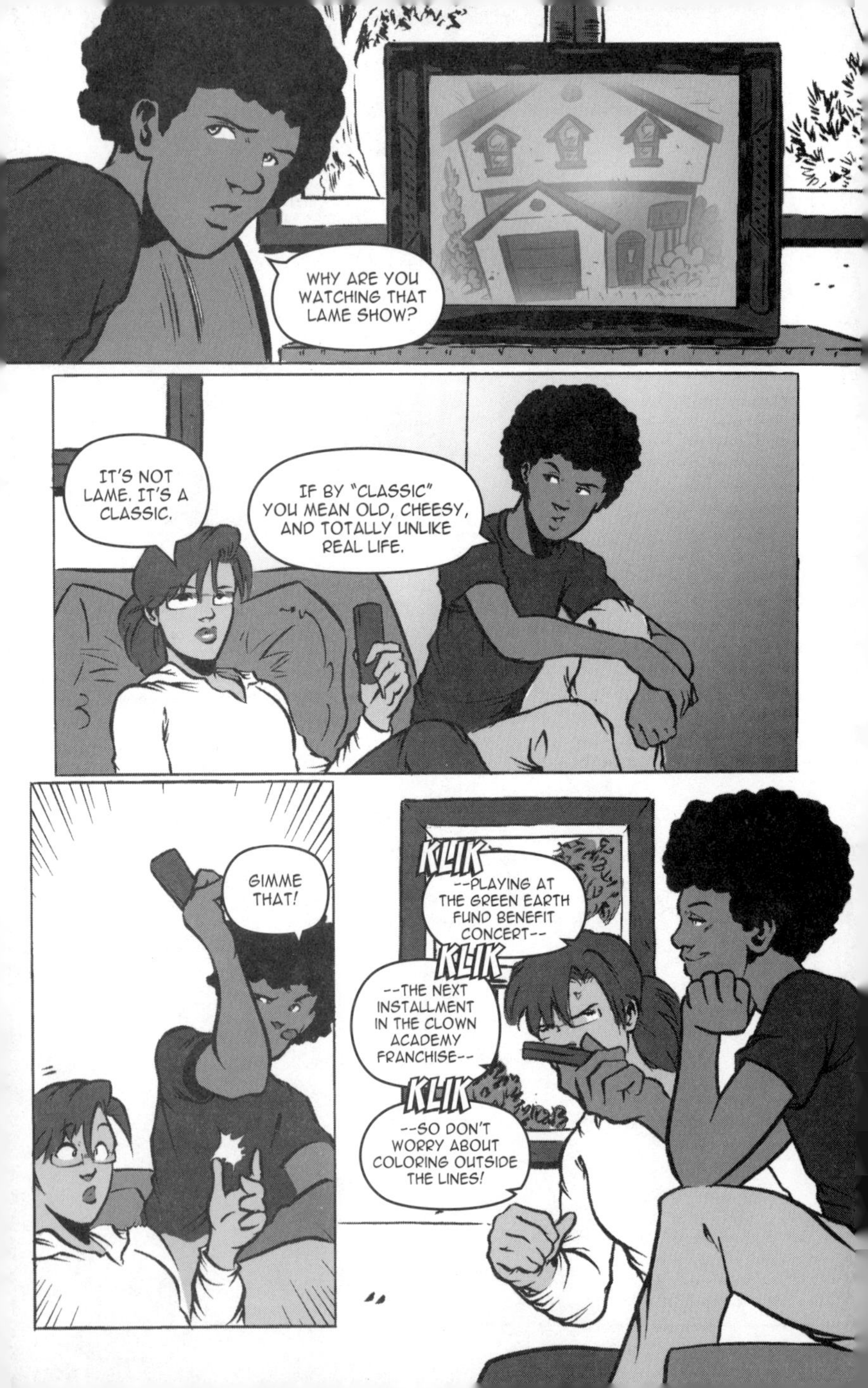
WHY ARE YOU WATCHING THAT LAME SHOW?
IT'S NOT LAME. IT'S A CLASSIC.
IF BY "CLASSIC" YOU MEAN OLD, CHEESY, AND TOTALLY UNLIKE REAL LIFE.
GIMME THAT!
KLIK
--PLAYING AT THE GREEN EARTH FUND BENEFIT CONCERT--
KLIK
--THE NEXT INSTALLMENT IN THE CLOWN ACADEMY FRANCHISE--
KLIK
--SO DON'T WORRY ABOUT COLORING OUTSIDE THE LINES!

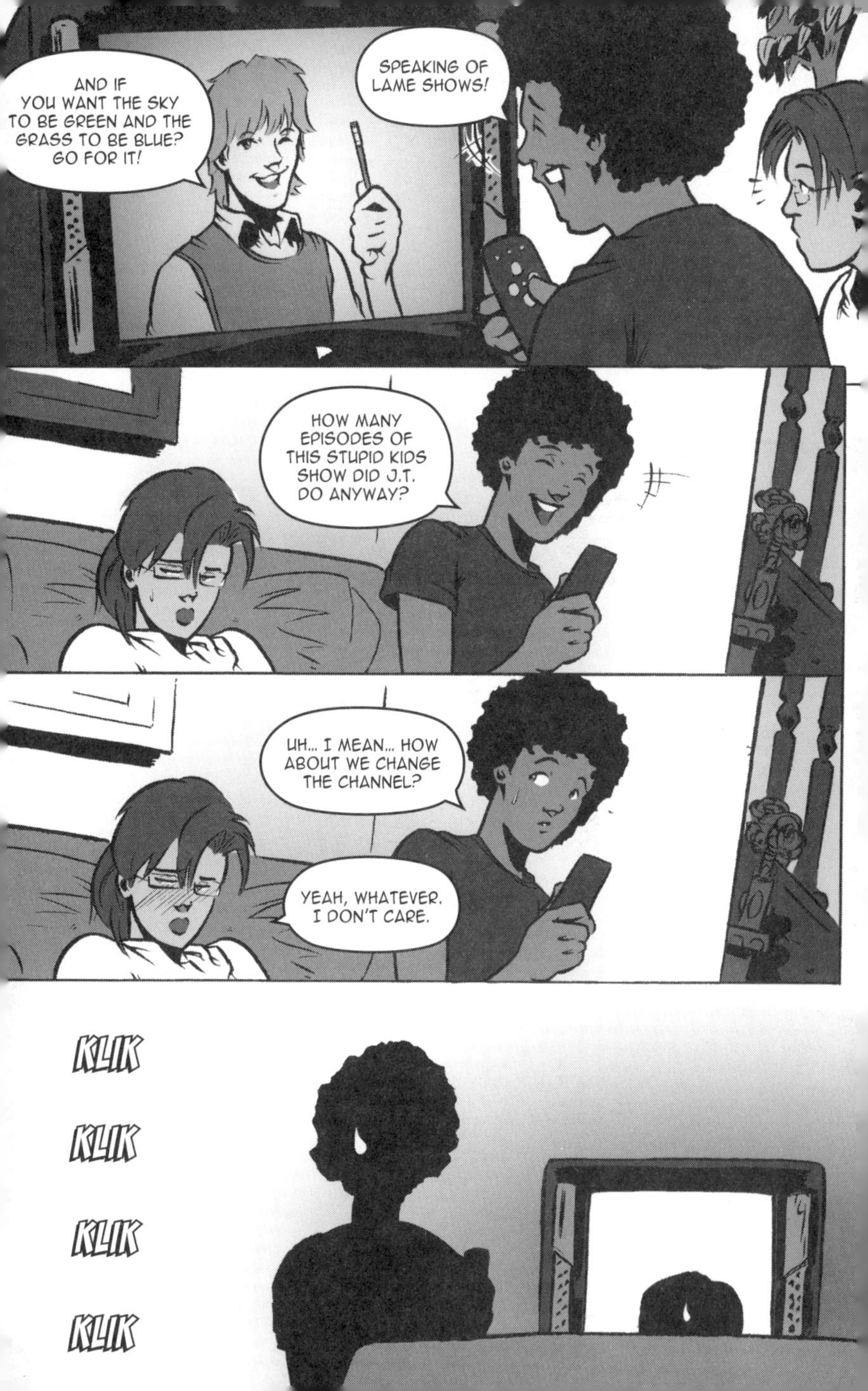
AND IF YOU WANT THE SKY TO BE GREEN AND THE GRASS TO BE BLUE? GO FOR IT!
SPEAKING OF LAME SHOWS!
HOW MANY EPISODES OF THIS STUPID KIDS SHOW DID J.T. DO ANYWAY?
UH... I MEAN... HOW ABOUT WE CHANGE THE CHANNEL?
YEAH, WHATEVER. I DON'T CARE.
KLIK
KLIK
KLIK
KLIK

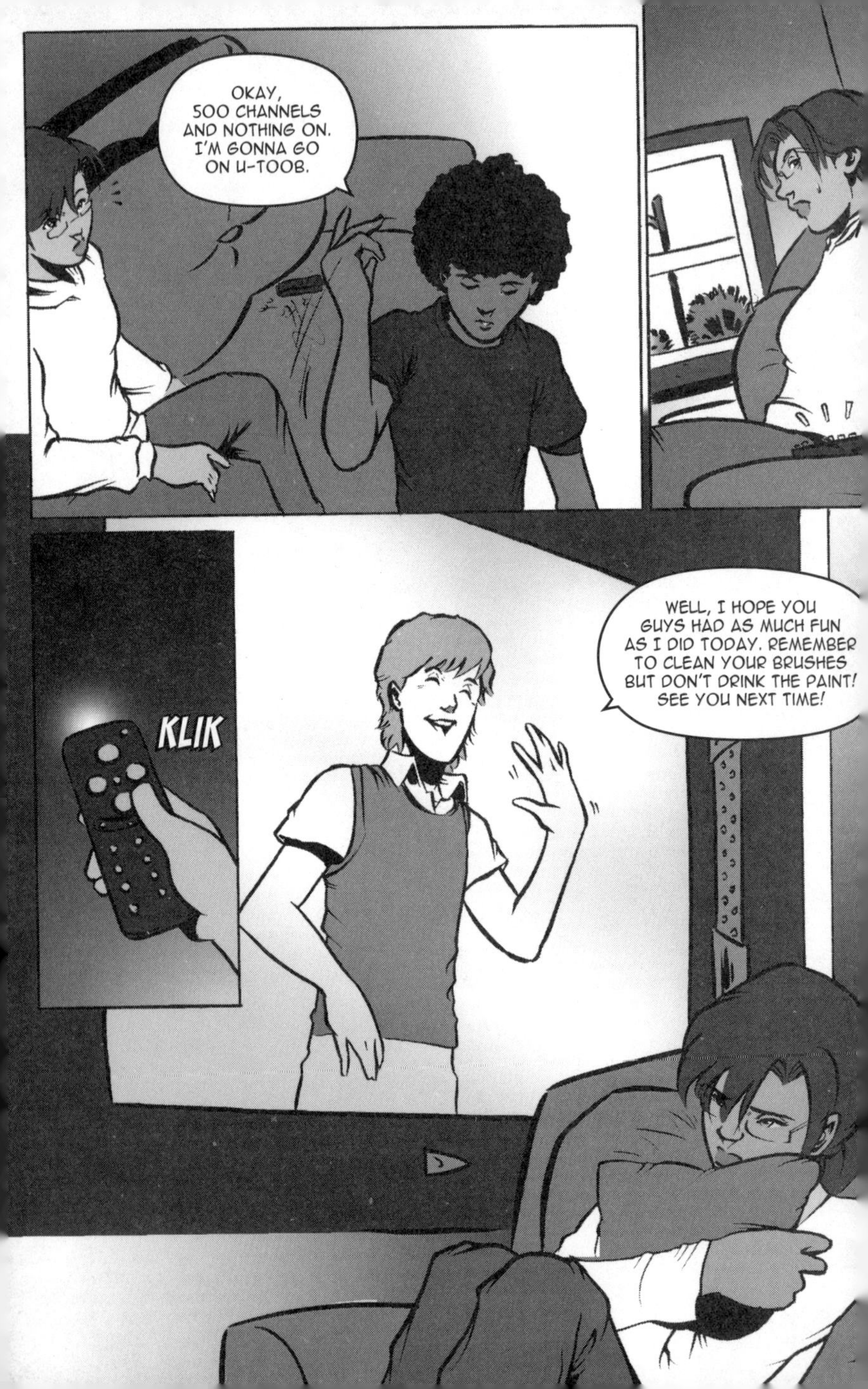
OKAY, 500 CHANNELS AND NOTHING ON. I'M GONNA GO ON U-TOOB.
KLIK
WELL, I HOPE YOU GUYS HAD AS MUCH FUN AS I DID TODAY. REMEMBER TO CLEAN YOUR BRUSHES BUT DON'T DRINK THE PAINT! SEE YOU NEXT TIME!

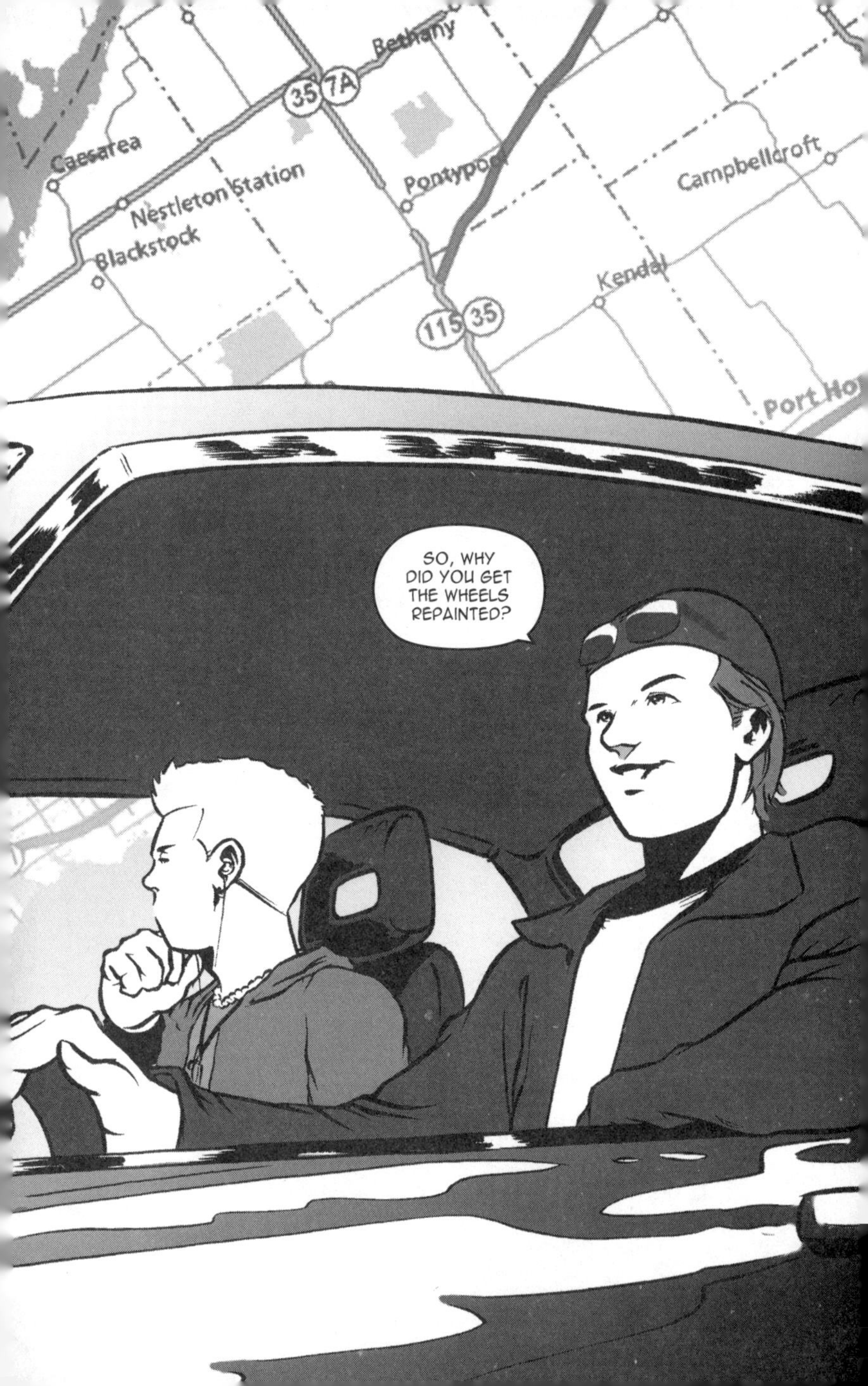
Bethany
35
7A
Caesarea
Nestleton Station
Blackstock
Pontypool
Campbellcroft
Kendal
115
35
Port Ho
SO, WHY DID YOU GET THE WHEELS REPAINTED?

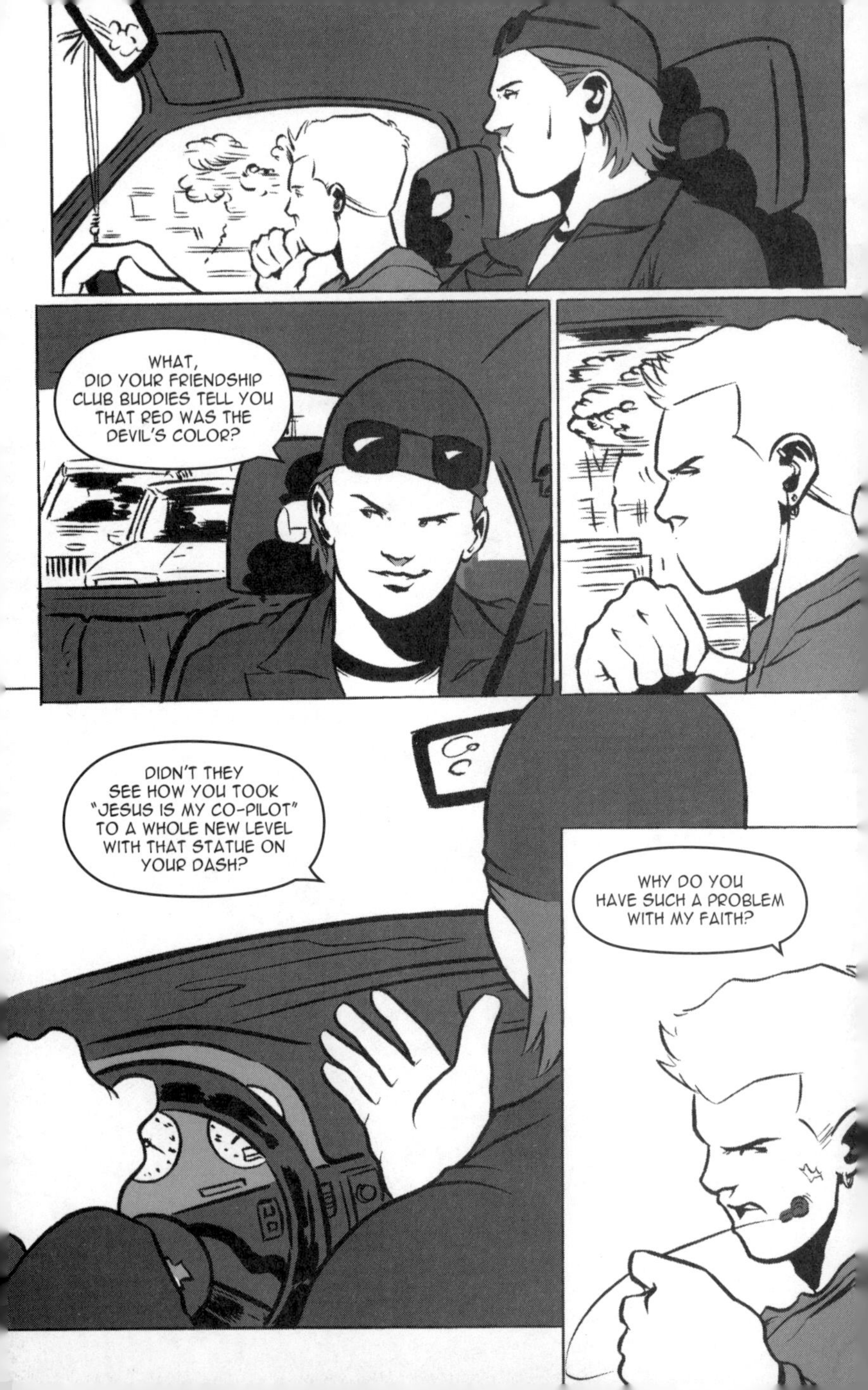
WHAT, DID YOUR FRIENDSHIP CLUB BUDDIES TELL YOU THAT RED WAS THE DEVIL'S COLOR?
DIDN'T THEY SEE HOW YOU TOOK "JESUS IS MY CO-PILOT" TO A WHOLE NEW LEVEL WITH THAT STATUE ON YOUR DASH?
WHY DO YOU HAVE SUCH A PROBLEM WITH MY FAITH?

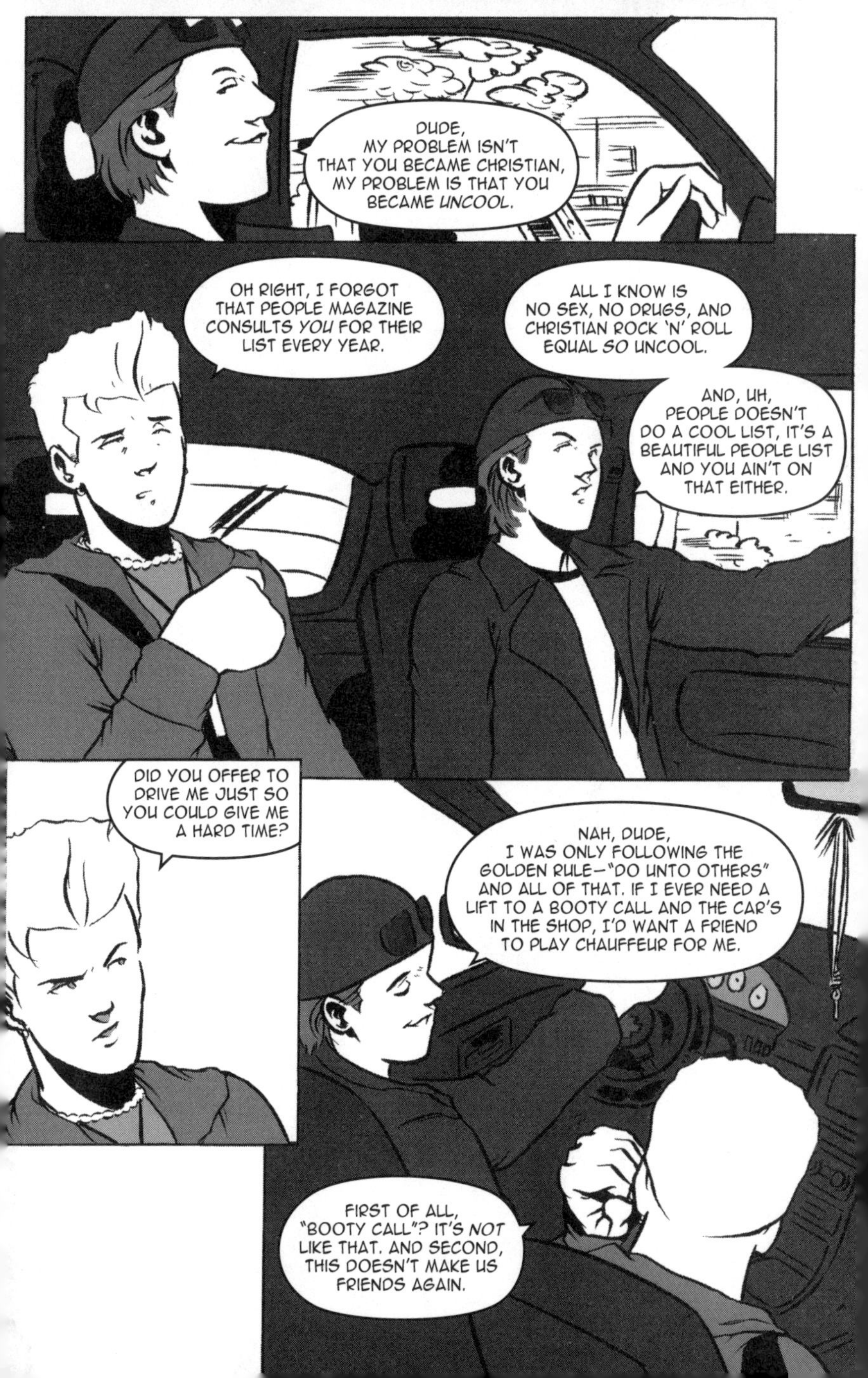
DUDE, MY PROBLEM ISN'T THAT YOU BECAME CHRISTIAN, MY PROBLEM IS THAT YOU BECAME *UNCOOL*.
OH RIGHT, I FORGOT THAT PEOPLE MAGAZINE CONSULTS *YOU* FOR THEIR LIST EVERY YEAR.
ALL I KNOW IS NO SEX, NO DRUGS, AND CHRISTIAN ROCK 'N' ROLL EQUAL *SO* UNCOOL.
AND, UH, PEOPLE DOESN'T DO A COOL LIST, IT'S A BEAUTIFUL PEOPLE LIST AND YOU AIN'T ON THAT EITHER.
DID YOU OFFER TO DRIVE ME JUST SO YOU COULD GIVE ME A HARD TIME?
NAH, DUDE, I WAS ONLY FOLLOWING THE GOLDEN RULE—"DO UNTO OTHERS" AND ALL OF THAT. IF I EVER NEED A LIFT TO A BOOTY CALL AND THE CAR'S IN THE SHOP, I'D WANT A FRIEND TO PLAY CHAUFFEUR FOR ME.
FIRST OF ALL, "BOOTY CALL"? IT'S *NOT* LIKE THAT. AND SECOND, THIS DOESN'T MAKE US FRIENDS AGAIN.

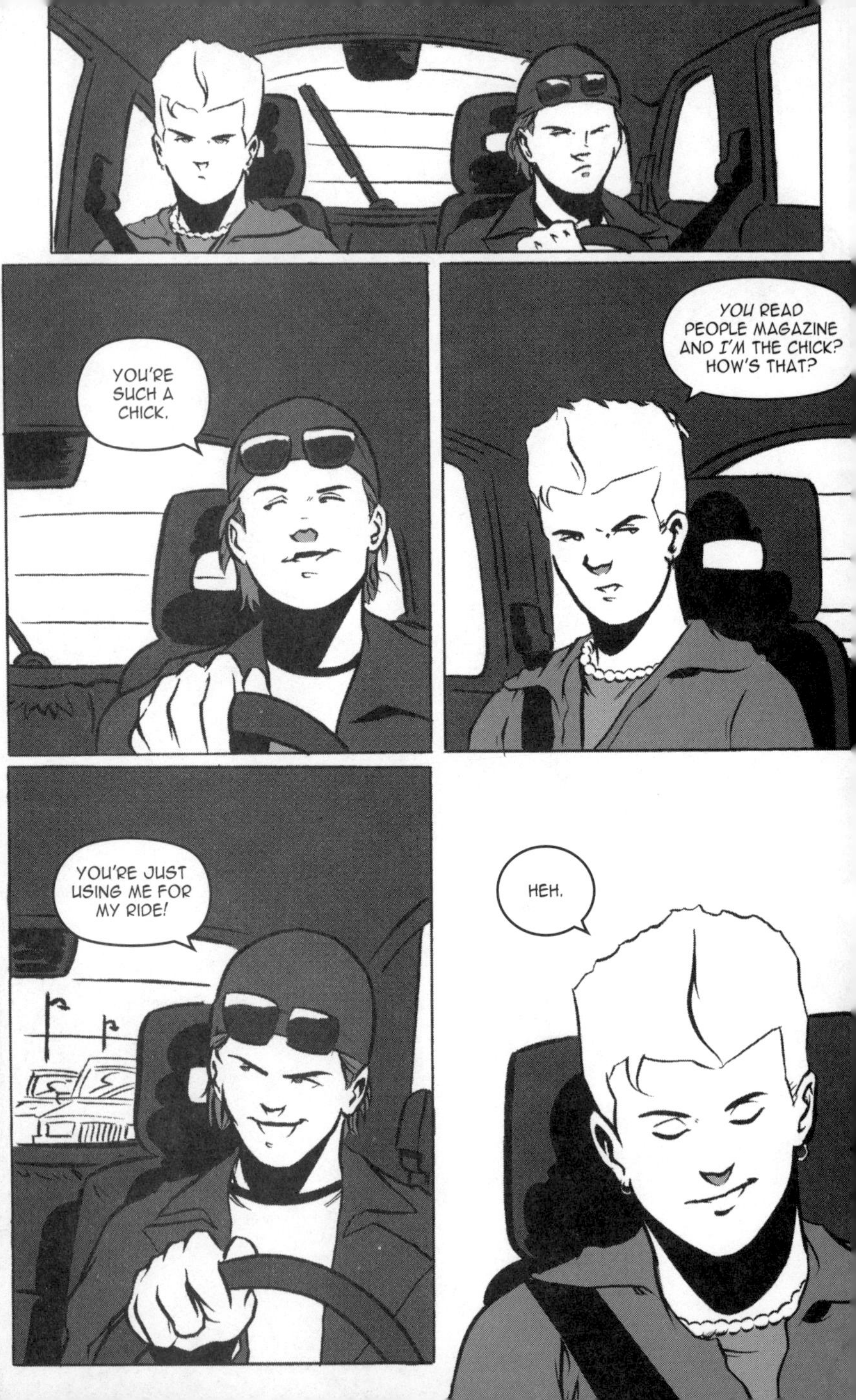
YOU'RE SUCH A CHICK.
YOU READ PEOPLE MAGAZINE AND I'M THE CHICK? HOW'S THAT?
YOU'RE JUST USING ME FOR MY RIDE!
HEH.

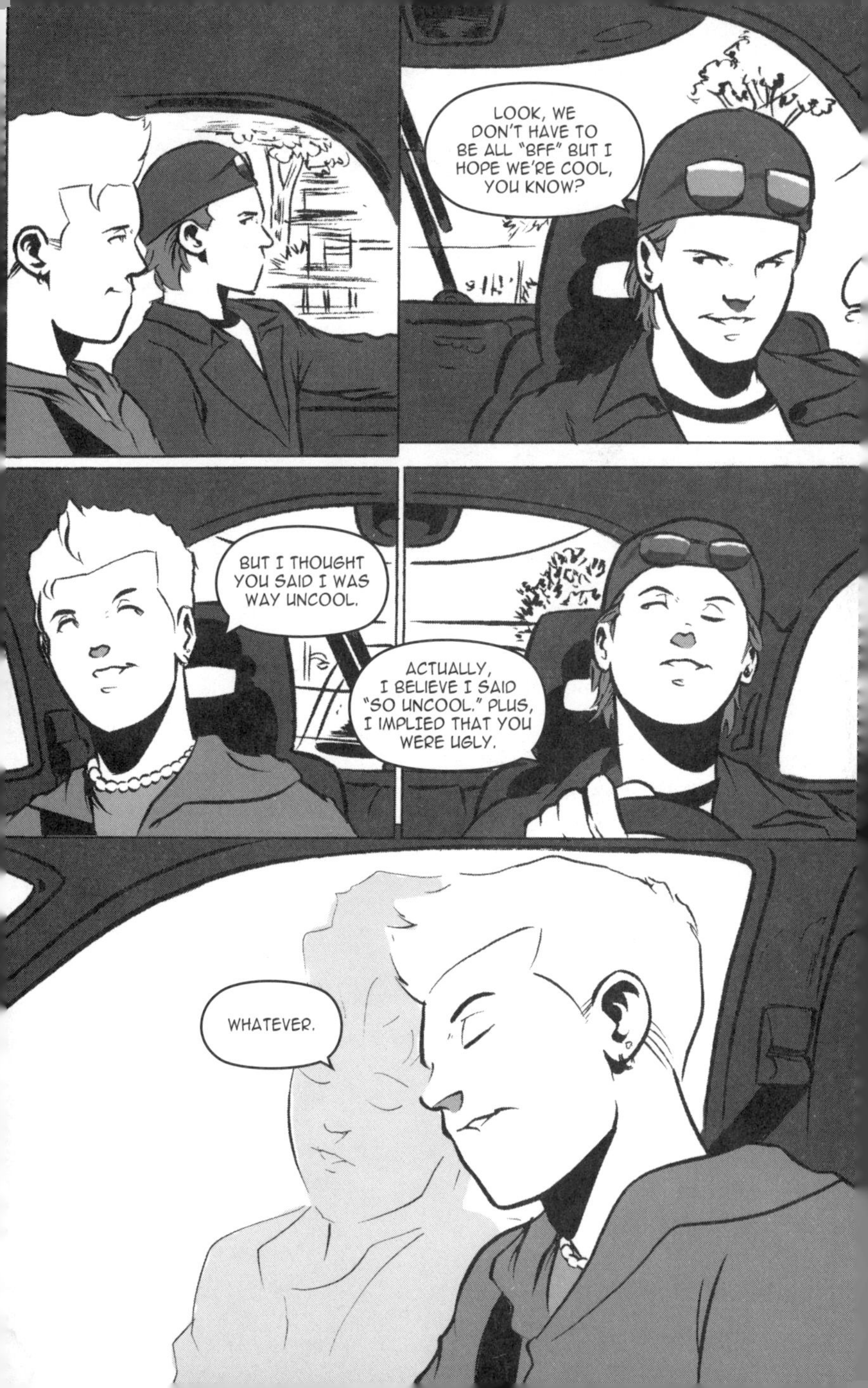
LOOK, WE DON'T HAVE TO BE ALL "BFF" BUT I HOPE WE'RE COOL, YOU KNOW?
BUT I THOUGHT YOU SAID I WAS WAY UNCOOL.
ACTUALLY, I BELIEVE I SAID "SO UNCOOL." PLUS, I IMPLIED THAT YOU WERE UGLY.
WHATEVER.

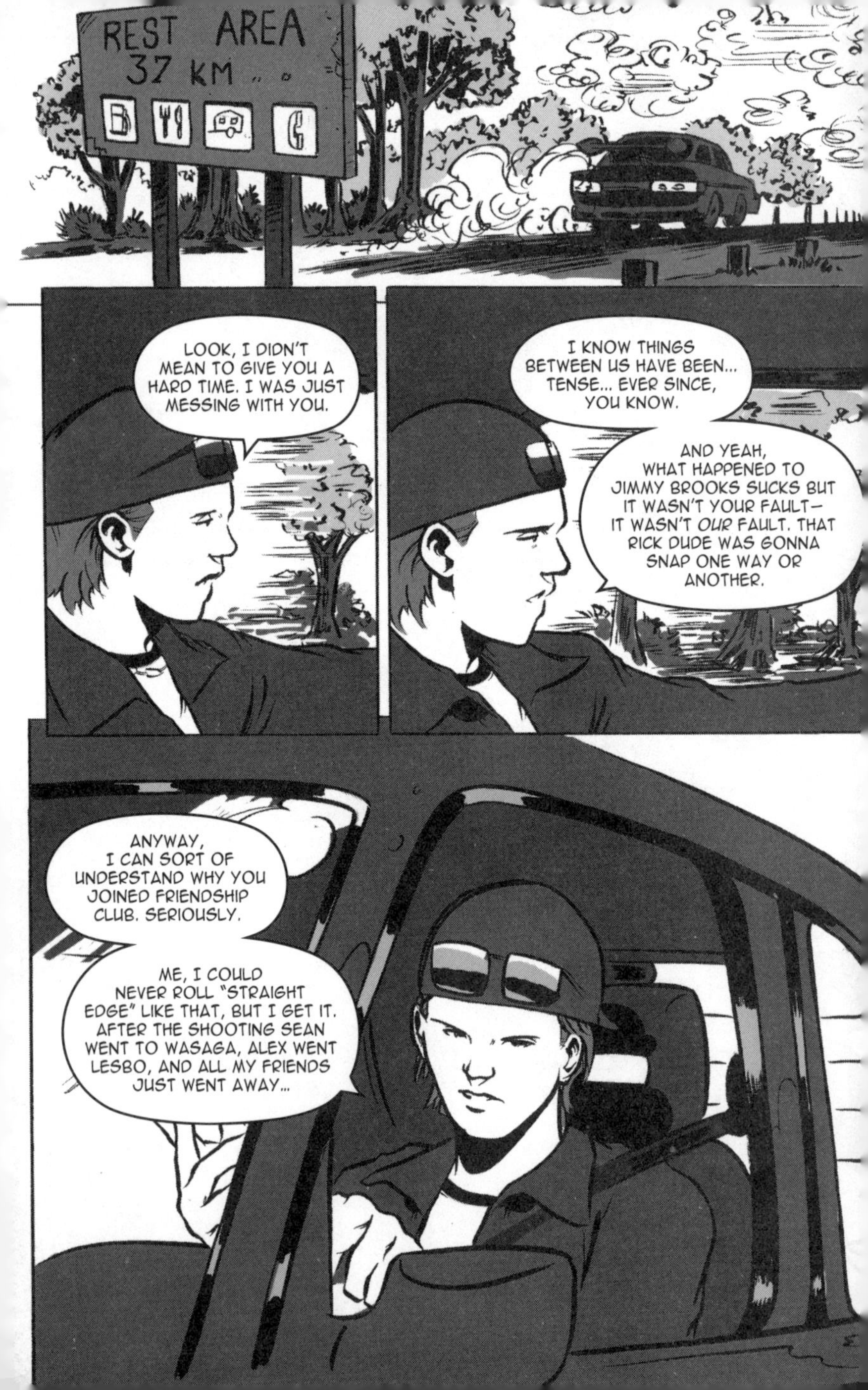
REST AREA
37 KM
LOOK, I DIDN'T MEAN TO GIVE YOU A HARD TIME. I WAS JUST MESSING WITH YOU.
I KNOW THINGS BETWEEN US HAVE BEEN... TENSE... EVER SINCE, YOU KNOW.
AND YEAH, WHAT HAPPENED TO JIMMY BROOKS SUCKS BUT IT WASN'T YOUR FAULT— IT WASN'T *OUR* FAULT. THAT RICK DUDE WAS GONNA SNAP ONE WAY OR ANOTHER.
ANYWAY, I CAN SORT OF UNDERSTAND WHY YOU JOINED FRIENDSHIP CLUB. SERIOUSLY.
ME, I COULD NEVER ROLL "STRAIGHT EDGE" LIKE THAT, BUT I GET IT. AFTER THE SHOOTING SEAN WENT TO WASAGA, ALEX WENT LESBO, AND ALL MY FRIENDS JUST WENT AWAY...

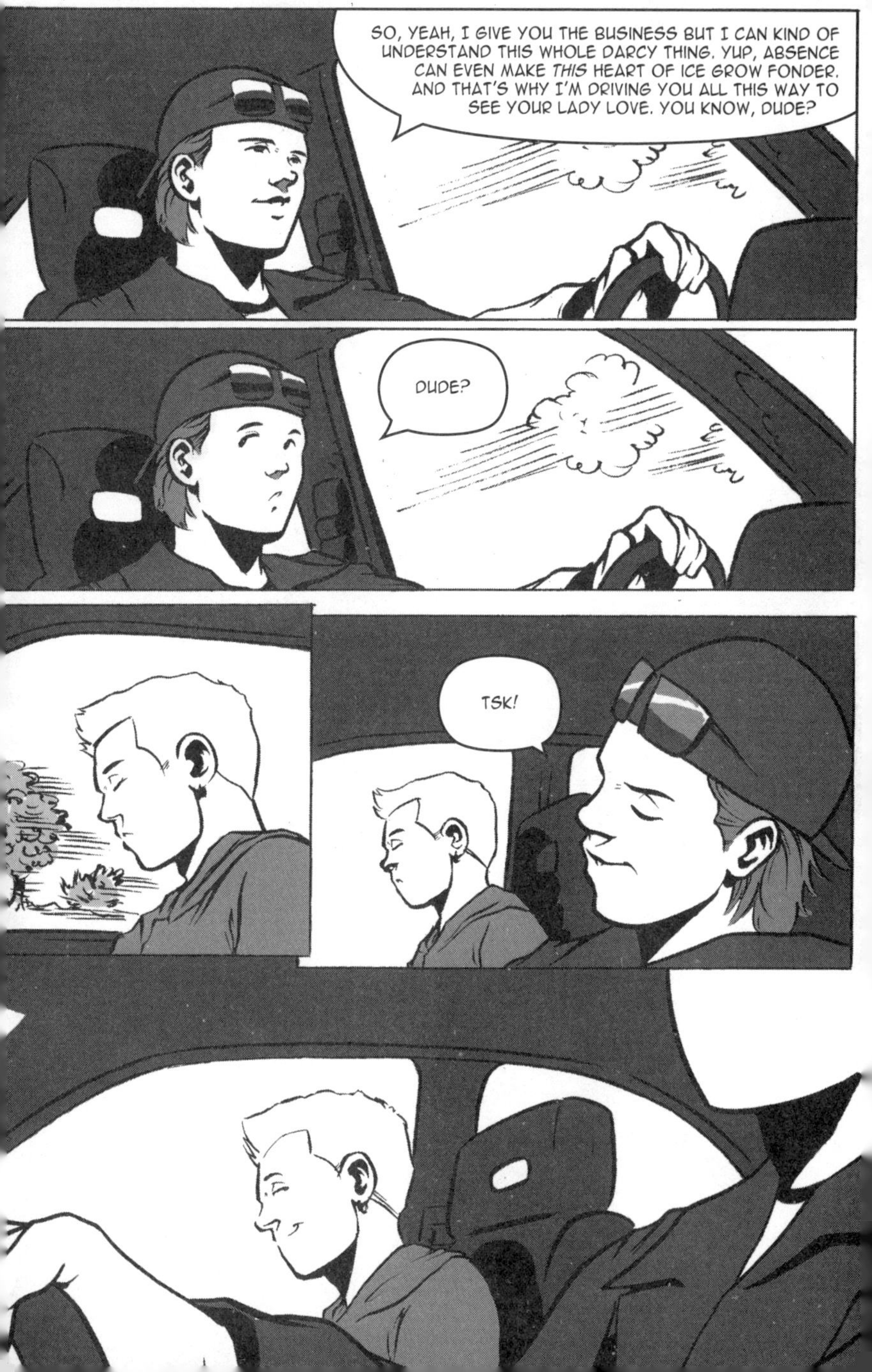
SO, YEAH, I GIVE YOU THE BUSINESS BUT I CAN KIND OF UNDERSTAND THIS WHOLE DARCY THING. YUP, ABSENCE CAN EVEN MAKE *THIS* HEART OF ICE GROW FONDER. AND THAT'S WHY I'M DRIVING YOU ALL THIS WAY TO SEE YOUR LADY LOVE. YOU KNOW, DUDE?
DUDE?
TSK!

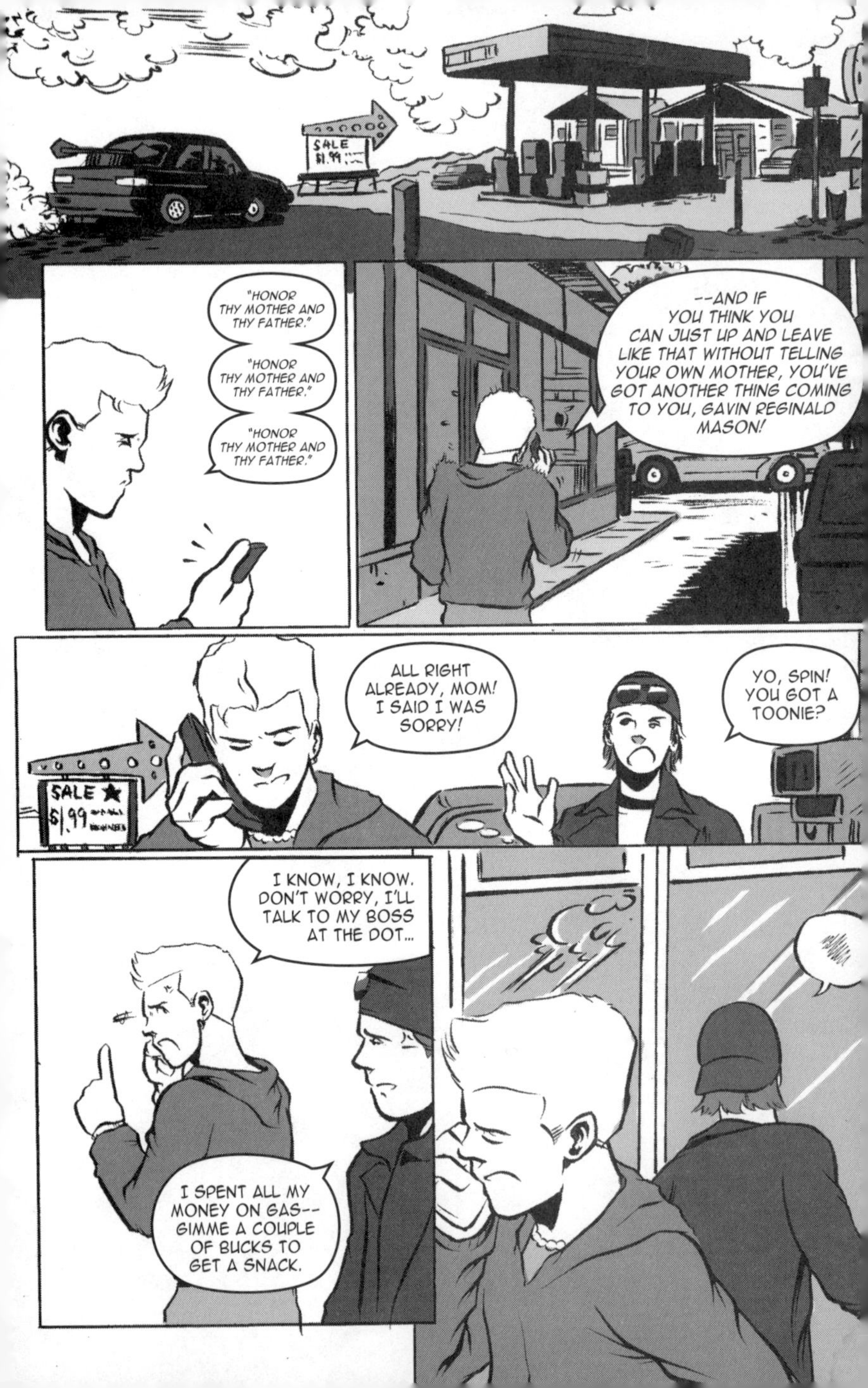

SALE $1.99
"HONOR THY MOTHER AND THY FATHER."
"HONOR THY MOTHER AND THY FATHER."
"HONOR THY MOTHER AND THY FATHER."
--AND IF YOU THINK YOU CAN JUST UP AND LEAVE LIKE THAT WITHOUT TELLING YOUR OWN MOTHER, YOU'VE GOT ANOTHER THING COMING TO YOU, GAVIN REGINALD MASON!
SALE $1.99
ALL RIGHT ALREADY, MOM! I SAID I WAS SORRY!
YO, SPIN! YOU GOT A TOONIE?
I KNOW, I KNOW. DON'T WORRY, I'LL TALK TO MY BOSS AT THE DOT...
I SPENT ALL MY MONEY ON GAS-- GIMME A COUPLE OF BUCKS TO GET A SNACK.

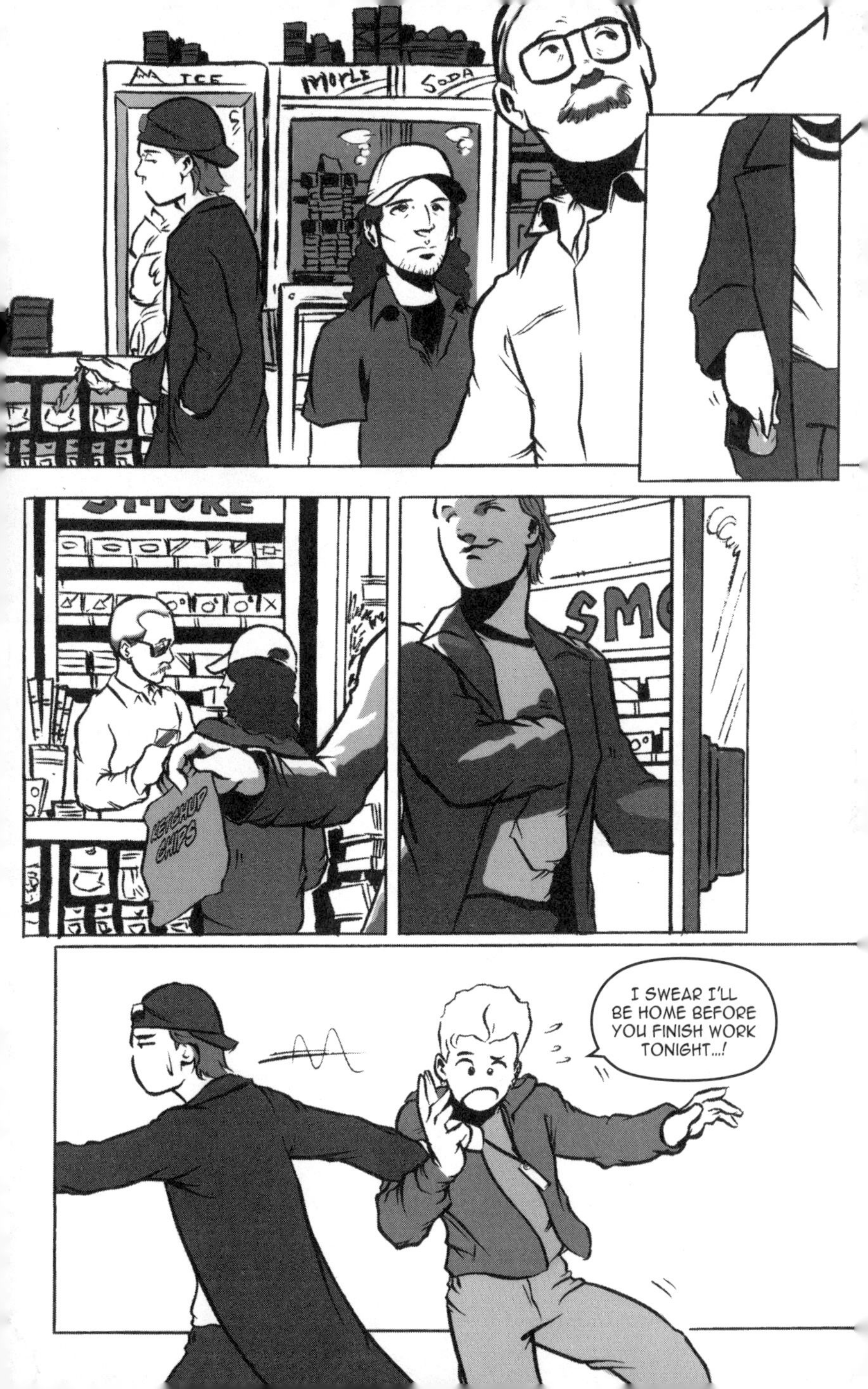
ICE
SODA
SMOKE
KETCHUP CHIPS
SMO
I SWEAR I'LL BE HOME BEFORE YOU FINISH WORK TONIGHT...!

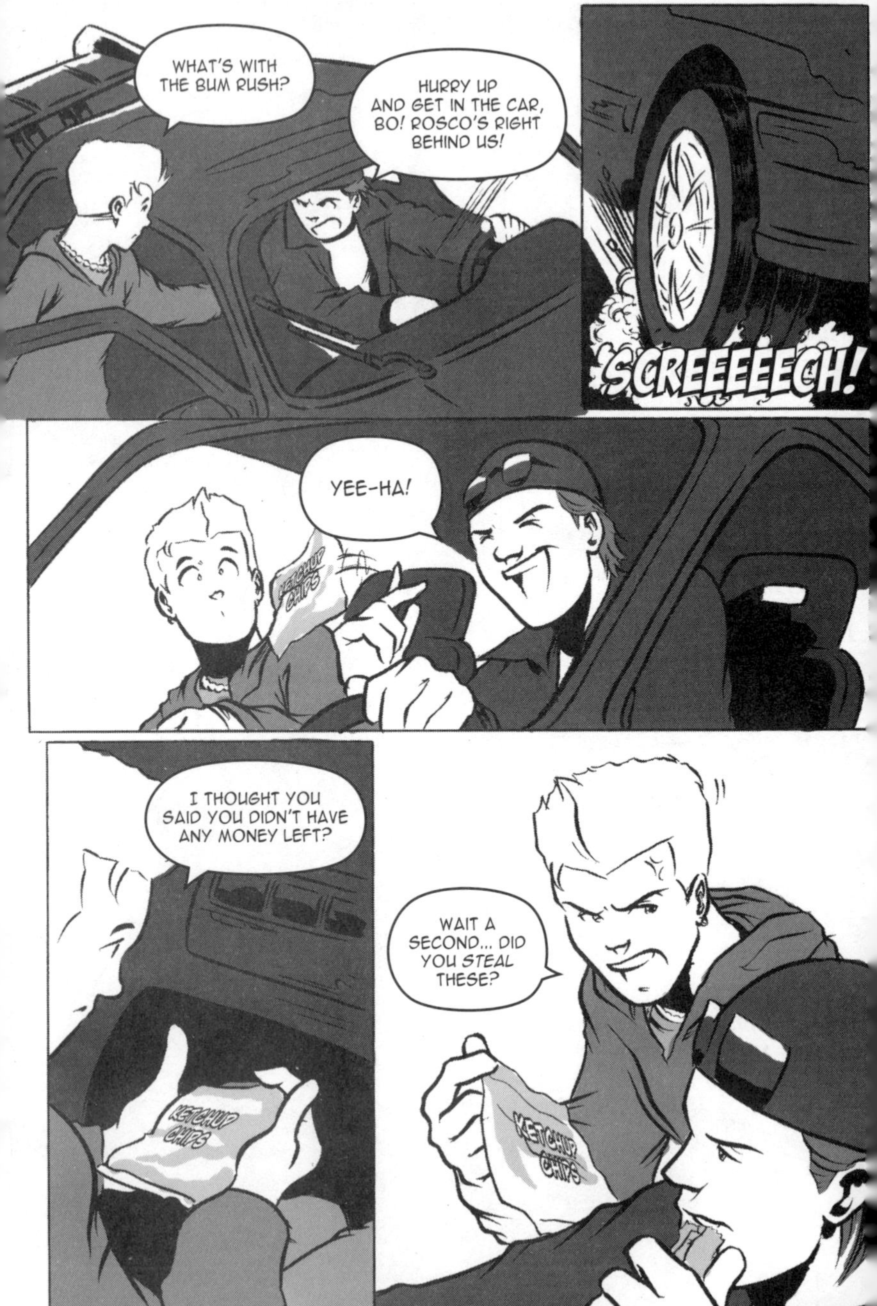
WHAT'S WITH THE BUM RUSH?
HURRY UP AND GET IN THE CAR, BO! ROSCO'S RIGHT BEHIND US!
SCREEEEEECH!
YEE-HA!
KETCHUP CHIPS
I THOUGHT YOU SAID YOU DIDN'T HAVE ANY MONEY LEFT?
KETCHUP CHIPS
WAIT A SECOND... DID YOU STEAL THESE?
KETCHUP CHIPS

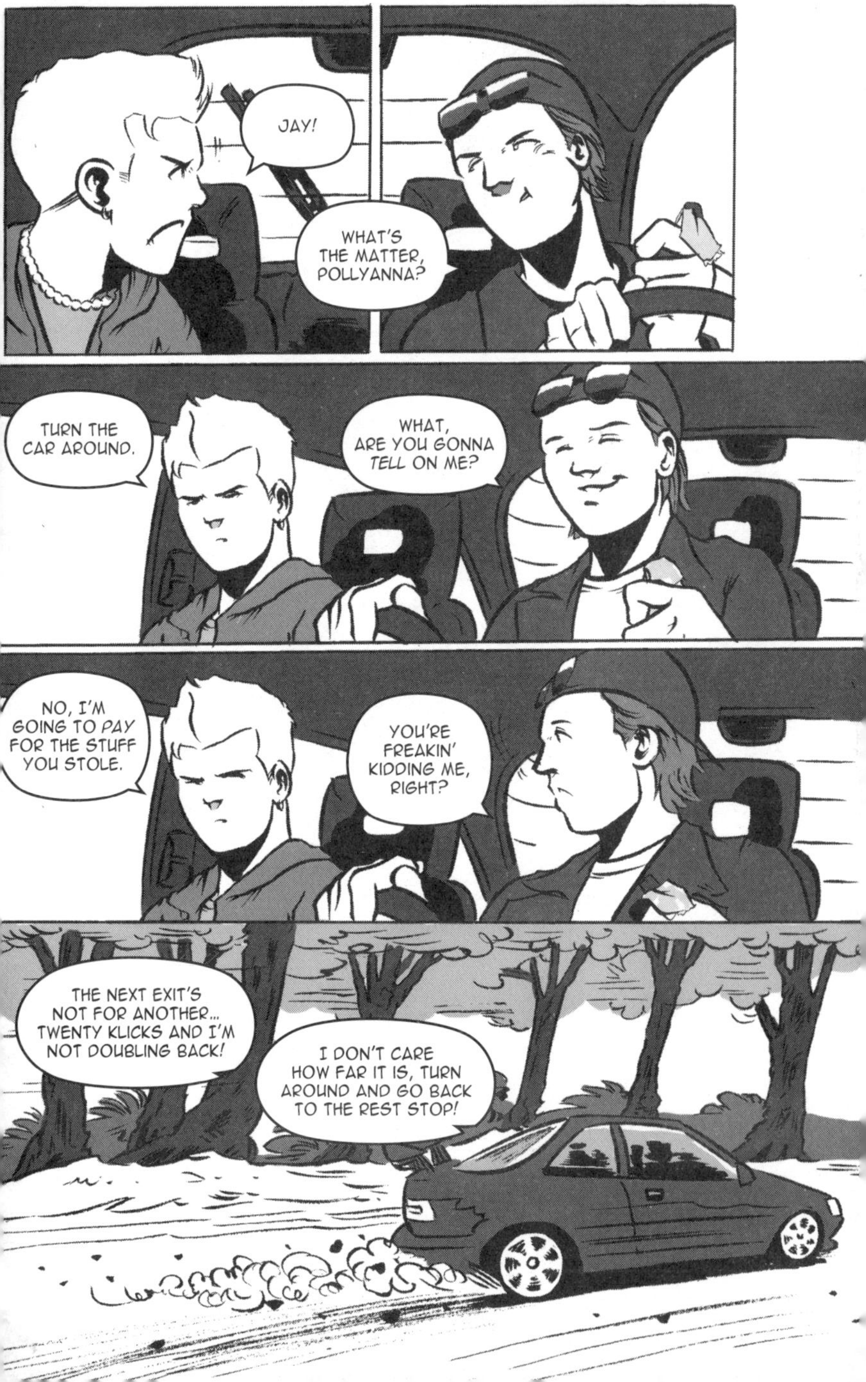
JAY!
WHAT'S THE MATTER, POLLYANNA?
TURN THE CAR AROUND.
WHAT, ARE YOU GONNA *TELL* ON ME?
NO, I'M GOING TO *PAY* FOR THE STUFF YOU STOLE.
YOU'RE FREAKIN' KIDDING ME, RIGHT?
THE NEXT EXIT'S NOT FOR ANOTHER... TWENTY KLICKS AND I'M NOT DOUBLING BACK!
I DON'T CARE HOW FAR IT IS, TURN AROUND AND GO BACK TO THE REST STOP!

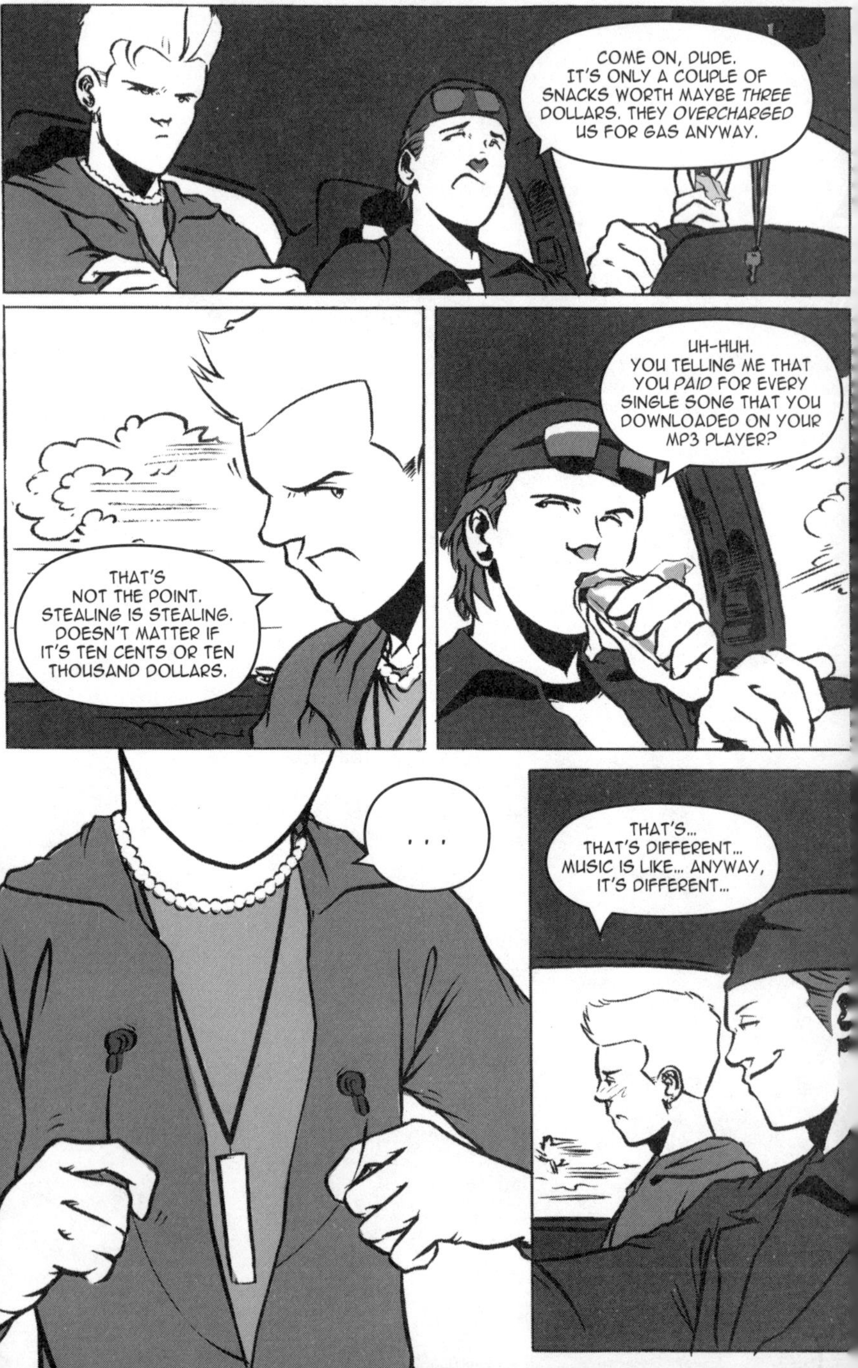
COME ON, DUDE. IT'S ONLY A COUPLE OF SNACKS WORTH MAYBE *THREE* DOLLARS. THEY *OVERCHARGED* US FOR GAS ANYWAY.
THAT'S NOT THE POINT. STEALING IS STEALING. DOESN'T MATTER IF IT'S TEN CENTS OR TEN THOUSAND DOLLARS.
UH-HUH. YOU TELLING ME THAT YOU *PAID* FOR EVERY SINGLE SONG THAT YOU DOWNLOADED ON YOUR MP3 PLAYER?
. . .
THAT'S... THAT'S DIFFERENT... MUSIC IS LIKE... ANYWAY, IT'S DIFFERENT...

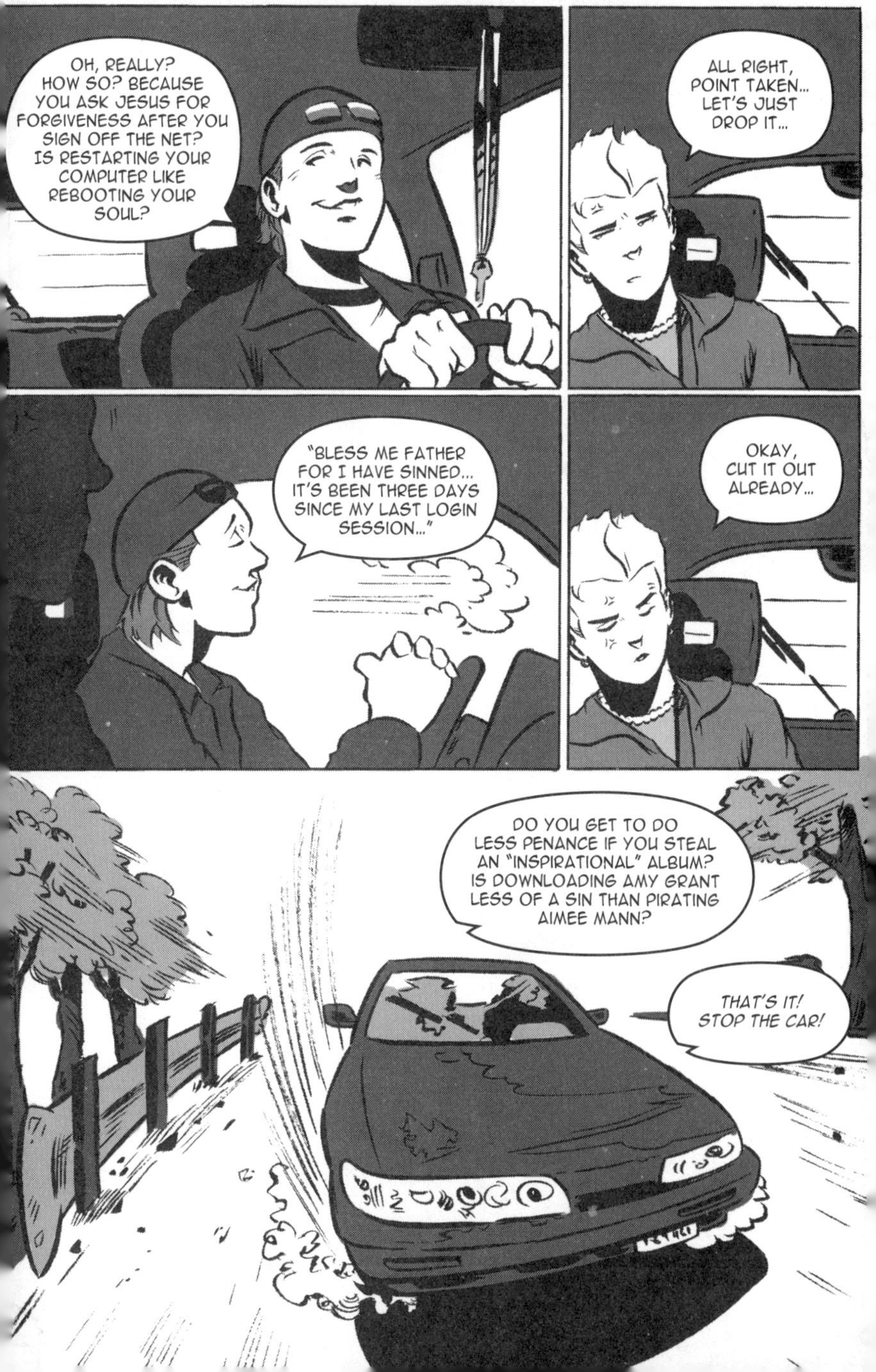
OH, REALLY? HOW SO? BECAUSE YOU ASK JESUS FOR FORGIVENESS AFTER YOU SIGN OFF THE NET? IS RESTARTING YOUR COMPUTER LIKE REBOOTING YOUR SOUL?
ALL RIGHT, POINT TAKEN... LET'S JUST DROP IT...
"BLESS ME FATHER FOR I HAVE SINNED... IT'S BEEN THREE DAYS SINCE MY LAST LOGIN SESSION..."
OKAY, CUT IT OUT ALREADY...
DO YOU GET TO DO LESS PENANCE IF YOU STEAL AN "INSPIRATIONAL" ALBUM? IS DOWNLOADING AMY GRANT LESS OF A SIN THAN PIRATING AIMEE MANN?
THAT'S IT! STOP THE CAR!

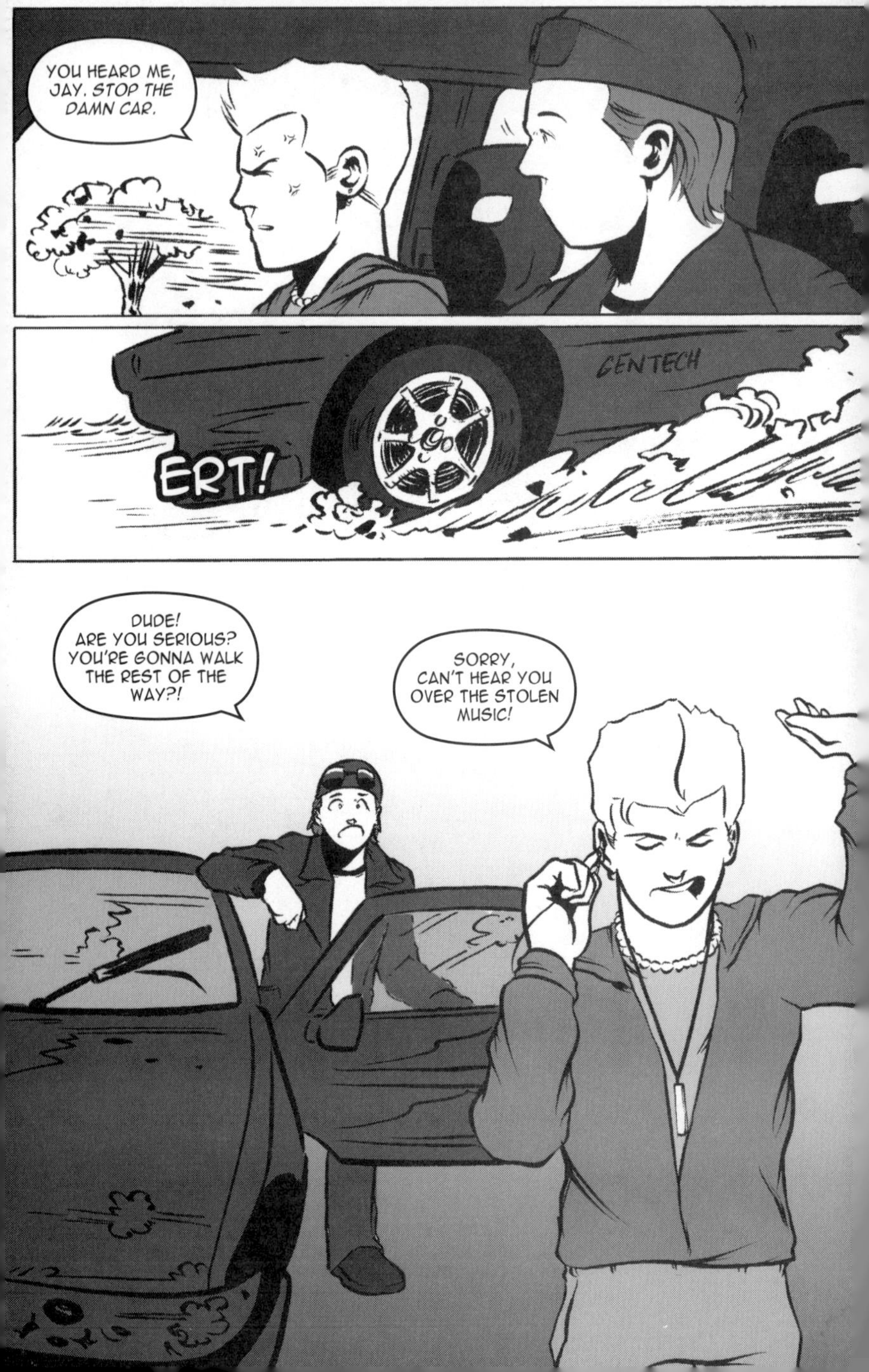
YOU HEARD ME, JAY. STOP THE DAMN CAR.
GENTECH
ERT!
DUDE! ARE YOU SERIOUS? YOU'RE GONNA WALK THE REST OF THE WAY?!
SORRY, CAN'T HEAR YOU OVER THE STOLEN MUSIC!

ACT 3

"You don't know how desperate I've become,
And it looks like I'm losing this fight."

— John Waite

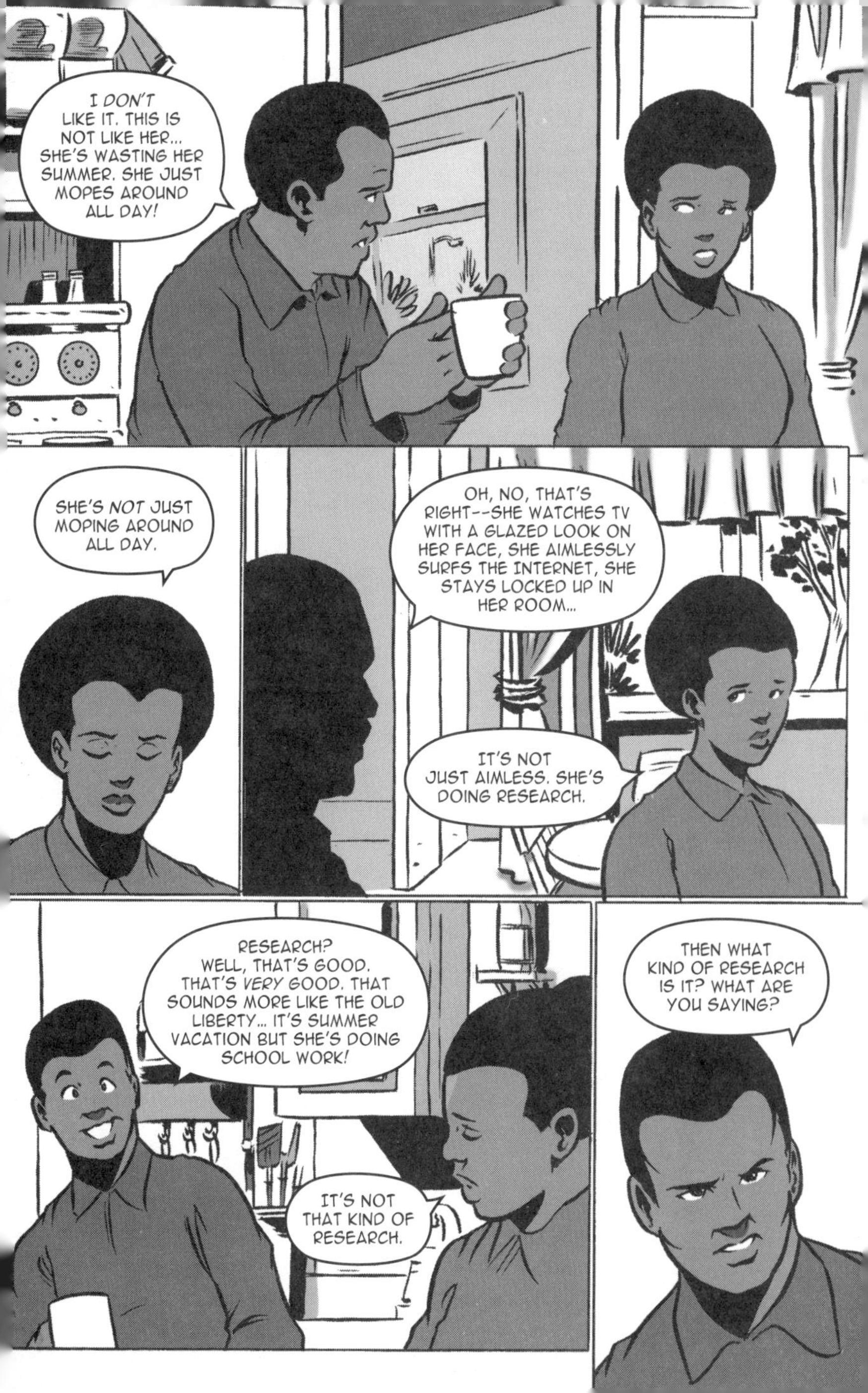
I *DON'T* LIKE IT. THIS IS NOT LIKE HER... SHE'S WASTING HER SUMMER. SHE JUST MOPES AROUND ALL DAY!
SHE'S *NOT* JUST MOPING AROUND ALL DAY.
OH, NO, THAT'S RIGHT--SHE WATCHES TV WITH A GLAZED LOOK ON HER FACE, SHE AIMLESSLY SURFS THE INTERNET, SHE STAYS LOCKED UP IN HER ROOM...
IT'S NOT JUST AIMLESS. SHE'S DOING RESEARCH.
RESEARCH? WELL, THAT'S GOOD. THAT'S *VERY* GOOD. THAT SOUNDS MORE LIKE THE OLD LIBERTY... IT'S SUMMER VACATION BUT SHE'S DOING SCHOOL WORK!
IT'S NOT THAT KIND OF RESEARCH.
THEN WHAT KIND OF RESEARCH IS IT? WHAT ARE YOU SAYING?

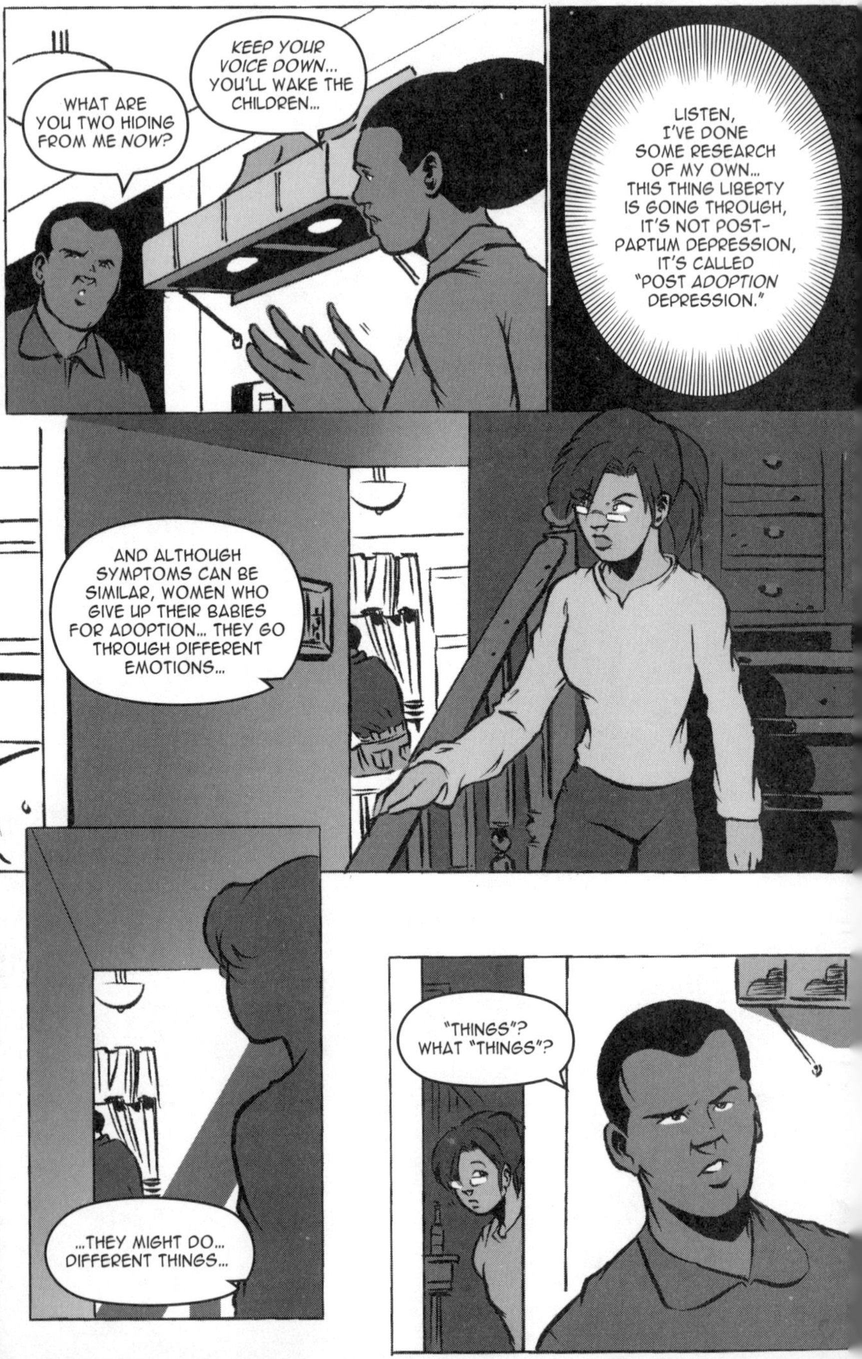
WHAT ARE YOU TWO HIDING FROM ME NOW?
KEEP YOUR VOICE DOWN... YOU'LL WAKE THE CHILDREN...
LISTEN, I'VE DONE SOME RESEARCH OF MY OWN... THIS THING LIBERTY IS GOING THROUGH, IT'S NOT POST-PARTUM DEPRESSION, IT'S CALLED "POST ADOPTION DEPRESSION."
AND ALTHOUGH SYMPTOMS CAN BE SIMILAR, WOMEN WHO GIVE UP THEIR BABIES FOR ADOPTION... THEY GO THROUGH DIFFERENT EMOTIONS...
...THEY MIGHT DO... DIFFERENT THINGS...
"THINGS"? WHAT "THINGS"?

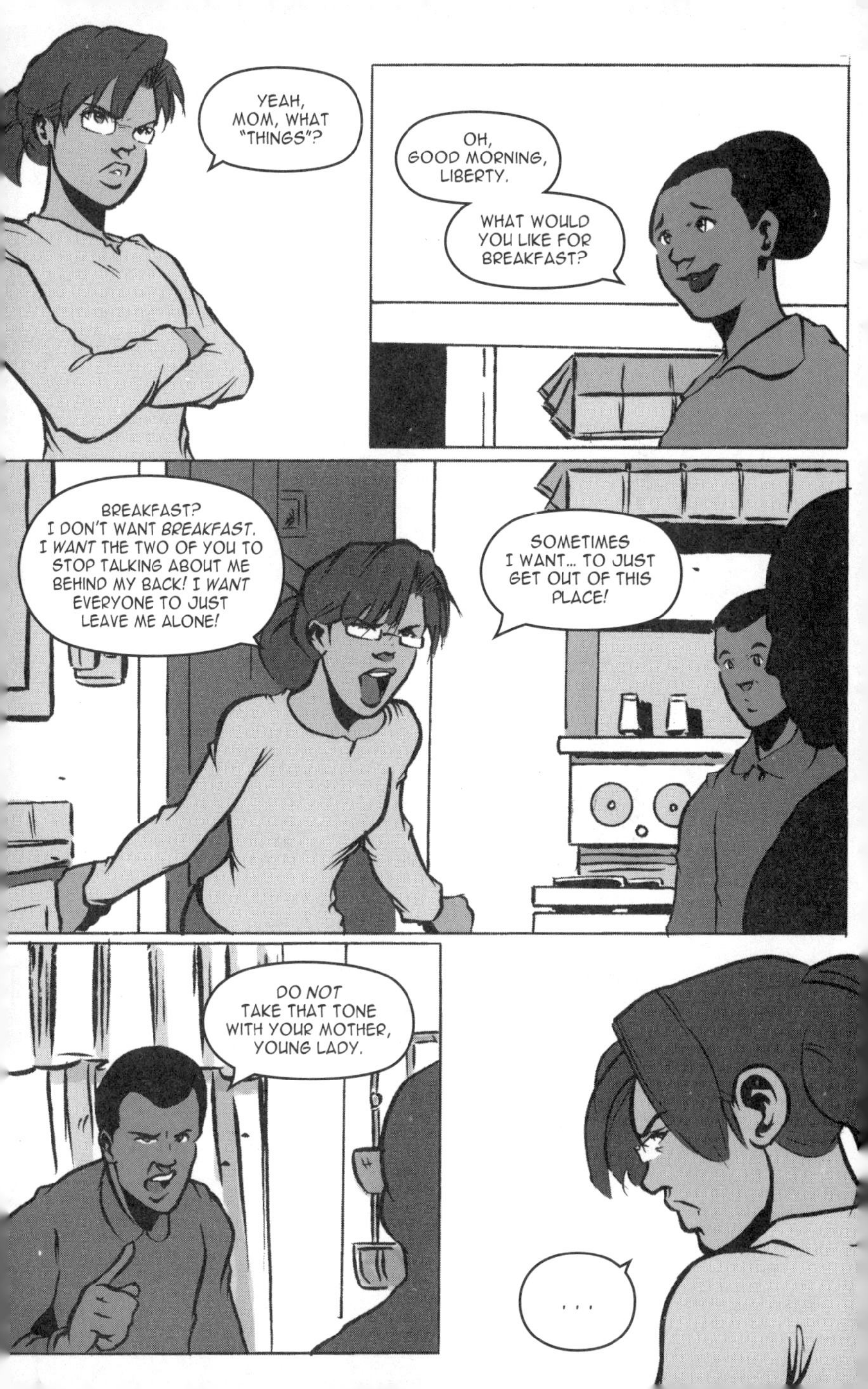
YEAH, MOM, WHAT "THINGS"?
OH, GOOD MORNING, LIBERTY.
WHAT WOULD YOU LIKE FOR BREAKFAST?
BREAKFAST? I DON'T WANT *BREAKFAST*. I *WANT* THE TWO OF YOU TO STOP TALKING ABOUT ME BEHIND MY BACK! I *WANT* EVERYONE TO JUST LEAVE ME ALONE!
SOMETIMES I WANT... TO JUST GET OUT OF THIS PLACE!
DO *NOT* TAKE THAT TONE WITH YOUR MOTHER, YOUNG LADY.
. . .

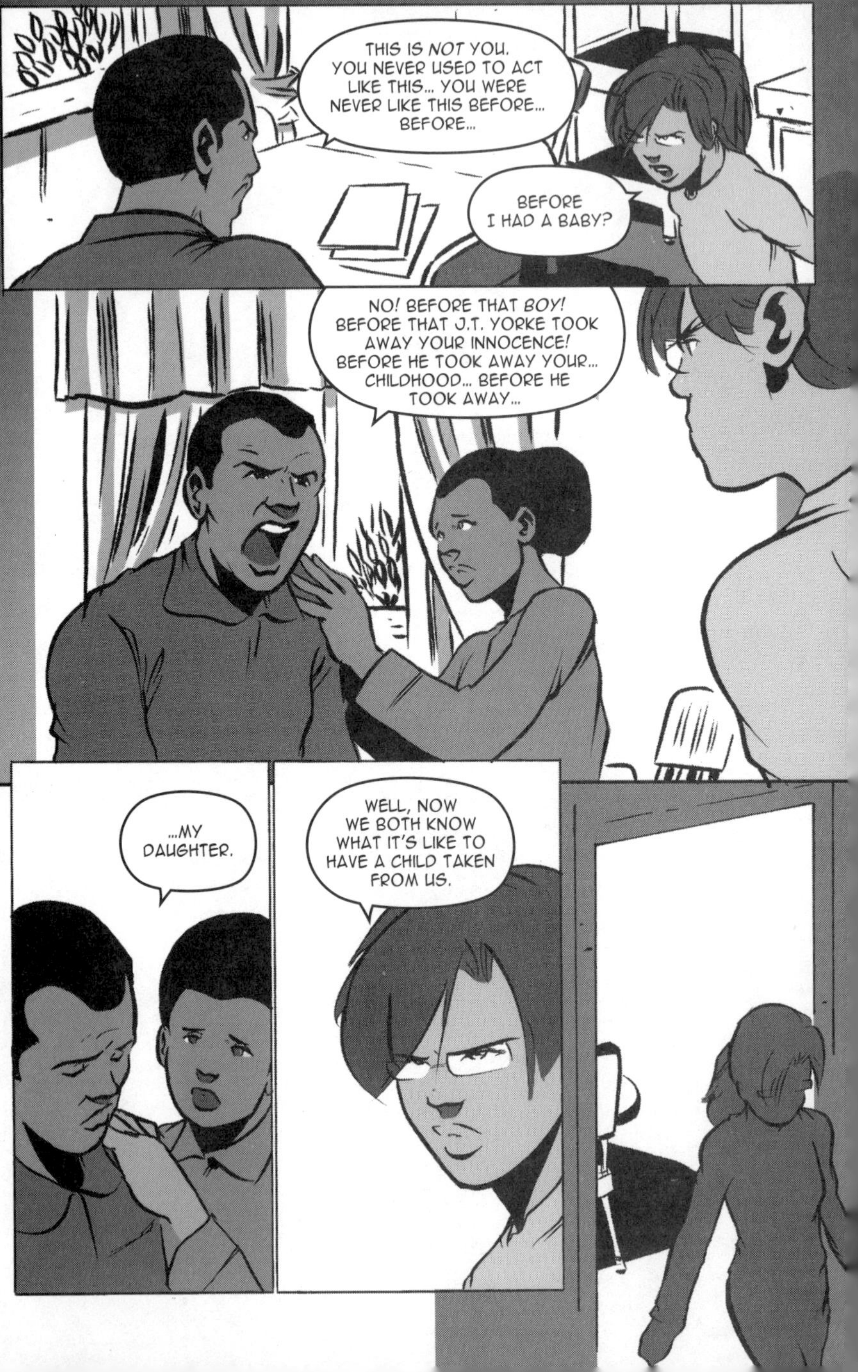
THIS IS NOT YOU. YOU NEVER USED TO ACT LIKE THIS... YOU WERE NEVER LIKE THIS BEFORE... BEFORE...
BEFORE I HAD A BABY?
NO! BEFORE THAT BOY! BEFORE THAT J.T. YORKE TOOK AWAY YOUR INNOCENCE! BEFORE HE TOOK AWAY YOUR... CHILDHOOD... BEFORE HE TOOK AWAY...
...MY DAUGHTER.
WELL, NOW WE BOTH KNOW WHAT IT'S LIKE TO HAVE A CHILD TAKEN FROM US.

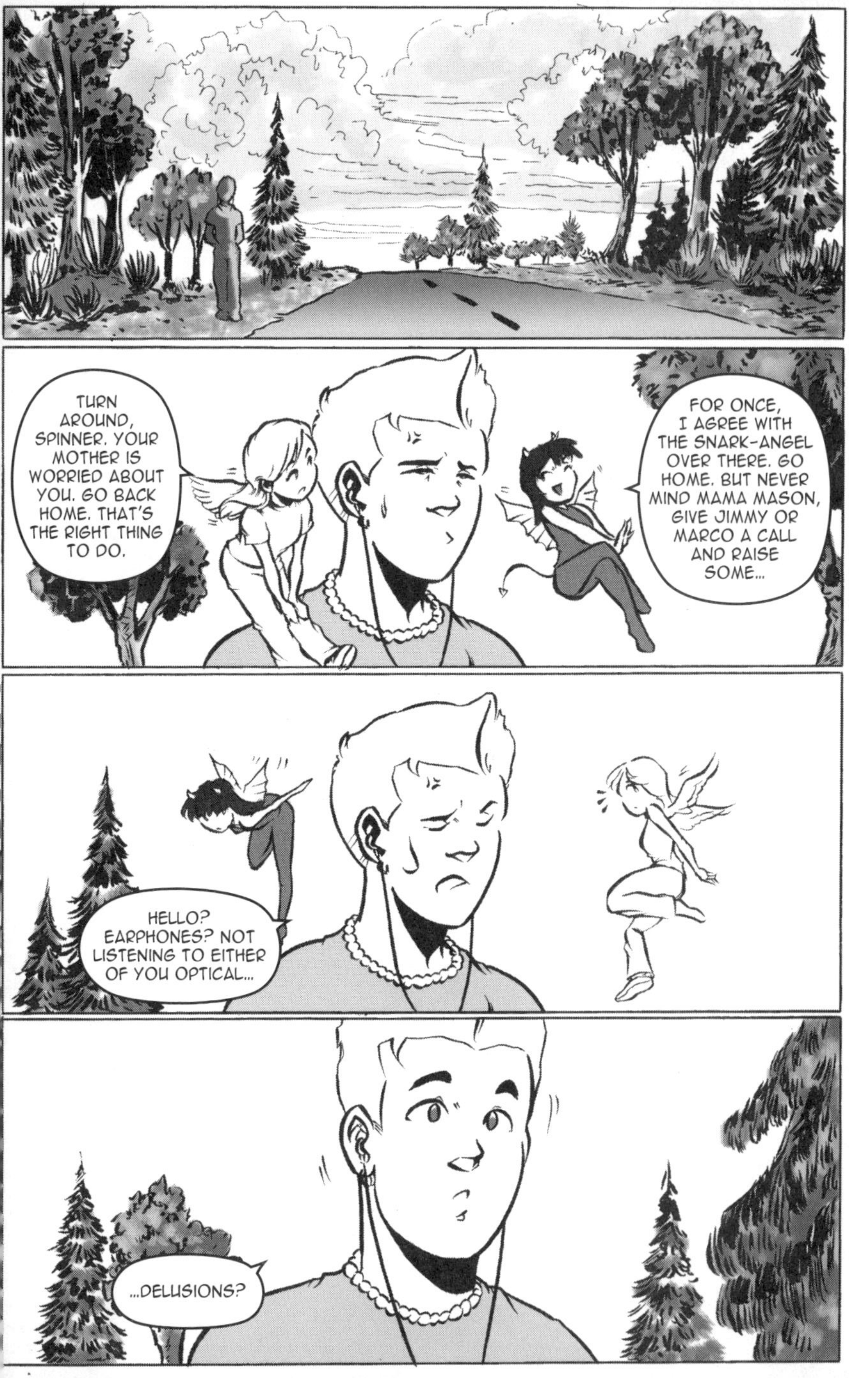
TURN AROUND, SPINNER. YOUR MOTHER IS WORRIED ABOUT YOU. GO BACK HOME. THAT'S THE RIGHT THING TO DO.
FOR ONCE, I AGREE WITH THE SNARK-ANGEL OVER THERE. GO HOME. BUT NEVER MIND MAMA MASON, GIVE JIMMY OR MARCO A CALL AND RAISE SOME...
HELLO? EARPHONES? NOT LISTENING TO EITHER OF YOU OPTICAL...
...DELUSIONS?

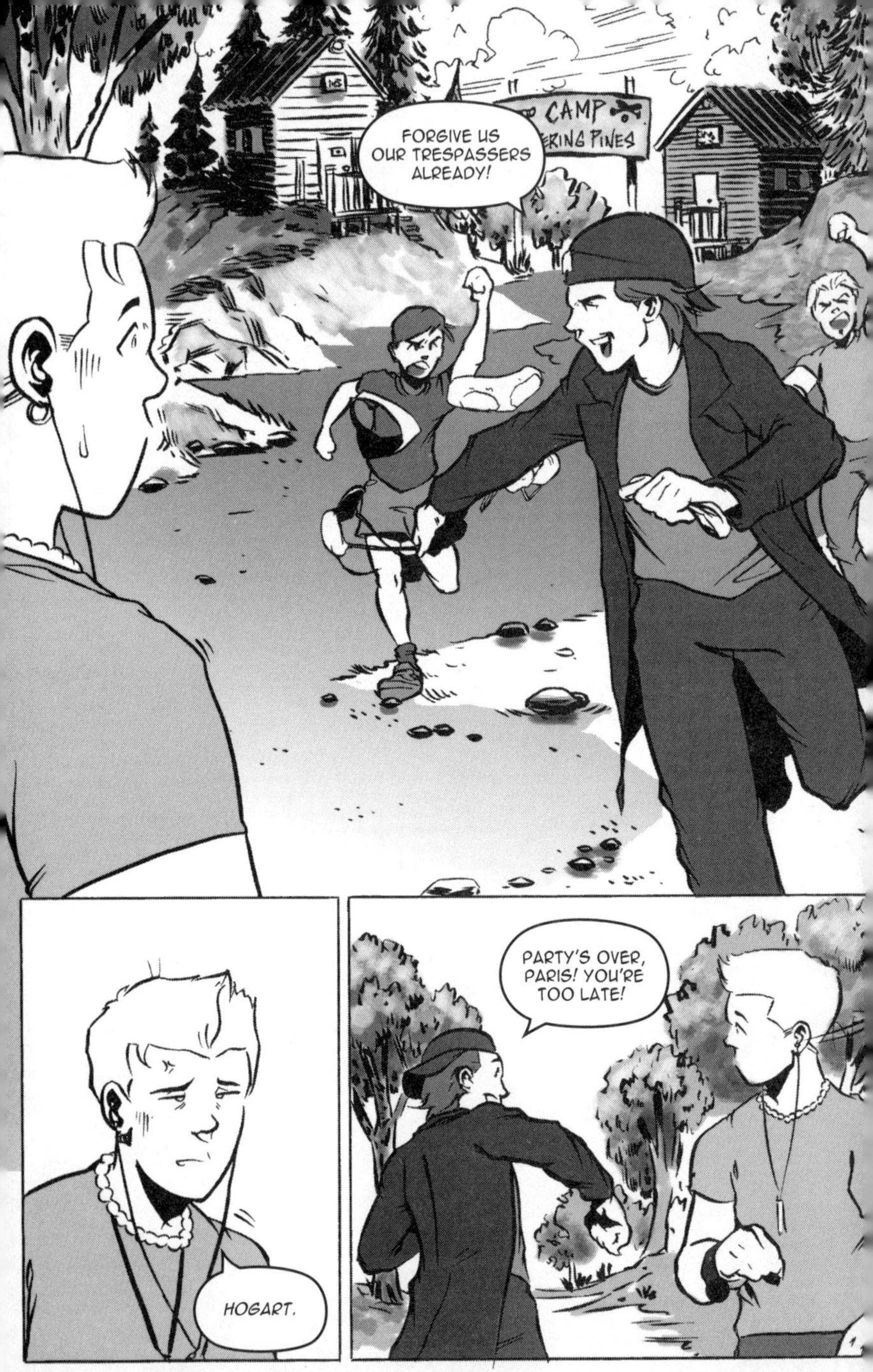
CAMP
FORGIVE US OUR TRESPASSERS ALREADY!
HOGART.
PARTY'S OVER, PARIS! YOU'RE TOO LATE!

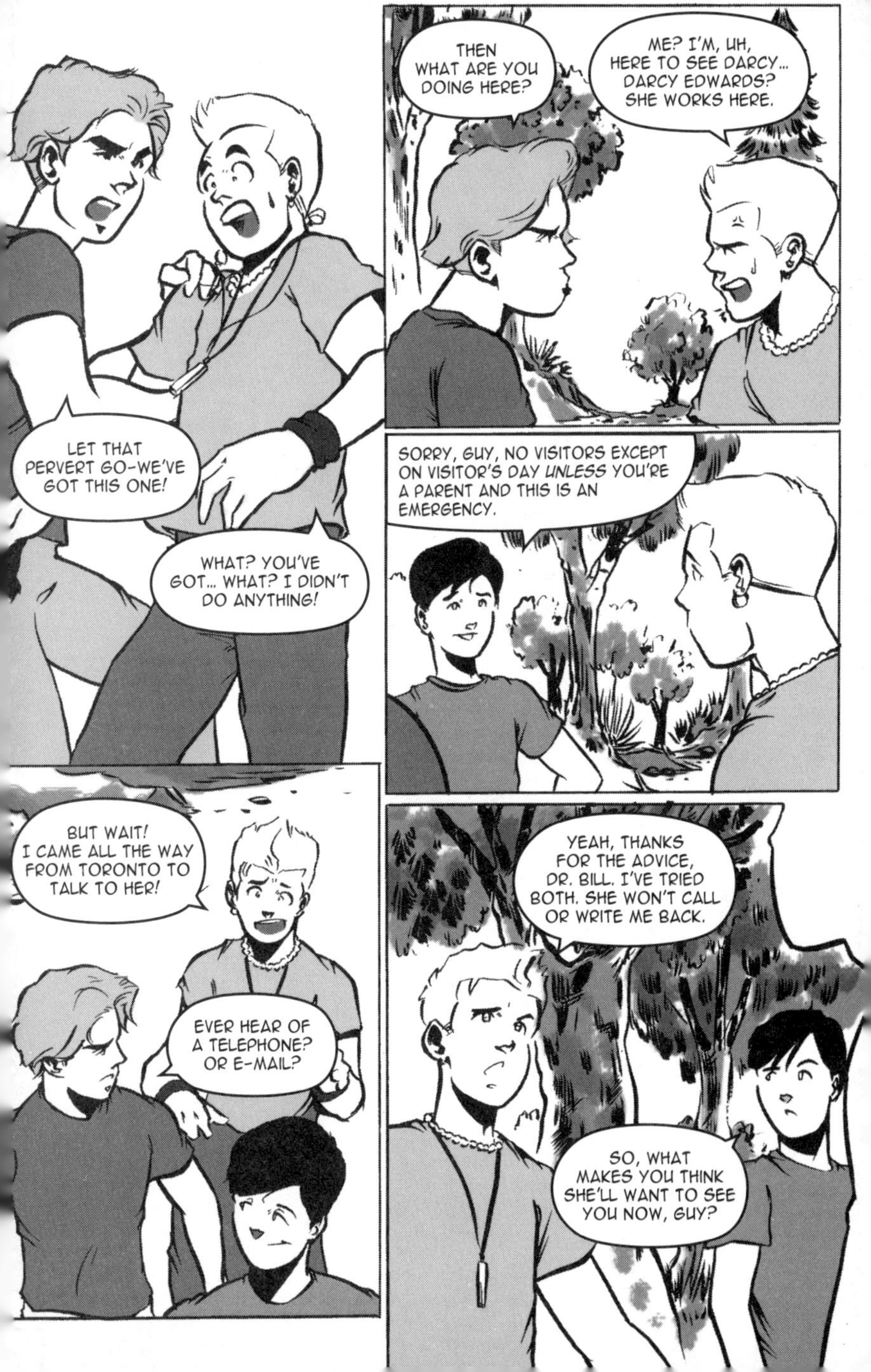
LET THAT PERVERT GO–WE'VE GOT THIS ONE!
WHAT? YOU'VE GOT... WHAT? I DIDN'T DO ANYTHING!
BUT WAIT! I CAME ALL THE WAY FROM TORONTO TO TALK TO HER!
EVER HEAR OF A TELEPHONE? OR E-MAIL?
THEN WHAT ARE YOU DOING HERE?
ME? I'M, UH, HERE TO SEE DARCY... DARCY EDWARDS? SHE WORKS HERE.
SORRY, GUY, NO VISITORS EXCEPT ON VISITOR'S DAY *UNLESS* YOU'RE A PARENT AND THIS IS AN EMERGENCY.
YEAH, THANKS FOR THE ADVICE, DR. BILL. I'VE TRIED BOTH. SHE WON'T CALL OR WRITE ME BACK.
SO, WHAT MAKES YOU THINK SHE'LL WANT TO SEE YOU NOW, GUY?

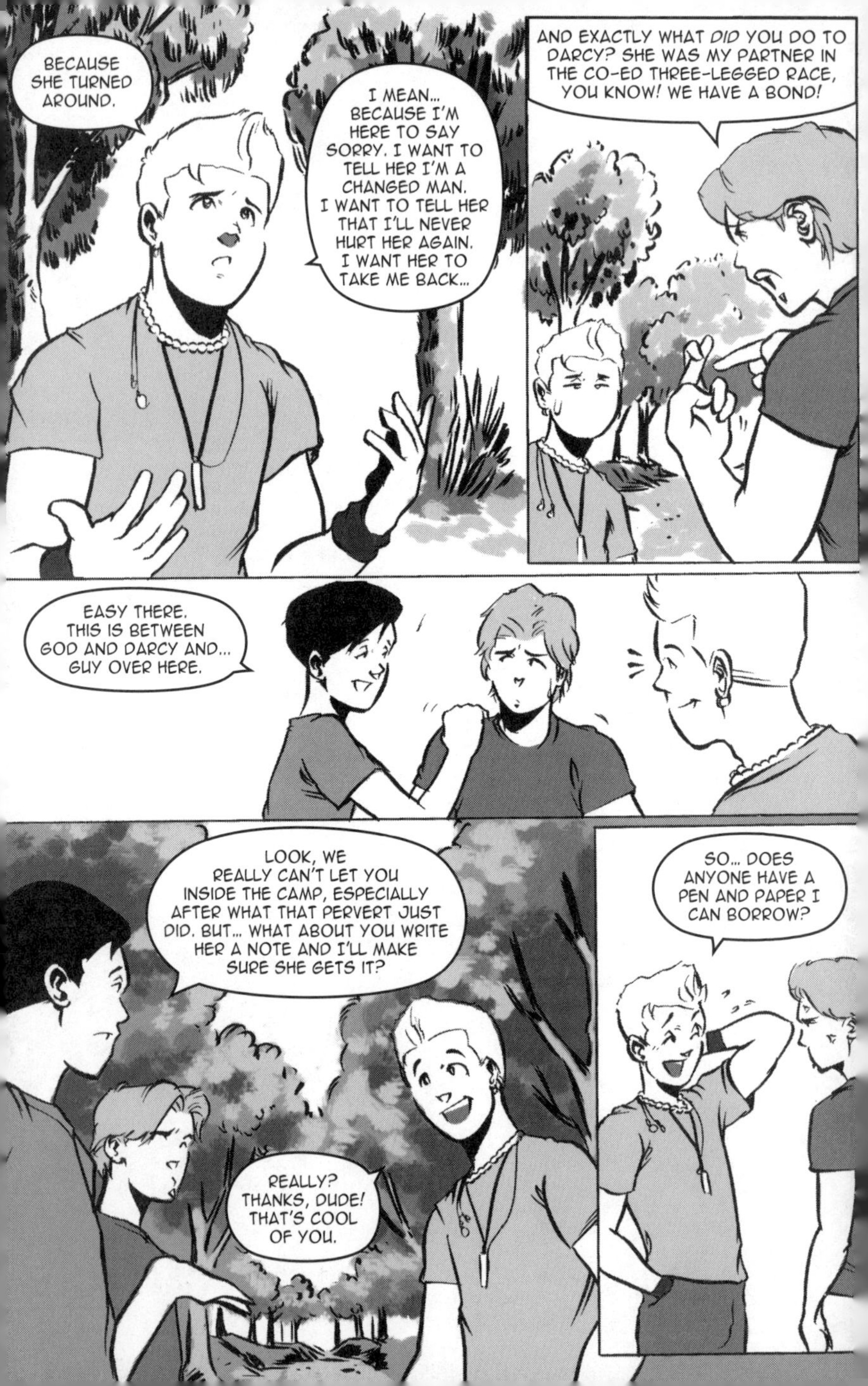
BECAUSE SHE TURNED AROUND.
I MEAN... BECAUSE I'M HERE TO SAY SORRY. I WANT TO TELL HER I'M A CHANGED MAN. I WANT TO TELL HER THAT I'LL NEVER HURT HER AGAIN. I WANT HER TO TAKE ME BACK...
AND EXACTLY WHAT *DID* YOU DO TO DARCY? SHE WAS MY PARTNER IN THE CO-ED THREE-LEGGED RACE, YOU KNOW! WE HAVE A BOND!
EASY THERE. THIS IS BETWEEN GOD AND DARCY AND... GUY OVER HERE.
LOOK, WE REALLY CAN'T LET YOU INSIDE THE CAMP, ESPECIALLY AFTER WHAT THAT PERVERT JUST DID. BUT... WHAT ABOUT YOU WRITE HER A NOTE AND I'LL MAKE SURE SHE GETS IT?
REALLY? THANKS, DUDE! THAT'S COOL OF YOU.
SO... DOES ANYONE HAVE A PEN AND PAPER I CAN BORROW?

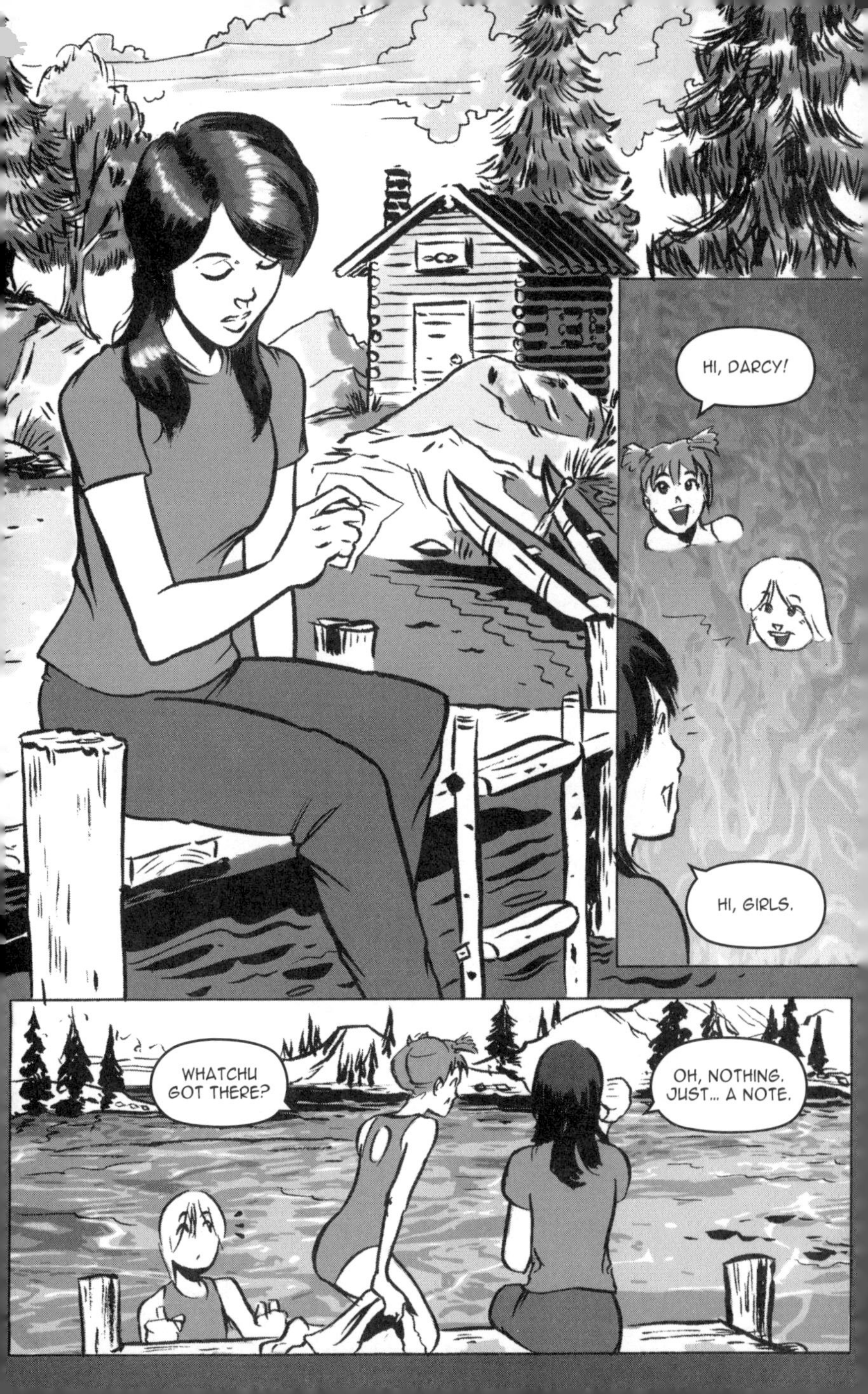
HI, DARCY!
HI, GIRLS.
WHATCHU GOT THERE?
OH, NOTHING. JUST... A NOTE.

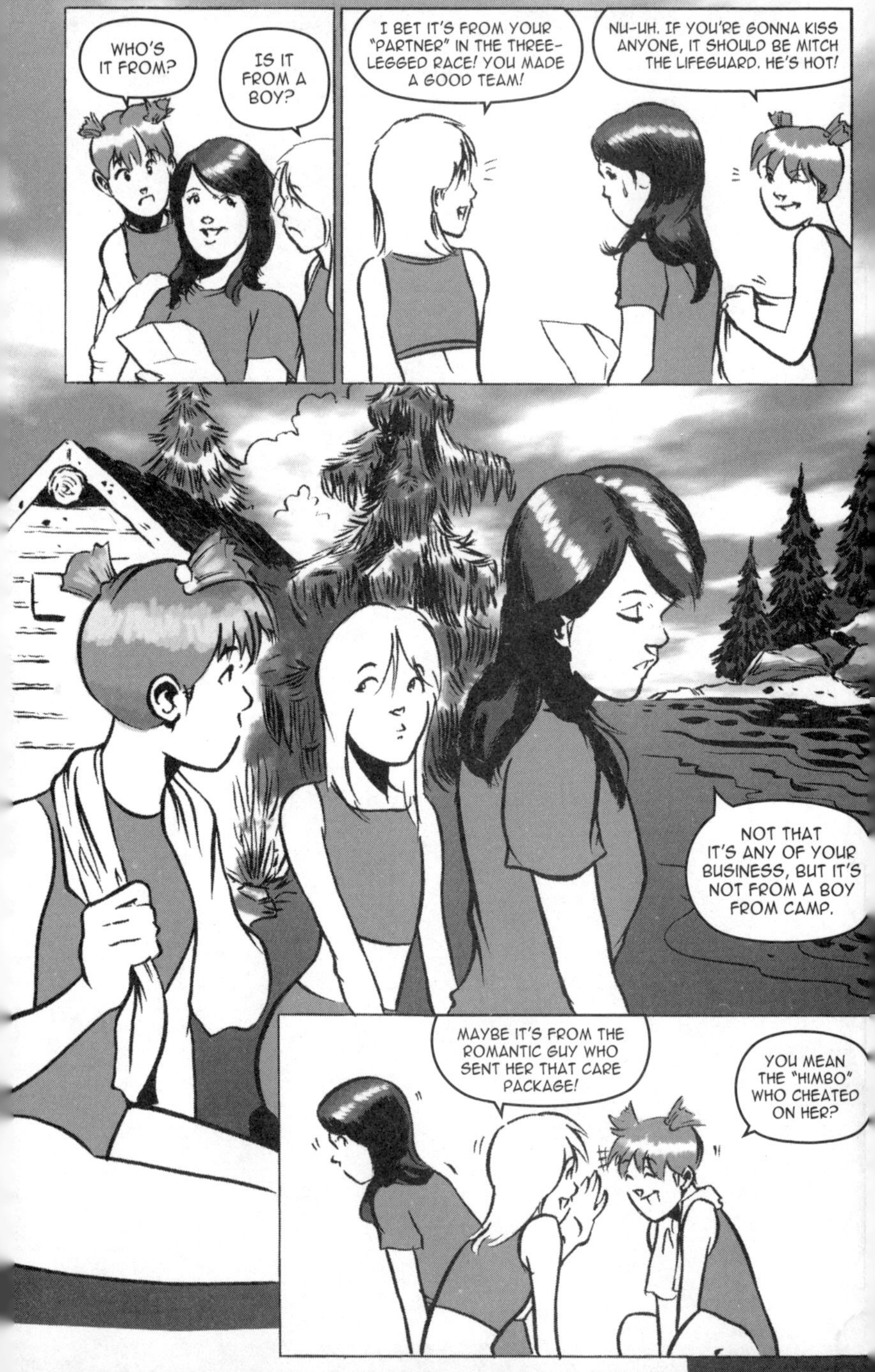

WHO'S IT FROM?
IS IT FROM A BOY?
I BET IT'S FROM YOUR "PARTNER" IN THE THREE-LEGGED RACE! YOU MADE A GOOD TEAM!
NU-UH. IF YOU'RE GONNA KISS ANYONE, IT SHOULD BE MITCH THE LIFEGUARD. HE'S HOT!
NOT THAT IT'S ANY OF YOUR BUSINESS, BUT IT'S NOT FROM A BOY FROM CAMP.
MAYBE IT'S FROM THE ROMANTIC GUY WHO SENT HER THAT CARE PACKAGE!
YOU MEAN THE "HIMBO" WHO CHEATED ON HER?

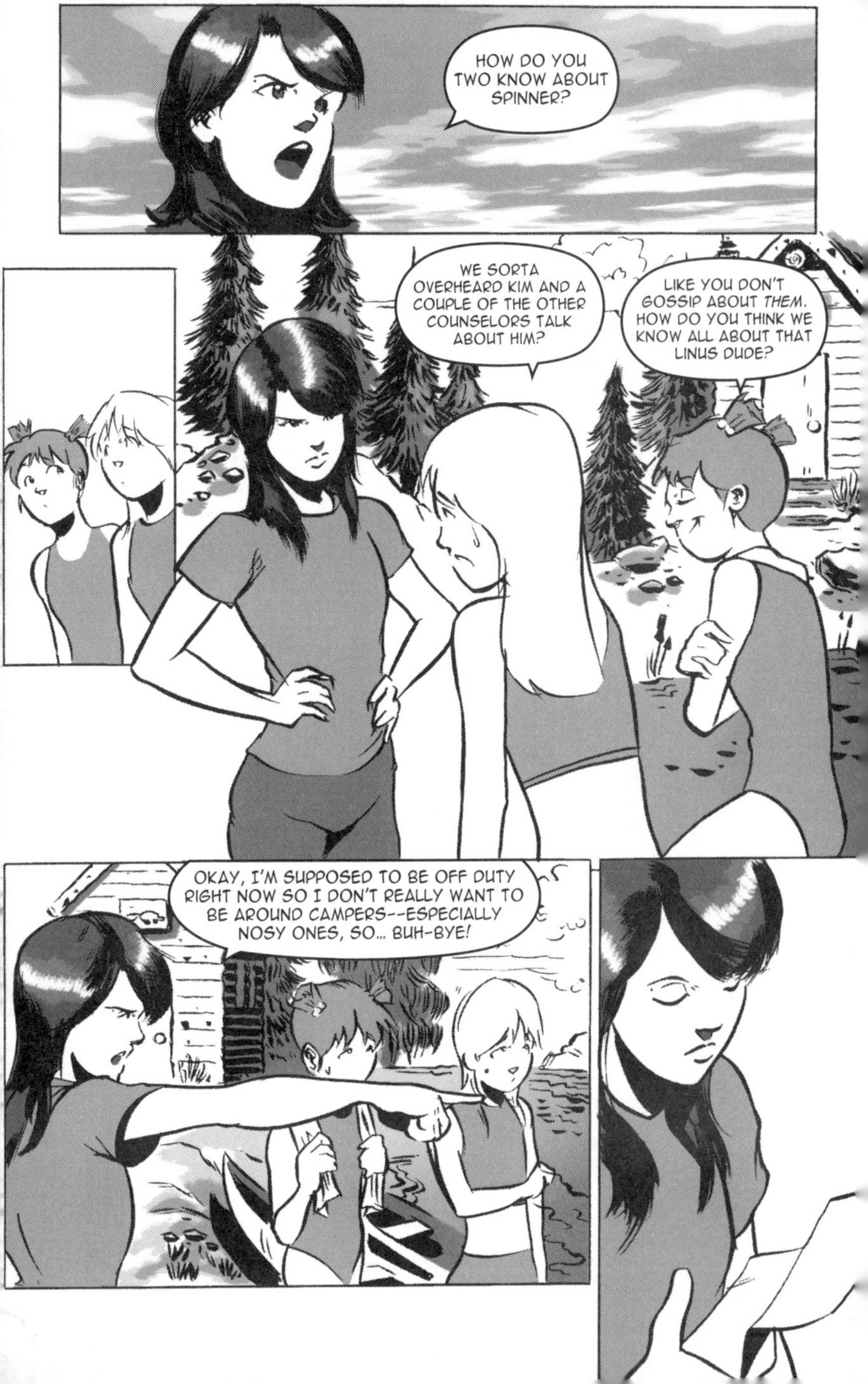
HOW DO YOU TWO KNOW ABOUT SPINNER?
WE SORTA OVERHEARD KIM AND A COUPLE OF THE OTHER COUNSELORS TALK ABOUT HIM?
LIKE YOU DON'T GOSSIP ABOUT *THEM*. HOW DO YOU THINK WE KNOW ALL ABOUT THAT LINUS DUDE?
OKAY, I'M SUPPOSED TO BE OFF DUTY RIGHT NOW SO I DON'T REALLY WANT TO BE AROUND CAMPERS--ESPECIALLY NOSY ONES, SO... BUH-BYE!

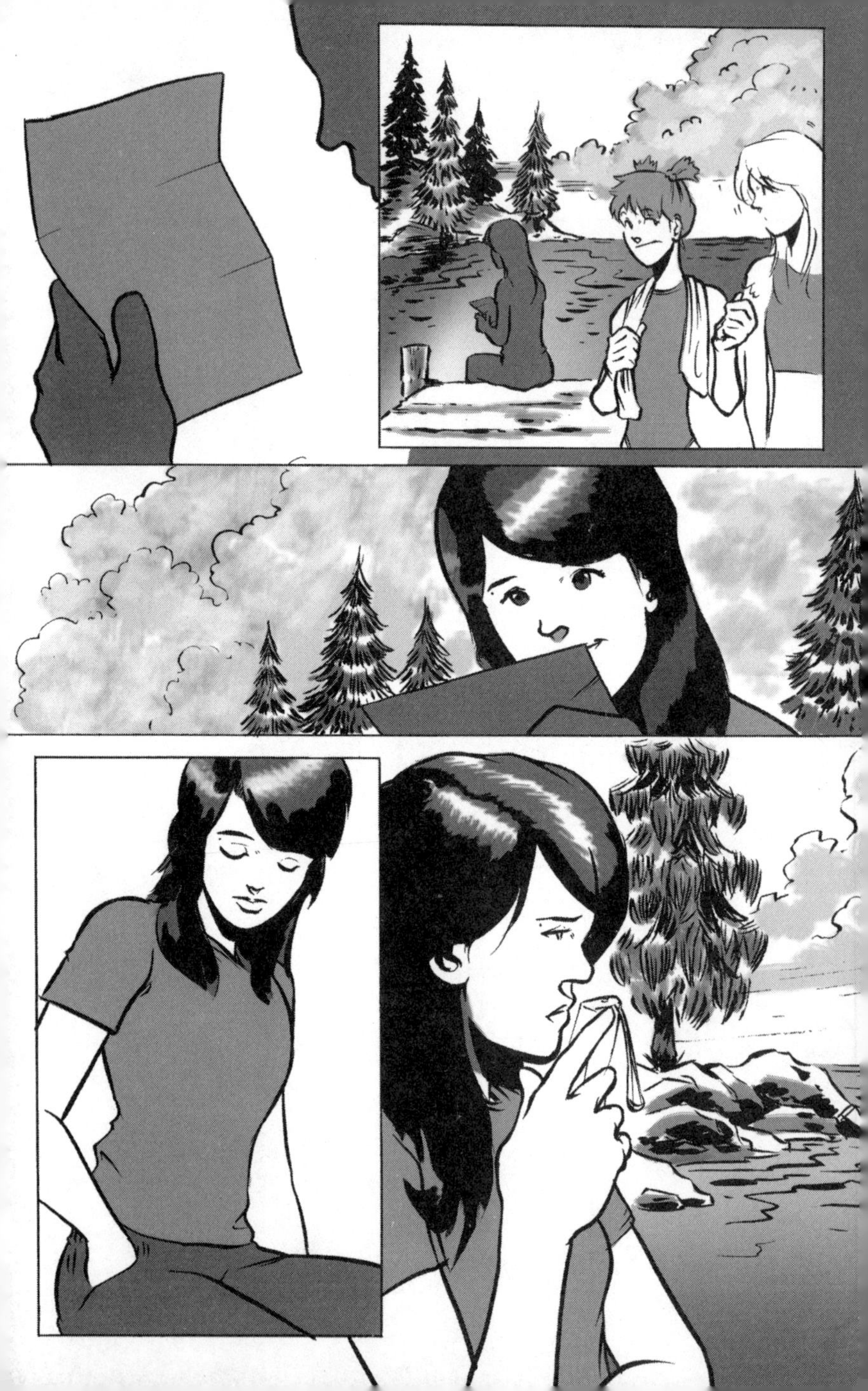

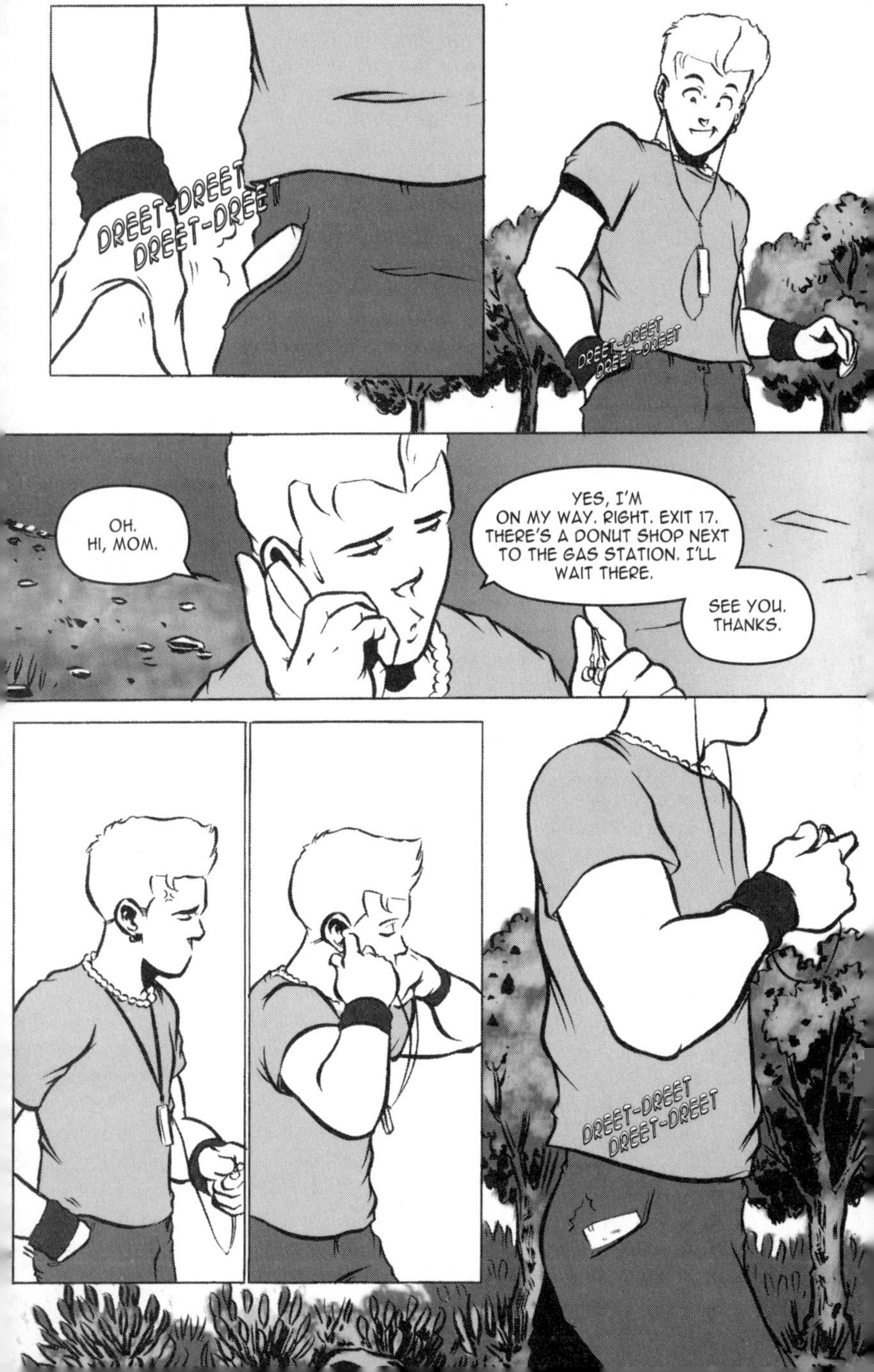
DREET-DREET DREET-DREET
DREET-DREET DREET-DREET
OH. HI, MOM.
YES, I'M ON MY WAY. RIGHT. EXIT 17. THERE'S A DONUT SHOP NEXT TO THE GAS STATION. I'LL WAIT THERE.
SEE YOU. THANKS.
DREET-DREET DREET-DREET

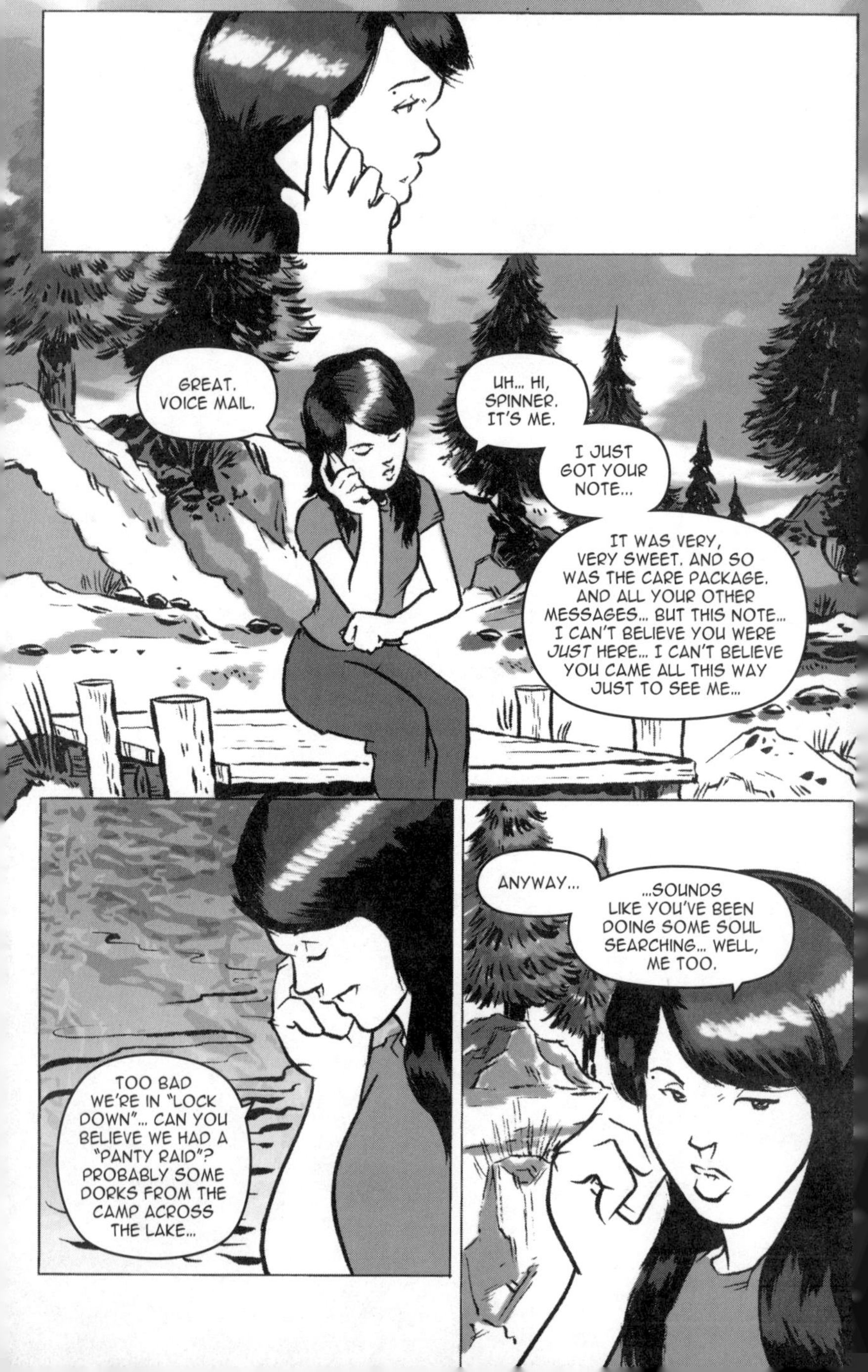
GREAT. VOICE MAIL.
UH... HI, SPINNER. IT'S ME.
I JUST GOT YOUR NOTE...
IT WAS VERY, VERY SWEET. AND SO WAS THE CARE PACKAGE. AND ALL YOUR OTHER MESSAGES... BUT THIS NOTE... I CAN'T BELIEVE YOU WERE *JUST* HERE... I CAN'T BELIEVE YOU CAME ALL THIS WAY JUST TO SEE ME...
TOO BAD WE'RE IN "LOCK DOWN"... CAN YOU BELIEVE WE HAD A "PANTY RAID"? PROBABLY SOME DORKS FROM THE CAMP ACROSS THE LAKE...
ANYWAY...
...SOUNDS LIKE YOU'VE BEEN DOING SOME SOUL SEARCHING... WELL, ME TOO.

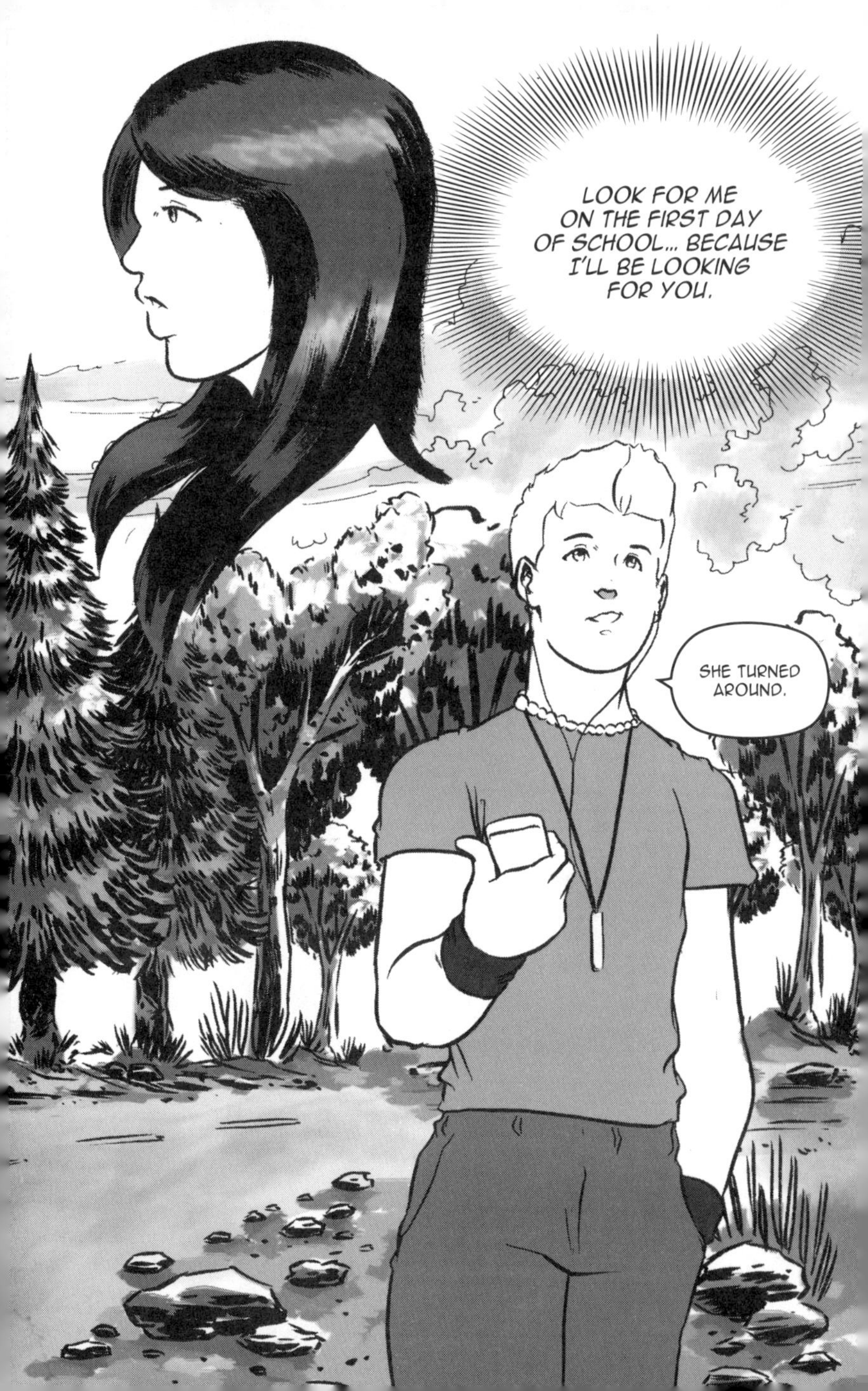
LOOK FOR ME ON THE FIRST DAY OF SCHOOL... BECAUSE I'LL BE LOOKING FOR YOU.
SHE TURNED AROUND.

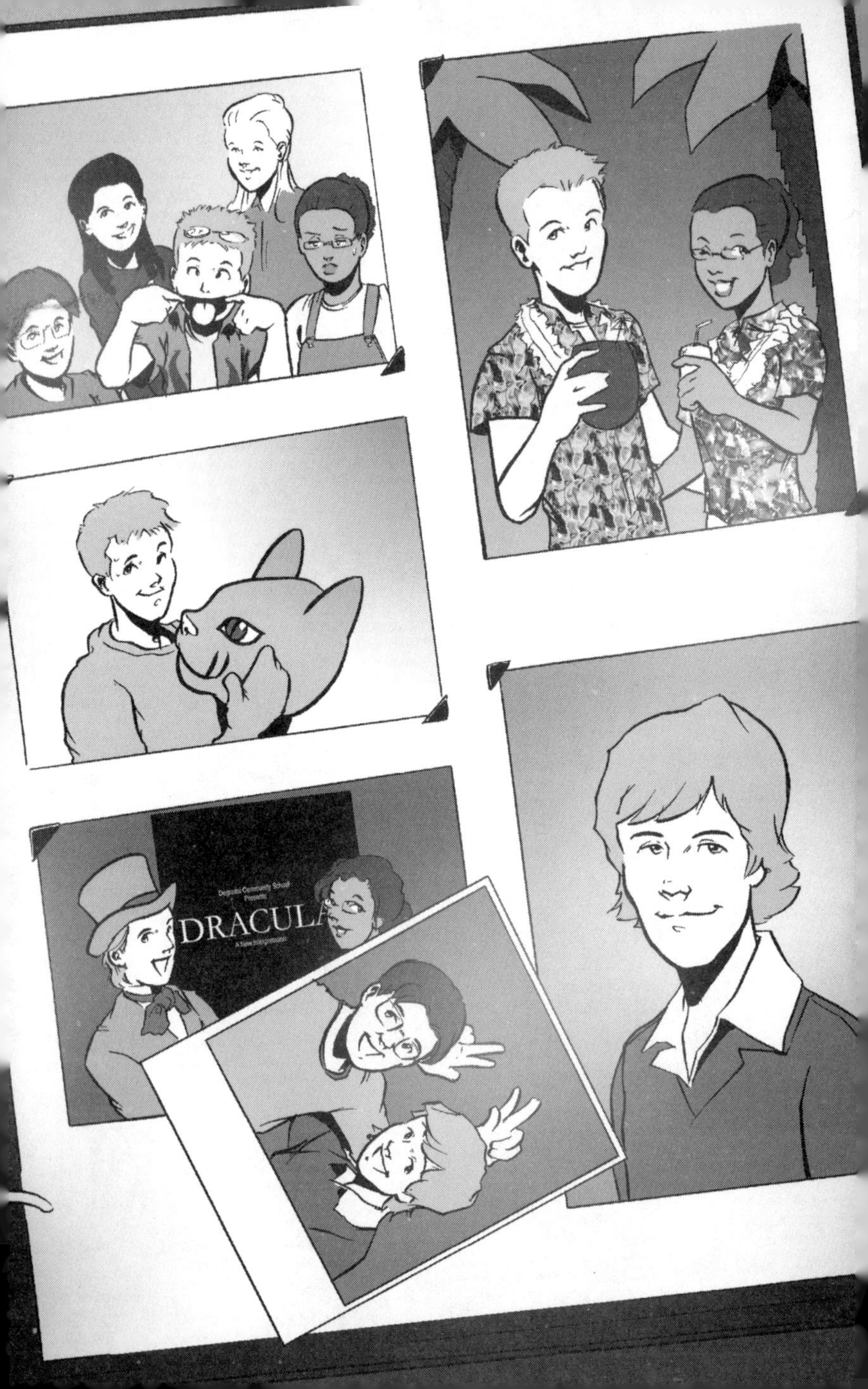
DRACULA

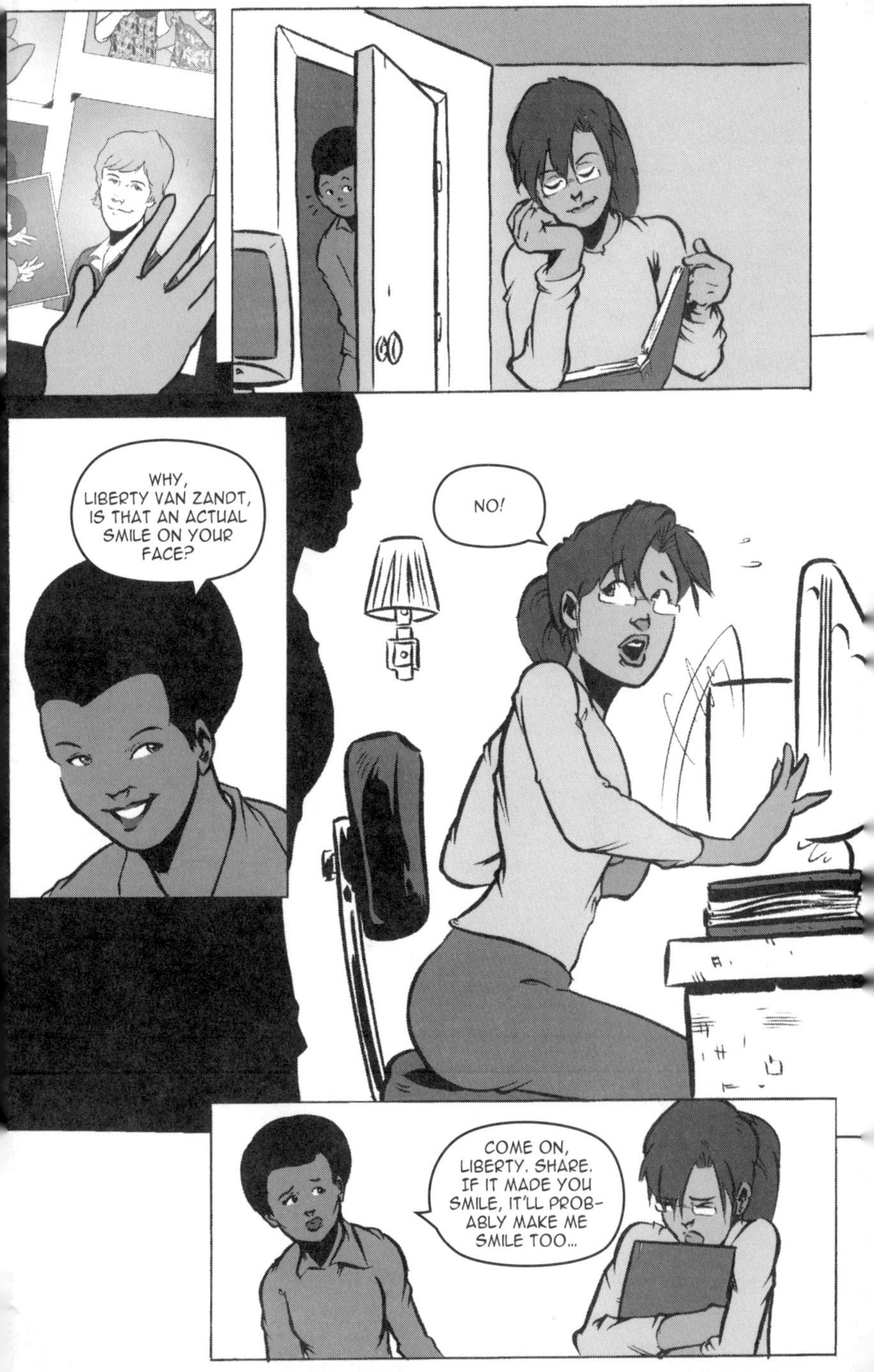
WHY, LIBERTY VAN ZANDT, IS THAT AN ACTUAL SMILE ON YOUR FACE?
NO!
COME ON, LIBERTY. SHARE. IF IT MADE YOU SMILE, IT'LL PROB- ABLY MAKE ME SMILE TOO...

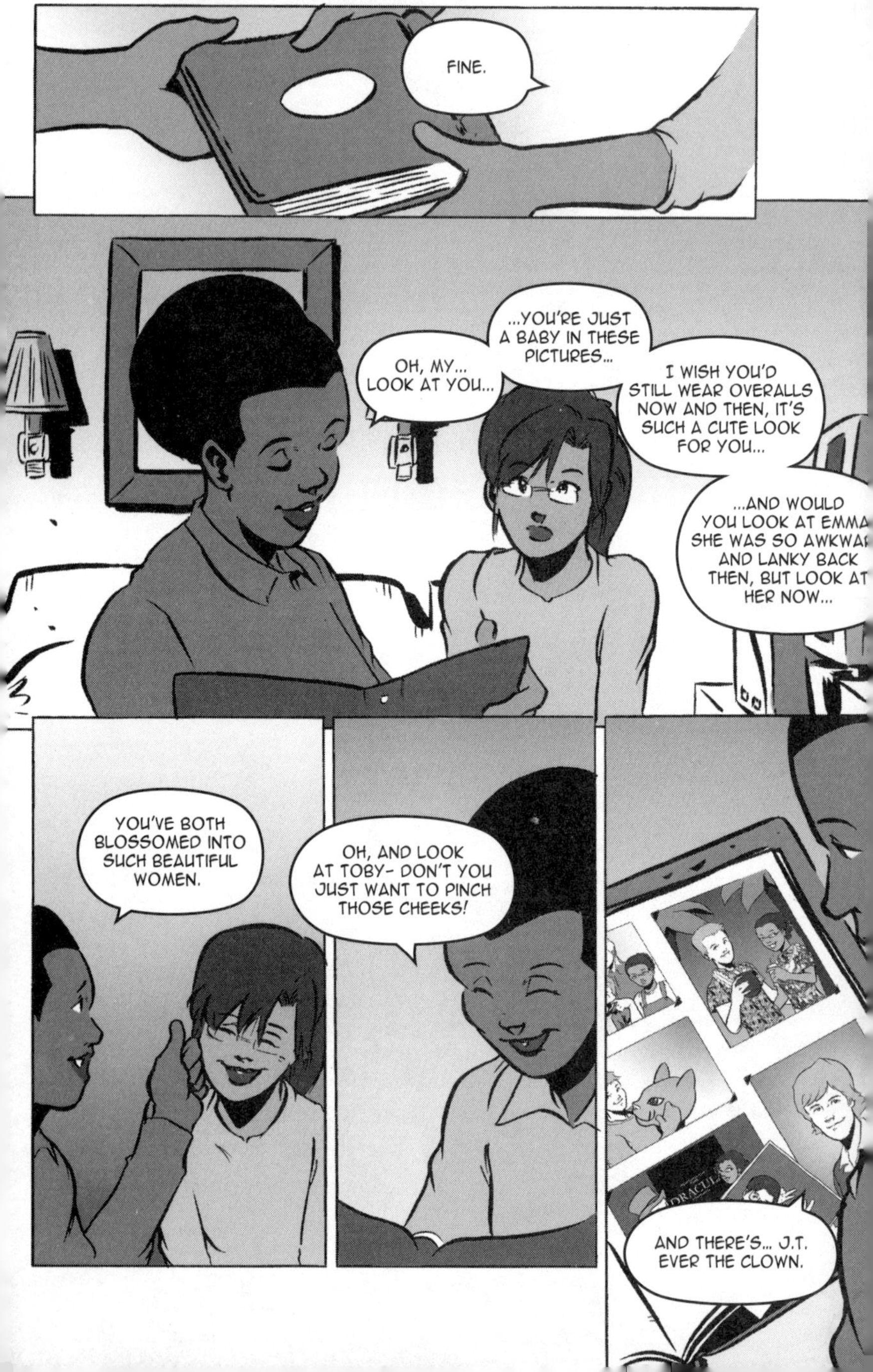
FINE.
OH, MY... LOOK AT YOU...
...YOU'RE JUST A BABY IN THESE PICTURES...
I WISH YOU'D STILL WEAR OVERALLS NOW AND THEN, IT'S SUCH A CUTE LOOK FOR YOU...
...AND WOULD YOU LOOK AT EMMA SHE WAS SO AWKWA AND LANKY BACK THEN, BUT LOOK AT HER NOW...
YOU'VE BOTH BLOSSOMED INTO SUCH BEAUTIFUL WOMEN.
OH, AND LOOK AT TOBY- DON'T YOU JUST WANT TO PINCH THOSE CHEEKS!
AND THERE'S... J.T. EVER THE CLOWN.

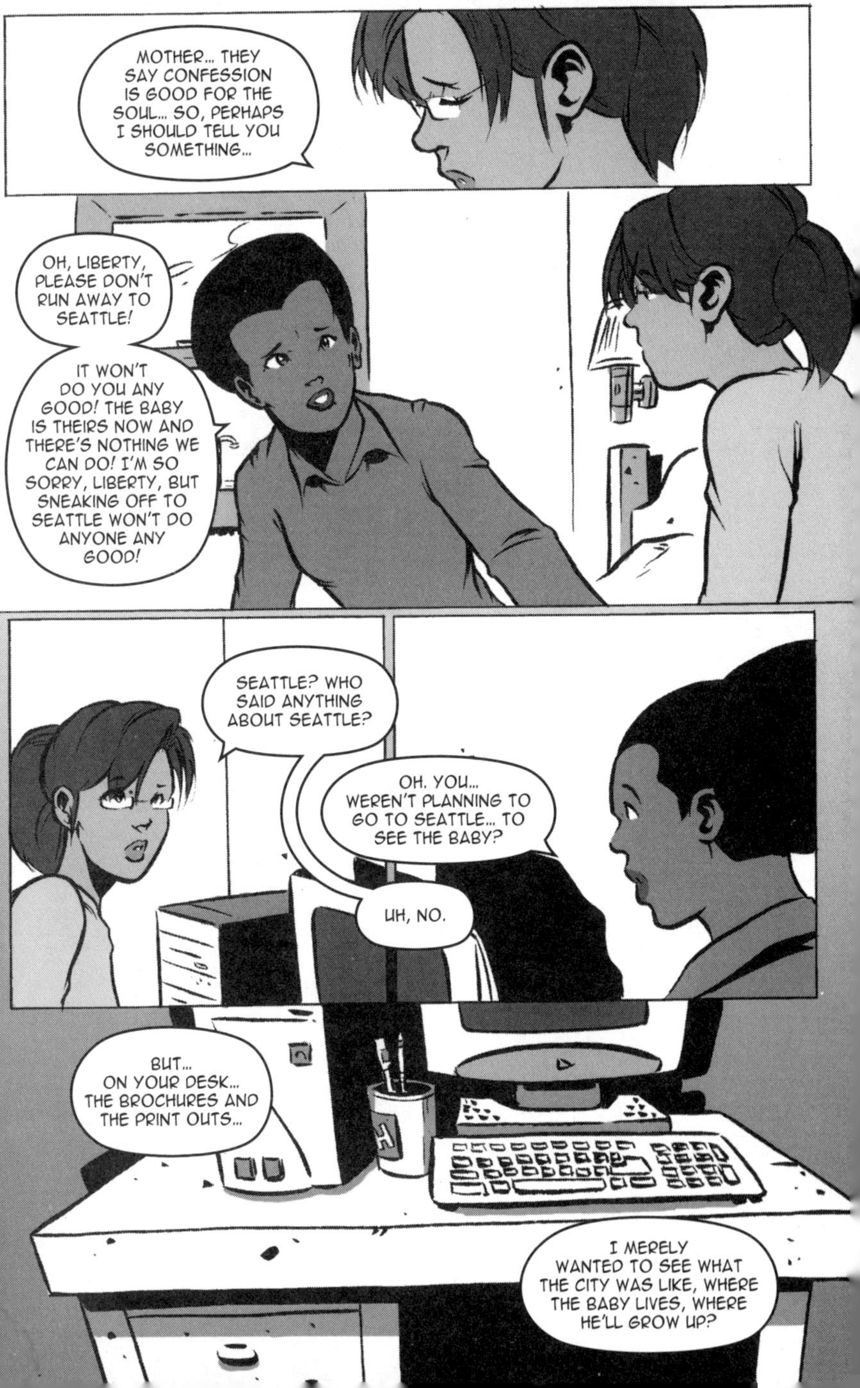
MOTHER... THEY SAY CONFESSION IS GOOD FOR THE SOUL... SO, PERHAPS I SHOULD TELL YOU SOMETHING...
OH, LIBERTY, PLEASE DON'T RUN AWAY TO SEATTLE!
IT WON'T DO YOU ANY GOOD! THE BABY IS THEIRS NOW AND THERE'S NOTHING WE CAN DO! I'M SO SORRY, LIBERTY, BUT SNEAKING OFF TO SEATTLE WON'T DO ANYONE ANY GOOD!
SEATTLE? WHO SAID ANYTHING ABOUT SEATTLE?
OH. YOU... WEREN'T PLANNING TO GO TO SEATTLE... TO SEE THE BABY?
UH, NO.
BUT... ON YOUR DESK... THE BROCHURES AND THE PRINT OUTS...
I MERELY WANTED TO SEE WHAT THE CITY WAS LIKE, WHERE THE BABY LIVES, WHERE HE'LL GROW UP?

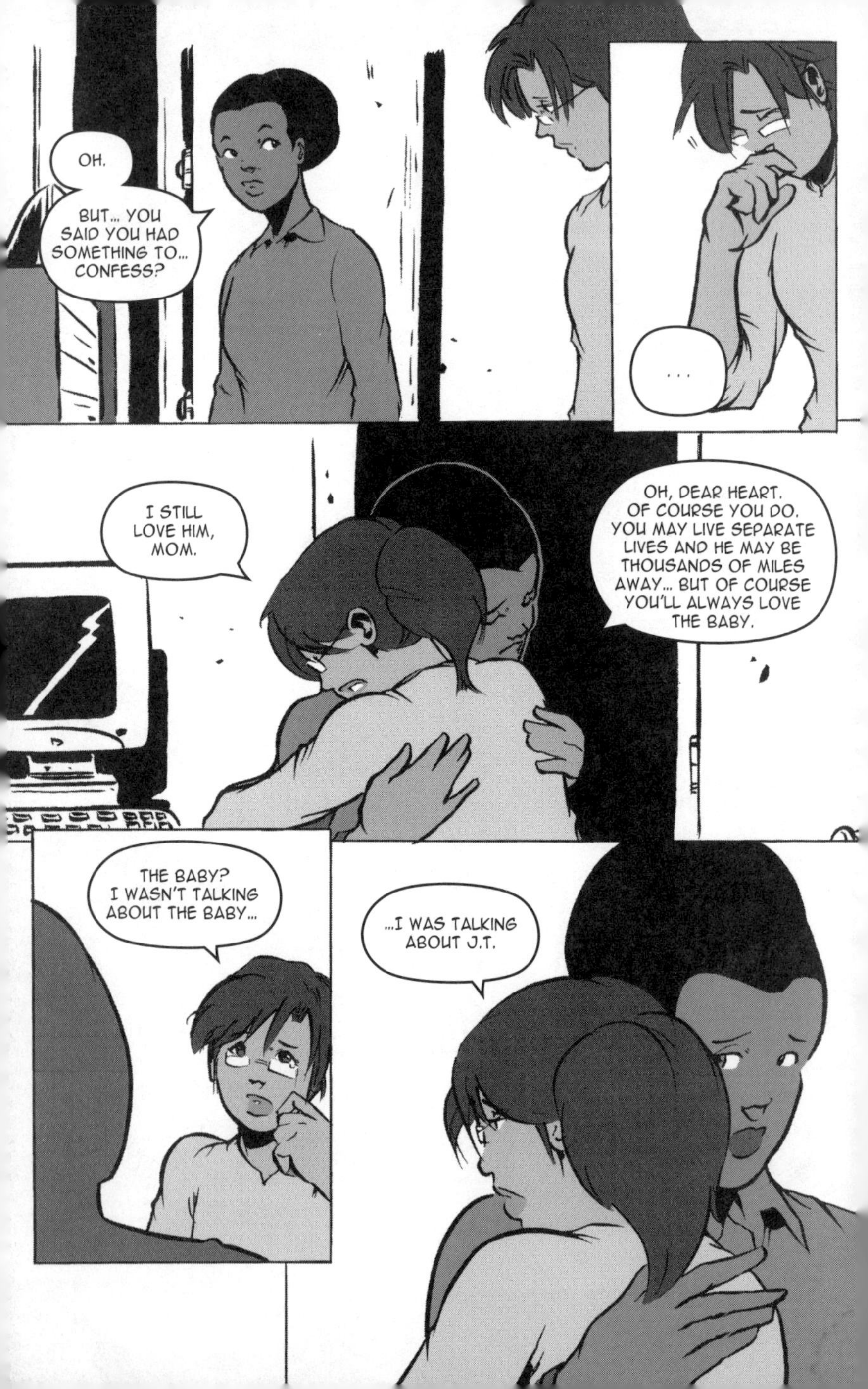
OH.
BUT... YOU SAID YOU HAD SOMETHING TO... CONFESS?
. . .
I STILL LOVE HIM, MOM.
OH, DEAR HEART. OF COURSE YOU DO. YOU MAY LIVE SEPARATE LIVES AND HE MAY BE THOUSANDS OF MILES AWAY... BUT OF COURSE YOU'LL ALWAYS LOVE THE BABY.
THE BABY? I WASN'T TALKING ABOUT THE BABY...
...I WAS TALKING ABOUT J.T.

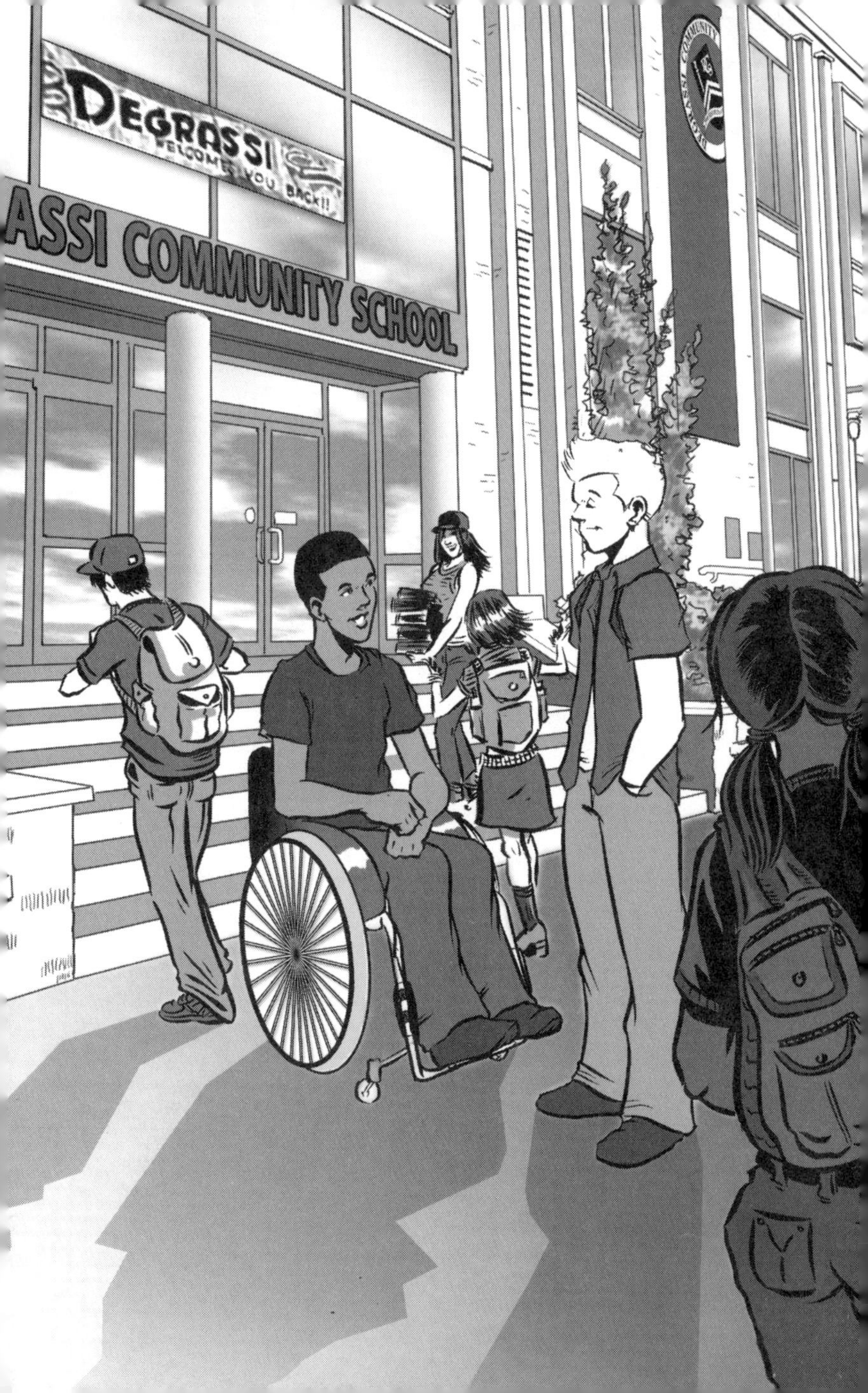
DEGRASSI
WELCOMES YOU BACK!!
ASSI COMMUNITY SCHOOL

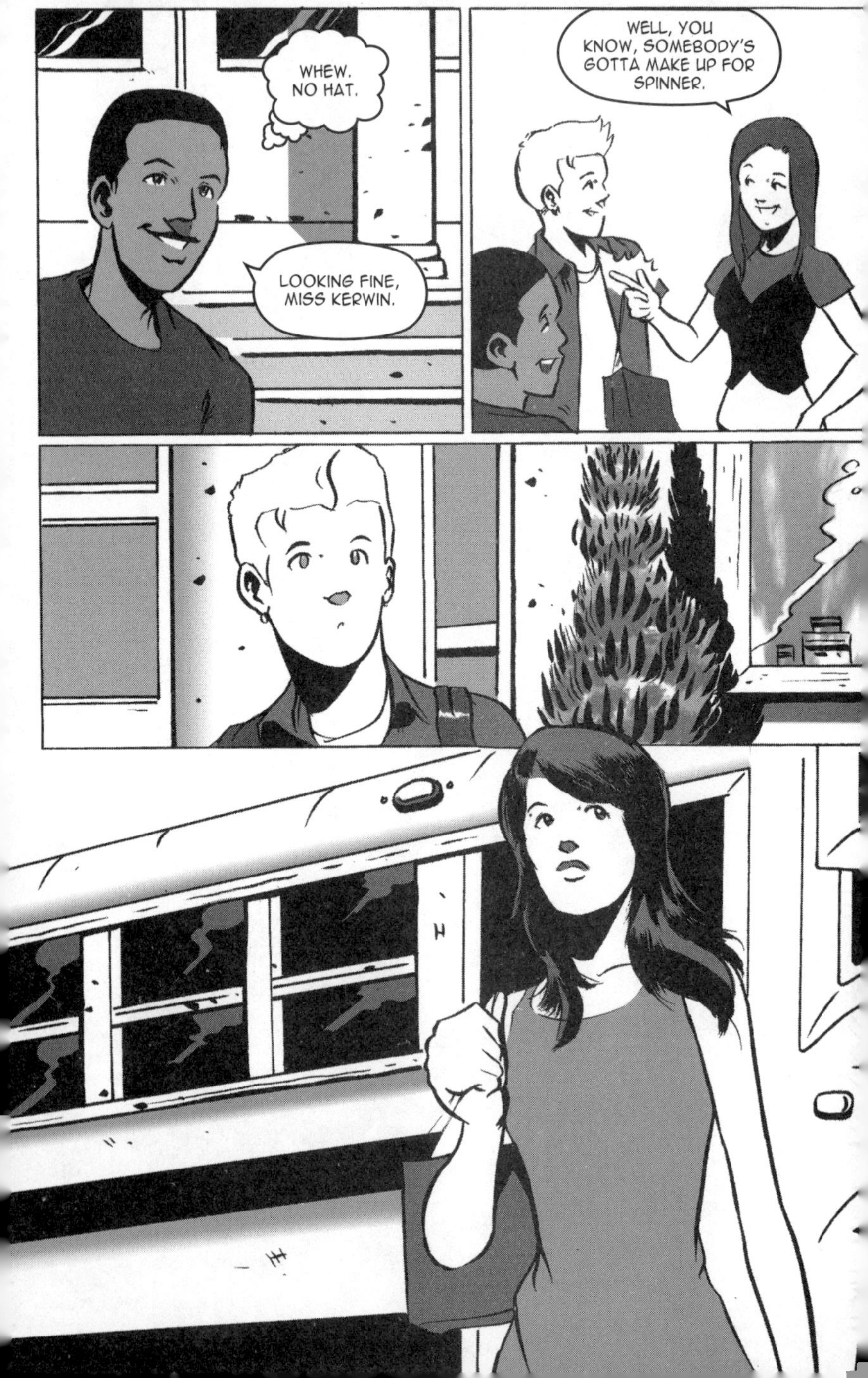
WHEW. NO HAT.
LOOKING FINE, MISS KERWIN.
WELL, YOU KNOW, SOMEBODY'S GOTTA MAKE UP FOR SPINNER.

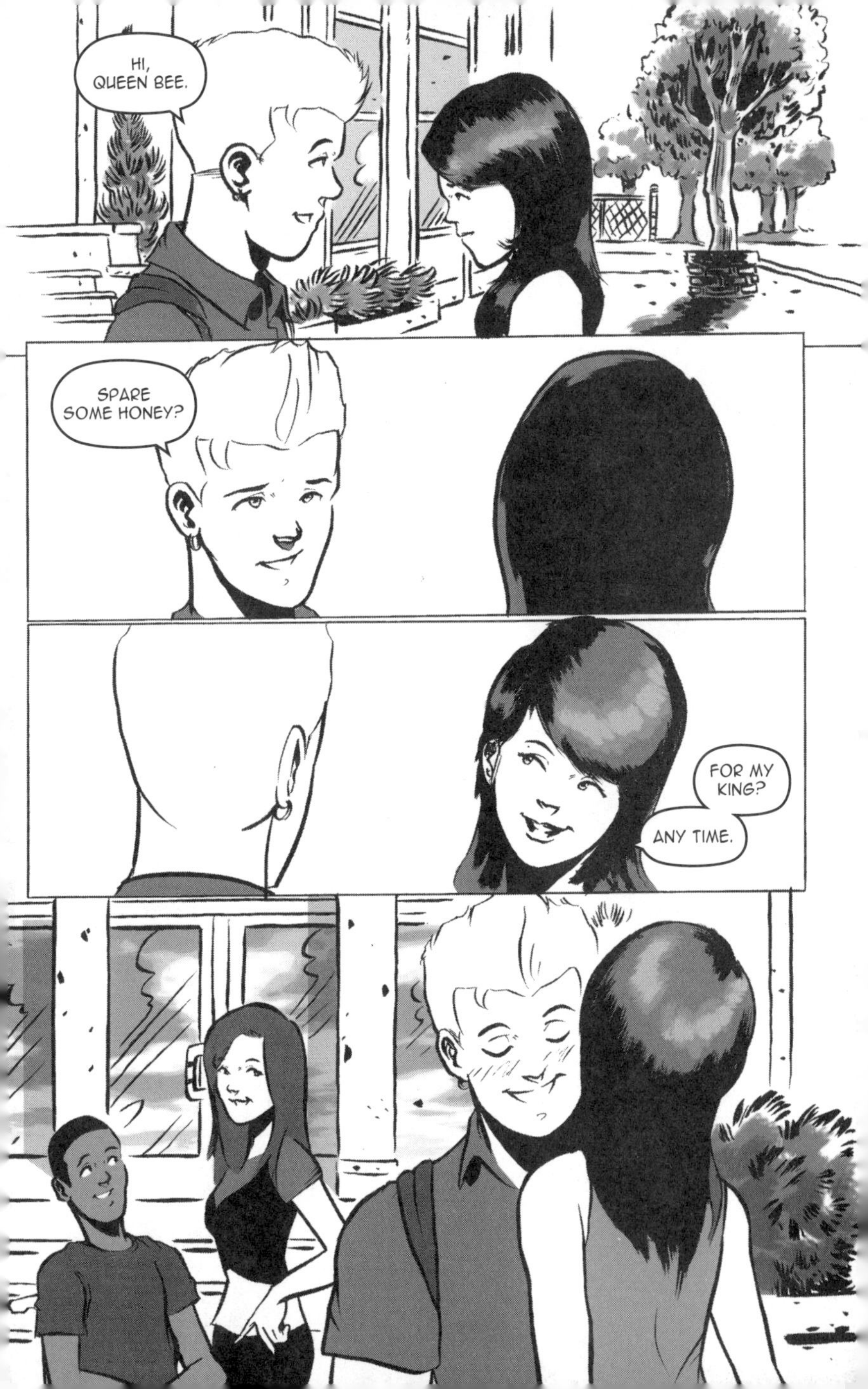
HI, QUEEN BEE.
SPARE SOME HONEY?
FOR MY KING?
ANY TIME.

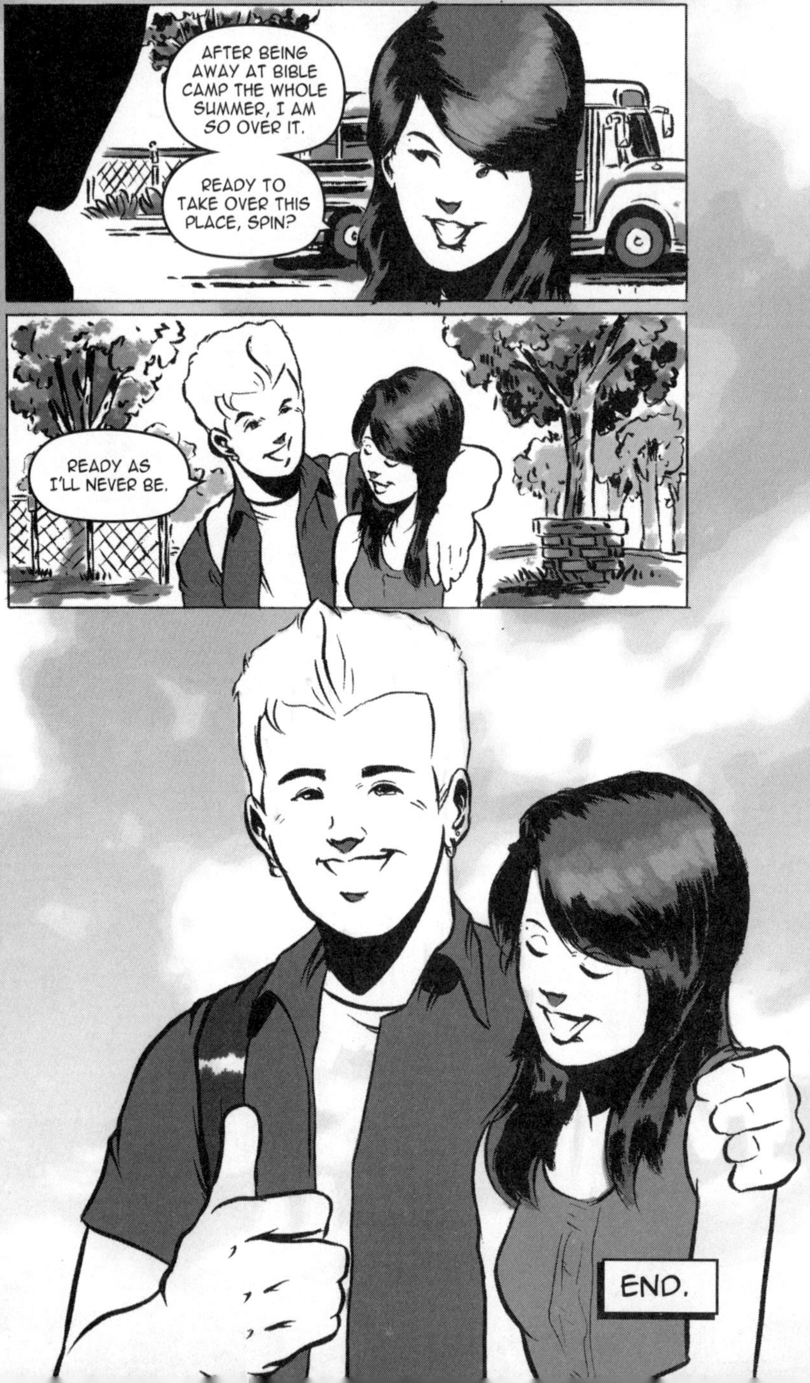
AFTER BEING AWAY AT BIBLE CAMP THE WHOLE SUMMER, I AM SO OVER IT.
READY TO TAKE OVER THIS PLACE, SPIN?
READY AS I'LL NEVER BE.
END.

Degrassi
THE NEXT GENERATION
EXTRA CREDIT

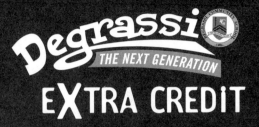

THE CREATORS

J. TORRES writes **NINJA SCROLL** and **TEEN TITANS GO** for DC Comics, and also contributes to **BATMAN STRIKES** and **LEGION OF SUPER HEROES IN THE 31ST CENTURY**. His other graphic novels include **ALISON DARE, DAYS LIKE THIS, SIDEKICKS** and the award-winning **LOVE AS A FOREIGN LANGUAGE**.

ERIC KIM collaborated with J. Torres on the Shuster Award-winning series **LOVE AS A FOREIGN LANGUAGE**. He has also worked in other media, such as film and video games. His other credits include **BATTLE ACADEMY** for Brand New Planet.

Inking
Eric Kim

Toning
Andy Belanger

Cover Art
Ed Northcott

Lettering
Chris Butcher

Additional Toning
Deryk Ousley

ACKNOWLEDGMENTS

My gratitude and appreciation to everyone at Epitome, Madison, Fenn, Simon & Schuster and Pearson Education Canada who helped make *Extra Credit* possible — with special thanks to Linda Schuyler, Stephen Stohn and Christopher Jackson for the hall passes; Brendon Yorke, James Hurst, Aaron Martin, Kate Miles Melville and Sean Reycraft for letting me copy their notes; Stephanie Cohen and Shernold Edwards for helping me with my homework; and Hye-Young Im for going to the prom with me. Also, thanks to Diana Sullada and Wanda Nowakowska for helping me get through those finals. — **J. Torres**

Holy COW! There are a lot of people to thank for this work. Everyone on this project has shown tremendous respect, dedication and devotion. Frankly, it's a little awe-inspiring! I'm grateful to Andy Belanger, Deryk Ousley of Canvas, Christopher Butcher and Anthony Brennan; thank you for your tremendous work. To Diana Sullada and Wanda Nowakowska at Madison; and to Christopher Jackson at Epitome — thank you for your support and for the time (and overtime) we spent in working on this project. Lastly, special thanks to J. Torres for once again giving me the opportunity to work on a project with him. It's been a blast! — **Eric Kim**

Madison Press Books would like to thank Linda Schuyler, Stephen Stohn, Christopher Jackson, Stephanie Cohen and Shernold Edwards at Epitome Pictures for their support and crucial feedback. We would also like to thank the cast of *Degrassi: The Next Generation.*

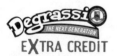

Degrassi THE NEXT GENERATION
EXTRA CREDIT

was produced by **Madison Press Books**

Art Director Diana Sullada
Editorial Director Wanda Nowakowska
Production Manager Sandra L. Hall

Vice President, Finance & Production Susan Barrable
President & Publisher Oliver Salzmann